KT-227-601

BLITZFREEZE

SVEN HASSEL

Translated from the Danish by
Tim Bowie

CASSELL

Cassell Military Paperbacks

Cassell
Wellington House, 125 Strand
London WC2R 0BB

Copyright © Sven Hassel 1973
Translation copyright © Transworld Publishers 1975
Translated from the Danish by Tim Bowie

First published in Great Britain in 1975
by Corgi Books
This Cassell Military Paperbacks edition 2004

All rights reserved. No part of this book may be reproduced or
transmitted in any form of by any means electronic or mechanical
including photocopying, recording or any information storage and
retrieval system without permission in writing from the publisher.

Sven Hassel
has asserted his right to be identified
as the Author of this work.

British Library Cataloguing-in-Publication Data.
A catalogue record for this book is available
from the British Library.

ISBN 0 304 36687 0

Typeset by Deltatype Ltd, Birkenhead, Merseyside
Printed and bound in Great Britain by
Clays Ltd, St Ives plc

www.orionbooks.co.uk

'I am leading you towards wonderful times.'
            Hitler in a speech on 3 June 1937.

The dead metallic crackle of machine-guns
Echoed in the cold silence.
The tramp of boots, sounding like shots,
The yelp of a dog,
Human screams.
Crying children, murdered women
In the last sunlight of a dying day.
Never forget it, the blood of the murdered,
It was war –
            To Dorthe, my life's companion.

> 'Once the Germans have accepted the Bolshevik doctrines, I will move my headquarters from Moscow to Berlin, because in the coming world revolution the Germans will make much better cadre than the Russians.'
>
> Lenin to the Turkish Ambassador,
> Ali Fuad Pascha on 14 January 1921.

In the '30s SS-Overgruppenführer Heydrich laid a crafty plan, designed to break the back of the Red Army. Using Gestapo agents, within the GPU, he filtered information through to Stalin naming traitors in the highest posts in Russian defence. Stalin's sick suspicions were aroused and the results far exceeded Heydrich's greatest expectations. Stalin and Police Minister Beria sent a wave of terror rolling across the giant Soviet state. Some of the most talented military leaders of the times were executed: Marshals Tuchatschewskij, Blücher and Iegorow, Army-commanders Uborewitsch and Jakir and the chiefs of the Red Fleet, Admirals Orlon and Wiktorow. With them went the commanders of every Military District and ninety-eight percent of the Corps and Divisional commanders. Almost every Regimental and Battalion commander was removed from his post and despatched to a forced labour camp as an enemy of the people. SS-Obergruppenführer Heydrich rubbed his hands in satisfaction. Stalin himself had eliminated the brains of the Russian Army and replaced them with useless sycophants and hypocrites capable at most of leading a machine-gun section.

In the course of one night several thousand incompetent captains and majors were promoted to General rank. Some had not even attended an officer's school and none had ever seen Frunse Academy. Countless frontier incidents took place before June 1941. German planes penetrated deeply into Russia on overt reconaissance, but Stalin had forbidden that they be shot at. The slightest provocation on the part of Russian frontier regiments was punished by death. Quite simply, Stalin forbade the Russian soldier to defend himself. 'Why?' asks Major-General Grigorenko. Yes, why? Most of those who could have answered this question were executed in the first two months of the war. Stalin and Beria were busy. Busy silencing witnesses to the greatest blunder in history. 'Or was it treason?' asks Pjort Grigorenko.

1 | The Girl Sergeant

'What's wrong with you?' the lieutenant asks.

'I can't do it,' says the girl sergeant.

'You won't!'

'I can't tell you.'

'Tell me why you won't,' the lieutenant begs softly. He smooths her hair, and her forage cap falls to the ground.

'You're unreasonable. A girl can't do it when she's feeling down in the mouth.'

'That's a lot of nonsense. Even when you're wounded you can do it. I once did it with both legs in plaster.'

'When did *you* have both legs in plaster?'

'When I was serving with the Soviet Laplanders. The time the Finns attacked us.'

'Were *you* there? I didn't know you'd been garrisoned in Leningrad. Stop it, Oleg! I can't, I tell you!'

'You mean you won't! You don't like doing it. I'm a holder of the *Krasnoe Znamja*,* you know.'

'Do you think a girl flops into bed with a man, just because he's got a *Krasnoe Znamja*? Where did you win it, anyway?'

'Suomussalmi.'

'Where's that? Out east? There's always war out there.'

'No, Finland. It's where we crushed the Finnish fascists and imperialists.'

* *Krasnoe Znamja.* (Russian): The Order of the Red Banner.

2

'Do you mean the big tank battle?'

'Yes. They destroyed the division. But then the Commander-in-Chief sent in the whole army corps. We drove deep into their flanks, and got six decorations for bravery.'

'And *you* got one of them?'

'Yes!' He tries to slip his hand up under her potato-brown army skirt.

She closes her legs. They roll about in the tall maize.

'You mustn't, she whispers hoarsely. 'I tell you I can't. I'm a soldier like you. All that filthy perversity'll have to wait till we've crushed the occupation force.'

'Oh, I understand you thoroughly,' growls the lieutenant bitterly. 'Hell! *how* I understand you. I understand you night and day, every hour, morning and evening. Especially evenings when I sit alone in that blasted battlewagon. I understand you the way the devil understands Karl Marx. *Job Tvojemadj!*'*

'Do you have to talk filth?' she says quietly. She straightens her military skirt and shifts the belt supporting the Nagan† to a more comfortable position.

'I'm a soldier,' she repeats, 'a tankman like yourself.'

'You're a soldier, yes, a telegraphist in a battlewagon, Jelena Vladimirovna.' He catches her by the neck and throws her on her back in the golden maize.

She kicks out at him, resists violently. Her skirt slides up, and a pair of well-formed thighs in khaki stockings come to view. 'Hell, stop it,' she snarls savagely. 'I'll report you to the Sampolit!'‡

'Do you think I'm afraid of those swine? If we don't crush the Nazis before they get into Moscow, all the Sampolits will be swinging in the breeze. They're shaking with fright, every one of them, and with reason. We're not *going* to beat the fascists!'

---

* *Job Tvojemadj.* (Russian): Go home and fuck your mother!
† Nagan. Russian military pistol.
‡ Sampolit. The unit commander's representative in political matters.

'Have you gone mad, Oleg Grigorjewitsch? Do you doubt the victory? That'll cost you your head if I report you!'

'Jelena Vladimirovna, can't you be honest with me? You doubt the victory too! Hitler's manhunters have been chasing us around like frightened chickens since June. Thousands upon thousands have fallen in just a few months. Countless others are behind barbed wire in Germany. Impregnable fortifications have gone down before we knew what was hunting us. We're finished! Hitler and his generals will be in the Kremlin before Christmas. Where's General Bagramja and his unbeatable Division of Guards? Crushed, Jelena! We stand on lost positions.

'We've been at war three months and Hitler's panzer divisions are little more than 200 miles from Moscow. If the weather holds, and it looks as if it will, fascist tanks will be in the Kremlin in less than a week. Did you hear the enemy radio the other day:

'"Panzer, forward march! Let the tracks roll! Don't stop till they're striking sparks from the cobblestones of Moscow. Crush international Communism! Didn't you hear it, Jelena? The Germans are devils. They've never been beaten. Any-where! You've seen their yellow tanks crushing everything before them. For every one of their's that went up in flames a hundred of ours went. Our own tank brigade has been destroyed and re-formed five times. Do you think *that* can go on? I heard this morning that they were packing up all ready to evacuate the Kremlin. Josef Stalin lets *us* be liquidated to save himself. He's as brutal as Hitler. It's a question which of the two is Russian's greatest scourge. You know the order: He who retreats is a traitor and will be shot! If we surrender, they shoot our families."'

'I'd rather die than surrender,' whispers Jelena hoarsely.

'Don't be too sure of that. Death doesn't seem so frightening at a distance. But up close even the bravest lose courage and choose life – if they have a choice at all. But who's to say we two'll *have* any choice. We haven't met

4

Hitler's SS yet. They're a thousand times worse than our own NKVD.'

'Impossible,' in a frightened groan from the girl. 'Nobody could be crueller than Beria's men.'

'You'll learn better! Wait till you meet the men with the skull on their caps. They kill for the love of it. It's said they get a pint of blood to drink every morning. Soviet blood, Jelena Vladimirovna.'

'It's said too, that they eat young children,' she mumbles, paling.

'Half a million babies disappeared in Berlin alone. Jewish babies,' she added after a moment.

'No, not Jewish, the SS definitely wouldn't eat them!' he protests – indignantly.

'Do you really think we're losing the great patriotic war?'

'We *have* lost it, Jelena Vladimirovna, God help and pity us!'

'You believe in God, Oleg? A Soviet officer passed out of Frunse Academy?'

'Yes, since the battle of Minsk I believe in God. He is our only hope. Jelena Vladimirovna, I love you! I've loved you from the moment you joined the regiment, and were put in my unit. Come on, girl! There's a war on. Who knows if we'll still be alive by evening?'

'Stop it, I can't, I won't! I'm engaged!'

'No you bloody well aren't,' he shouts mockingly. 'I know there's something between you and Captain Anna Skrjabina. The whole brigade knows it. They say a T-34 is what'll come out of it.' He throws back his head with a roar of laughter. 'You're Captain Anna Skrjabina's mistress. Everybody knows that cow's crazy about girls. But did you know, too, that they disappear but fast when the old witch gets tired of them? She'll soon be finished with the unit at Sampolit. Colonel Botapov doesn't like her.'

'He can't touch Anna. She has connections right up to the *Stavka*.'*

* *Stavka*. Russian High Command, instituted 23 June 1941.

'You're in love with her!'

'So what? Do I have to get my section commander's permission?'

'What do you do with one another?'

'Do you think I'm perverse?'

'No, just a lesbian. You nauseate me, Jelena Vladimirovna.'

'Good, then let me go, *tovaritsch* lieutenant! They certainly didn't hand out manners together with medals at Suomussalmi.'

'Are you knocking the Order of the Red Banner?'

'Report me, if you want to. I can answer for myself! If I'm to be stood up against a wall I'll see to it I get you for company!'

'Oh, I'm sure you'll get by, Jelena. Just crawl into Anna's little bed. She's the one who handles all the reports.'

'You're an animal. I curse you tenfold – by the Holy Mother of Kazan!'

'I'm sorry, Jelena, I didn't mean it but you drive me mad. I *will* have you, cost what it may!'

'No, I tell you I won't I won't have anything to do with you. Not like that!'

Suddenly he is on top of her. The maize sways. The thick stalks snap noisily.

'I'm going to have you now, if it's the last thing I do in my life! Fritz'll be here before sundown, and that'll be it. The orders are "stand and die"' With one movement he rips off her summer blouse. 'Afterwards you can go running to Anna and tell the old witch that it's a lot better having it with a man!'

'Fuckin' arseholes!' rumbles Tiny in his deep belly bass. 'It's enough to get a jack up on a neutered nigger with a paralysed pisspin! See the way that traitor to the Soviet's gettin' across her *now*! And him as 'as doubts about the final victory. Ought to be stuck up in front of a firin' squad! Bleedin' dog's dinner like 'im want perforatin'!'

6

'It's the bitch who's gonna get perforated,' sniggers Porta delightedly. 'If they knew who was lying here taking the piss out of them! War's a terrible thing! Just one shocking thing after another!'

'Christ, now he's moving up into the jungle,' whispers Stege ecstatically, wiping the sweat from his forehead.

'Cut it out, you lecherous monkeys,' rasps the Old Man, moving forward his LMG,* one of the new type with a bayonet for close-quarter fighting.

Barcelona Blom chuckles lasciviously and screws the cover off a hand-grenade.

'He'd better get a move on, that humpty-backed frog. It'll be his last bang, before we come tapping on the door.'

The girl has pulled herself free again. Her breasts are bared. She is breathing heavily and smacks the lieutenant resoundingly across the face. But this only excites him even more. She aims a kick at his crutch.

'She should've taken a course at the military academy judo school,' opines Porta, 'then she could've tossed that *alik*† straight over to us.'

'That'd stop 'is fartin' in church,' grins Tiny. 'His nice little officer's prick'd shrivel up at the sight of us, and 'e'd shoot a load about the size of a sparrer's tear.'

The two wrestle briefly in the swaying corn. Her skirt has been torn away. The heavy Nagan and white frilly pants seem ludicrous in contrast.

Panting they fall to the grass. Something white flutters into the air and ends on a branch.

'There go 'er arse-curtains,' reports Tiny gleefully.

We grin delightedly, all except the Old Man and the Legionnaire. Porta emits a long shrill whistle.

'What was that?' asks Jelena nervously.

'A reed warbler crying to its mate,' Oleg calms her.

'A Red warrior crying for his cunt, you bastard,' Tiny grins unrestrainedly, his face pressed hard to the ground.

* LMG. (Leichtes Maschingewehr) (German): Light automatic rifle.
† *Alik*. (Russian): Slang for the male sexual organ.

7

'Right up,' Porta laughs lustfully and scratches his crutch with his combat knife.

'No!' cries the girl hysterically, 'why should I?'

'To please me,' he laughs.

'I won't! Can't you hear? Leave me alone, I tell you!'

'Just once, what difference can it make?' he pleads.

There is silence for a moment. Betraying moans come from the bushes. A stifled scream. Jumbled words.

We are dumb with excitement, our breath comes pantingly, we stare greedy-eyed.

Porta wriggles forward to Tiny.

'Holy Mother of Kazan,' he whispers breathlessly. 'Ain't this something? Here we go knocking the Red Army, when in fact it's us who've joined the wrong army. Ivan understands things. He takes uniformed cunt with him right into the thick of battle. Maybe us two hard-tried Prussian veterans ought to let the faded eagle take off and follow the Communist star? These men are fighting for a holy cause.'

'Are they 'oly?' asks Tiny disappointedly. His experience with the missions has been uniformly bad.

'Like fuck they are,' grins Porta. 'No more than the devil is in the arse-part. But they're made of rougher stuff than our Party bums who want to serve both God and the Devil, and try to keep the latter connection a secret like the Pharisee in the Bible. I've heard that every Communist Obergefreiter has a piece of *allotjka** to press his pants whenever her superior feels the need.'

'If that's true,' mumbles Tiny with a hectic flush rising on his cheeks and eyes shining, 'then we've already wasted too much of our time in Hitler's connin' army.'

'Shall we let them finish before we turn it on?' asks Stege in a whisper.

The Old Man makes no reply, pulls nervously at his ear and plays with the 'stovepipe'. He is not interested in what is happening in the scrub in front of us.

* *Allotjka.* (Russian): Cunt.

The girl stands up and begins to order her uniform. Wraps her skirt around her. Now she is again a sergeant of the Guards in the Red Army's tank arm.

'I must go,' she smiles, with a flash of white teeth, 'but I'll come back to you after roll-call.'

'No you won't,' answers the lieutenant. 'You'll never come back to me!'

'He must be a bloody fortune-teller,' whispers Porta in amazement. 'Can he know we're here?'

'I'll come,' laughs the girl and disappears into the maize. She goes over towards the four Russian BT-5s* standing behind the maize-stalks by the sunflower thicket. If they had been painted yellow like ours you couldn't have seen them.

Russia is all yellow at this time of the year. Even the people seem to take on a slightly yellowish tinge when September is past. Now the green of the tanks shows up strongly against all the yellow and brown.

'They ought to paint their vehicles four times a year like we do,' mumbles Porta. 'Twice ain't enough in combat conditions.'

'They really ought to be painted every month,' was Stege's opinion. 'January snow is quite different from December snow, and the powdery snow in November can't be compared with the old February snow, and in March there are five different shades of white. So you can see that even in winter when white is white, it's only worth painting vehicles once. When you get to spring, the green is changing almost every week. What good is it riding around in a happy spring green wagon in the middle of all that tired-out old summer green. A wagon like that stands out like a young bint in the middle of a crowd of old men. No, if we really understood how to camouflage ourselves we'd live longer. Just look at our uniforms! Grey-green! Apart from the dust on the roads where do you find that colour? And the boys from the other FPO shag around in their winter khaki well into the spring. Uniform colours are chosen by idiots sitting in offices.'

* BT-5: Medium tank.

'In the old days they all wore red and blue,' explains Tiny, shaking his head.

'That was to frighten the enemy,' says Barcelona. 'A line of men with fixed bayonets advancing side by side in scarlet uniforms was enough to frighten the shit out of the bravest. It was like a wave of blood sweeping forward.'

'If there was anybody barmy enough to attack like that, I'd soon have this ol' chatter box tuned in to lullaby music an' make a nice row o' scarlet corpses,' grins Tiny mockingly.

'Dope,' sneers Barcelona contemptuously, 'they didn't have automatic weapons then, only muskets that had to be loaded again every time.'

'Wot, no SMGs?* asks Tiny unbelievingly. 'Must've been a funny kind of war. Almost 'armless. Didn't they 'ave no mine-throwers nor mortars with jumpin' jacks neither?'

'Nah!' answers Barcelona with a superior expression. 'Nothing like that at all.'

'Well, they'd 'ave a coupla naphtha bombs on 'and, I suppose, for if things got rough?'

'Petrol wasn't even discovered then,' answers Barcelona.

'Why the 'ell didn't they stay at 'ome? That wasn't nothin' to do with war, even if they did 'ave red jackets on. More like a bleedin' *demonstration*, like what we 'ad before the war when we wanted more money and 'ad to fight the Schupos,† who 'ad green 'elmets on special for the day. You could put 'em out on it dead easy by givin' 'em one on top o' the elmet so it come down over their bleedin' ears. I'm dead good at 'ammerin' Schupo lids down. Easy as scratchin' your arse in a beer-bar.'

The Russian lieutenant is lying on his back in the grass with a maize-straw waggling in his mouth. He laughs with satisfaction. His summer tunic is unbuttoned. A ladybird moves busily across the yellow star on his Boudionovka.‡ He has closed his eyes. Not until the Legionnaire's shadow

---

* SMG (Schweres Maschinengewehr) (German): Heavy machine-gun.

† Schupo (Schützpolizie) (German): Uniformed police.

‡ Boudionovka: Soviet spiked helmet of cloth.

10

falls across him does he realize that he is in danger. Then he is dead. A last frightened bubbling comes from the slashed throat. The Legionnaire wipes his Moorish knife casually on the lieutenant's summer tunic. We hurry past with the Panzerfausts* over our shoulders. A smell of coffee comes from the Russian tank crew's encampment.

'Holy Moses!' whispers Porta, eyes wide-open. 'Coffee! Real coffee! These Communists've got every bloody thing! I am slowly beginning to like this: Workers of the world, unite!' Porta loves coffee. He knows of nothing better. More than once he has jeopardized his life to get hold of coffee beans. The Old Man says Porta would sell the entire company for a pound of coffee. And he is probably not far from the truth. Porta is a coffee-maniac. Tiny, who is well in front of us with the heavy Panzerfaust nonchalantly under his arm, drops down suddenly into the maize and signals to us. Soundlessly we crawl forward to him. He points silently. A Russian tankman is sitting by a small fire, on which a large pot is steaming. Blissfully Porta inhales the penetrating coffee aroma. 'Holy Guns!' mumbles Julius Heide in a horrified tone. 'Four BT-5s!'

'Five,' Porta corrects him. 'There's a KW-1† behind the stack, the command vehicle.'

'Pissin' arseholes,' says Tiny ecstatically. 'We'll *smash* 'em with one great lovely bang.' He pats the magnetic grenade and pushes it into the Panzerfaust. 'This'll shove their ball-bearin's up into their throats, so they'll never be able to shag a soldier's mare no more. Bleedin' traitors, wot doubts the final victory! If Ol' Joe in the Kremlin knew what we was up to 'e'd be tackin' medals on us!'

'It is forbidden to wear Soviet decorations, remember,' Heide instructs him coldly.

'I ain't got any yet, so wot's the problem?' replies Tiny drily and raises his Panzerfaust to the firing position.

---

* Panzerfaust: Rocket firing apparatus. (Bazooka.)
† KW-1: 43-ton tank.

'Stop that,' whispers the Old Man irritably. 'Put down that pipe! Nobody fires until I give the order!'

From the tank soldiers bivouac comes the cheerful laughter of women and men.

'D'you think they know there's a war on?' Porta asks, astonished. 'They go on as if they were on their way to a Turkish whorehouse. They'll have a stroke when we turn it on them.'

A woman's voice cuts sharply through the general noise. A harsh, guttural commanding voice.

'The prickless captain,' Barcelona states, withdrawing 'silent death' from his pocket. 'It's mine. I'll give it a last bang-up, before I strangle it.'

'No, I'll 'ave it,' growls Tiny. 'That bitch-captain's gonna find out what kind of guests 'er country's gettin' now.'

'If you could just keep your trap shut,' whispers the Old Man sourly. 'Let's get closer. We're a long way from the vehicles yet. All five boxes've got to go up in one go! Barcelona, you cover the foreground with the MG!* Kill the lot! Not one reaches the bridge. If they blow it, it's a court-martial for us. Everything hangs on that bridge. There's at least a ton of explosive under it.'

'What a lovely noise it'd make!' Tiny dreams aloud. He loves everything that is loud and noisy. 'A ton o' HE! Fuckin' arseholes! You could 'ear it all the way to Greenland. It'd make the lice on a' Eskimo whore's belly dance the can-can!'

Shortly after the Russian tank crews are called in and served a mess-tin of coffee.

'If only to liberate that coffee, we've got to blow their candles out,' gasps Porta nervously. 'I only hope they don't guzzle the bloody lot down 'em first.'

'Nah, they wouldn't be *that* nasty,' Tiny comforts him. 'They'll leave us a drop. Wonder where they cornered it?'

'They're Guards,' explains Heide, always well-informed. 'They get special rations.'

* MG (Maschinengewehr) (German): Machine-gun.

'How d'you know they're bloody Guards?' irritatedly from Porta.

'Green summer tunics with silver shoulder straps,' comes knowledgeably from Heide.

'I can't understand why *you* don't know that. Haven't you read May orders, in which you were told it was your duty to know the uniforms of the enemy?'

'I usually wipe my arse on orders,' sneers Porta. 'They're softer than corn-cobs.'

'That's sabotage!' growls Heide, gruffly.

'Wiping my arse?' asks Porta with his supercilious street-boy grin.

'You know what I mean, Obergefreiter Porta. It is my duty to report you to the NSFO.'*

'I reckon it's *my* duty to blow your bloody earholes through from side to side and get your brain moving,' sneers Porta.

'Come on,' orders the Old Man and begins to crawl forward. The Russians are sitting in a circle, chewing at thick slices of bread, which they wash down with aromatic coffee.

The light is fading. Beyond the river, the sky is a rosy red. One of the Russians begins to play a balalaika. The others sing:

> Long in his grave
> Your father has slept.
> In exile, in thralldom
> In cold Siberia,
> Your brother toils.
> Under the nagajka's†
> Biting lash,
> Chained hand and foot.

* NSFO (Nationalsozialistischer Führungoffizier) (German): Nazi Political officer.

† *Nagajka* (Russian): Siberian whip, issued to prison camp guards.

In Russia they have sung these sad songs for centuries. For as long as there have been prison camps in Siberia.

'What a wicked bleedin' song,' mumbles Tiny and shrugs his shoulders as if chilled.

In the distance artillery thunders. We are old hands at the front, and can distinguish clearly the sound of air-bursts. It is the German heavy artillery at work now. It presages an attack. It's not pleasant to be on the receiving end of those coal-boxes. We feel with the fellows from the other FPO. They're curled up like hedgehogs behind a bit of an earth-work. Their only defence against death. We've been through it ourselves. We too are only soldiers. The human butcher's-meat of the new age.

'*Muss i denn, muss i denn, zum Städtele hinaus!*' hums Tiny.

The light from the Russian tankmen's fire throws a fantastic glow over the scene. There is nothing quite so spectral as the dark trunks of fir-trees seen by firelight.

'Slip me a swig of poor man's schnapps,' requires Porta, and holds his hand out demandingly towards Barcelona, who passes him the big French water-bottle.

The gunfire intensifies. The sky flames violently in the distance. Both the Russians and we look to the north. It means death, mangling death, for both sides. Shells can't tell the difference. 'Forward, what the hell do you think you were born for?' Engines drone. Tanks roll forward with infantry running alongside them. Every man of them is sick with fear. Irresponsible politicians have named them the backbone of the nation.

The advance speeds up. The tank has to pass a minefield. Nobody bothers about the grenadier running alongside hanging onto the towrope. He falls, is dragged, makes it to his feet again, shoots at a helmet sticking up over the lip of a trench.

This is war, friend. Kill some other mother's son, before he can kill you, and you have won a prize in death's lottery.

If you live through all the madness you will go home a hero, but don't forget that nothing disappears so quickly

14

from this earth as a hero. Two months after the war is over they'll be laughing at you. I speak from experience. Never volunteer to be a hero. You'll be disappointed with it.

Straight above our heads rocket batteries draw fiery trails. The Russians are listening now. Their nervousness infects us. Rockets fall far beyond the river. The summer-dry maize fields begin to burn. Apart from flame-throwers there is nothing we hate more than rockets. Porta says they are made of hair from the Devil's tail.

'Ready to march!' announces a hard commanding Russian voice. A tall officer, no longer in his first youth, gives the command. He too is wearing one of the queer old-fashioned Boudionovkas with a blue cavalry star.

Tiny decides he will liberate that cap. The Legionnaire says it's his. 'Stop your nattering,' snaps the Old Man.

I say nothing but I am quite decided that *I* am going to get the Boudionovka with the blue star. Everybody's collecting them, because they're on their way out in favour of flat-tops. I already own a Boudionovka with the green and black artillery star. The tall officer snaps out orders.

'What's he saying?' asks the Old Man, who can't – or won't – understand Russian.

'He says to get their fingers out and climb in the coffins,' Porta translates loosely.

'I bet 'e's one o' them trigger-'appy bastards, as don't just shoot to 'ear the bang,' says Tiny.

We crawl forward to a better firing position.

I lay the 'stove-pipe' on my shoulder and screen in on the nearest tank. Tiny lets out a sigh of anticipation. Porta, seemingly quite unmoved, chews on the butt of a liver sausage. Heide screws at his rocket. Every movement is as laid down in the HDV.* He is a walking dummy stuffed with army regulations. He isn't killing human beings with his magnetic rockets, but just dispersing unimportant concentrations of atoms in which he is personally uninterested. He'd

---

* HDV (Heeres-Dienst-Vorschrift) (German): Army Service Manual.

cut any throat at all if ordered to. And if you reproached him for it he'd think you were out of your mind.

In his opinion orders should never be questioned or even wondered at. Ordered to march to the moon he would pack his kit as regimentally perfectly as a recruit, swing his gun over his left shoulder, draw eight weeks march rations, crack his heels together and turn smartly to the left. Erect as if he had a broomstick stuck up his back he would march in the direction of the moon and keep on marching, either until he dropped dead or somebody gave a counter-order. Unfortunately for normal people there are a lot of NCOs like Julius Heide around. You find them everywhere. You cant get away from them. But Porta says these regulations robots are indispensable. Without them things would go all to pot. Without a bit of the 'fear of God' behind them, people got superiority complexes.

'Mount!' commands the Russian officer. With practiced movements the tank crews swing themselves up into their vehicles.

'Start up!'

With a howl the diesel engines start. Soon they are turning over smoothly, bubbling in anticipation of movement. Only one of them continues racing madly.

A tall powerful woman, in a green uniform with captain's badges, shouts angrily at the commander of the leading tank.

Immediately the driver lifts his foot from the accelerator pedal.

'Ready!' orders the Old Man.

All five Panzerfausts are aimed.

'Come death, come—,' whispers the Legionnaire between his teeth.

'Dawai, dawai,'* the commander of the lead tank chases the laggards collecting the cooking utensils. Soldiers always have difficulty tearing themselves away from a camp. In a good camp one forgets the war.

* *Dawai* (Russian): Faster.

'Where's Oleg?' the girl-sergeant cries suddenly, and looks around fearfully.

'Yes, where's Oleg?' repeats the commander of the third tank.

'Time to get into 'em,' says Porta.

'Fire!' commands the Old Man, chopping his arm forward.

The commanders in their turrets turn towards us as if at an order.

The bazookas roar simultaneously. Five fiery-tailed comets speed towards their goal. A deafening explosion cuts through the woods. All five shots are hits. At thirty metres the Panzerfaust is destructive to all types of tank. Glowing splinters of steel hurtle between the trees. The men in the turrets are thrown high into the air. They seem to balance momentarily, supported on the flame of the explosion. Then their bodies shatter in the force of the blast.

A whole turret with its long gun-barrel whirls above the trees. Burning oil spurts many yards away.

The girl-sergeant stumbles about in a sea of fire. The young soldier who had made the coffee runs headless through the trees. We used to wonder at the distance a human being can run without a head. We don't anymore. When you've experienced war for a while you don't wonder at anything. The other day we saw a man run without legs. His screams rasped at your nerves. He was a German Oberleutnant, an older reservist. It was comical, seeing him run without legs. Afterwards we discussed the phenomenon. Tiny thought people might be like lice which can still run even after you've nipped their legs off.

Heide, that irritating know-all, gave us a long lecture on the nervous system, which it seems becomes particularly strong under the influence of the National Socialist health diet. A Soviet *untermensch*, not to mention a Jew, would never be able to run without legs like that German Oberleutnant. Now we were all hoping we *would* run across a Russian who could run just as fast as a German without legs. That'd shut

17

Julius up. A Russian running along without a head didn't move *him* at all. A chicken could do that!

We storm forward, between the burning sunflowers, shooting at everything that moves. A little white dog dashes about barking madly. Barcelona catches it. It struggles madly and snaps a piece out of his nose. He throws it from him with a howl of pain, into a pool of petrol where it burns like a torch.

Porta considers Barcelona much handsomer without a nose. Heide clamps it in place. Of course, he *would* have surgical clamps with him. It was in orders back in 1939. He's had them with him ever since, in a shiny little metal box hidden in the field dressing pocket of his greatcoat. It's a certainty that ten minutes after we're back with the regiment he'll have drawn replacements, and it's just as certain that he has six metres of gauze bandage in his individual first-aid pack. Not a millimetre more or less.

We catch the woman captain alive. She goes for Stege like a hungry wolf. Porta trips her and she rolls like a ball. She tries to stab Tiny with a needle-sharp Caucasian dagger, but he kicks her on the knee and brings his gun down on the back of her neck. She isn't finished yet. Comes back like a released spring and goes for the Old Man. Six subs speak at once.

She falls down, screaming. Blood spurts from her mouth. She's a long time dying. We daren't go near her. She could have a pistol on a Bowden cable up her arm. Bend over her to wipe the blood from her lips and give her a slug of vodka, and she could lift her arm and nail you through the kisser with a 6.5. We've seen it often enough. The Eastern Front is like no other. Even in death they still kill out here. Tiny takes a thoughtful bite out of a mutton sausage and swills it down with slivovitz. Porta slices at a goatsmilk cheese he has found in the Russian camp. I chew at a chunk of Russian army bread, dipping it from time to time in a large tin of sardines in oil I have found. The Old Man bites on a gherkin. We aren't insensitive animals, we're just hungry. So that we drive at the supplies the Russians have left us. I can't remember when I last saw sardines in oil. I love them – and the best bread in the world is Russian army bread. The woman captain writhes in agony.

'Shall I turn her off?' asks Tiny and pulls his Nagan from the yellow leather holster which he has strapped to his thigh in real commissar style. 'None of that,' snarls the Old Man, 'or I'll turn you in for killing a prisoner!'

'The pain's comin' in stabs,' explains Tiny. 'She's turnin' 'er toes up! I can't stand seein' a nice-lookin' bint like 'er suffer. Let me rock 'er into 'ell, Old'un, so we can get movin'!'

'Go on,' we all cried in agreement, 'give it her in the neck!' The Old Man springs smartly backwards. The submachine-gun's wicked mouth gapes at us.

'The man who kills her, I kill! Put that gun away, Tiny!'

'You ought'a be in command of a flock o' bleedin' nuns,' growls Tiny and rams the Nagan crossly back into its yellow holster.

The woman captain ends it herself. She did have a pistol on a Bowden up her arm.

'And I was ready to go over and give her a swig of vodka,' bursts out Stege in a scared voice.

'Never do it, mon ami,' warns the Legionnaire. 'Always put a bullet into a body before going near it and you will lengthen your miserable life on this military dung-heap appreciably. Thank Allah for all dead enemies. They cannot hurt you anymore!'

Naturally Porta finds a sack of coffee. He swings it over his shoulder with a happy look on his face.

'Squad, fall in!' commands the Old Man. Tiny stands with the burnt remains of the very desirable Boudionovka in his hand.

'Oughta 'ave that spike rammed up 'is jacksey an' broke off smartly! Wot 'd 'e want to go standin' on the top of all that explodin' petrol for? Bleedin' officers, I don't know! Wouldn't give us gun-fodder the shit from under their nails even when there's a war on!'

He slings the charred cap away amongst the trees.

19

'You picked up five gold teeth,' I say and haul him away with me. The others are already well ahead.

They are easy to track. The aroma of coffee from Porta's sack hangs like a banner behind them.

Above the trees the rocket batteries draw lines of fire on the sky. The Russians are using Stalin Organs.

'Where them there 'its,' says Tiny and points toward a long row of fiery streaks, 'there won't be as much as a button left. Queer, when you come to think of it, 'ow it's possible to chuck a bleedin' great chunk of iron up in the air an' 'ave it drop just where you want it to.'

'It's something they've been a long time working out,' I explain.

'I *am* aware o' that,' says Tiny heavily. 'I am *aware* that they didn't pull it all out of a bloody top 'at. But I still say they wasn't sittin' right at the back of class when brains was dished out. Think o' bein' able to shoot a bleedin' ton o' steel miles an' miles through the air, an' 'ave it fall bang on top of a general's bleedin' nut whenever you feel like it! Bleedin' wunnerful is that *that* is! *Bleedin'* wunnerful!'

> 'A strange man, this Hitler, but Chancellor, not to speak of Commander-in-Chief of the Army, he will never be. At the most he could perhaps be used as Postmaster-General.'
>
> President Paul von Hindenburg in a conversation with General von Schleicher, 4 October 1931.

Marshal Malinovski writes in *Wojenno-isoritschesskij-jurnal* nr. 6 1961: The zenith of Stalin's stupidity came when he ordered the Russian troops to remain in garrison and at training bases far behind the front line even after he had been given positive proof that Hitler was preparing an attack. Three months before X-day, more than a million German soldiers were concentrated on the Russian-Polish frontier. The defence plan, worked out to the smallest detail by the Russian General Staff and confirmed by Stalin, was *by his own orders* never put into operation, and the various divisions and army corps were so stupidly disposed that the German panzer forces destroyed them as easily as if merely carrying out an exercise. The craziest disposition of all occurred on Saturday evening, 21 June 1941, when the tank divisions were withdrawn from their infantry to be formed into new tank brigades. The old BT-5s and -7s were drawn up on the parade grounds and their crews marched away to troop training grounds. On Monday, when the Germans arrived, these specialist troops had not even infantry weapons with which to defend themselves. They were ready-made columns of prisoners served up on a plate by Stalin to the Germans. In the first three days of the war, 90% of the Russian Air Force, forbidden by Stalin to leave the ground, was crushed by the German bombers. During the first six hours of 22 June Stalin forbade the Red Army's frontier divisions to open fire. But as Pjort Grigorenko ironically says: Thank God for the 'undisciplined' soldiers of the Red Army who opened fire against orders.

Stalin refused to believe that German troops had crossed the Russian border on Hitler's orders. Even in August he was still convinced that the whole thing was a mistake, and provoked by the German Junkers.

He kept on saying: It cannot be true! Adolf Hitler would not break his word! Foreign Minister Ribbentropp has assured me of Germany's friendship.

Slowly Moscow recovered from the shock, and began to send out attack orders.

Defence Minister Timoschenko still thought he was living in the revolutionary days of 1917 and ordered: 'Attack with cold steel'.

Front commanders begged to be allowed to move under cover of night.

But no! Stalin ordered attack, and the troops moved forward to their deaths. Easy prey for the Luftwaffe. The remnants of the tank army were sacrificed in a witches' cauldron stirred by Stalin.

In the Kiev cauldron, the 5th Tank Army battled desperately to avoid complete destruction, and would have won through but for foolish orders given by Stalin and his sycophants in the Kremlin. Thousands and thousands of brave Russian soldiers were slaughtered because of this stupidity.

When all was over, and courageous men had brought some semblance of order out of chaos, the responsible leaders busied themselves looking for scapegoats. The officers of the Western Military District went first – all of them! One of the youngest – and best – army commanders, Colonel-General Kirponis, was executed. His Chief-of-Staff, Lieutenant-General Tupikov met the same fate. Throughout the gigantic land the rifles of the firing-squads crashed. Major-General Grigorenko states that 80,000 higher-ranking officers were executed without benefit of trial in the course of a fortnight. The witnesses to Kremlin stupidity had been wiped out. Stalin took the title of Generalissimo!

2 | Herr Niebelspang's Via Dolorosa

Before we take over the white castle, the GPU has used it as Staff HQ. There are 200 neck-shot bodies in the cellars. The next day the PK* people are swarming all over it. When they've finished snapping their shutters the dead are buried in the flower-beds. The earth is softest there. We get the feeling that there are a lot of bodies in that park, and that more are on the way; for when we march out SS-Gruppen-führer Heydrich's Special Detachment marches in. We don't talk about it, but we all know what the job of the SD-units is.

Most of us are very young but have never enjoyed youth's light-hearted freedom. They threw us into the war before we even began to live. Something big is cooking. Every second hour we test motors. With the aristocratic Maybach engine this is a necessity. If it stands too long without turning over it won't start, and Panzer troops never know when they will have to move off. Just when you're lying there having it good and have almost got to believing the war is over, or that the infantry will do the rest, you get the order: 'Mount! Start up! Panzer march!' And then you're in the thick of it again, and comrades you sat talking to only a short while ago are already turned into burnt mummies. Sometimes it's quick. If the crew's been soused with petrol, for example. It's worst when oil from the flame-throwers boils them slowly to a soup. Sometimes when you get to them they're still alive. You touch them and the flesh falls away from their bones. They shouldn't be picked up, really, for they'll die anyway, and they die easiest when they lie, once they've got out of the tank. But Army Medical Regulations say they must be taken to the Medical Aid Centre. And it is wisest for a soldier to obey service regulations blindly.

'In the Forces there must be order,' says Porta, 'otherwise going to war at all would be out of the question. Every so

* PK: Propaganda Company.

often a great nation *has* to go to war if only so that their next-door neighbours can see they're *still* a great nation. Where'd we be if any slave could do what he liked? To put it bluntly, the 'Fatherland's Moments of Destiny would be shat upon.' All the bloody footsloggers'd down tools after the first day at war, and neither the generals nor the politicians could put up with that. Think of all the trouble they've been at, arranging it all. War's a serious business! You'll do well to take note of that,' Porta ends, and slams the driver's slot shut.

It's pitch-dark the night we break camp. Rain is pouring down and a gut-wrenching stink of diesel oil penetrates everywhere. The Panzer infantry come over to us wet and chilly with groundsheets pulled about them and caps down round their ears. The veterans have wrapped their weapons in oiled paper. Ninety-nine alarms out of a hundred are false alarms so why get your arms dirty. It's forbidden to use oiled paper but no platoon commander ever takes notice of it. To be quite honest we do a lot of things which are forbidden.

Take rape for example. *That's* forbidden. *Strictly* forbidden. The penalty is hanging but it's seldom anyone gets hanged for it. In the village of Drogobusch the other day, we found a lovely long-legged girl who'd been treated pretty roughly. She said 25 men had raped her. The medical officer who examined her said it could well be true. But no action was taken. Not a single 'Watch-dog'* turned up, and they're there for a certainty every time a threat arises to the interests of Greater Germany's Defence Forces.

'Stretcher!' comes a complaining cry from the darkness. 'My hand.'

It happens every time there's an alarm. Some fool lays his hand unthinkingly on the exhaust-pipe. There's a sizzle and a stench of burnt meat. When he pulls back his hand it's a skeleton claw. He'll be punished for his stupidity but what's six weeks hard in comparison with the front-line? Summer at the seaside! A stretcher-bearer threatens harshly with courts-martial. Self-inflicted wound.

---

* Watch-dog (slang): Field Police, who wear a chain around their necks.

If the chap's unlucky they might even shoot him – when the medics have brought him back to perfect health. We executed one last Sunday. A fellow who'd had both legs amputated. They tied him to a board so that we could shoot him standing up. Executions have to be carried out standing, in accordance with regulations.

'They'll neck 'im,' predicts Tiny ominously, tearing open *die eiserne Portion** and consuming the contents in three colossal gulps.

'Where the devil do you put it?' asks the Old Man astonishedly.

'Put what?' asks Tiny blankly.

'Put a couple of pounds of grub at that speed?'

'Never thought on it. When I was eight years old I'd swaller a 'ole chicken with legs an' the lot. You soon learn it when y'ave to get it down quick an' under cover.'

'Remember the time we ate Hauptfeldwebel Edel's Christmas ducks?' chuckles Porta.

We'll never forget those ducks. When the Secret Police turned up to investigate the theft of eight corn-fed army ducks they fed the entire company emetics to find the guilty party. The ducks shot out of us in pieces almost big enough to quack at the four leather coated investigators with the turned down hat-brims.

We were escorted to HQ Company, where two offices had been placed at the disposal of the interrogators, but there it turned out that the hat-brims boss was an Obergefreiter pal of Porta's and the interrogation turned into a crap-shooting session which sent the investigators home without their leather coats.

'Panzer, forward march!' comes over the communicator.

Maybach engines roar thunderously.

The Old Man pulls his goggles down over his eyes. From the wood comes distant sounds of armed contact. Our grenadiers have run into the enemy infantry. Field artillery

* *Die eiserne Portion* (German): Iron rations (only to be opened on special orders).

ploughs up the defence positions and soon they are nothing but heaps of clay and stone.

'We should never have gone into Russia,' sighs Stege pessimistically and fits a new belt into the machine-gun. He is always pessimistic before going into combat.

MGs chatter madly and 80 mm mortars spit their bombs towards the machine-gun posts.

'Plop! plop!' sounds incessantly. Geysers of earth spout up all around us. A polished track runs straight as a ruler along the edge of the wood and disappears in a milky curtain covering the village of Pocinok. We have never been in Pocinok but we know every inch of it. We know where they have positioned their PAK* without being told. If they have tanks they'll be dug in behind the school. The ideal position. They don't even need to dig them in. With our short-range equipment we can't touch their heavy KW-1s and -2s. The PAK will be next to Party HQ and the Komsomol†. Party HQ is the last thing they abandon.

Gods, how it rains! Rain is coming in through the gas-ventilators. If rain can get through them gas can too! Involuntarily I look towards my gas-mask hanging over by the periscope. It has two filters. One of them has been used for distilling spirits and smells sweetly of alcohol. It ought to be a great help in a gas attack. You'd be half cut before you'd even noticed you were choking on chlorine.

At the roadside, half in the ditch, a lorry lies on its side. One of the big three-axled heavy artillery jobs. Its howitzers have been blown over into the orchard. One wheel has disappeared completely. The strike has torn up a whole row of fruit-trees. Ripe apples are lying everywhere. 1941 was a good year for fruit. The apple-pickers had been hard at work when the air-borne mine arrived. A ladder has been cut across as neatly as if with a circular saw. An apple-girl has been blasted inextricably into it. She has been blown almost completely out of her clothes. One shoe hangs from her left

---

* PAK. (Panzer-Abwehr-Kanonen) (German): Anti-tank guns.
† Komsomol. Russian Youth Organization.

foot and a piece of amber on a chain is still round her neck. A piece of a rung has gone through her stomach and sticks out of her back. Dead artillerymen lie around the lorry. One of them still clutches a bottle of wine in his hand. He met death in the middle of a swig.

By the gate lies the body of a German infantryman. He cannot be more than seventeen years of age. Both fists are buried in his entrails as if he were trying to retain them. His ribs are bared. They look like polished ivory. In the black crater, blasted by the mine, water chuckles pleasantly, washing away blood and torn remnants of humanity.

'Odd how wars always start in the autumn, and how they slow down in the spring,' Porta philosophies. 'Wonder why?'

When summer begins to wane war begins in all seriousness. Then the infantry skirmishing is over. It usually starts with the sound of engines starting up night after night over on the other side.

Suddenly, just before some dawn, things start to move. The first twenty-four hours are always the worst. There are so many casualties. After a couple of days things begin to ease off. Not because the war itself gets any easier. Just the opposite. What happens is that we get used to living with death.

During the last three weeks fresh troops have been pouring in. Night and day boots have marched past our white castle. Companies, battalions, regiments, divisions. In the beginning we watched them curiously. They smelt of France. We all longed to be back in France. Then we were wealthy. Porta and Tiny did big business. In partnership with a Marineobermaat they once sold a fully-armed torpedo-boat. Tiny reckoned on receiving an English decoration when the war was over. The two shady gentlemen who had bought the torpedo-boat had promised him one.

We thunder through the village without meeting resistance. The heat from the exhaust makes us sleepy. Porta has the greatest of difficulty in keeping the heavy tank moving straight between the lines of troops marching on both sides of the road. A moment's inattention and he could flatten an entire company.

Our own infantry are lying on the back of the tank half-unconscious from the carbon-monoxide. It is dangerous to lie on top of the engine between the two big exhaust-pipes, but they still do it. It's so lovely and warm.

Tiny sprawls on his ammunition and curses in his sleep. His snores are almost enough to drown the noise of the motor. Four fat lice race across his face. They are the rare kind with cross-markings on their backs. They are said to be particularly dangerous.

They give us a Deutschmark for every good specimen we turn in to the medical orderly. He puts them in a test-tube and sends them to Germany. We've never found out what they do with them back there. Porta has a theory that they wind up in a concentration camp for lice in which scientists are attempting to breed a special Aryan louse just intelligent enough to lift its front legs in the Nazi salute if Adolf should happen to pass by. Heide walked off in disgust when this theory was promulgated. The Old Man wakes Tiny and informs him of the fortune he has running around on him. He manages to catch three, but the fourth, and largest, specimen drops onto Porta's neck. Naturally, he immediately declares it his personal property. They pin them to the rubber of the periscope mounting, ready to hand over when they run across the medical orderly.

A colossal orange fire-ball springs upwards with unbelievable force from the bushes close to the leading P-IV. The Panzer infantry throw themselves from the vehicles and take cover. With frightened eyes and hammering hearts they wait for death. An automatic cannon sprays the terrain. 20 mm projectiles ricochet from the steel sides of the tanks. A great wall of fire rises up in front of us. A flaming roller-curtain rolling the wrong way. It comes from the woods, shoots skyward in thousands of coruscating colour nuances, bends forward, and falls in our direction.

'Stalin Organ,' mumbles Heide frightenedly, and ducks reflexively under the Funker-MG.*

In a long-drawn horrifying thunder the rockets fall. Buildings are literally shaved off the face of the earth.

'Panzer, forward march!' snarls a hoarse voice through the speaker. But before the drivers can get into gear, the next salvo falls.

Porta speeds up his motor. We burst forward through mud and water. The Maybach screams at full power. Tracks whip at the mud, throwing great clods of earth high into the air.

In Spas-Demensk the streets are all ablaze. As we pass a large house the roof falls inwards and a rain of sparks and burning wood is thrown out over the Panzer column. A piece of burning wood falls through the hatch of our tank and sets fire to a pack. A sugar factory burns with a blinding white flame. Immediately after we have passed it a sugar-tank explodes and sprays glowing sugar far and wide. A P-III explodes right in the middle of the boiling mass.

The Panzer column halts for a moment and the guns roar. Burst-flames spring up everywhere. Artillery, grenade-throwers, machine-guns and tanks in a hell of death and destruction.

Shovels and picks ring. The wide tracks scream deafeningly. Tanks move slowly forward through fallen walls and twisted girders. Thick strangling smoke covers them.

The forward units guide us by wireless. No other army in the world is so well-trained in keeping contact as is the German. We even maintain contact with the heavy artillery far behind us. Our 75 mm guns cannot touch the giant Russian KW-2s, and our tactic is to hang on to them, worry them, smash their tracks until they cannot move, and then call on the heavy artillery and direct its fire by wireless until the giant is smashed.

No. 1. Battalion is in contact with the enemy trenches and PAK. Hordes of blood-spattered soldiers rush past us on the road. Our infantry has already suffered terrible losses.

* Funker-MG. Telegraphist's machine-gun.

Step by step we move forward. Porta takes his cue from the exhaust flame of the lead-tank. A frightful explosion shatters a P-III. It lights up with a blueish flame, then breaks up and disappears in a coal-black blanket of smoke. Trails of tracer hasten questingly towards the enemy position.

A BT-6* comes charging out from a side-road. It shoots up over an earthwork into the air and lands again with a deafening crash ramming a P-III and turning it on its side. It spins like a top and makes for us.

I just manage to catch it in the periscope and fire without aiming. Our shell bursts on the turret in a shower of sparks. With a crash both tanks ram one another, and we tumble around inside our vehicle.

The Old Man tears open the hatch and pops up simultaneously with the commander of the BT-6. The Old Man is quickest. He fires first. Tiny springs from the side door with an S-mine clutched in his hands. He scrambles across the tanks and lobs his mine through the BT-6's open hatch. Seconds later fire jets from its slits and it becomes a heap of junk.

With the help of tow-wires the Legionnaire pulls us free of the wreck. Raging, our company officer, Oberleutnant Moser, chases us.

A 37 mm PAK comes down on us. It is inside a house shooting through a window.

'Aim four o'clock, enemy PAK 125 metres! Explosive shells! Fire!' It's too easy. I can hardly be bothered to take aim properly. The turret whirrs. The long barrel of the gun swings round. The PAK fires again. They might as well be using pea-shooters. Muzzle and impact explosions sound almost simultaneously. The house and the PAK disappear – nothing is left of them.

'Any more for any more?' questions Porta, moving slowly forward. With a lurch the tank tips into a deep shell-hole. Its nose bores into soft earth.

* BT-6: Russian medium tank.

Porta changes swiftly into back gear, but the tracks only whip around without taking hold. He tries to wobble us free but we are caught. Tiny has a long slash on his face from the corner of an ammunition locker. He has fallen forward together with his shells on top of Heide who is jammed between the wireless and the Funker-MG. He is yelling that his hand has been torn off. Later it turns out that he has broken a finger. Annoying when there *has* to be a casualty that it should only be a broken finger. Not enough to get you out of the wagon for a couple of days.

The Old Man slides over the ammunition basket and gets his arm jammed under the oil-pressure gauge. I have fallen over Porta and get the gear-lever in the crutch. I'm going mad with the pain but it won't get me a hospital ticket.

It takes Barcelona's wagon almost fifteen minutes to pull us out. Oberleutnant Moser's language can be heard far and wide. He is certain we did it on purpose.

'One more of those and you're for a court-martial!' he rages.

'His mother must have been pissed when she got him,' Porta mutters contemptuously. 'He talks as if he's nearly ready to spew his lights up!'

We take up position close by the burnt-out hospital. Nobody really knows what is happening. The company's twenty-two tanks are drawn up in one long open row. The guns point expectantly and threateningly forward. We can hear No. 8 Company taking up position on the other side of the river. The rest of the battalion is in readiness down by the sugar factory.

Morning breaks, heavily veiled in fog. That's the worst of being close to water. Morning and night you're wrapped in an impenetrable witch's broth of mist. The heavy weapons are silent. A couple of MGs on the other side of the water are all that can be heard. Nobody has any idea where the infantry is. We don't even know if they've got through the enemy lines. We have a frightful feeling of being all alone in the hugeness of Russia. Slowly the fog lifts and darkness

31

recedes. Houses and trees take on a shadowy outline and form.

The Panzer infantry moves up in single file, close to the houses, and groups by the tanks. Our guns and MGs break out in a thundering, flaming barrage. The earth shakes and shivers under the bellowing cannonade, long flames shoot from gun-muzzles. An umbrella of tracer covers the terrain.

The regular infantry makes ground in short advances. We shoot just above their heads in a precisely calculated covering fire. It's no fun moving with shells howling overhead. If they drop short the infantry gets it in the neck and it *can* happen that the soldier behind the gun is an incompetent fool. It doesn't help the man on the receiving end of a shell to know the gunner behind him will be court-martialled for dropping short.

A long way forward brown uniformed figures are running away from us. They disappear into the fog. Over a hundred tanks hammer shells into the enemy ranks. Disorganized and panic stricken the Russians withdraw to prepared positions.

We are drawn up in ranks as if at firing-practice. Only here the targets are live. Carelessly we leave all hatches open but suddenly a storm of enemy artillery fire breaks over our attacking infantry. They scuttle about digging themselves in. Shells hail from the heavens. Bodies are thrown again and again into the air. Red-hot shell fragments slash terrible wounds. Screams and moans rise from the fox-holes.

A new surprise awaits us. A long line of enemy anti-tank guns move into position. Quickly they range in on us and in the course of a few moments the action develops into a raging duel between our and their guns. The first two PAKs fly to pieces but the others know their job. One of No. 8 Company's tanks blows up.

Barcelona reports a hit on the turret. His gun is out of commission and he must go back to workshops.

A second later we are on the receiving end of a direct hit on our forward shielding. The screaming clang of the explosion is so loud that we are totally deaf for several minutes. An oil lead bursts and drowns the cabin with heavy oil. If we had not reinforced the front shield ourselves with sections of track the shell would have penetrated it and blown us to pieces. It would have gone straight through Porta and struck the ammunition rack behind me.

Shortly after, the Legionnaire reports hits in the underbelly and damage to his gun. He too must go back to workshops. Three of No. 4 Section's wagons are on fire. They explode before any of the crew can get out.

A new hit shatters the gear-box and we can no longer manoeuvre. This is the worst thing that can happen to a tank. When it loses its mobility it becomes a sitting duck for a PAK.

Porta jogs us slowly into cover behind a hill. We get to work on the gear-box with our emergency tools. We bang away with the sweat pouring off us. We have to change three links in the tracks as well. A hell of a job. Luckily a workshop truck turns up with special tools and a crane, and things go more quickly. In half an hour we are back in position and helping in the attack on the Russian PAK. But in short order seven of our tanks are reduced to wreckage.

Grey beetles creep forward in line from the edge of the woods. Momentarily we believe them to be self-propelled anti-tank guns. We are undeceived when No. 3 Section swings round to take them on. They are far more dangerous opponents. Five T-34s and ten T-60s. At 800 metres the leading T-60s go up in blue flames. Like factory chimneys they send black oily smoke up into the sky.

We twist madly to avoid the well-aimed shells from the T-34s. This tank is the most dangerous of all; the Red Army's finest weapon. Three of our P-IVs are in flames. Two others withdraw seriously damaged. A P-III is hit by two shells simultaneously. An 88 mm FLAK battery comes to our aid. In the course of a few minutes the enemy armour is destroyed. These heavy anti-aircraft guns are wonderful anti-tank weapons. The new shells they are using are highly penetrative.

The 27th Panzer Regiment attacks in full force and in a

short time the enemy anti-tank guns are overcome. The regiment rolls over them.

Our vehicle has to go into field workshops. The turret is jammed and must be lifted off for new rings to be mounted. The rollers on one side need complete replacement.

'Attack, attack!' comes continually from Division. The enemy must under no circumstances be allowed to regroup. Keep him constantly on the move.

We are ready to drop from fatigue; nervous blotches break out all over our bodies; we stagger like drunkards; answer wildly when spoken to.

Every town we pass through is a smoking heap of ruins; on both sides of the track countless wrecks of tanks and stacks of bodies. Skinny dogs chew at the flesh of the dead and hens squabble over the entrails. We used to shoot at them. No more.

Telephone-poles crash to the ground. Copper wire tangles in our tracks. Houses are ploughed down in whole rows, and the fleeing inhabitants pulped under the advancing tanks.

'Move, moujiks, the Liberators are bringing you the new age! You're to become Germans! Which is a great advantage! Or so they say in Berlin!'

Infantrymen run panting alongside the vehicles, the tracks spattering them with mud. Automatic weapons send tracers tracking light across the terrain. Incendiary shells turn enemy nests of resistance to seas of flame.

We pause briefly and carry out service tasks on the vehicle: change oil, clean ventilators and filters, tighten tracks. No time for sleep. The order comes as soon as our tasks are completed: 'Panzer march!' comes through the loud-speaker.

A few hundred yards on a swarm of Jabos attack us. Their rockets skip over the fields. No. 1 Company is wiped out in the first minutes of the attack. Every tank is affire. The Panzer infantry flees in panic as a wave of Russian soldiers rises from the clover-fields.

'*Uhraeh Stalino, uhraeh Stalino!*'

34

Young GPU troops with the green cross on their caps, political fanatics, storm forward with bayonets at the ready.

'300 metres, straight in front, enemy firing line!' comes from the speaker. 'Explosive shells and all automatic weapons! Fire!'

Two hundred machine-guns and a hundred cannon thunder. All sixteen of the regiment's companies have moved into line. The first row of young khaki-clad soldiers drops, but new ones take their place, as if rising from the earth, form up and advance.

Artillery behind us gets the range. The attacking Guards disappear in fire and screaming steel. The sky itself seems to blaze. Every living thing is killed under the tracks. Some dive into foxholes. When we see them we stop over the hole and see-saw the wagon until the screaming soldier in it is crushed. This short, bloody, engagement will not even be mentioned in the daily report, so unimportant is it, even though it has cost several thousand humans their lives. No, sorry, not humans, merely soldiers. They've no connection with humanity.

We are now moving directly north-east and reach the Smolensk-Moscow motor road. Straight as a string it runs, through swamp and forest, over rivers, swinging in smooth curves as it by-passes towns. On the way we overtake endless columns of marching infantry and horse-drawn artillery. The motorized units are further on. You can tell by the wrecked vehicles lying at the sides of the road. We pass a spot where an entire regiment has been killed with one strike. 'Blast bombs,' says the Old Man quietly. These wicked things, which are shot from emplaced heavy mortars, literally tear the lungs out of their victims. The regiment lies there in good order. In companies and platoons. It's as if they've been given the order:

'Fall out dead!'

A single tree with naked branches remains standing in the wood. A dead horse hangs high up in it.

'I hope this war ends soon,' says Barcelona. 'There's no

end to the hellish weapons they'll discover if it goes on much longer.'

'Might even last that long we'll 'ave nothin' left to shoot *with* an'll 'ave to go at it with clubs,' surmises Tiny. 'Glad I ain't one o' them Tiny Tims!'

Tired, sour fog comes down over everything in a heavy shroud, reminding us of death. The infantry marches in single file down the motor road. They sleep as they march. The old sweats are masters at it. The fog comes from the marshes, and is a real pea-souper. Visibility three feet, no more. The torsoes of the marching column are all that can be seen of them. Where the road dips they disappear entirely and suddenly pop up again on the other side. We drive along with hatches open. The drivers can see nothing and have to be directed by wireless. To an advancing army nothing is worse than fog. Continually we expect to meet the other side. They could attack and butcher us with pocket-knives before we knew they'd even arrived.

In front of us three tanks crash into one another. One turns over on its side, and immediately the cry goes up:

'Sabotage! Court-martial!'

Confusion spreads past us and far behind.

Two soldiers have been crushed under the overturned tank. A Luftwaffe lorry coming from the opposite direction, brakes, skids and sweeps an entire company of infantry off the road. A Jaeger officer and a Luftwaffe Leutnant quarrel wildly. 'This'll cost you your head,' screams the flier hysterically. 'The Luftwaffe won't stand for it any more. The Army has been blackening our name since the days of St Wenceslas. Telegraphist here!' He shouts to his men who are standing forlornly around the wrecked lorry. 'Call the Reichmarschall's Chief-of-Staff!' he commands.

'Sir, the wireless is out of commission,' the Obergefreiter lisps in a pleased tone.

'Sabotage!' screams the Leutnant into the fog.

'Yes, sir, sabotage, sir!' echoes the Obergefreiter with complete indifference.

36

'I command you to call the Reichmarschall,' screams the Leutnant, his voice cracking. 'If your instrument has been sabotaged, then shout man! Or march to Berlin! My order must be carried out!'

'Yes sir,' the telegraphist replies unexcitedly. He turns smartly on his heel and begins to march towards the west. He pauses alongside our wagon. Porta is lying, languidly resting across one of the tracks, chewing on a quivering chunk of brawn. He follows Churchill's motto:

'Don't stand up if you can sit down! Don't sit down if you can lie down!'

'D'you know the way to Berlin, chum?'

'Y-e-e-ep!' replies Porta forcing a large piece of brawn into his mouth. 'Is the Obergefreiter on his way to Berlin?'

'Your parents must have been fortune-tellers,' grins the Luftwaffe Obergefreiter.

'It'll take some time if you intend to go on foot,' smiles Porta. 'Come with us to Moscow. It's not a hundred miles. You could probably get the use of a telephone there!'

'That sounds sensible,' replies the Luftwaffe Obergefreiter, 'but my boss has ordered me to march to Berlin and tell the Reichsmarschall that he wants to speak to him.'

'Well, I suppose then you must go to Berlin,' decides Porta. 'An order's an order. We Germans learn that right from the cradle. March straight down the motor road until you reach Smolensk. Follow the signposts to Minsk, but don't over night in Tolsjeski. Those pigs will put the authorities on to you, and that will delay you at least two days. The military mind thinks slowly. When you reach Minsk look for the fountain: "The Pissing Lady". Everybody knows where that is. Across from the statue is the cabaret called "Ludmilla's Smile." Contact Alexandrovna who owns it. She'll fix you up with vodka. You can get a bed from the dealer in flour, Ivan Domasliki, an outcast Czech who lives at 9 Romaschka Street. Don't forget to have a look at Minsk while you're there. It's an historically interesting town, where a great many different armies have been bashed about through the centuries. But

37

watch your socks! The bastards who live there consider it their *duty* to steal from strangers. Never give them the impression that you own anything at all. Let them think you own nothing but your personal skin and bones. If you don't you can count on getting sold either to the "Watch-dogs" or to the partisans. Whichever of them pays most'll get you. 50 to 100 marks. For an Obergefreiter from the Luftwaffe I'd think the partisans would pay top-price. Army boys like us are only worth 50 marks. SS-men they just won't accept. They only cause trouble.'

'You don't really mean to say that we airmen are worth all that much?' asks the Obergefreiter with assumed pride.

'Of course,' Porta grins across a mouthful of brawn. 'You're a rarity out here in the war. We only see you lot when decorations or supplies are being dished out.'

'I know,' replies the Obergefreiter honestly.

'When you get tired of Minsk,' Porta goes on, 'there's three roads you can choose between. Through Brest-Litovsk is the quickest but I wouldn't take it myself. You're bound to run into trouble. Better to nip through Brohobitz near Lemberg. If we'd taken Charkov you could've gone that way and carried on along the Black Sea through Bulgaria and Rumania. Might've got a lift on one of the Danube boats right through to Vienna. From there there's the autobahn to Berlin via Munich and Plon. Plenty of nice rest-stations along the road. You *can* go north along the Baltic, but that'd mean going through Reval where the SS and the Jews annoy one another. I wouldn't recommend it. As a member of the Luftwaffe you wouldn't be made welcome by either lot. It'd be all up with you. Neither the hooks nor the SS are sympathetic towards your Reichmarschall.'

'It's a dangerous world we live in,' says the Luftwaffe Obergefreiter worried.

'You couldn't be more right,' replies Porta. 'Take old Herr Niebelspang who used to deal in used bottles in Berlin-Moabitt. He once had to travel to Bielefeld, on account of the death of an aunt and a letter about it from an attorney. The letter read like this:

Dear Herr Niebelspang,

Your aunt, Frau Leopoldine Schluckebier has departed this life by fastening her neighbour's clothes-line around her neck and thereafter attempting to step down from a blue kitchen-chair.

As sole heir you must inform me immediately whether or not you accept the inheritance with the assets and liabilities of the deceased. In this connection I can inform you that the neighbour has demanded replacement of the clothes-line.

'"Hurra!" shouted the bottle-dealer from Moabitt in undisguised glee over the old lady's departure by way of the clothes-line. All he thought of was the inheritance until his friend Fuppermann, who was a "No. 7"* in an upper-class district of the town, drew his attention to the innocent little word "liabilities".

'"Yes, but she was such a nice old lady who lived quietly behind drawn curtains," explained the happy heir.

'"There y'are," grinned the No. 7 "Drawn curtains! What was they drawn *for*, I asks? For that the nice people *out*side shouldn't see what was goin' on *in*side! Don't be the least bit surprised if it turns out your nice old auntie was just an old drunk as pissed persistently on the parson's prize pelargonias. You'd never believe the wicked things that come out after a sudden death like that."

'But Herr Niebelspang wouldn't listen to the No. 7's words of wisdom. He took the Berlin-Bielefeld passenger train, changing at Kassel, and arrived at Bielefeld on a dark night, snowing something cruel. It was a Wednesday and he had to be back in Berlin-Moabitt on the Friday to take delivery of a consignment of bottles he was expecting from Leipzig. So that he steamed straight over to the attorney's place without

* No. 7: A rag-and-bone merchant who uses a hook shaped like a figure 7.

39

thinking of how late it was and rang the bell. There was a sign that said: Ring and wait! Open the door when the buzzer sounds! But the door didn't buzz. Instead a coarse, irritable voice said:

'"What bloody idiot's that who's ringing the bloody doorbell at this time of bloody night?"

'"Herr Niebelspang from Berlin," answered the bottle-dealer truthfully. "I have come to accept the assets and liabilities of my aunt, Frau Leopoldine Schluckebier, deceased."

'"Get the bloody hell out of here after your fucked-up aunt! And when you find her shit on her and rub it in for me!" roared the voice with true German courtesy.

'Herr Niebelspang withdrew in haste and passed the night on a bench in a park belonging to the Nunnery of God's Own Sisters. He felt that a holy place was most suitable now that Aunt Leopoldine had passed away.

'Stiff with cold he arrived at the solicitor's office next day, and signed a statement accepting his aunt's assets and liabilities. *Then* they explained to him that his entire inheritance consisted of a large debt. He was ruined and had only one choice left: the Army, the last refuge of the luckless social loser. He joined the 46th Infantry Regiment at Neumunster, and with this fine body of men he left for France with the rank of Unterfeldwebel. God's hand protected him. The very first day he was honestly wounded, the German artillery dropped a barrage short and massacred the unfortunate 46th, and since there were only a few left on whom to hand the Iron Crosses which 10th Army Corps had sent down, Unterfeldwebel Niebelspang was one of those so decorated. When he came out of sick-bay they sent him to 9th Army Corps as a despatch rider. There his troubles really began.

'He was given a BMW solo job with reverse gear and horizontal valves and sent rushing around with messages of vital importance. It was nice in the summer, but then the winter came with snow and ice and rain and hail and skidmarks in the Wehrmacht underpants. One day the Unterfeld-webel was sent on a secret mission to Berlin. They gave him a lovely black briefcase with eagles on it so that nobody could be in doubt about his being a traveller in military secrets. But very soon he and his official briefcase had the men in black suits after them. Good friends advised him to travel by way of Stuttgart. The people there have only one thing in their heads: Mercedes cars. But the dummkopf chose, unluckily for him, to go via Hamburg. In Bremen the Schupos picked him up at a check-point. It took them four days to find out that they needed a government warrant to sniff about in the briefcase. They didn't get it, but instead were given strict orders to release the despatch rider and the briefcase, and my unfortunate friend sputtered away again along his Via Dolorosa on his BMW solo job with reverse gear and horizontal valves.

'At Hamburg he ran into an SS road-block. They were shadowy men from the SS-regiment "Der Führer". Since the "day of awakening" in '33 they had regarded Hamburg as their personal property, and they dragged him off to Lange-horn Barracks. There they only kept him for three days while the SS-men used his arse for football practice.

'Without pausing he continued his journey with briefcase and BMW. At Trave on the Lübeck autobahn he was beaten up by the Security Police for not lifting his arm high enough in the Nazi salute. By mysterious and complicated side-roads he at last arrived at the autobahn leading to Halle, where he had no reason to be at all. There he met a homeless prostitute and gave her a lift. She was on the run with the Vice Squad nipping at her neat little arse. He would've done better to think of his briefcase and leave the Halle pro' to the tender mercies of the cunt-hounds. Just before Willmannstadt, there where the old Gallows Hill lies, the district police were standing around waiting for something to turn up. "*Halten sie sofort, oder ich schiesse!**" screamed an Unterwachtmeister

---

* *Halten sie* etc. (German): Halt at once or I fire!

who was under his wife's thumb. He was a bit of a twirp who'd had one of his balls shot off by the Frenchies in the Battle of the Somme in 1916. I should mention that his name was Unterwachtmeister Müller *II* since there was another Unterwachtmeister with the District whose name was also Müller.

'"You are a spy!" screamed Müller II in a voice which sent the crows fluttering up from the ancient Gallows Oak close by. They disappeared in the direction of Poland cawing excitedly as if denying the accusation.

'"Anything whatever you say will be used against you! You are not required to make a statement but I would advise you to confess at once, you traitorous schweinhund! You don't know me, and you are going to wish you'd never met me. I am Unterwachtmeister Müller II, Herbert Carl of the 7th Police District, Halle. I have caught bigger crooks than you in my time: two murderers, four larcenists, three embezzlers and a traitor. Every one of 'em lost his top!" he added with an enjoyable policeman's smile.

'"Herr Unter . . ." my friend attempted.

'"Keep your mouth shut until you're told to open it!" screamed Unterwachtmeister Müller II. "In Halle we maintain order. Make a note of that! You have the right to refuse to make a statement but don't try to exercise it or you'll wish you'd never been born. We'll make mincemeat of you and serve you up for Saturday supper. So you admit you're a Soviet spy? Your scoundrelly face gives you away. You want to undermine the Fatherland. You are an enemy of the people. Gentlemen of the 7th District, beat the bastard up!"

'The squad drew their truncheons and my friend was in a happy state of unconsciousness when they dragged him into the No. 7 District station. Gendarm-Rittmeister Sauerfleisch went to town in a big way on Unterwachtmeister Müller II after a pleasant conversation with General-Commando III in Berlin.

'Afterwards Unterwachtmeister Müller II and my friend went over to "The Crooked Cop", on the corner of Erika

Strasse and Hermanngasse, for a quiet lager. On the way home they sang blissfully:

> Oh Lord, don't let me stand
> Outside your pearly gate.
> Oh Lord, give me your hand
> Don't say I've come too late!

'"Our society is built on our mistakes," hiccups Polizei-Unterwachtmeister Müller II before they fall asleep, happily arm-in-arm.'

'Why are you telling me all this?' asks the Luftwaffe Obergefreiter quietly.

'To prepare you for your march to Berlin. You'll go through some terrible experiences on your pilgrimage through our three dimensional National Socialist state.'

'I protest!' cries Julius indignantly. 'High treason, enemy propaganda!'

'What the hell kind of spook's that?' asks the Luftwaffe Obergefreiter in surprise.

'There's a clown in every good circus,' smiles Porta. 'In No. 5 Company we have Unteroffizier Julius Heide.'

'The kooky types you do meet in the forces,' sighs the Obergefreiter apathetically. 'Did your friend ever get to Berlin with his express message, by the way?'

'Yes, he got there in the end,' continues Porta, 'but the Chief-of-Staff's adjutant got a funny look on his face when he looked at the date on the messages. If they had got there in time they could've changed the history of the world. My friend was arrested and locked up in Gross-Lichterfelde. You should've *seen* the charge-sheet they made out for him. He found out just how much easier and less risky it was to deal in used bottles than to be despatch-rider for a German General Command. The Judge Advocate enjoyed himself with him for three or four weeks. A carpenter came and measured him for a wooden one-piece to be delivered immediately after receipt of twelve rifle-bullets. Then 9th

Army Corps required him sent to Strassburg. He'd been posted in orders with the MPs as a deserter for quite a long time, and now to their surprise he turns up in III General Commando's jug. This they found a bit annoying. In Leipzig he met Herr Luske who ran a blackmarket slaughter-house and invited him to dine on "nervous pork with sauerkraut" washed down with poor-man's champagne. Whilst they sat filling themselves with fat pork . . . .'

'What are you doing here still?' comes an enraged shout.

'Didn't I order you to report to the Reichsmarschall? Down on your face! Twenty push-ups.'

With unbelievable slowness and complete indifference the Luftwaffe Obergefreiter drops down in front of his officer and carries out the required twenty push-ups.

'Don't bend your elbows so much,' whispers Porta. 'It takes more energy to come up.'

'Up, Obergefreiter!' shouts the Leutnant hoarsely, realizing suddenly that he is only making himself a laughing-stock.

For a moment the Obergefreiter lies motionless, simulating unconsciousness. It almost always works. Push-ups are forbidden in the Prussian Army. They've cost too many broken blood vessels over the years and if a story like this gets to the ears of a court-martial it can have unpleasant consequences.

'Your officer wants you to stand to attention,' says Porta with his mouth full of brawn.

The Leutnant goes for Porta without thinking.

'You! Obergefreiter there! Keep your mouth shut! Can't you see you're addressing an oficer of the Luftwaffe?'

'No sir, sorry sir, I don't see anything for the moment, I've got my eyes closed, sir. Closed by order of my CO, sir, Oberst Hinka, sir. According to HDV no tank driver must be irritated or ordered to carry out work of an unproductive nature. As soon as the vehicle stops the driver must rest!'

The officer makes odd noises. His eyes roll in his head and his colour changes.

Porta regards him with an adoring expression. As if the Leutnant were his newly-returned beloved prodigal brother.

'Request to be allowed to ask the Leutnant, sir, if the Leutnant knows Herr Judge Advocate Plazek from Wiener-Neustadt?'

The Luftwaffe officer regards Porta with a look of wonderment.

'Judge Advocate Plazek was the life and soul of the garrison prison,' continues Porta with a friendly smile. 'Each new arrival was met with the following beautiful speech: Confess, you criminal, and you'll get on well here. Refuse and God and the Church will turn from you in horror. The reason for your being here does not interest me. *I* want to know what you were doing *before* the authorities uncovered you? Tell me everything about the murder at 27 Kärtner Strasse! Then you will find in me a faithful friend who will stand by you in court.

'Most often prisoners refused to confess but sometimes Herr Plazek met a sensible person. There was, for example, Waffenmeister Kleinhammer who took great pleasure in confessing. He confessed not only to the murder in Kärtner Strasse but also to countless other unsolved murders throughout Central Europe. The Judge Advocate and the Waffenmeister had fun with one another for several months. But when the court-martial began to check up mathematically they found that Herr Kleinhammer must have committed a murder every single day of his life from the age of three. This was no great problem for the lawyers and the court psychiatrists. But to make matters worse the defending officer proved that Herr Waffenmeister Kleinhammer had never been out of the Tyrol. Born in Innsbruck, he had gone to school at Innsbruck, and been officially enrolled in the 6th Artillery Regt. at Innsbruck. The nearest he had ever been to a foreign country was a period as a frontier guard on the Brenner. It made a great noise when the court dismissed the mass-murderer, who had been talked about for months, with only a warning.

'The defending officer got a terrible rocket for insulting the Army by getting his client off. They sent him to Salzburg where a court-martial worked him over. The President of the Court was transferred to Klagenfurt, where he was stabbed by a chap from Trieste in '39. An ordinary murder for gain made out to be a political assassination for the sake of appearances. They hung the black-eyed scoundrel who did it, in reprisal for something else. I don't remember exactly for what but I think it was something to do with a Herr Giodonni from one of the islands where they make glass.'

'That's enough of that, you, you – Obergefreiter,' screams the Leutnant desperately and begins to gabble quite horribly.

'I order you to march to Berlin,' he squeaks finally.

'Sorry sir, sorry, but I'm sorry to say that I'm afraid that can't be done,' smiles Porta patiently. 'There's nowhere I'd rather be than in Berlin. D'you know "The Sitting Bear" in Bernauergasse? There's a pavement-pounder there called Long Lean Lily who has a regular beat between "The Gypsy Cellar" and "The Bear". In the winter you can meet her playing the lady in the Turkish Mocca Room, where they hold their cups daintily with only two fingers. The same thing happened to her as to Herr Pampel in Fasanenstrasse who put water in the beer . . .'

But the officer has had enough, and runs, sobbing weakly, back to his overturned lorry.

From the distance Porta's voice·follows him:

'This Herr Pampel fell into the clutches of Judge Advocate Liebe at Sennelager. They shot him at the back of the Panzer Barracks at Paderborn. You know sir, you know, he *cried* when they shot him.'

'That's the way it always goes,' Porta turns to the soldiers crowded around the tank, 'they arrive, puffed-up and self-assured with their swords clanking against their legs, and dried-up and deflated we send them away. If I was an officer I'd never have anything to do with Obergefreiters. I'd carry on my war without 'em!'

'Then you'd lose your war,' grins Barcelona.

'I'd do *that* anyway,' replies Porta, 'but if I kept away from Obergefreiters I'd lose it without being made a laughing-stock of.' Slowly Porta takes his leather gauntlet off and looks at his right hand with slowly-dawning recognition. 'Jesus and Mary,' he breaks out in pretended astonishment, 'there you are you pretty little chap!' He pats the hand tenderly. 'You've grown since I saw you last, you little devil you!'

Hauptfeldwebel Edel comes slowly over towards the P-IV. In true Hauptfeldwebel style he plants both clenched fists on his hips. He stops by the P-IV and sends Porta a killing look.

Porta lies to attention.

'Herr Hauptfeldwebel, Obergefreiter Porta reports complying with CO's instructions: Resting as soon as becomes possible.'

'Porta,' snarls Edel viciously through thin, pale lips. 'You'll end your days dangling at the end of a good, stout Wehrmacht rope. I'd be a liar if I said I won't be glad to see you dangling. The cleverest thing you can do is to get yourself a hero's death p.d.q., Obergefreiter Porta. You are a shameful blot on the Greater German Wehrmacht. If the Führer ever gets to know that you're a member of his Armed Forces, he'll retire immediately and go home to Austria.'

'Request Herr Hauptfeldwebel's permission to send a postcard?' Hauptfeldwebel Edel turns on his heel and stalks off. From bitter experience he knows how unwise it is to enter into a discussion with Porta.

Porta turns back to the large ring of soldiers round the P-IV and speaks to them of the new times and the happiness which comes to the cheerful in heart.

He goes on to speak of the ties of blood, the brilliance and warmth of the sun, and ends with a ringing Amen and a 'Hail the Great Ones of the Earth!'

Then the MPs turn up, but before they get to the P-IV, Russian mortar-bombs begin to fall and the order comes to move off. Grinning all over his face Porta slides down through the hatch. The Maybachs roar out. Tracks creak. The tank drops a curtsey to the war, which is knocking at our door again.

> **'I have often felt bitter pain when considering the German people; how worthy the individual, how wretched the nation as a whole.'**
>
> Johann Wolfgang von Göethe.

The Sampolit* Malajin walked down the field hospital ward, tore bandages from wounds and in the face of protests from the medical staff hustled the solider patients down to the assembly hall where uniforms and equipment lay stacked.

'Malingering swine!' he screamed. 'You deserve to be liquidated, every one of you. But I am not a cruel man. I leave that sort of thing to the Fascists. I intend to make examples only of the worst of you!' Quickly he chose ten young soldiers, every one of them with a large blood-soaked dressing on some part of his body.

He pulled hard at his cigarette and blew a stream of smoke slowly through his nostrils.

'You bastards lie there taking it easy in your hospital beds while every other Soviet citizen is fighting for our Fatherland and Comrade Stalin!'

'I'm wounded, tovaritsch major,' said the soldier, Andrej Rutych, just eighteen years of age that day.

'You've still got a head on your shoulders, haven't you?' roared the Sampolit, 'and haven't you still got both your arms and your legs?'

'Yes,' replied Andrej, 'but I have a lung wound.'

'Use the other!' The Sampolit turned to a Colonel.

'These ten are condemned to death!' He tightened his belt, straightened his flat cap and spat out his cigarette-butt.

'Get it over quickly! Liquidate them at the crossroads! I want as many as possible to see it!'

* Sampolit: (Russian) Divisional Commissar.

49

'Very good,' replied the Colonel. 'I'll have them shot as soon as it's light.'

'Fine!' grinned the Commissar and left the hospital with his four Siberian special service men at his heels.

'All over!' thought the young soldier Andrej Rutych, whose father was commander of a regiment. 'Nobody will ever find my grave. They'll throw me into a hole like a stray dog and stamp down the earth above me so that no trace is left.'

A grey dawn crept from under the veil of night. They were led to the crossroads. All the wounded from the hospital were lined up against the walls of the house. Many had to be supported by nurses. They dragged the first of them forward and threw a cloth over his face.

Three submachine-guns chattered. Ten times the pattern was repeated. Andrej Rutych came last. They had to carry him to the execution post. He had fainted when the two before him were shot. But regulations must be adhered to. A doctor was called to bring him back to consciousness before they tied him to the post and threw the cloth over his head.

Three hours later the regimental commander, Colonel Kujbyschew, was informed that the Sampolit, Major Malanjin, had fallen in battle.

'It looked for all the world like suicide,' said the adjutant, confidentially.

'That devil went up against a tank with nothing but his side arm and was crushed under the tracks.'

'That son-of-a-bitch!' snarled the Colonel. 'He's cost me half the regiment. We withdraw. It's madness to stay here. Withdraw,' he repeated, 'but fast!'

With his men behind him in close column he ran straight into the Soviet Security Force. They opened fire with machine guns and mowed the Colonel and his 436th Omsk Rifle Regiment down without mercy. Only a few escaped with their lives. They were neck-shot some days later.

'*Nitschewo*,' said an old militia-man. 'They should've known what to expect. That's what always happens. I've seen it often enough. Next time I'll get my hands up smartly and give Fritz my most friendly greetings. It's the safest. Staying on this side is certain death.'

3 | Anti-tank

I position my throat mike. The PAKs, which have been pulled into position under cover of darkness, open fire on us. A reverberating roar seems to send the entire wood flying end over end. Whole trees are uprooted and thrown into the air. The leading tank flies to pieces in a fiercely expanding cloud. Bent and buckled scraps of steel are all that remain of it.

A scarlet curtain of fire climbs towards the clouds and spreads across the road. They're using naphtha shells with pre-contact detonators. The forest is on fire. The flames spread to engulf the overripe unharvested maize fields. Soldiers who have taken cover in them are converted in a moment to living torches, running desperately in circles. Through our observation slots we watch them indifferently. It is a long time since we have been moved by human suffering.

A rain of explosive shells roll across the road and sweeps away an entire company of infantry. It is impossible to differentiate between the sound of discharge and impact. Two P-IVs disappear in one thunderous detonation. The charred remains of an anti-tank crew swing to and fro in a tall fir tree in an oddly casual way. A column of yellow-black smoke mushrooms towards the sky.

'Panzer, march!' commands Oberst Hinka over the loud-speaker.

Company commanders signal with raised hand. Section leaders repeat.

The two hundred and sixty tanks form into line. In the van and on the flanks P-IVs. In depth P-IIIs, with their obsolescent 50 mms. P-IIs and Skodas follow, snapping like bad-tempered fox-terriers.

The air quivers nervously with the noise of motors.

Russian positions are ironed flat. Hundreds of enemy soldiers are crushed beneath the tracks. A haze of poisonous smoke hangs behind the steel giants.

The tank jerks to a halt. The gun recoils and a spear of flame shoots from the oddly shaped muzzle-brake. Shot and sound of impact occur almost simultaneously.

Flames flare up where the phosphorous shell strikes. We alternate with phosphorous and HE, and with terrible effect. We roll forward, mashing wounded and dead into the mud!

A Russian captain attempts to save himself by hanging on to our tow-line. The ragged steel of the cable tears the flesh from his hands. He falls behind us, his legs crushed, thrown off like a piece of garbage.

Concentrated fire from a Russian anti-tank group stops our advance.

'Back to the road!' orders the Old Man. 'Cover with flame-throwers and the forward MG!' He peeps cautiously over the edge of the hatch, and kicks Porta gently with his foot; the signal for full speed forward. The P-IV roars at the road.

I catch sight of a T-34 partly concealed in a clump of trees. The turret swings round, but the long gun-barrel knocks against a stout fir-bole and is stopped. The turret gunner becomes nervous. Attempts to force the tree over with the gun barrel.

I rotate our own turret fast. Figures and lines jump in the sighting lens. The T-34 needs to back only a little to be in position to release a shot, and if it does we'll be nuts and bolts. Long before we can touch it with our weaker armament it will have destroyed us. Our strength lies only in our superior speed. The Russians have committed the unforgivable error of manning a T-34 with a crew of only four men, so that the tank-commander also has to act as turret gunner.

The fifth man, the observer and objective-finder, is badly missed. Invaluable time is wasted while the turret gunner is finding the objective and at the same time must direct the tank's movements.

'T-34 at 200 metres! Armour-piercing!' orders the Old Man. 'Loaded, ready,' shouts Tiny monotonously.

A yellow-white spurt of flame; black smoke expanding to a giant mushroom. The explosion tears the T-34 to pieces. In a procession of glowing balls wreckage rolls across the road. A human body is thrown against our tank and bursts like a ripe marrow. A phosphorous shell explodes immediately behind the smashed T-34. We search the area with our eyes, looking for concealed Panzer grenadiers, and then rumble forward over the wreck. A group of wounded hold their arms out towards us as if trying to stop us with their bare hands.

We meet the road at an angle. A shell from a PAK whistles close above us. The left track throws earth and grass into the air. The tank fights like a drunkard to maintain its balance. Porta, cursing foully, wrenches at the gears and accelerates fiercely.

The tracks clatter on the surface of the road. The long-barrelled 75 mm spews out shot after shot. A platoon of infantry is wiped out. The wounded try to duck away before the tracks can churn over them. The battle area is bathed in the corpse-white glare of the tanks' searchlights.

'Loaded, ready,' mumbles Tiny mechanically. He shouts with pain. He has forgotten he is not wearing his leather helmet and has knocked the safety in with his forehead.

'Jesus Christ!' he howls smearing blood across his face.

'Bloody 'ell! That 'urt!'

'Stop your boasting!' jeers Porta. 'A head as thick as yours pain can't penetrate! All that's alive inside it is a bloody woodpecker that thinks he's found a hollow tree.'

'It flew straight in up his arse without him even feeling it,' sniggers Heide.

Tiny throws his battle-knife at him, missing him by a hair as he ducks. 'You could've killed me, you silly bastard,' shouts Heide, raging.

'No worry,' grins Tiny, on top again.

'Range 500 metres!' commands the Old Man. 'With HE! Load! Fire!'

Like a gaping beast the breech gulps the shell.

'Loaded, ready!' rasps Tiny aiming a kick at Heide which drapes him over the wireless.

'You did that deliberately,' shouts Heide.

'It wasn't me, it was me foot did it,' grins Tiny. 'All the limbs of me body lives together in self-governin' freedom an' brother'ood.' He begins to sing in an excruciatingly cracked bass:

> *Wählt den Nationalsozialisten*
> *den Freund des Volkes!*
> *Täglich wechseldnes Programm!*
> *Urkomisch! Zum Totlachen!*
> *Kinder and Militär vom Feldweben abwärts*
> *halbe Preise!**

'God knows what the Führer would say to such traitorous filth,' screams Heide, shocked.

In a long roaring line the tanks roll forward. An enemy PAK is smashed. The barrel flies through the air, a wheel thumps against a tank turret. The gun-crew is left a bloody tangled clump of meat. The next gun sends a fireball howling at a P-IV. The Russian gun is served by only two men. The aimer and the commander. The rest of the crew lie dead around it. It is a brand-new gun and corporal Pjotr Waska is very proud of it. His militia regiment was formed only eight days ago and has already been destroyed.

'Bravo, Alex!' screams Pjotr enthusiastically. 'That's the fourth fascist bastard we've taken!'

---

* *Wählt den etc. (German)*
  Vote for National Socialism
  The peoples friend!
  New programmes daily
  Lots of fun – laugh yourself to death!
  Children and soldiers
  From Feldwebel down
  Half-price!

A new shell flies into the breech. Ammunition is heaped high behind them. The heap of empty casings is even higher.

'Smack 'em in the teeth, the German swine!' he roars and throws his green steel-helmet towards a wrecked tank. He intends to obey the regimental commissar's order: 'Stand fast! Don't give an inch!'

The two Russian anti-tank men are covered in mud. They look like devils risen from the swamp. They make two more hits. The torn-off head of a German grenadier, still wearing its steel-helmet, lands with a thump beside them. They roar with laughter and take it for a good omen. They plant the head on top of their gun-shield.

'Shoot the arse off 'em!' screams Pjotr, fanatically.

The two soldiers work with machine-like accuracy. Their bodies bend, lift, stretch at their bloody work like automatons. They have no thought of flight. Anybody suggesting it would be shot down on the spot. The regimental commissar's words still ring in their ears: 'Comrades, kill the Fascist invaders! Crush them, destroy them like the vermin they are! Die before letting them pass. It is the duty of every Russian soldier to take a hundred Fascist swine with him. If you do not reach that target you are a traitor and your family will suffer for it! Long live Stalin! Long live the Red Army!'

'Enemy PAK straight in front!' sounds the Old Man's quiet voice as he sights Pjotr's anti-tank gun.

'Target acknowledged!' I echo.

Points dance in the sight. The green lamp blinks.

The hum of the turret stops. The PAK shows up clearly in the sighting mechanism. The gun-muzzle winks hungrily at the Russian position. There is a short violent explosion of light and sound and the gun commander is flying away from us, the gun turning and twisting end over end until it lands a pile of scrap. As we drive over the position the gunner is caught in the tracks and dragged after us. An arm drops to one side a leg to the other. The lower part of his body catches on the off-side light cowl.

The incident is over. Forgotten!

A party of infantry appears in front of us. One of them throws his machine-gun at us in desperation. He dies under the tracks together with his comrades.

'If only blood wasn't so sticky,' grumbles Porta. 'Can't get it off. If God'd thought of tanks when He created the world He'd've made blood that wasn't sticky, and could be washed off with plain water before inspection.'

Heide enters into a complicated explanation, involving red and white blood corpuscles, of just why blood sticks to tanks.

Slowly we fight our way through the village. Two companies of the 41st Infantry have been liquidated – neck-shot.

Propaganda says it's the NKVD, but there are a lot of Mpi* cases round the bodies. There's a rumour that they're would-be deserters shot down by the SD Special Commando. When we go to have a closer look at the bodies we get chased off. A mortar bomb drops into the middle of a group of SD-men. A torn-off arm, the hand still gripping a pistol, is thrown through the driver's hatch into Porta's lap. He picks it up and waves it admiringly.

'Look at that, boys! That's the way we fight in Adolf the Mighty's army! Even a torn-off arm hangs on to its bloody weapon! Reminds me of when my biological father went off to war with the 67th Potsdam Infantry who were so inspired by the thought of dying for the Fatherland that they marched away decorated with roses in black and white organdie.† The third day in action they deserted to the enemy. They'd had enough of fighting for the Fatherland, but before they left they gave themselves time to beat up some Austrians from Vienna who were shouting traitorously:

Down with the Prussians!

'"Hurra, hurra, long live the King!" cried the 67th as they ran across no-man's-land.

* Mpi: Maschinen-pistole (German) submachine-gun.
† Black and white: The Prussian colours.

'The officers never dreamt what these fervent patriotic cries really meant. They thought these coolies were shouting for Wilhelm, King of Prussia. But the Berliners were thinking of Peter of Serbia. The 67th had a drunken Feldwebel called Mateka who had been in front of a court-martial in irons several times, and had it explained to him equally often that a bigger fool than himself had never existed. The Feldwebel's trouble was that he was a Sudeten German, and as such was forced to change his allegiance the way other people change buses; without feeling any particular interest in either the new or the old one.'

'Where'd 'e come from?' asks Tiny who is sitting on a body eating a tomato.

'He was from Prague,' explains Porta. 'His mother was a Pole from Lemberg who'd lived with a Jew horse-trader from Libau who bought Russian horses for the Scandinavian market.

'These nags from the steppes were so old the Jew had to dye their muzzles before he loaded them. On the way he salted their food so much that they always arrived with nice round bellies from drinking all the time. The oldest of them he doctored with a shot of pepper up the arse to make 'im seem frisky on arrival. If any of them had been cut out for sale by the Cossacks because they were lame in a leg, this was no problem for him either. The Jew lamed 'em on the *other* side so the purchaser wouldn't notice it. If pepper-stick couldn't liven 'em up he'd gave 'em a dose of schnapps laced with arsenic and believe you me *that* made 'em jump about as lively as crickets!'

'Come *on!* What *about* Feldwebel Mateka?' interrupted the Old Man impatiently.

'Jesus! I nearly forgot *him!* He reported to a Persian Rittmeister of dragoons who handed him over to the care of Polizei-Watchtmeister Joseph Malán. Malán was the type of policeman who was continually beating his own record for idiocy.

'After the first bottle of Slivovitz they were calling one

57

another traitors and deserters and swore that each of them would be on the end of a good hempen rope before the evening meal. By the time they opened the third bottle they'd got to singing good patriotic songs and compiling crazy reports and despatching them to places far outside that particular police district. Then they went off arm-in-arm singing away down the Libjatkastrasse. I don't suppose anything would have come of all this is they hadn't run into the wife of the CO of the regiment, and slipping their hands up under her dress remarked that it was like feeling-up a frozen Polish cow on a rainy day in November. The well-born officer's lady rushed straight to the Oberst of dragoons who rang to the Rittmeister of police and demanded that order be kept in the district so that God-fearing married women could walk the streets in safety without the risk of being compared to Polish cows.

'The Rittmeister of police was well away when the dragoon Oberst rang to complain about the treatment his wife had received here in the middle of a war. After opening a new bottle of Tokay and thinking about it for a while, he paraded his force and numbered the men in threes. Nos. 1 received a slash across the face from his riding-whip, as was usual when officers and gentlemen, as happened occasionally, ran across the rank and file. Nos. 2 were given a regimentally correct kick in the pants. Nos. 3 got a punch on the jaw for being last in numbering-off.

'"You villains! You're not Royal Serbian Police at all!" roared the Rittmeister. "You're nothing but a shower of flat-footed pot-bellied parsons in uniform. You're the Royal Austrian Steers!" he added thoughtfully as he looked at his sleepy herd.

'The Rittmeister was generally known as a notorious nut-case who sprayed insults and curses around whenever he was under the influence. Which was almost always.

'"I hate the bloody sight of you!" he continued. "You stand here on parade thinking all the time that the Father-land and the war effort can all get fucked as far as you are

58

concerned. But the Fatherland has no intention whatever of getting fucked! You would be surprised what the Fatherland *does* intend and *will* do! With *you* however it will have nothing whatsoever to do"

'He went on to speak of discipline and regulations.

'"Presumptuous persons, who put their hands up under the skirts of officers' wives in the public streets, shall be handcuffed and taken to the police-station. The lady will also be taken to the station as a witness, but *not* handcuffed, you witless fools! At the station the crime can be reconstructed for the report!"

'He withdrew a circular from his cuff and began to read aloud:

'"From the All-Highest Royal Ministry of War it is made known that it is not beyond the bounds of possibility that spies and similar criminals are operating, by reason of the present war, within the country. It is the Royal Police's highest duty to apprehend these suspicious persons and make provision, according to the law, for their being hanged."

'The Rittmeister of police from the Zagreb Military District was, all-in-all, a highly respected idiot who every Saturday evening at the officers' weekend parties stripped himself completely naked. He was close to disgrace once, when he lay down in front of the Tihomil statue in Petersplatz with a kipper stuck up his backside and explained to passers-by that he was a mermaid on tour to Monte Negro. It wouldn't have been half so bad if the drunken fool hadn't had his sabre with ceremonial trappings clanking around his naked loins, and if he hadn't had his garrison cap hanging on his dick. He explained this later as being due to personal modesty. They took him to the main guardroom where the warrant officer in charge of the cells, Brieler, ordered him to be hung in irons and gave him a thorough going-over with the bastinado.

'"We'll teach a civilian bastard like you not to take the piss out of the fighting forces. Lying down in front of King Tihomil and farting straight up in his noble granite features!"

'The next day the warrant officer was broken two grades and fined a quarter's pay for disrespect to an officer. His excuse, that the Rittmeister was naked and in this condition bore a remarkable resemblance to a civilian, did not help him in the least. Further, he suffered from piles. This latter was, however, deleted from the report to save the face of the Army. No officer could possibly be afflicted with piles. This affair cost the Rittmeister a packet. He was posted to a miserable frontier district, where the people were so suspicious of one another that they took their bikes in to church with them, which is a thing they do in certain parts of France. . . .'

'Can it, Porta!' sighs the Old Man, '*and* climb aboard! We're moving!'

'This war's getting on my bloody nerves,' shouts Porta furiously. 'What the bloody hell's it got to do with me, anyway! It's just the same as with old Levinsky, the gents' bloody tailor from Königsallee in Düsseldorf, who was a specialist in turning jackets. When you turn a jacket, naturally the breast-pocket comes out on the wrong side. There was one hell of a row over that in the Kaiser's War in 1916, one Monday. Herr Oberstleutnant von Schletwein had had this civilian jacket turned. The first time he wore it he met a major of hussars who asked him interestedly what it felt like to pull a fountain-pen out of the wrong side of a jacket. That's when the Obersleutnant discovered that there were problems involved in having a jacket turned.'

'Shut your great gob!' yelled the Old Man. 'We don't give a sod for your Düsseldorf tailor and your Oberstleutnant! Start the bloody *motor*!'

'Don't you even want to know what happened to Levinsky when he was called up in the 7th Uhlans, which had been turned into a foot regiment because all the horses had been eaten. Their Oberst wasn't too clever where war was concerned and advanced in column of route. He was against all the new-fangled stuff they were teaching the young officers.

'"Machine-guns are of no importance," he explained to his adjutant, "and I'll prove this by making my advance in column of route. When these Frenchmen recognize our blue Uhlan uniforms advancing towards them they'll run from their *machine-guns* like *rabbits*."

'It was a costly proof for the cavalry Oberst and his Uhlans. The Frenchies mowed the lot of them down with those same machine-guns. Even as he lay dying the Oberst still sobbed! "Machine-guns are of *no* importance in war. . . ." The only man of that regiment who got out alive was Levinsky the tailor who was discharged for the loss of a leg, and this . . .'

'One word more,' hisses the Old Man, pressing his revolver muzzle against Porta's neck, 'and I'll blow your bloody brains out!'

A 100 mm anti-tank gun is dug-in in the ditch alongside the road, behind a heap of agricultural machines and burnt-out lorries. 'Fire!' the gun commander's hand chops down. The shell flies above the leading T-34. Too high! A slight correction is made to the sights. The next shot is a hit. The gun crew are jubilant and thump the aimer on the back. He is an old soldier with nerves of steel. A necessity for a good anti-tank man.

It's a hit, all right. But the only result is a shower of fat sparks struck from the tank turret as the shell bounces off.

'Fire!'

Another hit! Without effect! Again and again the anti-tank guns fire but they might as well be using pea-shooters.

'God have mercy on us!' pants the gun-commander fearfully.

'What the devil *is* that monster!' asks the loader nervously. He has never met a T-34 before. Until now they have only operated singly. This is a whole formation of them.

'And they say Ivan's finished!' mumbles the gunner. Shaking with fear the gun crew stare at the giant tank with the unbelievably broad tracks, the sloping green sides and the enormous gun projecting from the round turret with the red Soviet star on each side.

'Fire,' roars the anti-tank NCO in despair. 'Maximum rapid! Try to hit the swine in the same place every time!'

But the results are equally ineffective. The fear of death comes over the gunners. They send shot after shot at the steel monster rocking and roaring evilly on the same spot. A loaded lorry is crushed, unnoticed beneath its 38 tons weight.

The twenty-fifth shot crashes from the PAK-gun and glances off the enemy tank with as little effect as all the others.

Suddenly the turret opens. A leatherclad figure appears and threatens the German positions with a clenched fist.

The German gun crew is morally defeated. All eleven feel themselves doomed and only await the stroke of death. They are beasts pushed into the arena to be slaughtered and the toreador is the T-34.

Ammunition bearer nr. 2 is the first to panic. He breaks desperately for the woods. A line of tracer spits from the T-34s turret and ends in the running figure. The four men in the tank laugh aloud. This is revenge for Brest-Litovsky where their BT class tanks were crushed like eggshells.

'Why doesn't he move forward and make an end of it?' asks the gun commander.

'He's enjoying himself,' answers the loader, and Obergefreiter who has been in the service since '39.

The turret of the T-34 turns slowly. The long 76.5 mm gun sinks.

A fiery howl, a flaming burst at the edge of the wood, and a German machine-gun group is wiped out of existence. Again the gun thunders and a mortar group is blasted to bits.

The diesels rattle. Tongues of flame shoot from the gaping exhausts. A stench of burnt diesel oil blows, like a charnel breath of death, over the anti-tank crew at the road block.

The loader lights a cigarette from a burning fir-twig, sits down on an ammunition box, looks thoughtfully up at the grey clouds driving overhead and sucks the smoke deep into his lungs. With a sketchy smile he inspects the T-34 then jabs a thumb between the gun commander's ribs.

'Lenau, you've lost your war! Before long you'll be manuring the Russian sunflower fields, and next summer the women street sweepers of Moscow will eat you in the form of Stalin Chocolate. The Herrenvolk's bravest soldiers eaten by the *untermensch!*'

He hands his water-bottle to his comrade. 'Take a swig! If you're drunk enough maybe you won't feel the kiss of death.'

'Do you think dying is painful?' asks the gun commander staring fearfully at the T-34 which is sending a finger of light from its turret projector, searching to the left of the group.

'I've never tried it,' laughs the loader carelessly. 'But I've seen a few go off. Some of them just gulped and died. Others howled something fierce. If our friend in the steel coffin hits us clean with the tracks we won't even know we're dead, but if he just nips our legs off, it won't be so pleasant.'

'I'm going to finish it myself,' says the gun commander releasing the catch of his P-38.

'Adolf certainly won't like that,' sneers the loader. 'Two years ago you were the battalion hero, named in orders, and now you're about to blow your brains out for fear of an *untermensch!* What *are* you thinking about, man? You'll bring shame on the Fatherland!'

'Shut the hell up with that goddam Nazi shit!' curses the commander. 'Those Soviet pigs are going to massacre us in a minute.'

'Did you expect anything else?' grins the loader. 'Were you one of those who thought the other side didn't use bullets and gave in as soon as they saw a German steel-helmet?'

'Your goddam cynicism gets on my nerves,' says the gun commander in a shaking voice. 'Aren't you afraid of dying?'

'Yes. It's a sod dying only 150 miles from Moscow and victory.'

'You believe, then, we're going to win the war?'

'What I believe? Winning's saying a lot, but it won't be pleasant for us if we do lose. Being a German won't be good. What about sticking up our hands and waiting for the final victory in one of their prison camps?'

'The Bolshies'd liquidate us,' says Lenau darkly.

'Balls, Ivan isn't so bad at bottom. My father was a prisoner eight years in the last war, so I know all about that. He even became a Communist because of it.'

'What'd Adolf's boys have to say to that?' asks Lenau interestedly.

'They sent the old fellow to Fuhlsbüttel.* He crossed the white line one day and SS-Oberscharführer Zach set his man-eating alsatian on him. I'll get Zach for that some day!'

'I didn't think alsatians ate people,' inserts Lenau wonder-ingly.

'Believe you me! You can train them to do anything. They were the only dogs we could teach to run with mines at the anti-tank school. We started with English dogs but they just sniffed at the mines and went home with their tails between their legs. They weren't going for it. But our German police-dogs only needed a little speech about the Fatherland and the Führer, a couple of cracks across the neck and a kick in the arse and off they went with the mines. They're the only dogs in the world you can teach to march. Have you ever seen how the dog companies train them? The first dog dashes forward and barks twice. This means: Centre here! All the other German dogs place themselves accordingly.'

The T-34 is now only a few yards from the road block. It stops for a second. Both machine-guns chatter and an infantry patrol is wiped out. Like a steel mountain the colossus rises above the anti-tank gun. Hot oil fumes beat down on the terrified gun crew. Steel and wood crackle under the broad tracks. Slowly the tank tilts forward but the tracks cannot get a proper purchase.

The gun commander throws a hand grenade but it does no damage. With a crash the T-34 tips forward and down.

* Fuhlsbüttel: Prison just outside Hamburg.

64

The PAK-gun is crushed to scrap. Water, blood, dirt and earth mixed to a gruel. The loader rolls away, the only survivor. Cold-bloodedly he ties three hand-grenades round a petrol bottle and runs after the T-34 which is engaged in the massacre of a machine-gun group. He slips and falls in blood and shredded flesh, comes to his feet wiping blood and slime from his face. He is alongside the monster. He has only one thought. To avenge the gun commander, his friend. The rest of the crew mean nothing to him. They are newcomers, arrived just before the attack on Russia. He grasps the tank's infantry-grip but stumbles and is dragged alongside it. He rips out the arming string with his teeth, throws the bomb and drops flat. Rolls to cover, and watches from behind the wreck of something which was once a lorry.

There is a hollow explosion and two rollers fly through the air together with a piece of track.

The T-34 stops. The motor races but the monster only scuttles round on the same spot like an insect with its legs torn off.

The loader takes cover behind a corpse with his Mpi at the ready. The turret hatches are thrown open. Three leatherclad figures jump out and commence making repairs. Only the driver remains in the tank.

The loader opens fire. All three fall together.

Only the commander is still alive when he reaches the tank.

Carefully he plants a foot between the Russian's eyes. Blood and brains spurt out over the heavy army boot. This is what it was designed for. The tracks of the Prussian boot are lined with corpses and slaves! Long live the Kaiser! Sieg Heil! From behind the horizon rises the German sun! Look out, enemy! We'll be back!

The loader withdraws a hand-grenade from his boot and unscrews the cap. With his eyes on the driver's hatch he lights a cigarette he has found on a body. He has almost finished it before the hatch goes back and the driver appears to look for his comrades.

'*Dassvidánja tovaritsch,*'* the loader says with a grin and throws the grenade through the hatch.

'*Njet!*' cries the driver in terror before a column of fire throws him out of the hatch opening. The loader wanders dazedly towards the wood. He doesn't even see the German P-IV, which crashes through the underbrush, until it is on top of him crushing him under its tracks. All that is left of him is a messy pool and a flattened steel-helmet.

'Hurra!' roar the grenadiers following in the wake of the tanks. According to regulations they are supposed to shout 'Hurra' when advancing. But they do it to keep up their courage as well. Now they die cheering. What they should be shouting is: 'Hurra, we're going to die! We're going to die, hurra!'

Rank after rank falls to the Russian waist-high machine-gun fire. the forward positions are overrun; the fighting is merciless; with knives, bayonets and entrenching tools. He who stabs first lives longest.

The flame-thrower operators move forward to relieve them. Jets of flame hiss along the ground. The stink of burnt flesh nauseates us. A 20 mm gun barks angrily, spouting tracer at us. A Maxim hammers from the steps of a cellar.

Under cover of our two MGs the grenadiers storm the burning Party HQ. A group emerges from it with hands above their heads. We mow them down without mercy. We are no longer human beings but blood-crazed monsters who want to kill, kill, kill!

The tanks rumble through burning ruins crushing everything under their tracks. A company presses itself up against a wall. Both machine-guns stammer together.

'Say your prayers, *moujik!*' cheers Heide fanatically. 'We've no room for you in the new age!' He empties the whole belt into the company.

'They're our own men you're flattening you slavering Nazi idiot!' rates Porta. 'Can't you tell field-grey from khaki any more?'

* *Dassvidánja tovaritsch* (Russian): So long, comrade.

66

'Jesus!' gasps Heide in a strangled voice.

'Your Leader wouldn't approve of your calling on a Jew for aid,' smiles Porta sociably.

'Jesus wasn't a Jew,' protests Heide. 'Alfred Rosenberg spoke to us on that subject at the Nazi youth school. Jesus was a German. His family came from Bielefeld, the German Bethlehem.'

'That's a bloody new 'un,' shouts the Old Man from the turret doubling up with laughter.

'Do you really believe that yourself, Heide?'

'Of course,' replies Heide with conviction. 'If you read the Bible properly you'll see how much it resembles "Mein Kampf". Jesus was the first National Socialist but he didn't clearly understand the Jewish peril threatening from Moscow.'

'You're nutty as a fuckin' woodpecker!' shouts Tiny bringing a water-bottle down on Heide's head. 'They shoulda 'ung you up on one side o' Jesus the bleedin' partisan, 'stead o' the bleedin' prophet Elias.'

Tiny's always a bit uncertain on the story of the Bible but we know the man he means.

'You're insulting the Aryan race!' screams Heide hysterically. A thunderous crash stops the conversation. The tank lifts from the road and almost topples. A feed-pipe has broken and petrol spurts all over the combat cabin.

'Wrecked left track,' reports Porta calmly. 'Vehicle immovable!' He stops his motor, drops the back of his seat and takes a long pull at the vodka bottle which hangs by the fire extinguisher. The Old Man opens the hatch cautiously. Alongside us two other P-IVs are on fire giving off billows of black nauseating smoke. The charred bodies of their crews are hanging out of the hatches. By the village well lie a group of dead grenadiers. They look as if they are sleeping. Just a little blood around the mouths of a couple of them. Killed by the blast bombs which have only recently been taken into use.

Porta takes another swig at the vodka bottle, scratches at

his red mop of hair, and screws his cracked monocle into his eye.

'So it's forward again to honours and distinctions in battle for the Fatherland,' he drawls arrogantly. 'Comrades, children in schools everywhere will read of your deeds. Thank God for the good fortune that allowed you to take a part in all this.'

'Good day for suicide,' mumbles Stege dejectedly.

'Turn off them negative waves,' orders Tiny, sourly.

Oberst Hinka sits in his open turret with his grey-painted field glasses directed towards the T-34s, which are opening out for attack.

It is the first time we have seen T-34s in closed formation. Up to now we have only seen them used in sections as infantry support.

Oberst Hinka reaches for his microphone and sends to all vehicles: 'Hear me,' says the quiet voice. 'Our only chance of taking those T-34s lies in movement. Don't lose your heads! Go forward with all the speed you're capable of! We've got to get inside 400 metres. Then swing round and put your shots up their backside! The T-34s weak points are the turret rings and the tracks! But movement, above all movement! Don't stop even to fire. Shoot on the run!'

We pass a demolished roadblock and our section is the first to meet the leading T-34s. They roll forward in a V-formation which they have learnt from us. In June we were attacking confused novices but now in September we are meeting experienced specialists.

No. 2 Section's tanks roll forward at top speed straight through houses and blockades. Water and mud spurt up behind us from the tracks.

'Faster, faster!' comes from the company commander, Oberleutnant Moser.

The Russian tank commanders in the T-34s turrets cheer triumphantly as they see the German tanks press forward to get within range. Captain Gorelik feels himself already a conquering hero in his new T-34 which for some years will be the world's finest tank, purely because of its amazingly far-sighted design. The engineers must have had the Silurian period in mind when they created this deadly monster. Its tracks were so broad that at first sight they seemed almost comical, but the idea behind the construction was soon taken up by foreign manufacturers.

It was flat without sharp angles like a tortoise, and its 76.5 mm gun with its long oversized barrel was a wonder. A mile from the T-34s waiting position the German tanks stick fast in the mud. They back and swing desperately but the more they struggle the deeper they bore themselves into the ooze. The Russian artillery lays down a worrying fire but for every pioneer who falls it seems a dozen others come from the woods to take up the work of the dead. Felled trees tied in bundles are rolled forward under the tracks of the tanks.

'Do what they will, we'll destroy them!' laughs Captain Gorelik confidently.

Warrant Officer Tarsis, who is a section commander in Captain Gorelik's company, is impatient for the battle to begin. He is an old soldier, a holder of the *Zolostaja Zvezda*,* and left a safe job as Garrison WO three days after the war began to volunteer for front service. With a malicious smile on his tight lips he watches the German tanks bucking and sliding helplessly around in the mud. He leans back in his leather seat with a feeling of satisfaction. He has plenty of time. Let the fascist dogs do battle with *Rasputiza*† first. That ought to wear them out. The rest of the battle should be child's-play for the T-34s.

He laughs heartily as he watches the German tanks through his periscope burrowing deeper and deeper into the mud. Revenge is at hand for the dreadful day when he had to abandon his Christi tank at Kiev. He was a prisoner of the fascists for four days. The very thought of his disgrace still sickened him. He had personally beaten up three of his soldiers for having worked for the occupying troops. When

* *Zolostaja Zvezda*: Hero of the Soviet Union.
† *Rasputiza* (Russian): bottomless mud.

he got back to the Russian lines after escaping he reported them as collaborators. Their fate was sealed should they ever return home. Their families had no doubt been seen to already. In the Soviet Union there is room only for true believers.

'Kill them!' Ilja Ehrenburg had said speaking to the tank troops before they left. 'Kill them in their mother's womb!' That was the way to talk.

'Hönig!' shouts Oberst Hinka to the commander of No. 1 Battalion. 'I ordered you to attack in arrow-head! What are you doing clumped together in that hole?'

'Herr Oberst,' groans Major Hönig desperately. 'My whole battalion's stuck in that goddam mud. They're slipping sideways and blocking one another in. Only No. 2 Company has a partially clear field of fire and at any minute Ivan may start up and turn us all to junk!'

'Cool down,' says the Oberst calmly. 'I'll send you a couple of cranes. No. 2 Battalion'll cover you.'

'Ivan has learnt a few things from us,' groans the major. My No. 4 Company has been shot to pieces. Every one of their shots is a hit.'

'Pull yourself together, man!' answers Hinka sharply. 'Get under cover. Use everything you've got in the way of smoke-shells. The enemy's short of ammunition. He'll shoot only when certain of a hit!'

No. 1 Battalion disappears under a dirty-yellow veil of smoke, but soon after the T-34s attack. They thunder forward in a seemingly irresistible V of steel. Without taking heed of the terrain they disappear into No. 1 Battalion's smoke-screen. They seem to skim across the mud on their broad tracks.

Flashes brighten the smoke. It's rough in there. Explosion follows explosion.

At a range of 40 yards we pump shell after shell into the T-34s. We swing, turn and back. We don't stand still a second. In speed and manoeuverability we are superior to the Russians.

In a few minutes the Russian tanks are in wild confusion.

'*Djavolls!*' * roars Captain Gorelik, frothing at the sight of his burning T-34s. He knows what this means for him. The execution wall or degradation to a penal regiment. 'Load faster, you dog!' he screams at his loader. Straight in front of the periscope, right in the gun's sight-line, a blood-red cloud blooms. Lieutenant Sinewirskij's tank has been hit. Soon three more T-34s glow in a sparkling sea of fire.

The captain sees what is coming. They had all put their faith in the new T-34. It would sweep the Nazis from the face of the earth, had Marshal Tsdukow rashly promised.

Warrant Officer Tarsis sits in the turret of his tank pale with suppressed rage. He has missed twenty times even when he has had a fascist dog right in his sights.

'Tarsis, what do you suggest?' asks the captain nervously over the wireless.

The Warrant Officer's spirits rise appreciably. It is the first time an officer, a captain by the mark and an acting battalion commander, has asked his advice. He swallows the gob of spittle he has been about to eject onto the neck of his driver. He even spares the lives of three German infantrymen who run straight across in front of his machine-gun. He opens the turret hatch and elbows himself upwards. Under his black leather helmet his white teeth show in a satisfied grin. It is the high-spot of his life, this conceited captain asking him for advice.

'*Tovaritsch kamandir*,'† he answers superciliously into the microphone. 'Let us use the new flame-throwers! *They* should frighten the dogs. Then into the woods and turn! They'll think they've got us on the run and we'll bang a few shots up their backsides! They're used to an enemy running from them. A real stand-up fight will confuse them and get their tails between their legs.'

Captain Gorelik is shaking with nervousness. All round him the battalion's tanks are exploding. A few yards behind

---

* *Djavolls* (Russian): Devils.
† *Tovaritsch kamandir* (Russian): Comrade Commander.

each green T-34 lies a yellow fascist tank spitting flame and steel at its enemy's rear.

'How the devil do they do it?' mumbles the captain to himself half aloud. 'They're not stupid, these Kraut lice!'

He gives his battalion the order to withdraw. Take cover in the woods. He realizes that this is going to be a narrow victory – if a victory at all.

The remaining T-34s take up position behind a dyke but the German P-IV's are on their heels. Now there is firm ground under the tracks. When a tank catches fire the crew evacuates it and continues the fight with side-arms.

Our vehicle bursts into flames just before we reach the mouth of the river. I hardly catch the Old Man's order:

'Tank on fire! Dismount!'

We lie at a little distance from the burning tank. He don't dare to leave before it is burnt out. The Old Man is in a state of considerable excitement. He is the first who'll be hanged if the vehicle isn't a total wreck before we leave it. But it won't catch fire properly. There's a lot of smoke but no flames.

'Goddam it!' hisses Porta. 'When you don't want them to they catch so fast you're passing St Peter before you're finished shitting your pants!'

Tiny arms a T-mine determinedly and throws it through the turret hatch. A whole series of explosions wreck the tank. Only the red-glowing undercarriage is left.

We pick up our Mpis and run towards the hazel bushes, where three dead horses are lying. Porta takes time to cut a couple of hefty chunks from them.

Suddenly a machine-gun is throwing long salvos at us and a T-34 breaks through the hedge so violently that we only just manage to escape its whipping tracks.

Desperately I dig myself into a large mud-hole. As if in a slow-motion-film I see the commander in his turret; his black leather uniform coat shining wetly from the mist in the woods.

Like a weasel Porta springs on to the T-34 and throws a

72

potato-masher down into the turret hatch behind the commander.

A hollow explosion and the commander is thrown a hundred feet into the air to burst like a star-shell.

The T-34 jerks to a stop and the crew, living torches, jump from the vehicle. They roll madly on the ground in an attempt to extinguish the flames.

'Take 'em!' shouts the Old Man pulling his 08.

Mpis crash and the Russian tank-men die.

We take up position in a deserted machine-gun nest in an orchard. Tiny takes over a black-mouthed SMG gaping skywards. Tracer rattles towards the Russian infantry.

'Back!' cries the Old Man appalled.

Behind us three T-34s burst through the brush.

A green under-belly rocks forward and I feel steel slide forward over my back pressing the breath from my lungs. I see the grey heavens again and feel the rain whip at my face. I am still alive . . . .

> 'The Germans are a nation with principles. Once an idea has taken hold of them they become completely convinced of its truth and do not give it up willingly.'
>
> Lenin to the Turkish Ambassador Ali Fuad Pascha,
> Moscow, 3 April 1921.

Corps and Divisional Commanders had taken their places in the great salon. The light from the chandeliers blinked from uniform buttons and decorations. Cigar smoke curled towards the ceiling. Feelings were animated and high. Champagne fizzed and sparkled. The toast was: 'A quick end to the war!'

General-Oberst Guderian slapped dust from his long black leather overcoat, pressed Generalfeldmarschall von Bock's hand in comradely fashion. The two high-ranking officers spoke in low voices of the latest events. The Feldmarschall moved over to the table and leafed through some documents.

'Gentlemen, the Führer has ordered the attack on Moscow!' he began with gladness in his voice. 'This magnificently conceived campaign is now entering its final and decisive phase. With the fall of Moscow we will have achieved the greatest victory in all history. Our army has been given the great honour of smashing the Communist monster and forcing Bolshevism to unconditional surrender.' The Feldmarschall went over to the large wall-chart.

'Operation TAIFUN will be carried out in two phases. First we break through the Soviet western front, north and south of the Smolensk-Moscow autobahn. After this the tank groups consolidate at Vjasma. Then we round-up any escaped enemy forces, destroy them, move straight on to Moscow, surround it and take it. A bold and clearly conceived plan, gentlemen. 24 tank divisions and 46 infantry divisions will take part in the storming of Moscow. The army has three weeks in which to cover 200 miles. There is plenty of time. In four weeks time we will hold a victory parade for the Führer on the Red Square, and will re-christen it Adolf Hitler Platz.' The aging Feldmarschall clasped his hands behind his back, stuck his eagle-nose forward into the faces of his officers, bounced elegantly forward and back on the tips of his beautifully polished boots and said in an almost convivial tone:

'The Führer is a genius!'

'There's many a true word. . . .' whispered Panzer-General von Hünersdorff confidentially to General Hoepner.

Hoepner laughed quietly.

'If he was he wouldn't have stopped at Smolensk in July when Moscow lay wide open to our Panzer divisions. Clausewitz says:

'"Departures from the original conception should only be made in conditions of extreme necessity."'

'The Führer has studied Clausewitz,' General-Leutenant Conradi broke in. 'He had his reasons for sending our troops into the Ukraine instead of continuing towards Moscow. We haven't his breadth of vision. I believe in the Führer,' he added threateningly and stared sharply at the now patently nervous General Hoepner.

'What do you think of the attack?' von Hünersdorff turned to General Strauss.

'Officially we shall succeed. What else?' laughed the artillery general.

'And unofficially?' asked Hünersdorff with a crooked smile.

'If I were to say what I think I'd be asking for a court-martial,' smiled Strauss.

'You're in doubt, then?' Hünersdorff pressed him.

'The Bohemian Corporal's waited too long,' mumbled Strauss. 'The plan is not only boldly and clearly conceived. It's also crazy. We're into autumn and the rains are already threatening.'

'If the rains come we might as well give up,' broke out General-Major von Hünersdorff.

'The Russians will block us wherever they can,' continued Strauss. 'They know what it's all about. If they don't hold Moscow their prestige is gone. For that very reason they'll fight like madmen. Stalin and his people aren't soft. They'll throw in everything they can scrape together.'

'We're the strongest army in the world,' said von Hünersdorff proudly. 'If the weather holds we'll make it. But we'll have to make it at a hell of a pace, every bit of speed we can get out of our tracks will be needed to make Moscow before the winter mud catches us.'

'What about the winter equipment?' asked General Hube cautiously.

'The Führer has stopped manufacture of winter equipment,' answered the Feldmarschall with a fatherly smile. 'Talk of winter clothing is defeatism. The campaign will be over long before we need mittens and woollen helmets. Any winter equipment which has already been issued is to be withdrawn and returned to depot. That is the Führer's order, gentlemen!'

Several generals looked at one another silently but not one protested.

4 | Porta helps the padre

We are lying in the shade from a row of fruit-trees. The autumn leaves fall gently on and around us. It is a beautifully warm autumn day, one of those late summery days which only occur in Russia.

The regiment is well behind the front line waiting to be reorganized. Of our two hundred tanks only sixteen are left. More than sixty-eight percent casualties amongst the men.

New tanks have already started to arrive. We've been here five days now. Some of us feel they're the best five days of the whole war. The supplies people have made a fortunate mistake. The company is still getting supplies for 220 men and that's not bad when we number no more than about 60.

At the canteen the QM's going crazy with only 60 men to consume all those rations.

'What the hell can I do?' he cries in despair. 'I've *signed* for 220 *men*! And those bastards who ain't here 've let themselves get killed by the bloody *untermensch* and who's it to *go* to? Somebody ought to get the wall for this!'

'Give us the bloody lot,' shouts Porta happily from the queue. 'You'll be surprised how fast *we'll* get rid of it!'

A hot discussion commences. The QM can't make up his mind what to do. Not even when Tiny offers to beat his brains out if he doesn't pass the rations on.

Anything might have happened if Oberst Hinka hadn't come past and ordered the QM to distribute the lot to the men.

The QM goes amok! The Old Man gets an extra stick of chewing tobacco, and the rest of us two cigars over the ration. *Porta*, of course, gets a whole carton of cognac.

And now we're lying stretched out under the apple trees. We've put on half a stone in weight in under a couple of hours.

Porta looks as if he's on the verge of giving birth. Twins at least. He's not only eaten his own rations, but has also been over to No. 4 Company and finished up all their leavings.

He is sitting on an oil-drum which he uses as a latrine. We're doing things the high society way. Puffing at big cigars. Using our military ranks when we address one another; and drinking cognac from real glasses. But when Porta begins to use a knife and fork we give up and send for the medical orderly and a strait-jacket.

Porta is wearing his monocle in honour of the day and Tiny has fixed a hen's wing to each side of his bowler. He feels it gives him a distinguished appearance. Our boots are off for the first time in six weeks and it feels good.

'Our padre's a bleedin' drunk,' remarks Tiny suddenly between two slugs of cognac which he chases down with a beer.

'Which one?' asks Porta interestedly. 'The one with the yellow badges or the white one?'*

' 'Is riverence with the white pipin',' answers Tiny, rolling

---

* Yellow and white badges: Yellow for Catholic padres, white for Protestant.

his eyes skywards in the manner appropriate when referring to holy things or to persons belonging to the holy hierarchy.

'I hope for your own sake that you can prove your accusation against this virtuous officer, Obergefreiter Creutzfeldt,' threateningly from Porta.

'Goddamn it, I *can*!' shouts Tiny. 'That bleedin' biblepuncher was pissed as a coot yesterday, an' 'ad 'is 'and up the clouts of that 'umpty-backed old 'ore of a *babuschka** down at the bleedin' ferry. *An'* 'e'd got a look on 'is face like a Jew with 'is 'and fulla bleedin' gold ducats. 'Ard luck it was gettin' dark so I 'eard more'n I seen, but 'e was soakin' the piss up like a sponge.'

'How d'you know that, if it was dark?' asks Barcelona suspiciously.

'I got all 'is empties over where I was lyin' listenin',' answers Tiny injuredly. 'They went orf singin'. 'Im tellin' ol' 'umpty as 'ow she was 'is only true love an' 'ad bin sent from Garwd. It's true, by Christ, as 'e was sent to the front for 'ittin' the piss. Nobody'd 'ave nothin' to do with 'im in Leipzig because of it. When 'e was preachin' 'is last sermon in the garrison church there, 'e fell outa the bleedin' pulpit into the Commandin' General's bleedin' lap as 'e was explainin' the parable o' the man sick o' the bleedin' palsy. 'E'd just got to the well-known words: "Pluck up thy pailliase and piss orf promptly!" when over the railin' 'e goes an' picks up 'is ticket to points east!'

'It reminds me,' Porta takes up the thread, 'of the time I was chief clerk to Padre Kurt Winfuss of the 7th ID at München. He was what you'd call a happy maniac with his nose into everything he should've kept it out of. One evening he decided to make a check on the prevailing rumours of drunkenness and immorality in München and we started at the Hofbräuhaus where the good citizens and the villains meet over sauerkraut and beer and where you can slip your dicky into a few fur coat without too much difficulty. We got

* *Babuschka* (Russian): Grandma.

there about eight o'clock, when the crowd waiting to get in is always at its worst. You couldn't hardly've got a postage stamp in edgewise. Everybody and his brothers and sisters were there!

'"We're all right now, boys," shouted a well-oiled infantry-man, "there's a sky-pilot in the party so neither the wallop *nor* the crumpet'll go off tonight."

'"They've come to set up an altar to the god of Germany right here in the Hofbräuhaus!"

'And all these rude soldiers began to sing:

> *Onward Christian soldiers*
> *Onward as to war*
> *With the cross of Jesus*
> *Going on before* . . . . .

'If I could've got through the mob I'd have sent that pig of an infantryman for a burton. My padre took it pretty hard.

'They were at him all the time we were in that queue. I was promising bashings right, left and centre but they couldn't've cared less. Booze and bints was all they'd got in their heads.

'We got inside eventually, the soul-saver and me, in the posh part of course, up on the first floor. There we planned our campaign against drink and immortality. We stood in a corner so's not to get pissed on by the customers as they came swaying in.

'"Porta," said the padre, "I trust you. You are a young, intelligent man in whom I find much that is good and laudable. You are hard-working, modest and have attained an understanding of the work of the Church in the military field. You have never made a muddle of things as did my earlier assistants. I have never seen you smoke or drink. During the period in which you have filled the position of chief clerk with me not a drop of altar wine has ever 'evaporated' and we have never 'run short'. You do not gamble and where women are concerned your papers are unsmirched. As far as I am aware you have no debts, and you are a good comrade, often helping those who are in need. The pay sergeant tells me that you have never asked for an advance of pay. I have been happy to find that you are quick and efficient at paperwork and your handwriting is as good as an academician's. It has been of satisfaction to me, furthermore, to note that you are economical with paper and turn envelopes so that they may be used twice. You allow nothing to go to waste. You are the first to arrive at our field services, straighten and snuff the candles and call to order those who spit on the floor during our holy celebrations. You type almost without error on any make of machine. No sacristan could be an improvement on you. And at High Mass you never go wrong in the singing. My last assistant always got Our Father and the Creed mixed up. Your uniform is perfect, your boots well-polished, your neck-cloth clean and white. I will, therefore, now confide to you a great and dangerous task, but do not allow yourself to fall into temptation! The Devil is everywhere in this the Sodom of Bayern. You will now go down into the common hall and observe what is happening. Here is 100 marks for your expenses since I do not wish you to use your own money. I will go up to the Ludwigssaal which the officers use. Tomorrow we will write a report on what we have seen and heard. We meet at nine at the Field Chapel."

'"Jawohl, Herr Padre!" I roared in a voice which lifted three drunks, coughing and farting in chorus, up in their chairs. We didn't take any notice of this, the padre being of the opinion that farting was a human reaction condoned by circumstances and surroundings.

'I went down to Pay-Sergeant Balko who sat waiting for me in the middle of a lively party. I let him order a 4-litre* tankard for me before asking him for my outstandings – 700 marks.'

'Were you an eighty percent man even then?' Barcelona Blom asks with interest.

* 4-litre tankard: Almost 1 gallon.

'I was *that* long before I got to the Divisional Chapel at München and took over the souls of the infantry there.'

'Didn't your religious superior know about this?' asks the Old Man with a glint of humour in his eye.

'No,' grins Porta. 'He only knew what I felt he ought to know – about me.

'But it was Balko's night, so he started immediately with a new loan of 700 marks. I did pretty good business whilst I was with the Army Soul Service.

'We drove back to barracks in horse-drawn carriages and by the time we got home the horses were as drunk as we were. They even whinnied in tune with the choruses of *"Oh du schöner Westerwoll"*. They slept it off down behind the guard-house. They wouldn't come up with us.

'But my holy boss had fallen in with bad company. A party of officers had fixed him with raspberry juice which they'd "blessed" in advance, so that he was well cut when we met in the Field Chapel around midday. He promised me the hand of a sister I knew he hadn't got, and then he tried to get me into bed with him in the belief that I was Louise from Zell-am-See. Later on he confided to me a great deal about the sex life of John the Baptist. Finally he began to cry and asked me to beat him for he had sinned. I fulfilled his wish but unfortunately hit him too hard and *he* wound up in the garrison infirmary and *I* wound up on a charge. He accused me of having shit in his dress boots but he'd done that himself. The officers at the Hofbräuhaus had given him laxative pills instead of aspirins when he'd become dizzy during the party.

'On CO's orders I was sentenced to 21 days for having struck the padre. Our Oberst wouldn't hear of any heavier punishment. As I was marched away between two guards with loaded rifles and fixed bayonets there stood the padre in his field uniform, waiting for me outside the garrison gaol.

'"You are a lying scoundrel," he raged at me with an expression on his face like that of a martyr being torn with glowing pincers outside the gates of Rome. "God and I will have nothing further to do with you," he stated, and pointed towards the clouds where he thought God lived. "It will go badly for you if you continue on the broad path leading to damnation!"

'After a while he became more human and gave me two packets of Juno. He was rash enough to promise that Jesus would forgive me if I soon returned to the Lord's little vineyard. He followed me right into the guard-house and ordered the glass-house Warrant Officer to treat me well and without brutality. I must be allowed to keep the cigarettes. I was a God-fearing man who had been tempted into evil ways by low persons. Next day he sent his batman with a basket of extra rations. In amongst all the sausages there was a Field Bible bound in green, the colour of hope. On the fly-leaf he had written: Soldier, Turn towards God! Do not forget to pray! And the star of Hope will illumine your dark cell. We had light enough from the carbide-lamp so Jesus was saved the trouble.

'The Glass-house WO moved into my cell as soon as he discovered this horn of plenty.

'My cell-mate, a transport soldier, who looked for all the world like an export-quality pig, could imitate all kinds of animals. He had been on the stage before he became a soldier and had been a favourite in the country districts where the rustics think it funny to hear a city dweller grunt like a pig or cackle like an old hen.

'At two in the morning there were complaints about the noise from the gaol-house. We answered them with:

> Mein Hut, der hat drei Ecken,
> drei Ecken hat mein Hut,
> und hat er nicht drei Ecken,
> dann ist er nicht mein Hut.

'Then we moved on to the song of the 10th British Hussars "Moses in Egypt". The transport soldier did the trumpet. The Warrant Officer imitated horses' hooves with two mess-tins

82

and I did the kettle-drums. What a row! It sounded as if a whole regiment of cavalry was drilling in the gaolhouse. But we were having a wonderful time. We got schnapps and beer sent over from the café "Friends of Gaiety". The cell we were using was really the death cell. There were a lot of interesting things written on the walls. One of the newest was a crisp military message:

> Calling all bastards!
> Feldwebel Paul Schlüntz.
> Born on the Führer's birthday, 20th April.
> Leaving 3rd May (1938).
> Unfortunately he will not be accompanying me.

'On the other side of the wall was written in very large letters:

> SS-man Boris Brause, shot by
> Swamp Germans 7.4.38.
> "They said I would go to Valhalla,
> But I couldn't accept their views.
> So I've booked myself a ticket
> For the Paradise of the Jews,
> And Oberstürmbahnführer Ritter,
> Can shove that up his shitter!
> Every Christmas!
> Heil Me!

'Under the window a short sharp missive:

> I go at 4 o'clock tomorrow.
> With a German Weidersehen.
> Helmut Wenzel, SS-Sturmmann.
> P.S. You can all kiss my arse!

'For emphasis he had drawn two swastikas one on each side of his name. A political philosopher amongst the inmates of Cell 9 had written on the ceiling:

What is Marxism in reality?
It is National Socialism's non-aryan
grandmother!

'Now we three were sitting here, in this pleasant cell with its sad memories, enjoying ourselves so much that the prisoners on the other three floors sent a collective complaint to the Garrison Commander about the noise we were making after lights-out. The party widened and became even noisier with the arrival of Hauptfeldwebel Putkammer. He was on his way home from a wedding after being thrown out for having three times attempted to rape the bride: once during the meat course; once after the dessert; and the third time in the bath-tub. He rang the bell at the door and demanded entrance in a loud, commanding voice. Nobody heard him, and he knocked again with the point of his sabre. He was in full dress uniform.

'Still getting no answer he threw a stone through a window and fired three shots into the air, shooting down the official blue light over the entrance door.

'We named him prisoner-of-honour in Cell 9.

Deutschland, Deutschland, ohne alles,
ohne Butter, ohne Speck,
und das bisschen Marmelade
frisst uns die Verwaltung weg. *

'Our song echoed back from the stables on the other side of the square where the dragoons slept with their horses.

'"Brothers, we meet at last on the scaffold," shouted the Haupfeldwebel, beating his breast.

'*Dulce est decipere in loco.*† Later on he got rough and

---

* *Deutschland, Deutschland etc:*
  '*Germany, Germany without everything*
  Without butter, without meat;
  Even our little bit of jam
  The Civil Servants eat.'
† *Dulce est* etc: A joke is a good thing in its right place.

84

claimed we were a pack of rogues who were leading him astray.

'On the fourth day the padre visited us and to please our benefactor we agreed to be confirmed. It was such a solemn affair that the transport man got an attack of sobbing and grunted like a pig. The service was conducted in the Garrison Church. The CO was furious when he heard about it and gave us eight days extra for making fun of the Church. The padre was posted to a far distant and very grim border town. He excommunicated us just before he climbed onto the train.

'"By God, I'll confirm you," our Oberst promised us on CO's orders. "More than you'll fancy too. I'll cram your prayer-books down your gullets and haul 'em up and down again on a piece of barbed wire, you wicked men!"'

In closely-packed sections the khaki figures of Russian infantry swarm across the steppe. Thousands upon thousands of them. A wave of humanity sweeping forward through the waving grass. The field-grey German infantry looks insignificant in comparison with these enormous brown hordes. They press forward with fixed bayonets taking no apparent notice of our concentrated machine-gun fire.

Our infantry are retreating in panic from their positions. Officers try to stop them. German bullets kill German soldiers, but nothing can stop the fear-maddened flight from the trenches. Officers who stand their ground are trodden into the earth.

It's no longer the Fatherland we are fighting for but our very lives. Red flares shoot up signalling to the artillery. A barrage of unbelievable power hammers down in front of the Russian regiments. Hundreds of machine-guns stammer tracer into the advancing hordes.

Our company takes cover behind a tile-works. Shells sweep the steppe like fiery brooms.

We move our tanks slowly forward up onto a height from which we can observe clearly many miles to the west. In the distance Russian troops can be seen marching in close column.

In a wide V-formation the tanks move forward, without infantry support, crunching through walls and ruins. Our machine-guns spit continuously. A horse-drawn battery runs away. The guns swing crazily behind the horses, until these fall under the rain of shells and guns and limbers go flying over them to land in a tangled heap of metal, wood and human and animal flesh. The ventilators hum softly, sucking acrid powder fumes out of our combat cabin. Sack after sack of casings is emptied out of the hatches. The tank shakes and shivers from the continuous shocks of firing. We are in the grip of a kind of hunting fever; laugh when we see we've made a hit. We have no thought of the fact that we are killing human beings. Time stands still. The heat is unbearable. It's an unusually hot autumn day. Have we been fighting one hour or five? We've no idea.

Infantry fire drums deafeningly against the vehicle's steel sides. Several times tank-killers try to get alongside us with magnetic bombs but we see them and our flame throwers burn them to cinders.

'Enemy tank attack!' comes the alarm from the loud-speaker. Three or four hundred T-34s come crawling up over the hills away towards the horizon. With a terrific crash the regiment opens fire with all guns. The earth flames. The leading T-34s go up in an inferno of fire and smoke but very shortly terribly many P-IVs are exploding into whitely glowing bonfires. Black oily smoke climbs up towards the clear blue of the heavens.

Shell after shell leaves the long barrels of the guns to bore whiningly into the mass of enemy tanks.

More and more tanks on both sides explode and break apart.

Only a few crews get away. Most of them die in the flames. This is the lot of the tank soldier.

Suddenly the enemy tanks turn and disappear at full speed over the hills. For a moment we believe they are running from us but we soon see what they are after. They swing round again and roll without stopping through out thinly-manned infantry positions a few miles to the north. They are using German tactics. Punch through where resistance is least. To put it short: Blitzkrieg!

Oberst Hinka sees the danger at once and gives the order for immediate withdrawal.

'Panzer withdraw. March, march!'

The boys in the trenches are left to their fate. The tanks leave as fast as their tracks can take them.

We stop for a moment to pick up wounded. They are piled up on our rear shielding in layers, more like sacks of flour than human beings. There is no time to be careful. They can thank their stars they are being moved at all.

They lie all over us. On the front shields, on the turret, on the runway, where they need almost superhuman strength to hold on as the tank bounces and slithers over the uneven terrain.

'Comrades, take us with you!' they scream to us, those whom we must leave behind. 'Don't leave us!' Pleadingly they stretch their hands out towards us.

We look the other way and they disappear in a cloud of dust and exhaust fumes as Porta puts on speed. There is no room for more on the vehicle and if we get into combat those who *are* aboard will be sitting ducks for the enemy MGs.

At a terrific pace we crash through brush and ditches. The 25 ton P-IV sways like a ship in a rough sea.

Without slackening speed we smash straight through an artillery park. We can just make out the dust of the regiment far in front of us. It is a race with death. If the pincers close on us before we get through they'll be able to shoot us down like clay pigeons.

'Faster, faster!' comes continually from the loud-speaker. We stop to take Barcelona's damaged tank on tow. The wire breaks with a whining howl and the back lash chops the head off one of 'our' wounded. A Feldwebel. Sweating and cursing we make a new wire fast. With Barcelona's P-III on tow behind us we roll through a burning village at considerably reduced speed.

The artillery has done a job here. Bloody heaps of human meat lie everywhere. Flies, millions of them, rise in great buzzing swarms as we roll over the bodies. The stench is sickening.

Just outside the village a T-34 with its tracks shot off sends a shell to us. Barcelona's P-III is hit. Tracks and rollers damaged. Without thinking of the wounded aboard us I swing the gun around, and sight down on the enemy tank. Our shell rips away its turret. Two men jump out and are cut down by Heide's MG. One of them drops by the tracks, the other drops at the rear of the tank. He tries to crawl away but a string of tracer chases and catches him. The P-III is finished. The cable breaks in three places when we try to move it. Barcelona and his crew come over to us. Tiny throws a couple of grenades into the P-III and in a moment it goes up in flames.

With rattling tracks we disappear across the steppe, engine revving at top speed. Nothing but speed and surprise tactics can save us now. Over the air we can hear Oberst Hinka chewing the company commander up for having got his 38 ton Skoda caught fast in a marsh. He thought he could take a short-cut along the river. It might have come off with a P-IV, which has broader tracks than a Skoda.

'We'll try to pick you up tomorrow with a rescue truck,' shouts the CO irritably. 'You'll stay with the vehicle over-night, Moser!'

'That's his death warrant,' says Porta carelessly. 'He should never have reported getting caught with his backside in a marsh. Cleverer people would've blown the wagon, and then blown the coop smartly with a soldiers' farewell to Ivan. Afterwards a nice little report stating that a T-34 had smacked 'em in the eye with a shell. Luckily they haven't started checking our reports with the enemy yet, but they probably *will* do some day.'

'You have no feeling for your duty,' shouts Heide reproachfully. 'One does not blow up one's vehicle excepting in a case of the utmost necessity!'

'I've noted it,' grins Porta superciliously. 'But don't cry, mister Party hero, if *we* suddenly drop in the shit and are short a piece of track. It'll be interesting watching you play tag with our friends the enemy.'

'Cut out the negative thinking,' protests Tiny, shrugging his shoulders. 'Let's talk about somethin' positive like, for example, pussy.'

We thunder down a sunken road straight into a horse-drawn artillery unit. Soldiers and horses scatter in wild panic away from the tank which thunders forward spitting tracer from both MGs.

Porta goes head-down for a howitzer parked between two houses. Three artillery men are sitting petrified on its carriage with full bowls in their hands. One of them has a spoon in his mouth. They have apparently been surprised during a meal break. Everything disappears, crunched under the tracks.

In the rear-view mirrors we can see them crawling around on the ground and sending curses after us.

'Goddam and blast it all!' howls Porta soon after. 'She's going for a bloody burton! You can't even trust the engines these twisting Nazi manufacturers turn out!'

'What's happened!' asks the Old Man nervously.

'She's dropping her revs like a Jew on his way in to an SS-barracks,' answers Porta kicking angrily at the gear lever.

Quickly we pull the cowling off the motor. We can't find anything wrong. Everything we test seems to be working properly.

'Come down here,' shouts Porta pulling at my foot, 'but God help *you* if this coffin stalls or if you strip my gears!'

Roughly they throw me into Porta's seat to take over his job at the steering levers. From sheer nervousness I drive the wagon straight into a deep ditch and come close to tipping it over.

Porta and Heide go at the motor.

'The devil!' says the Old Man pulling at his ear. 'And this

has to happen on our way to a break-through between two attacking enemy columns. It couldn't be worse!'

'Oh I wouldn't say that,' answers Porta. 'I'd rather have a motor on the blink than a T-34 shell up my backside.'

'Call the Legionnaire,' the Old Man orders Heide. 'Tell him to stop and take us on tow.'

But the Legionnaire continues up over a height without hearing the wireless signal. At the same moment his P-IV explodes. A blue-white flame shoots high into the air. A hatch cover flies like a thrown discus far out over the steppe.

To our relief we see the Legionnaire and the Professor jump from the hatch. The three others are caught in the exploding hell inside the tank. It looks like a blast-furnace at work. The sound reaches us a little later like a long roll of thunder.

Porta is right inside the motor, hammering and screwing away. It sounds as if he is trying to smash the Maybach to pieces. In between he curses the Russians, the Party and in particular Julius Heide.

'It's all your bloody fault,' he shouts from the bowels of the engine.

'If your rotten bloody Party'd stuck to drinking beer in the Bürgerbräukeller instead of playing at politics we wouldn't have had any bloody war at all and I'd never have seen the inside of a bloody Maybach. *There's* where *you* go you little bent-up prick!' Two thundering clangs and a burnt-out valve flies towards Heide's head.

'That's it,' he mumbles finally and worms his way out of the motor. The Maybach purrs like a pleased cat.

We're off again and without stopping we drag the Legionnaire and the Professor up and into the cabin.

Russian machine-gun fire sweeps away the last of our wounded.

'Shall we stop and pick them up?' asks the Old Man uncertainly.

'Can't be done,' says Porta. 'The accelerator's stuck fast,

and will continue to be so until I see nice square German heads around me again!'

A hit fires the motor. Flames lick through the cowling into the cabin.

Tiny gets the automatic fire-extinguisher going with difficulty. The fire dies away. The motor thunders again. It's beautiful music to our ears. He wipes the sweat from his powder and oil blackened face.

'Bleedin' lucky we got them extinguishers,' he just manages to say before a bolt of lightning smashes down into the tank and tears the hatches from their hinges.

I am thrown from the gun-seat and a giant hand seems to press me into the deck under the gun. A thick jet of blood splashes down over my face, blinding me.

Tiny falls unconscious amongst his shells. The explosion throws him straight across the gun. His leather helmet splits open against the ammunition locker.

Barcelona's mouth is torn open. Along his cheeks the teeth are bared like those of a skull.

The Old Man thinks his back is broken but fortunately it is not quite that bad. Working together we get his joints back into place. His screams of agony could've been heard miles away.

'The old coffin's finished,' confirms Porta drily. 'I can't move her! Bugger all to do! Pull the chain and off we go.'

'Out!' orders the Old Man. 'Demolish vehicle!'

I am last man out and trigger the demolition charge in the turret.

'I do believe we'd do well to pick up our skirts and get out of here in one helluva rapid manner,' says Porta pointing to a small birch wood from which Russian soldiers are stretching their necks inquisitively and staring at us.

Barcelona is already over the top of the hill together with the other crews. We follow quickly. The blood races in our ears and we have difficulty in breathing. Our lungs hurt and our nasal membranes feel dry and rough from the heavy powder fumes in the compartment.

The Russians can see everything we're doing and could easily shoot us down.

'Move!' says the Old Man curtly. 'We've got to get over those heights. The others are already well ahead.'

'Why the devil isn't Ivan shooting at us?' asks Porta breathlessly. 'He could drop us like lame hares!'

Heide stumbles on a helmet and bangs his forehead against a large stone.

He is unconscious for a moment.

Tiny and I pull him to his feet.

'We might just as well stay here,' he moans, wiping the blood from his face. 'They'll mow us down with an MG any minute. We can't get away!'

'Get your bleedin' finger outa your nick, you Nazi super-man!' growls Tiny. 'Over that bleedin' 'ill-top there's a 'ole plateful of boiled swastikas waitin' for you and as a special treat we've 'ad 'em sprinkled over with essence of dried BDM-quim!'*

'I've had it!' gasps the Old Man worn out and letting himself fall. 'I'm too old for this piss. I can't run any more!'

'Turn your old cherry back over your shoulder, my old son,' grins Porta. 'And I do believe you'll feel in quite a hurry to get back to Uncle Adolf's chimney-corner!'

Now we understand why the Russians are holding their fire. They want us alive. Less than fifty yards behind us a section is coming up at the double.

The Old Man is on his feet with a speed which is quite amazing.

All tiredness is gone. We run like Olympic gold-medallists. Jesse Owens would get left behind, even with us in full battle order. A wounded Leutnant is lying in the tall grass. His left leg is crushed, bones showing whitely. We take him with us.

'Thanks comrades,' he says tears choking in his throat.

The Russians are overtaking us slowly and we have only bayonets and battle-knives to defend ourselves with. Our

* BDM (Bund Deutsches Mädels): Nazi Girls Association.

personal weapons are in the tank. The Leutnant has a Mauser but that isn't much against a whole platoon.

'If we only had an MG,' gasps Porta, out of breath. 'That'd make those Stalin cock-suckers find something better to do than chase after us. I'd fill 'em so full of rivets they'd think they'd got into a shipyard by mistake.'

'Don't leave me comrades,' cries the Leutnant hanging between Heide and me. He isn't more than nineteen and can't have been at the front long. Not even a combat medal decorates his green uniform coat, and they're generous enough with those even if you've done no more than wave to the neighbours.

'Fritz, Fritz, idisoder,'* the Russians call to us. 'We've got girls for you! Fritz, Fritz, idisoder! You come have pretty Russian lady for mattress!'

They are catching up on us. I look questioningly at Heide. He nods and makes an uncaring movement with the corner of his mouth. We drop the wounded Leutnant. He lets out a heartbreaking scream and hops a little way on his good leg before falling.

'No, no, take me with you, take me with you! Comrades, don't let Ivan get me!'

But our lives are at stake. The Leutnant tries to scrabble after us but soon gives up. He scratches earth over himself frantically in the hope that the Russians won't see him.

Breathless we reach the hill-top and look down into a valley four or five miles wide in which hundreds of white cows are grazing.

Crazily, half-running, half-tumbling we race down the hill towards the cows.

It's a wonder none of us breaks anything. Tiny goes over a ledge and falls almost forty feet. He drives his combat knife into the ground in a blind rage.

A couple of shots sound and bullets whistle wickedly, as we dash to cover amongst the cows. It would take artillery at least to get at us amongst all those living breastworks of meat.

* Idisoder (Russian): Come here.

A long, rough tongue licks my face as a cow examines me with friendly curiosity.

The Russians are shouting and screaming up on the hill. They form a dancing ring around the wounded Leutnant. Two shots from a Nagan sound faintly, followed by shouts of laughter.

'They've punctured him,' says Porta drily, patting a cow on the neck.

'Pity,' says the Old Man quietly. 'He wasn't much more than a kid.'

'He volunteered,' decides Porta shortly.

'How do you know?' asks Barcelona.

'Leutnant already, at that age!' smiles Porta. 'He took the helmet when he was sixteen. He *wanted* to be an officer.'

' 'E made it too,' sighs Tiny, shooting a spear of saliva at a bull which is examining him with a wondering expression in its black eyes. 'Only now 'e's a *dead* officer.'

'It's no fun to shuffle off with a bullet from a Nagan in your neck,' says Porta thoughtfully. 'There's so many nicer ways of sneaking off.'

'Bleedin' arseholes!' shouts Tiny in surprise. 'These four-legged Commies 've got milk in their distributors.' He throws himself down under a ruminating cow and seizing the udder directs a stream of milk into his mouth.

The Russians are doing something. They are cutting off the Leutnant's head and sticking it on a pole which they swing to and fro.

'Siberians,' says Porta, 'so we know what to expect if they get their hands on us. Where the devil have the rest got to?'

'The speed they was makin' they're in Berlin already,' says Tiny.

A machine-gun barks. Rifles snap angrily. Bullets smack into the cows, stampeding them. The whole of the great herd is soon in swaying motion and we go with it.

'Hang on to the gear lever,' howls Porta as he passes us clinging tightly to the tail of a terrified cow.

We follow his example and catch the tail of the nearest

cow and away we go with the wind whistling past our ears. Tiny's cow steers the wrong way, towards the Russians. He gets angry and, as always when this happens to him he stops thinking altogether. He catches the animal by the horns and tries to swing it round. The cow obviously thinks he wants to fight, and snorting and stamping wildly it butts him on to his back. Now he *really* gets mad. Head down he rushes at the animal which turns tail with a bawl of fear and gallops after the rest of the herd. But Tiny catches up with it and manages to swing himself up onto its back, and things really start moving. Like a crazy rodeo act the cow and Tiny buck off towards the west. Porta is the first to catch on. He picks on a little white cow, runs alongside it for a while, then swings his leg over its back. It circles and tries to buck him off but Porta hangs on like grim death with both arms around its neck. With a wild bawl it takes off after the others, head shaking from side to side and tail straight up. Somehow Porta hangs on to it.

We follow suit and go through the same experience as Porta. Heide falls off several times before managing to find out how to keep his seat. He nearly dies of fright when he discovers that the steed he has chosen is a bull. The Old Man gets a kick from two whirling hind legs which knocks the wind out of him. Barcelona is sent flying several yards through the air by a bull which is obviously defending its harem. It is about to attack him again when a Russian bullet fells it.

The Russians on the hill-top are almost dying with laughter and shout advice down to us. They fire shots in the air to make the herd wilder. Apparently they want to get as much as possible out of the free show we are giving them.

My cow is dancing around bucking and landing stiff-legged, and it feels as if my kidneys have been pushed up into my throat. I'm convinced that every bone in my body is broken. Suddenly it stops its cavorting and begins to run in zig-zags after the herd. The speed is frightening. None of us had ever dreamed cows could move so fast. We have all our work cut out to hang on to these living battering-rams, which gallop like racehorses over stick and stone, straight through thorn bushes, where we leave half our uniforms and skin hanging on the branches.

At a terrific pace we thunder straight through a Russian infantry group. The men stare in amazement and completely forget to open fire. In a billowing cloud of red dust we pass the German lines with the herd of cattle bawling at our heels. The fighting stops completely.

Russian heads pop up from their trenches to enjoy the fantastic sight. Some even cheer us.

A German regimental staff HQ, set up in a clearing, is sent head over heels, maps and papers flying around their ears. Before they know what has happened we've disappeared into a village where cooks and baggage troops fly from us as if we were some new Russian weapon.

> *Oh bury me not*
> *On the Lone Prairie-ie-ie . . .*

yips Porta waving his yellow top-hat above his head.

At this very moment of triumph his cow stops suddenly with both front legs planted stiffly in front of it. Its rump lifts straight up into the air until it looks almost like a man standing on his hands. Porta shoots straight on and up like a rocket and lands with a colossal splash in the middle of a stinking midden.

> '**But they are mistaken. I am not finished, as they imagine. They are all mistaken. They undervalue me because I come from the lower classes, the scum of the people; because I am not cultivated and do not know how to behave in the manner which, in their small sparrow brains, is considered right.**'
>
> Hitler in a conversation with the Senate President,
> Hermann Rauschning.

Hitler's harsh diabolical voice roared from the loudspeaker: 'German men, German women, I assure you that the power of our criminal enemy has been smashed completely by my invincible Wehrmacht. These untermensch will never rise again. . . .'

The loudspeakers crackled as applause crashed out from hundreds of beer-oiled throats. 'Behind my victorious troops lies a conquered area more than four times the size of the great German Reich in 1933, when I took over its leadership, and I can assure you that it will become a hundred times greater! Nothing can stop us! We take what we need! Those who stand in our way will be mercilessly annihilated!'

Still greater applause from the faithful Party comrades in the Bürgerbräukeller. The sweat and beer fumes could almost be sensed through the loudspeakers.

The applause would not stop.

'Heil! Heil! Heil!'

'I greet, and bow my head in respect, to the brave soldiers and officers of the great German Wehrmacht who now take up position for the greatest attack in all history. I promise you, my faithful comrades, that in three months, at the latest, this war will be over. By Christmas our mobilized forces will be sent home and it will be a thousand years before another war comes. If it ever comes.'

The applause seemed enough to make the loudspeakers fall from the walls.

'Sieg! Heil! Prosit! Sieg! Heil! Prosit!'

A wave of enthusiasm swept through the great beer-halls of Münich. Millions of Germans heard this fateful speech. Everyone had his own opinions on the matter, but nobody dared to express them. It was too easy to say the wrong thing in the day of the Third Reich. SS-Overgruppenführer Heydrich's Gestapo was everywhere, even in the marriage bed.

'Now we will give our infamous enemy the death-blow,' roared Hitler in a wild transport of ecstasy.

Sweat ran down his face. His blood-shot eyes were glassy and he hammered on the speaker's desk with clenched fists. His tie was crooked. The buttons of his shirt had burst open. 'Never more shall Stalin's hordes arise from this defeat! If they offer to capitulate we will not accept their offer! This is a Holy War! I swear to you that we will continue it until the Bolshevik monster is totally eradicated!'

General von Hünersdorff walked the floor listening to Hitler's words. The fantastic boastings of a sick man. Not one soldier in the German Wehrmacht undervalued the Russian opponent as did Adolf Hitler. Nobody seriously believed that this mighty enemy was beaten. The future held terrible things in store.

Von Hünersdorff took a document from the table and read half-aloud to his Chief-of-Staff, Oberst Laut: 'Every soldier, irrespective of rank, who, in opposition to my orders, retreats, will be court-martialled immediately and sentenced to death!'

The General's thoughts went irresistibly to the great Moltke: No operation can be constructed without reference to the weather. The time of year *must* be taken into consideration! And Hitler's operation TAIFUN is constructed without reference to the autumn, he thought, and saw defeat looming already on the horizon.

5 | The Tepluschka

The terrible November storms sweep over the Russian steppe driving great blankets of white snow before them.

Winter has arrived in all its might and majesty. The first snows on 10 October. Particularly early this year. All the powers of nature seem to be on the side of the godless.

The German armies are less than 90 miles from Moscow. If the weather had not broken we would have been there within twelve days. Now the battered Russian divisions gain time to pull themselves together and regroup. They are issued with brand-new winter equipment. We don't even get mittens and have to make shift with cloths cut from the uniforms of the dead. Instead of furs we use newspaper wadded next to the skin. A wisp of straw to put in your boots is an expensive commodity.

The General Staff says winter has surprised us, but the Russians, strangely enough, seem to have been informed well in advance of its arrival. If the gentlemen with the red tabs had studied the Russian people before attacking them they would have been warned against the winter. As soon as the grey-blue clouds appear on the eastern horizon and the waters of the rivers grow wilder, Ivan the peasant begins to pack the eaves of his hut with logs in readiness for the cruel winter which can come in the course of a single night. The *Babuschka* begins to cover the windows with paper, from 'New Russia' which is distributed free of charge and which every Russian citizen is wise to have lying about when the District Soviet comes visiting.

After only two days of winter, trees begin to split in the iron frost with a sound like a 75 mm field gun, and wolf packs trail about the skirts of the advancing German army. There are always stragglers to provide them with a meal. The first few days we shoot at them and kill some but after a while we lose interest. They keep away as long as we are marching in column but it doesn't do to go off alone even armed with a

98 carbine. The pack is on top of a man before he can get his second shot away.

The cold worsens hourly. Frozen bodies of men and animals lie everywhere. It is as if the whole of nature is moving into a state of frozen suspension to await the arrival of spring.

But who can think of spring at 50° below zero, with the storms driving crystals of ice cuttingly across the Russian steppe. Supplies fail to get through. The ersatz coffee freezes to ice in the containers. The German armies are short of everything needed to conduct a winter war. No anti-freeze lubricant for the weapons and ordinary oil freezes the working parts fast. Whole motorized columns stand abandoned at the wayside. Frost! After two hours standing idle, the motors are ruined.

'If Napoleon got a real beating from the Russian winter our Adolf's going to get a bigger one!' Porta tells the company loudly.

'Porta says your Führer's lost 'is war, Julius,' shouts Tiny. 'Get protestin' mate!'

Julius Heide looks at him with dead eyes which seem to have become even bluer and colder in the biting frost.

'Say somethin', Julius,' shouts Tiny stubbornly. 'E says Adolf the Great's fell on 'is arse on the bleedin' ice!'

'Reporting for duty,' groans Heide from somewhere far down in his chest.

'Holy Mother of Kazan be thanked,' shouts Stege relieved. 'We're not completely lost. The old warriors can still open their traps!'

'Give him a swastika on rye. It's good for his beliefs!' suggests Barcelona. 'Straight vitamins for old Nazis!'

'Sing!' comes a command from the flank.

'Striped pig!' crows Porta disrespectfully. 'Come over here and I'll knock the frozen shit out from between your ears, you dried-up dwarf!'

A General-Major comes rushing angrily down the column demanding to know who shouted.

'Don't get across me, you men!' he shouts furiously into the storm.

'Wouldn't fancy it,' mumbles Porta half-aloud.

'I require your company to sing,' the General-Major turns on Oberleutnant Moser. 'They're to sing so loud the Kremlin can hear we're coming!'

'A song,' commands Moser tiredly. 'Form in a column of threes! Space off!'

Unwillingly we extend our left arms to take our distance.

Weit ist der Weg zurück ins Heimatland, so weit, so weit!
Dort wo die Sterne stehn am Waldesrand, blüht die neue Zeit.
ja, neue Zeit.
Jeder brave Grenadier sehnt heimlich sich nach dir,
ja, weit ist der Weg zurück ins Heimatland, so weit, so weit!
Die Wolken ziehn dahin, daher, sie ziehn wohl übers Meer.
Der Mensch lebt nur einmal und dann nicht mehr!*

We had to do it four times before the Herr General-Major was satisfied.

Then he drives us in amongst the trees where the wolves get the shock of their lives and take off to parts where there are no song-happy German General-Majors to worry them.

After an hour the great man tires of his fun, and disappears in his Kübel surrounded by his Military Police escort. We spit after him and in loud tones wish him a slow death at Kolyma. The German armies have turned into a long grey-green snake, made up of dead souls, dragging itself towards the north-east. Moscow is the magnet that still draws us. The heart and soul of Russia.

With faces covered in a mask of rime we stare at the back

---

* *Long is the road to the Fatherland, so long, so long!*
There where the stars show at the woodland's edge, blooms the New Day,
yes, the New Day.
Each brave Grenadier longs in his heart for you,
yes, long is the road to the Fatherland, so long, so long!
The clouds come from it and to it, crossing even the sea.
Humans live but once and never more!

of the man in front of us. As long as he keeps moving we do. Two thousand paces is a kilometer and we are 140 of these from Moscow. Nothing to speak of in the normal way but in the Russian winter it's a stretch of unbelievable hell. If you invited the Devil on a trip like this he'd drop his tail between his legs and run for it merely at the thought. The few German soldiers who live through operation TAIFUN are frozen right through to their backbones and will never thaw out.

When we rest and put out sentries we have to relieve them every fifteen minutes. Otherwise we'd just be relieving corpses frozen into caricatures of humanity.

As the cold grows deeper we lost faith both in God and in Hitler.

'Hell's front yard,' says Porta swallowing a piece of frozen fish.

'Think of bein' with the partisans, an' 'avin' summer all the year long like in Spain or Africa,' Tiny dreams aloud.

'We should've stayed with them,' says Porta. 'It was dangerous but it was a wonderful time. The planes came over like motorized Father Christmases dropping supplies bang on the minute.'

'Think if we was to get just a little bit of all the good luck as is goin' round loose all over the world, an' got sent to the Kola peninsula,' says Tiny enthusiastically. 'We could fish for pearls in the breaks in the fighin' an' when the war was over we'd be off to 'Amburg with a bag-full of pearls enough to buy a nice little boozer. One with a long, long, bleedin' bar where all the boys could stand up at the same time with one foot on the brass rail an' a beer in their fists. Jesus Christ!' he adds after a pause. 'What I wouldn't give for a place like that, stinkin' somethin' lovely of 'ores scent, tobacco, 'n fresh-pulled wobble!'

'Are there pearls in the Kola river?' asks Stege wonder-ingly. He wasn't with us in '39–40 when we, German soldiers in Finnish uniforms, were operating behind the enemy lines under the command of the Lapp, Lieutenant Guri, in Russian uniforms. We changed uniforms so often we had a hard time remembering whose side we were really on.

'There aren't many in the Kola,' explains Porta. 'But there's more than a few in the Umba. They're bloody beautiful, oval with a kind of waist-belt. Some of them are almost blue. The Lapps have a special name for them, some word only a Lapp could get his tongue round. They've got tongues like reindeer up north there. We fetched these mussels up in ice and cold and almost forgot what we were really supposed to be doing on the Kola peninsula until the other lot started trying to ventilate us.'

'Yes, we had a lovely time in Finland,' says the Old Man with a happy sigh.

'In the evening we ate trout we'd caught on bent fishing rods. Guri the Lapp taught us how.'

'But the best was when we got back from a trip,' shouts Porta gleefully. 'If we weren't as bang on time as a crack express train those Goddamn Finns'd shoot us down.'

'Stoi!' they yelled if we were too late and banged away immediately whether we halted or not. But if God was on our side and we got back dead on time and were allowed through we were picked up in lorries and driven to the sauna so that all the enemy dirt could be steamed out of us. In the sauna we drank skimmed milk just like the Finns. But God how cold it was jumping into the lake. Your old pennywinkle'd disappear like a shot in the icy-cold water and the nurses used to ask us if we'd pawned him with Uncle Joe.'

'An' the cookies from the other units treated us like we was Obersts with coloured ribbons all over our 'ole bodies,' grins Tiny glowing. 'We was that tough we laughed at the infantry boys' job. That was a real bleedin' army, the Finnish! They even 'ad uniforms as fitted me.'

'Wonder what happened to Guri,' says the Old Man thoughtfully.

'Called up again I'd reckon and working with a new lot behind the enemy lines,' suggests Barcelona. 'Probably a captain by now.'

'Think we could get posted up there again?' asks Tiny. 'It's supposed to be a bit of all right in the summer. They fatten up on grouse. I 'eard it off a corporal in the reindeers.'

'And they take it out on the girls who bathe naked in the lakes,' interjects Porta with a lustful laugh. 'Call me a liar if I couldn't fancy a couple of hundred pounds of woman wobbling past right now. I'd fix her on the spot in the middle of a snowdrift and risk me old *tovaritsch* prick freezing to an icicle straight after.'

Many drop off in the snow as we march. We see them go with indifference. Even before the column is out of sight they are covered in light powdery snow. Very soon they are dead. Freezing to death isn't so bad. It's worst being saved. You don't know what pain is if you've never experienced frost gangrene. The stink is like a rotten tumour. Nothing smells quite like frost gangrene.

We halt in a ruined village. It must have been a small rail junction before the war. Everything is burnt out. We try to make something eatable out of the burnt maize in one of the granaries. We give up when Tiny breaks a tooth. It's like chewing on granite.

We find a row of *tepluschka* on a siding and wonder how they have avoided being burnt like everything else. We walk round them carefully. The sliding doors are heavily pad-locked.

Porta tests one of the locks with the butt of his Mpi but it is a heavy railway type lock and won't give way. He scratches thoughtfully at his tousled red thatch.

'There must be something of value in those boxes since they're so carefully locked. Maybe the Kremlin gold's inside,' he whispers with anticipation in his eyes. 'All my life I've wanted a real gold bar. Have you ever thought what you could buy for a lump of gold like that?'

'You could buy yourself a piece of cunt,' shouts Tiny lecherously and scratches himself in the crutch with the handle of a grenade.

'You could buy the whole knocking-shop and bang away till dust comes out of your ears,' grins Porta.

'I hope there's food inside,' mumbles Stege through the strap he's chewing away at. 'I'm hungry enough to eat a tree!'

'Look around you,' says Barcelona. 'There's enough of 'em here to keep you going if you live to be a thousand.'

We crowd round Porta. Our imaginations run riot. There's no end to what we can imagine the *tepluschka* to be loaded with.

Tiny suggests deep-frozen whores only requiring to be thawed out before use.

'Maybe they're filled with *balanda*,' shouts Porta. 'Holy Mother of Kazan, we'll be shitting a whole field of oats for the next three months!'

None of us is quite ready to shoot the locks off. *Tepluschka* should be treated with care.

There have been *tepluschka* in Russia for as long as there have been railways. They were, in fact, built for military purposes originally. They are large, solidly constructed, goods wagons, built of Siberian wood. In the middle of the floor there is a small iron stove with a pipe going up through the roof. Next to the stove is a hole in the floor, a WC without the W. Practical and simple like everything else in Russia. The wagons are reckoned to take 30 soldiers or 12 horses or 70 prisoners destined for Kolyma, Novosibirst, Chila or elsewhere; terminals for people not in agreement with the big fellows in the Kremlin. When soldiers were being carried backwards and forwards across the great, wonderfully beautiful but cruel reaches of Russia the *tepluschka* would smell of hay and straw. When prisoners were being carried the *tepluschka* stank of excrement. The pipe from the floor toilet soon froze solid and the fish soup which was the prisoners staple diet gave them diarrhoea. They died like flies. They were kicked, beaten, jabbed with bayonets, by everyone who wanted to demonstrate that *he* of all people was the last to sympathize with these lunatics. That's how it's always been in Russia and that's how it'll always be.

Tepluschka carried the soldiers, and the prisoners, of the Czars all over the Empire. What the Czar ordered was right, until one dark October day in 1917. Now it was the free men of yesterday who had to take their turn in the *tepluschka*. The Czarist eagle was replaced by the Red Star. All the *tepluschka* had one thing in common: Those inside them were destined to die for the Fatherland; either on the field of battle or in the lead mines.

Porta smashes the butt of his weapon down on the lock. With lifting-bars we prize away at the sliding doors.

'I'll eat my tin 'at if there ain't frozen meat in there,' shouts Tiny, licking his frost-cracked lips hungrily.

We've had nothing to eat for five days. The Russians blow their storehouses up as they retreat. It's an old Russian tactic. Withdraw fighting and burn everything behind you.

Slowly the doors give way. We jump back in alarm as a frozen corpse rolls out.

'It *was* frozen meat,' mumbles Tiny disappointedly. 'Pity we ain't bleedin' cannibals.'

Apathetically we squat in the snow and share out the remainder of the iron rations. In the woods a machine-gun barks wickedly. It's one of the new kind that sounds like a racing car-engine. Barcelona has quite lost his spirits at the disappointment with the *tepluschka*. He is crying silently. Tears are dangerous. If they turn to ice it can mean blindness. In the beginning ice and snowblind casualties were sent back to the advance medical stations, but now the orderlies don't even bother examining them. A man's finished if his friends don't take him in tow. Wherever you look your eye meets an endless field of white and you walk in circles as if dead drunk. A man without friends is pushed from the column and forgotten as quickly as the dead lying in the snow-drifts.

If he has any energy left he staggers on until he ends in a drift with the others. They say that 100,000 German soldiers lie frozen along the road to Moscow. The Führer's orders are that German casualties are not to be counted. Only cowards die. A German soldier will not allow himself to die. That one causes quite a lot of merriment.

The Professor, who keeps a diary, can't resist keeping count. We warn him. If the NSFO hears of it it will cost him his head, and informers are everywhere; people who are *forced* to inform. Nobody is safe from them. Particularly dangerous are the ones who have family members in the concentration camps. Hostages have been taken and used since 1933. When the Professor came to No. 5 Company he believed every word the National Socialists had told him. Now, like many others, he is cured. He believes only what he sees.

'With a *tepluschka* like these, a man could go anywhere, if only he had a red star on his cap,' groans the Old Man, dropping tiredly to the snow. He tries to get his ancient silver-lidded pipe alight.

'We'd fill up the wagon with beautiful straw and set a bubbling pot of Kascha over on the stove.' He closes his frost-rimmed eyes dreamily. 'Scalding hot Kascha! The Russians look after their slaves better. Have you ever met a moujik who didn't have *something* in his duffle?' With an angry movement the Old Man turns *his* inside out showing the white lining. 'And what've the Prussian heroes got? Five hundred pages of propaganda piss with golden promises of how good we're going to have it when we've won the war – and fuck-all else!' He manages to get his pipe going finally, blows out smoke with satisfaction, takes it out of his mouth and points the stem at us.

'Know what *I* think, kiddies?' Gröfass* has lost his war and we can be glad of it!'

'Trea . . . ,' is all Julius Heide has time to get out before Timy knocks him unconscious with a plank. When the Old Man speaks everybody else keeps his mouth shut, because the Old Man knows what he is talking about. No. 2 Section suddenly realizes that Adolf Hitler has lost his war seventy

---

* Gröfass (Grösster Feldherr aller Zeiten): The Greatest Military Leader of All Time (contemptuous nickname for Hitler).

miles from Moscow. We should have realized it long ago, but the countless ranting speeches have blinded us and the endless columns of prisoners filling the roads have made us believe in the victory. What do a couple of million men mean to Joe Stalin? A mere two or three armies. No more than a division means to us. For every Russian we kill there are ten waiting to take his place.

'The German Army is running itself into the ground,' continues the Old Man. 'Here *we* are. Panzer soldiers with a long and expensive training behind us running around as footsloggers. Our neighbour is wiser. He knows what a Panzer soldier is worth. As soon as a crew steps out of a wreck there's a new T-34 waiting for them and they've learnt something more about what *not* to do. Kiddies, kiddies! If we're going to get out of Russia with whole skins we've got to learn a lot from Ivan.'

'Doubter of the Victory, you're insulting the Führer,' screams Heide who has recovered from his meeting with Tiny's plank.

Tiny lifts a heavy log and is about to hit him again.

'Leave him be,' hisses the Old Man irritatedly.

'Why?' asks Tiny open-mouthed. 'If I snatch 'is bleedin' balls off 'e won't be able to make any more little Nazi bastards!'

'No. 5 Company fall in!' commands Oberleutnant Moser.

We get up crossly. We were just getting used to not marching.

'Wake up, man,' Stege rousts out Barcelona Blom who is lying in a snowdrift.

'Leave me be,' sobs Barcelona. 'Go to Moscow your bloody selves if you want to. It ain't my war!'

'Come along,' I say. 'You can't stay here!'

'Somebody pinched yer sweeties?' asks Tiny nudging him with his Mpi.

'That frozen bastard is resigning from the campaign,' says Stege. He kicks out at Barcelona, misses, loses his balance and rolls in the snow.

'Frost in 'is speculator,' reckons Tiny. 'We'll soon fix *'im* up.' He takes Barcelona by the front of his uniform smashes a fist into his frost-blue face and shoves him hard into a snowdrift. 'March, *march* you weedy bastard! Austria's Adolf the Great 'as ordered you to Moscow! Russia wants to come back to the Reich!' Barcelona struggles to his feet with difficulty and slowly wipes the blood from his nose and mouth.

'I'll send you to Torgau, Obergefreiter Creutzfeldt,' he snarls through his nose in a strange Feldwebel voice quite unlike his own.

'I'm crazy mad to get shoved into a warm cell at Torgau,' grins Tiny. 'I'd kiss Iron Gustav* right on the bleedin' mouth. I'd even kiss 'is bleedin' arse, if it'd get me back to Torgau!'

'You'll get to *know* me,' screams Barcelona in the same tightly screwed up voice.

'Tain't necessary,' answers Tiny pleasantly. 'I know you already, you squeezed-out ball-bag.'

Barcelona's Mpi is up and ready to shoot. There is a queer light in his eyes, the sign of a sickness which hits soldiers who have been in combat for too long. Battle madness!

'You dare to lay hands on a Feldwebel?' he snarls hoarsely. 'Goddam *you*!' He looks around him quickly as if to ensure himself that there are no witnesses. His Mpi comes up. He mumbles to himself. Jumbled sentences which have no connection with what is happening. We back towards the trees. Any minute he may get the idea we're Russians and let go at us.

'So a fuckin' Russian'll lay his hands on a German Feldwebel!' he shouts so loudly that every man in the company looks up at him and realizes what is happening.

In the twinkling of an eye the whole company is in amongst the trees. Nobody wants to get himself killed by a German Mpi.

Tiny is on his belly in the snow with his weapon at the

* Iron Gustav (Gustav Dürer): See 'March Battalion.'

109

ready. It'd be easy for him to shoot Barcelona down, but it isn't easy to bring yourself to shoot down a comrade even when he's raving mad and thinks he's surrounded by enemy soldiers.

'Listen to me Feldwebel Blom, peace has been signed,' says the Old Man. He walks towards Barcelona. 'The war is over. Throw down your gun! See I'm not armed.' He holds his open hands out to the side.

'You're trying something, you bloody Communist,' screams Barcelona, 'But I'm gonna blow the Goddam shit out of *you*!'

Tiny springs like a panther and pins him just as a hail of bullets rips up the snow at the Old Man's feet.

Barcelona bawls like a wild bull.

'Help me! The enemy's got me!' He takes Tiny for a Russian.

The company comes back to life. Everybody is shouting at the same time.

Some suggest shooting Barcelona immediately before he goes crazy again and thinks we're Russians he has to put to sleep.

The MO arrives on the run and shoots a hypo into him and soon he is himself again. He goes round offering his hand and apologizing to everybody. It's a characteristic of the sickness. They always do that as soon as the mad fit leaves them.

Not so long ago we had an Unteroffizier who went round talking about black angels with golden wings. He claimed he was Chief Mechanic in the garages of the Heavenly Mechanized Host. We kept a close watch on him, and were ready when his eyes started to glare, but we still weren't quick enough. He managed to kill five men before we disarmed him. *He* went round afterwards shaking hands and saying he was sorry. He even shook the five bodies by the hand and said he wasn't mad at them. The same evening it hit him again and he shot off over to the enemy to arrange an armistice. We never saw him again.

In front of us the heavens glow red, lit up by the almost continuous flashes of mighty explosions. An SS tank regiment thunders past us.

A few hours later we catch up with them, but now the tanks are smashed and the frozen twisted bodies of the SS-men hang from the hatches. In amongst the trees are shattered Russian tanks and the remains of an entire anti-tank battalion.

A dozen or so Russians have been neck-shot. Probably for trying to run for it when things got too hot. We're through their things faster than professional pickpockets but there are no great pickings. There's one thing common to both sides: We're hungry.

In a hut Porta finds a pot containing a little frozen *balanda*. There are five dead civilians in the room. All shot in the neck, faces torn away by the bullet exiting.

'Neck-shot Nagan,' confirms Stege shortly. 'Traitors, then!'

'Cut that traitor rubbish *out*,' says the Old Man irritably. 'It's the most overworked word in the language. Soon as the nationalists need a goat they smell out a traitor. Preferably a little one who can't answer back.' He points to the body of a young girl lying across a pile of wood. Her face has been torn away by the bullet and blood has run down over the logs. 'Think she ever dreamt of being a traitor? Who could *she* betray?'

'There's always traitors in wartime,' Tiny considers. 'In school they told us everybody in Alsace was a pack o' traitors as ought to be strung up. They fired on our soldiers when they marched through in 1914. My teacher who was 'oly, an' a 'oly terror with the cane, was there 'imself an' 'ad a bullet put through 'is 'oly shoulder by one o' them Alsace traitors.'

'*Merde!*'* shrugs the Legionnaire. 'The Alsatians were Frenchmen. It was their duty to shoot at German soldiers. But these border people are, like the proverbial louse, caught between two nails. In 1871 the people of Alsace suddenly

---

* *Merde* (French): Shit.

111

became Germans and had to take their orders from Berlin. In 1918 they became Frenchmen again and Paris gave the orders. In 1940 they went back to being Germans. You can bet your sweet life they'll be Frenchmen again as soon as we've lost this war. You cannot wonder at it being difficult for them to know where their allegiance lies.'

'No matter what they do the poor bastards are traitors!' grins Tiny. 'Thank Christ for livin' in bleedin' 'Amburg. No sweat bein' there. If you can't think for yourself they do it for you at Stadthausbrücke 8.'

'What's all this to do with *them*?' asks Barcelona, gesturing towards the five bodies. 'They're not from Alsace. They've always been Russians.'

'It's different with them,' answers the Old Man, puffing violently at his silver-lidded pipe. 'They were probably ordered to open fire on us, tried to discuss it, and the NKVD won the argument.'

'It's not *clever* startin' discussions with the NKVD *nor* the bleedin' Gestapo. You gotta work 'em a flanker,' says Tiny looking sly. '*I'd* a' said to these 'ere NKVD *tovaritsches*: Gimme a cannon, mates, an' see 'ow I'll neck them German-skij bastards. I'll 'ave 'em laid out in rows by the bleedin' company. Comin' 'ere without even bein' invited.'

'Do not forget who you are, and what uniform you are wearing,' comes threateningly from Heide.

The *balanda* was only enough for two spoons full each, and hunger gnaws worse than ever.

The cold becomes even more intense. We rest in a ruined tile-works. There are a lot of charred Russian bodies just inside the main gates.

'Flame-throwers,' comments Stege.

We drop to the floor half-dead from fatigue. Our feet feel like lead in our frozen boots. Nobody says a word. Not even Porta. I sit beside him inside one of the large ovens. We're out of the wind here, and inside the oven it is slightly warmer. Most of us sleep. Oberleutnant Moser lies rolled into a ball across a heap of ashes. He is wearing a Russian captain's fur coat. Risky if he is taken prisoner. The Old Man shoulders in beside us and takes something out of his padded coat. He hands it to us. A little sugar and a piece of mutton sausage.

'Where in the world did you get it?' I ask in amazement.

'Shut up and eat,' growls the Old Man. 'It's little enough for three. D'you want the others to hear?'

'Got any more?' asks Porta chewing away fiercely.

'A little sausage, a little bread and some soup powder,' nods the Old Man.

'Holy Mother of Kazan! We're the richest bloody soldiers in this man's army,' laughs Porta his eyes shining again. 'Let's have the rest of the sausage and the bread. We'll keep the soup till tomorrow.'

'Jesus, I think we're going to make it,' I say confidently as I feel the warmth spreading through my body.

'Reminds me of a butcher in Berlin-Moabitt,' says Porta. 'He had so much black sausage left on Christmas Eve that he had to *give* it away. He was from Breslau and thought they ate black pudding in Berlin too on Christmas Eve. Late in the afternoon he was standing outside his shop on Schlesischer Strasse with a box of black pud' in front of him shouting: Come one, come all! Free Christmas sausage! Free Christmas sausage!

'Three Schupos dropped down on him and dragged him off to the psychiatric section. The sausages they sent for chemical analysis. Their idea being that he was either stark staring bonkers or else he was a mass-murderer who was trying to depopulate Berlin with poisoned sausages. No normal Berlin butcher ever gives anything away.'

'Cold?' asks the Old Man laying his arm around my shoulders.

'As hell!' I answer pulling my thin summer coat closer about me. Winter equipment hasn't got to us.

'Turn your back towards me!'

His strong fingers take hold of my neck. He begins to massage me hard, at the same time blowing his warm breath down my neck. Slowly warmth comes back into my body.

When I'm quite warm I do the same for him. Then we both go to work on Porta. Now we feel good. We roll together in a heap like animals in the woods and fall into a heavy sleep. . . .

Nine men of the company freeze to death that night. A pity for them, since we wake up to a wonderful morning.

The cooks have got through to us with supplies. There's a whole herring per man and half a mess-tin of *Kipjatok*. Best of the lot we get half a pound of bread. We feel like multimillionaires.

'Kiddies, kiddies!' enthuses the Old Man skipping joyfully around. 'They've not written us off entirely yet!'

The rest of No. 2 Section sit round in a circle, every man with a frozen salted herring in his mouth. Not a morsel goes to waste and a frozen herring takes a long time to eat. You break off a small piece of it and put it in your mouth where it thaws out slowly. God how we enjoy it. A solemn silence sinks over us. We huddle close like fledglings, and feel the body heat from the man next to us. It is a long time since we've been so happy. Each piece of food goes into our mouths as if we were performing some holy rite. Slowly the herrings disappear; head, fins, bones, tail, every last part of them. Not an atom is left. Even a cat couldn't have done it better. We dip our bread in sugar and hold it in our mouths long enough for our own spittle to make it swell hugely. The sugar trickles down our throats in a wonderful stream and we feel its strength bubbling out into every corner of our body.

'Bread and sugar just about beats every other kind of eats in this whole damn world,' says Porta dipping a small piece of bread in sugar and handing it to the Old Man.

Suddenly a whole lot of bread and sugar goodies are on the way over to the Old Man. The Old Man is not only our section leader, he is our father and mother, this stocky little carpenter from the Berlin slums who has been forced into a Feldwebel's uniform. It's *our* lives that are at stake if anything happens to the Old Man. If we lost him our section's finished. We know that.

114

Oberleutnant Moser pushes in amongst us bringing tea with him. A big can. We get a swig apiece.

Porta digs out two cigarettes, and they go round three times!

> **'They know nothing about reality, these incompetent careerists, bureaucrats and adjutant-minded souls, all the high Wehrmacht officers, the leaders of the General Staff. They are now classified under one generic title: Adjutants. Have you noticed, how they tremble when they duck their heads before me?'**
>
> Hitler in a conversation with
> Obergruppenführer Heydrich 23.12.36.

'Tomorrow morning, gentlemen, we attack Borodino,' began General-Leutnant Weil. 'Here, on the historic ground on which we now stand, the Emperor Napoleon, on 7 August 1812, defeated the Russian General Kutusow. I am happy that we can repeat this victory and be spoken of in the history of our nation with honour and pride. When Borodino has fallen the way to the Kremlin is open, with only a few unimportant hindrances.' The General stopped for a moment and took out a cigar. A dozen lighters snapped out smartly. Outside, artillery roared. The little chateau trembled slightly. The glass of the chandeliers tinkled. The General smiling and well-satisfied, looked around at the officers.

'Gentlemen, I almost dare to say that it would be a fine thing to meet one's fate on this historic earth. We have . . .' His words were drowned in the roar of an explosion and a sun-burst of light illumined the scene. With a deafening crash half of the ceiling fell in.

Oberst Gabelsberg, commanding infantry, bent over the General and together with the chief-of-Staff carried him to a sofa. A shell splinter had torn open his back. The medical officer could do nothing to save him.

'Gentlemen and comrades, our General is dead,' said Oberst Gabelsberg quietly. 'Let us take leave of him in a proper manner.'

He brought his heels together and raised his hand to his cap in the salute. All the officers followed his example. 'Like the remarkably brave soldier he was, Herr General Weil has led our division, over a long period, from victory to victory. It is because of him that we have always been permitted to fight in the forefront of the battle. Thanks to him we have, in this present war, added many names to the great battles already named on our colours, which were present at Waterloo. Our General died the death he would have desired. God has ordered his discharge and has taken him into a greater army. Comrades, Sieg! Heil! Honour our dead heroes!'

The officers stood with their field service caps in their hands looking sorrowfully at the ground. It was expected of them.

'As senior line-officer I now take over the Division,' Oberst Gabelsberg hurried on. He had difficulty in concealing his delight at the General's death. 'Our Panzer Division has the noblest traditions of any in the Greater German Wehrmacht, and as Commander of the Division I shall see to it that this tradition continues. We will not mourn our dead but thank God that they died for the honour of the Division. Gentlemen, I would be proud to fall within the hour for my Führer, my Fatherland, my fellow countrymen!'

The farewells were solemn. A General had fallen on the field of honour. The occasion demanded the employment of tact.

Cigars were not lighted, and women were not mentioned. The German officer corps were cultured men.

The new Divisional Commander drove away in his Kübel, mud splashing behind the car. The heavy vehicle swung and slid over the bottomless mud plowing through ridges of dirty snow.

The driver sighed with relief when he felt the road firm at last under the wheels.

The Commander wrapped three blankets around him, pushed his feet into lambswool footwarmers, and pulled the fur collar of his great-coat up around his ears. A German Oberst didn't allow himself to become cold. He leaned back comfortably. He had time to take a nap. He would hand over the Regiment to Obersleutnant Reuff and then back to Division and a

117

real bed. Now the war would become a more pleasant affair. The Oberst felt that he deserved some refreshment. He took a long deep pull at his cognac flask.

Poor General Weil, he thought. He never saw Moscow. Now he, Oberst Gabelsberg, would lead the Division on to the Kremlin. He would be a General several years ahead of time. This wasn't such a bad war after all.

In the same instant a terrible explosion blew the Kübel into a thousand flying pieces. The bodies of the Oberst, his adjutant, and the driver were blown into the air and fell to drive deeply into the mud.

Shadowy figures disappeared quickly into the forest. The partisans had been laying mines.

6 | The Meat Depot

The Hauptfeldwebel sits staring stiffly in front of him. His arms are lying across the desk. He is wearing a fur-lined winter great-coat and a beautiful astrakhan cap decorates his large square head.

Porta and Tiny salute smartly, report their arrival, smash their heels together three times, raise their right arms stiffly in the Nazi salute and march noisily towards the Hauptfeldwebel. They grasp him firmly under the arms, lift him from his chair and send him flying in a beautiful curve straight through the window. He falls and remains in a sitting position in the snow. He looks so natural that two infantrymen salute him smartly as they pass by.

Porta and Tiny go through everything in the mobile office snatching up rubber stamps and blank forms. By the time they leave they are equipped with passes, stamps, and tickets enough to send a whole regiment on a sight-seeing tour of Europe five times over. They are already well past the frozen Hauptfeldwebel when Tiny stops as if struck by lightning.

'What the hell's wrong?' asks Porta nervously.

'I'm afraid you an' me must be gettin' old,' answers Tiny,

shaking his head worriedly. 'We forgot to look if ol' fatguts 'ad any gold in 'is chops!'

Without a word they go back to the body and tip it on its back.

A gun-muzzle between the teeth and a quick operation and Porta is in possession of two gold teeth.

'You've got to keep your wits about you when you're in a war,' he explains. 'There's valuables all around us. Old fatguts sits there and lets himself freeze to death. There was even ice in his mouth. Probably deliberate, to keep honest people like us from finding the gold in 'em.'

'Reckon we're gonna leave the army rich men?' smiles Tiny, putting the bag of teeth carefully into his breast pocket.

'No doubt about it,' Porta assures him. 'We went into this dam' war piss-poor but we'll get out of it rich as a couple of Jew gold-dealers and dressed up in tailor-mades with officer's boots shining like shit on a slate.'

'Think we'll get to be officers?' asks Tiny sceptically.

'No, I wouldn't consider it probable, but I wouldn't consider it *im*probable either. In the service of God and Prussia anything's possible!'

'I wouldn't 'alf like the chance of bein' some kind of Oberst,' Tiny grins with a revengeful glint in his eyes. 'Best'd be one of them big guns on the General Staff with the rosy-coloured stripes down their strides. I'd 'ave Hauptfeldwebel bleedin' 'Ofman crawlin' on 'is gut in pigshit eight hours a day. An' Julius soddin' 'Eide up in the 'ighest tree in the forest with orders to shout *"Sieg"*, *"Heil"*, from dawn to bleedin' dusk. With 'is gas-mask on, too!'

'You don't have to be more than a Leutnant to do that,' states Porta, 'and you'll make that quicker than you'll make Oberst. Learn to quote regulations backwards and forwards and you'll be a sword swallower before you even know it.'

'I can't 'ardly read, mate!' mumbles Tiny bitterly.

'Get some slave or other to teach you. Never admit you can't read. They won't believe you. They'll send you to the Gestapo and they'll rip pieces off you with red-hot tongs until you admit you *can* read. In the Party Programme it says all Germans can read, and *you're* a German *that* you can't deny. It's a kind of curse. If you can get it removed you get the right to shave the Devil's backside with a blunt razor blade!'

'I've never been proud of bein' born in the bleedin' Reich,' admits Tiny sourly. 'If I'da bin born somewhere else at least I wouldn't 'ave 'ad to go round with this barmy bleedin' bird on me bosom. I never could stand poultry!'

'What's that?' asks Porta suddenly and points to a large white sign.

They scrape the snow from it. Porta has finished reading it long before Tiny has even started spelling it out.

3rd ARMY CORPS
SUPPLY DEPOT

ENTRY STRICTLY FORBIDDEN
WITHOUT AUTHORIZATION

'This is something we must look into,' considers Porta.

'Long as they don't try to make 'oles in us,' says Tiny cautiously.

'I ain't got much time for these salami supermen. They get trigger-finger itch when they see strange faces sniffing around their bleedin' larders.'

'Dry your eyes, son! If Moses could lead a tribe of Yids through the Red Sea with old Pharaoh's Panzer divisions snapping at their butts then two of our kind can take over a German sausage depot with one hand tied behind us. Keep your trap shut and let me do the talking. Look like tough-nut SS-man with your left hand on your pistol-holster as if it'd grown there, and your old persuader under your right arm with one finger on the trigger.'

'Shall I open up?' asks Tiny happily cocking his sub-machine-gun.

'Jesus Christ, no!' shouts Porta. 'The salami's would be

120

crazy enough to fire back at us. We've got to get 'em paralysed with fright first, so no matter what they say to you, you just growl like a gorilla and roll your eyes. We'll do 'em the way we did the railways when we scared 'em into handing us over a locomotive.'

'Got it!' glows Tiny happily. 'think them iron 'orse cowboys are still sittin' in the clink?'

'I certainly hope so,' says Porta. 'If they're not we're wanted by everybody, from the International Police to the Salvation Army.'

'To 'ell with 'em,' grins Tiny unworriedly. 'The International Police ain't comin' to Russia while this weather lasts. It's too big an' it's too bleedin' cold.'

> Ich hab' mich ergeben mit Herz und mit Hand dir,
> land voll Lieb und Leben,
> mein Deutsches Vaterland.
> Mein Herz ist englommen, dir treu zugewandt,
> du Land der freien Frommen,
> du herrlich Herrmannsland.*

they sing as they march towards the Army Depot.

'Look around you, Obergefreiter Creutzfeldt,' says Porta and throws out his hand with a lordly gesture as if it all belonged to him.

After two hours marching they are inside the perimeter wire surrounding the enormous depot, a former Russian military camp.

They saunter calmly around getting the lay-out of the depot, until suddenly a Feldwebel blocks their path.

He is about the size of an anti-tank barrier.

'What the hell are you two piss-ants doing here?' he yells

---

* I have given myself to you, my heart and my hand,
  You land full of love and of life,
  My German Fatherland.
  My heart is bursting with love for my land,
  The land of the free, the brave wonderful
  Herrmannsland.

waving his Mpi in the air. "Don't you fucked-up sons-of-bitches know this is out of bounds to scum like you?'

Porta straddles in front of him. Tiny, a stony-faced giant, stands directly behind him. He dips at the knees, down and up in SS fashion, and spits, narrowly missing the Feldwebel's boots.

'Listen to me you son of a blown-up bitch that dropped her miscarriage in a sewer. I'm looking for a Soviet turd I can fill your cock-sucking mouth with before I put you on the next train to Iron Gustav at Torgau you sow-bellied lump of striped shit. Message ended!'

The Feldwebel was only a soldier, and that is a terrible thing to be. He didn't know what to do. Scream at them or slink off quietly. One thing he did know. An Obergefreiter who dared to throw a mouthful like that at a serving Feldwebel was no ordinary Obergefreiter. He decided to slink away.

'See,' explains Porta to Tiny as they saunter on around the strictly out of bounds depot area. 'Use the language of an alley whore and they shut up. In ten seconds from now all the salami bosses'll be shitting themselves with fright. They'll fall apart like jerry-built war memorials built on sand. Now we'll show these kaffirs that we're in no hurry!'

'Like the Gestapo 'untin' people on a dark night,' shouts Tiny and bends over whooping with laughter.

'That's it exactly,' smiles Porta appreciatively. 'You're not as dumb as you look.'

'What're we doin' 'ere anyway?' asks Tiny a little later. 'Why're we goin' to all this trouble to frighten the shit outa these bleedin' sausage-miners?'

Porta stops in his tracks and gazes at Tiny with an appearance of undisguised wonder.

'Obergefreiter Wolfgang Ewald Creutzfeldt aren't you hungry?'

'I'm *always* 'ungry,' admits Tiny. 'I've never yet been that full up I couldn't eat more.'

'We are now in the middle of the Army's kitchen, and you

122

ask me what we're doing here?' shouts Porta reprovingly. 'We're foraging, Creutzfeldt, and, since we are not in possession of a legitimate requisition form, we must make use of other means.'

'Terror!' grins Tiny slitting his eyes.

The camp telephone wires glow. The rumour spreads with the speed of a forest fire. A secret spot-check! A panic of works runs through the depot. Hidden tinned stores appear on the shelves again. Weighted scales are readjusted. Erasers work overtime on the books. Five 'lost' lorries suddenly appear, readied for delivery. The shelves in the almost empty fur depot fill up again in record time.

Watchful eyes follow the two 'auditors' movements through the snow-covered streets. It almost ends in catastrophe when they stop at the Petrol Depot and Tiny fills his lighter.

The WO[1]/c the Petrol Depot snatches his ready packed duffel bag and disappears through the back door into his three-axled Mercedes.

Nobody feels safe. The Feldwebel in charge of the bread store has swallowed an entire jar of nerve pills and smoked a whole packet of Gribas.

'An audit without warning is worse for these boys than getting a dose,' remarks Porta pointing to a nervous group of supply soldiers who have been sent out with brooms in their hands to act as observers. Most of them relax as the two mystery men enter the Meat Depot. They are not unhappy to see that it is Stabsfeldwebel Brumme who is to have the pleasure of this unexpected visit.

'God is good to us!' cries the baker, Feldwebel Willinsky, happily.

'The fat bastard'll get his arse in the slicer now for sure! Did you see that thin red-haired chap who seems to be in charge? He stinks of Gestapo a mile away! Christ Almighty, my piles nearly dried up when he looked at me. He's one of the toughs they use to keep the mill going. Those uniforms can't hide it. They're SS-officers in disguise.'

Supplies Stabsfeldwebel Brumme is the only man in the Army Depot who has not been advised of the arrival of the two disguised Gestapo auditors.

'It's all up with him,' promises Feldwebel Willinsky gleefully. 'They'll drag him away in irons before long! Maybe they'll liquidate him out on the parade-ground,' he adds, hopefully.

Porta and Tiny step into a huge room, where countless slaughtered carcasses hang in rows from hooks.

'Where's your chief?' demands Porta, in an inquisitorial manner, of an overfat Unteroffizier, who is sitting on a stool biting into a liver sausage of unheard of dimensions. Fat is running down over his neck.

With cold, fishy eyes he examines the two strangers and comes to the decision that they are not worth answering. Condescendingly he points the liver sausage towards a door at the far end of the slaughter-house.

With a lightning motion Tiny snatches the sausage from his hand stuffs it into his own huge mouth and swallows it with the speed and elegance of an anaconda despatching a pig.

'Don't cry, sonny,' he advises him. 'You look for all the world like a dopy tourist lookin' at the Eiffel Tower! Your banger's gone an' even if it come back up again you wouldn't like it any more. So don't cry over spilt sausage! If it'll make you 'appy son, it tasted real good! It was a *good* sausage!'

'Good work!' praises Porta. 'Now this pot-bellied porker knows better than to wave a sausage about like that. Besides which he's been taught how to answer a polite question. Where shall we send him? Glatz or Torgau?'*

'Germersheim's better,' considers Tiny, belching between each word. The Unteroffizier looks at them with a foolish expression on his face. The look of a backward child or a chronic imbecile. He manages, however, to throw a good-sized bone after Tiny, as the door to the Depot Office bangs behind them.

* Glatz, Torgau, Germersheim: Three notorious military prisons.

Supplies Stabsfeldwebel Brumme is not a small man. A good seven inches over six feet, with a chest like a carthorse . Set in his huge completely bald head are a pair of unbelievably wicked little eyes blazing like searchlights on each side of a flattened purple nose.

He is lying stretched out on a cutting board with a blue cushion under his bull neck, prizing around with a bayonet after a piece of meat stuck between two of his teeth.

Almost ten minutes go by before he condescends to notice the presence of the two strangers.

'What you two maggots want?' he asks with the air of a conceited prosecutor.

'Just a short talk, Herr Stabsfeldwebel,' grins Porta cheekily, calmly choosing a steak from a dish standing on a small wheeled table beside the grossly fat Stabsfeldwebel. 'I've been told you're a good sort of man and you like to help your friends.'

Brumme lifts himself on one elbow and spits out a great mouthful of meat which lands with a slap under the photograph of the Führer. He glares suspiciously for a moment at Porta, turns his wicked coals of eyes on Tiny, and then falls back on the cutting-board with a roar of laughter.

'Now I've heard everything,' he yells in a beery bass. 'The *maggots'll* be crawling up to Stabsfeldwebel Brumme for extra next! Who sent you two red-arsed monkeys to *me*? Must've been somebody who hated your guts and wanted to get rid of you. Even the bugs don't come interrupting *my* rest-hour. Don't you two underdeveloped bastards *know* that? Write it down in case you're absent-minded: I'm *not* a good fellow who does things for his friends. I ain't *got* any friends. I'm the Devil himself!'

With a bound he springs from the table and pushes a giant fist in front of Porta's nose, so closely that he has to move his head to see round it.

'Take a sniff of that!' he orders with a harsh cackle of laughter.

'When we got no more tanks left *I'll* be out there

smashing them fucked-up T-34s flat with one punch from this!'

'It's big,' admits Porta unimpressed, 'but as you may not be aware, dad, nobody ever won a war by effing and blinding and waving his dirty great fists in the air! We had a block-commander at Germersheim, Leutnant Liebe, who could hide a well-grown alley cat in his fist, and whilst he was hiding it he would call a prisoner to him and say: "Guess what I'm holding in my hand you twisted-up alcoholic. Guess right and I'll put you on the trusties team. Guess wrong and I'll chop your fucking yid snout off with my sabre."

'This went along without any trouble for a couple of years, until a Gestapo controller disguised as an Obergefreiter infiltrated Germersheim to check on things. The Führer wanted to know what was going on. It was a Monday morning, just like it is today. And it was snowing too. Leutnant Liebe hadn't been warned about the visit and, as if to spite his lovely name, went screaming and shouting about as usual. Before he knew what was happening he was leading a section of 75 mm horse-drawn artillery straight towards the front. He would no doubt have made a success of the job of forward artillery spotter which he was given. *If* he hadn't been killed, almost as soon as he took it up.'

'Herr Stabsfeldwebel,' Porta looks stern, 'Would *you* like to die for your Führer, Family and Fatherland?'

Stabsfeldwebel Brumme swallows a lump in his throat and tries hard to look patriotic. He can't feel sure whether these two are a couple of Ironheads from the SS or a pair of queer ducks flapping away desperately to try and save themselves. He finds it best to be extremely careful. If they *are* Ironheads then he's in the shit. He points to the opposite wall which is ornamented with a large photograph of Adolf Hitler.

'There hangs our Führer,' he says proudly.

'He hangs nicely!' grins Porta impertinently, sniffing hard at the air.

'I don't smell the odour of Valhalla or of heroic deeds here in your unit. I think we're in agreement. Enjoy life while you can and keep as far away as possible from all that noisy warfare.'

The Stabsfeldwebel stares thoughtfully for a moment at Porta's cunning rat face.

'Do you doubt the Final Victory?' asks Porta pointing accusingly at him.

'Of course not!' trumpets Brumme in confusion. A crazy question, he thinks. Only an idiot on his deathbed would answer in the negative.

'Did you listen to the Führer's last speech?' asks Porta with an inquisitorial air.

'Yes, *sir*,' lies Brumme. 'He spoke well.' He wonders desperately what kind of craziness Adolf had ranted last time.

'Are there Jews in your family?' continues Porta with a dangerous Gestapo look in his eyes. A threatening frown from Tiny accompanies the question.

'My Aryan certificate is in order,' replies Brumme, now noticeably nervous. Fearfully he remembers that it only goes back to his grandmother. He is from the Reichswehr where an Aryan Grandmother is enough. Those Goddam Jews!

'Do you know who your great-grandmother was?' Porta continues the inquisition. 'Her name was not, by any chance – Rachel?'

'No her name was Ruth,' comes quickly from Brumme.

He once had a golden-haired sweety called Ruth, and thinks it must be a good Aryan name.

'That sounds interesting,' smiles Porta with an explosion of merriment.

'It is the duty of every good German to report to the Racial Purity Commission the existence of Jewish seed in the Greater German Wehrmacht. It was in this way that General-Leutnant Hosenfelder was uncovered. He had adopted an Aryan nose but an Obergefreiter observed that the General never ate pork. He made a duty report, and one morning a pair of SS racial specialists arrived and took the Aryan-nosed General-Leutnant away with them. A traitor like that in a

General's uniform could have contaminated the entire German Army, so that we would never have got to Moscow. The proud German flag would never have flown above the Kremlin, and the proud German infantry never have had the chance to parade in Trafalgar Square, nor the Führer have achieved his wish to receive the toothless British lion in front of Buckingham Palace. Herr Stabsfeldwebel, would not such happenings be insupportable to we true Germans?'

'Sieg, Heil!' roars Stabsfeldwebel Brumme in his beery bass and in his excitement he raises both arms in the Nazi salute.

'Our brave men in field-grey shall take their part in the greatest of all Crusades of Liberation,' proclaims Porta patriotically. 'The goal of National Socialism is the destruction of the swamp-men and so to create *lebensraum* for the enslaved German people. Where the brown storm troopers of culture tread all other cultures are crushed. We Germans will decide what *the others* must think. They shall *not* think! the Führer will think for them!'

'This is one of the real Party nuts,' thinks Brumme despairingly. 'This kind of fanatic is deadly dangerous. He's ready to shout *Heil* at a sheep with its head cut off if only he thinks it just might be the Bohemian Corporal in disguise.'

'*Ein Volk, ein reich, ein Führer!*' roars Tiny in apparent enthusiasm.

He can't keep his mouth shut any longer.

There is a short moment of absolute stillness in the office. All three stare stiffly at one another. In the distance the thunder of the guns can be heard. Tiny brings his heels together with a bang and raises his right arm.

> *Die Fahne hoch,*
> *die Reihen fest geschlossen,*
> *SA marchiert . . .**

* With the flag above,
  In closed ranks
  The SA marches . . . .

He is screamingly off-key.

Standing to attention with hands stiffly raised, all three sing the song right through to the end. To an observer it would seem a solemn and patriotic sight.

'What do you think would happen, Herr Stabsfeldwebel, if you were to offer me a drink?' asks Porta in a buttery voice. 'Do you think I would refuse?'

Silently Brumme takes a healthy-sized jar from a shelf and, with a sour smile, pours the liquor into two large mugs which Tiny has helpfully placed on the table. Brumme promises himself that he will flatten those mugs later.

With a deep-felt 'A-a-a-ah!' Porta and Tiny empty them.

'What about another of those?' asks Porta. 'In a great age like this we should not limit ourselves!'

Glaring darkly Brumme pours again. If he had his way he would bang the cork back in and throw these two highwaymen out the door.

'Herr Stabsfeldwebel, you are in charge of the meat depot,' Porta confirms between satisfied belches. With impulsive suddenness he bangs his fist down the black ledgers which lie on the table. Stabsfeldwebel Brumme starts back in fright as if someone had said: 'Drag that swindler in front of a court-martial!'

'Leadership of a military meat depot is no easy job,' Porta continues gruffly. 'A job like that is not given to just anybody. In reality it should be regarded as a kind of holy mission on a par with the Padre Corps from General Staff 6.'

'Sex?' mumbles Brumme confusedly.

'I understand you, Stabsfeldwebel,' nods Porta in agreement. 'When I hear of G. 6, I myself do not connect it with the Padres, but with the field brothels. Have you, by the way, well-trained cutters on your staff? To succeed in war, experts are needed in every branch.'

'All my other ranks are first-class tradesmen from the School of Butchery at Dresden,' Brumme assures them eagerly.

'To cut meat is a profession which entails an equal

responsibility to that of an Army cartographer,' continues Porta in a schoolmasterish voice. 'It requires men with grey matter under their scalps who have an understanding of mathematics.'

'Mathematics?' stammers Brumme nervously and feels the sweat running down his spine. 'This is an Army Meat Depot I'm running, not an Artillery Mathematician's Section where they work out to a fraction of an inch where to drop shells and bombs on the enemy. I know *all* about meat and *fuck-all* about mathematics and that kind of shit. I can add and subtract, weigh in kilos and grammes; know a company needs 175 rations, half of which must be lean meat. You don't need to know any more than that in the Supply Corps. Ask Albert Speer. He's done two years with the Supply Corps Building Commission where they sent him that crazy he didn't know whether he was coming or going after he'd learnt too much mathematics. I've got my counting frame: 175 red balls over on the right and a company's got what its supposed to have according to the book.'

'How bloody wrong you are!' Porta ejaculates, with a grating peal of laughter. 'A military meat depot is a place where there is every necessity for mathematical ability. Before one begins to cut, waste must be calculated exactly. There is a lot of water in animals, as well as in soldiers. You receive, for example, 400 kgs of sow-meat into your stores. A pretty large percentage of it is water and bone to which a hungry soldier does not take kindly when it is handed out to him as meat, but you yourself have checked the weighing-in. You have taken 400 kgs in and you believe, too, that you have sent 400 kgs out at the other end of the depot. But when the auditors come and go through your books they find a criminal loss of thirty-five percent. And *you* are left holding the baby because you have not reckoned with this natural shrinkage.

'Carcasses are wicked things to have to do with. I learned this when I had the job of dismembering bodies in the cellars of the Charité Hospital. A murdered pig of a beer-swiller takes up a fair amount of room when he arrives feet first, but he has shrunk quite a bit after a few days. When we'd finished chopping at him and had burnt him he could go into a cigar-box. I never accepted them by weight.

'I gave a receipt for "one body" only. My predecessor, who signed for them by weight, got himself into a nice peck of trouble because of shrinkage. They thought he was hand-in-glove with the owner of a delicatessen in Spitalen-market whose extremely tasty sausages were found on analysis to contain human flesh.'

'I've never looked at cutting meat up in quite that light,' stammers Stabsfeldwebel Brumme, shifting his weight uneasily from one foot to the other. 'I've always weighted out the rations on regulation army decimal scales, and had a checker standing beside me. In my depot we use double entry bookkeeping,' he adds proudly, as if he himself were the inventor of that complicated system. 'So much lean meat, so much salvaged bone, so much by weight of severed sinews and uneatable offal. You can't go wrong!'

'But you *can!*' shouts Porta triumphantly. 'You receive 50 tons just before knocking-off time. You're busy, and you sign for 50 tons. Am I right!'

'Yes, of course,' answers Brumme and thinks of all the times they have fixed the scales and in reality received almost double the weight.

'The weight notes don't lie,' he adds after a short pause.

'And there we have it,' Porta laughs long and loud. 'The weighing-in document reveals the truth. Irrefutable proof to any court-martial. Not long ago I helped to shoot a poor unfortunate Stabsfeldwebel from 4 Army's Meat Depot. I can assure *you*, Herr Stabsfeldwebel, we really believed him when he screamed: "I am innocent. I'm an honest . . . !" Our twelve bullets struck his poor innocent Stabsfeldwebel body just as he got to the word – honest!'

'Have you served on a liquidation commando?' asks Brumme with a shiver of inward fear.

'Haven't I just!' boasts Porta with a superior grin. 'I've sent a good few Supplies people to a better world in my time. Ever seen a military execution, Herr Stabsfeldwebel? It's a nasty experience. You need a drink afterwards and even that doesn't wash away the memory immediately. But why think about these heavy punishments? They exist. Let us go back to the 50 tons of meat you've signed for so casually. You come to the depot the following morning, fresh and relaxed after a good honest cut. Result – 45 tons! You send for weight control to check your weights, but the Army weights function perfectly.

'*You* have signed for 50 tons of meat, but the poor hungry German soldier at the front is only going to get 45 tons. Whilst you have been asleep, dreaming perhaps of good business deals, your meat has lost 5 tons of moisture and since neither you nor your personnel know anything about this mysterious chemical process, you get into terrible trouble when the auditors arrive, without prior warning, to check on your little games. You are a careful and clever man, and you have found out, long before the commission arrives, that you are short of these five mysterious tons. From bitter experience you have discovered that all normal soldiers are thieves and you descend like a delayed whirlwind on your slaves.

'If you are fortunate enough to have a couple of decidedly feeble-minded persons amongst them you are saved. Fools like these are easily convinced that they have in fact stolen five tons of meat in the night. If *you* cannot make them confess then Iron Gustav *can*. He is a specialist at driving people into confessing. We once had a Wachtmeister from the Army Ammunition and Explosives Factory at Bamberg. He had been a lay-preacher before he was called to the service of the Fatherland. He insulted the Catholic Field Bishop with a number of hair-raising religious statements which could not be stomached without reprisal. He landed in Torgau and here it took Iron Gustav 9 minutes and 21 seconds by the clock to convince him that he was a blasphemer who deserved to swing at the end of a good German rope. I once saw Iron Gustav work-over a Quartermaster from 5 P.D. The fool hadn't admitted his guilt at the court-martial, even though Herr Stabsauditeur Vjebaba, who was famed for his persuasiveness, had done all he could to explain to him that a confession would be in his own interests. What the Stabsauditeur could not do Iron Gustav did in no time. The Quartermaster confessed that he himself had eaten the missing five tons of meat in the course of one night. They riddled him in Yard 4 fourteen days later. By God, Herr Stabsfeldwebel, the man who gets out of Iron Gustav's claws with a whole skin could piss his trousers without wetting himself. Pray you'll never make his acquaintance. He even sleeps in his tin-hat.'

'Lord preserve us,' sweats Brumme rolling his eyes.

Prussian eagles look to the west,
Tall, tall, stand our banners.

hums Tiny patriotically in the background. Long enforced silence bores him. He feels that a quiet interjection such as this can do no harm.

'But let us get back to our five tons of mysterious shrinkage,' continues Porta, serious as a judge about to pass the death sentence on a beautiful woman.

'Five tons of shrinkage!' Brumme attempts to bawl but it comes out in a hoarse whisper. His brain races like a runaway adding-machine. It doesn't take him long to arrive at the unpleasant result that there is a considerable shrinkage loss in his section. It flashes through his mind that he could kill both these iron headed bastards, put them through his new mincing-machine, and feed them to the hungry troops in small portions as sausage meat. It would be the perfect murder. The bodies would never be found. Brumme quite livens up at the thought and throws a sidelong glance at the great meat chopper lying not three yards from him.

Tiny follows his eyes and, with an understanding smile, takes possession of the chopper.

Brumme's nervousness visibly increases.

'Who *are* you gentlemen, actually? And where are you from?' he asks with painful interest and wipes the sweat from his forehead with a piece of meat.

'Obergefreiter Joseph Porta, Berlin-Moabitt,' Porta presents himself with excessive politeness. 'And my assistant, Obergefreiter Wolfgang Creutzfeldt, Königin Allee, Hamburg.'

'He's dropped the mask, the wicked swine,' thinks Brumme, feeling for the club fastened under the table. 'Königin Alleé! *Geheime Feldpolizei!** Berlin-Moabitt: The Quartermaster General's auditing service. A nasty pair of lice to have on your back.' He regrets bitterly that he did not follow his original thought this morning and go sick, together with a bottle of cognac. Then Stalle would have had command. And if any ape in uniform deserved to end in Germersheim it was Feldwebel Stalle.

'Herr Stabsfeldwebel, how many other ranks have you on strength as cutters?' enquires Porta coldly.

'Forty NCOs and men,' barks Brumme eager to be of service.

'Are they fully trained?' asks Porta, slitting his eyes.

'Best crew in the service,' assures Brumme eagerly. 'Every one of my men has been on the QM slaughtering and butchery course at Stettin. They work like well-oiled robots.'

'Here we have the typical bad example,' shouts Porta with satisfaction. 'A gang of Moses Dragoons† who work like robots. These Goddam imitation soldiers chop and hack away at good meat wherever it's easiest. The Holy Mother of Kazan would cross herself at the quality of the works carried out by these know-nothing gut-scrapers. *Robots*, in the Devil's name! That kind should be punished.'

'Squashed, like a frog under a tank,' comes in a friendly voice from Tiny in the background. 'Kicked up the arse, too!'

'These tie-wearing bastards have joined the Supply Services merely to hide away from the front line,' shouts Porta

---

* *Geheime Feldpolizei*: The Field Security Police.

† Moses Dragoons: Supplies Service soldiers who had been to the Army School at München, where most of the students were Jews.

indignantly, as he points a cutting knife accusingly at Brumme. 'Here there are no bullets. The greatest risk is getting smothered under a carcase. But they're *wrong* these funny little blubber dicers. There is more to it in the Army than these clowns realize. Cutting up meat is not *funny*! They need brains under their lousy wigs! Any imbecile from a madhouse can cut and chop away with bones and sinews flying about his ears, but to cut properly so that fine hams and cutlets can come out of a lousy, streaky sow. *That's* the art! Sausage isn't *just* sausage even when it *is*! Herr Stabsfeldwebel! When you mix black pudding do you stir it to the right or to the left?'

'Stir?' groans Brumme, his whole body a living expression of complete confusion.

'No German idiot with the weakest glimmerings of intelligence would stir to the left. Only the English could bring themselves to do *that*,' shouts Porta convincingly. 'It reduces the rotational speed and the blood will clot. These robots of yours, Herr Stabsfeldwebel, you have the responsibility for them. You are in charge of the work. Am I right or am I wrong?'

'Right,' mumbles Brumme weakly, his brain almost boiling with the effort of trying to follow what this mysterious Obergefreiter is leading up to with all his strange hints.

'I have no doubt that the work you were studying when we entered was *Mein Kampf*,' Porta states in a voice not to be gainsaid.

'Naturally,' lies Brumme self-consciously, pushing that interesting work "The Woman Taxi-driver" under a piece of suet. The author's name was Levi! Reading books like that could put you in front of a Racial Purity Commission and those boys there could turn a full-blooded Eskimo with blubber oozing out of his ears into a hook-nosed Israelite dehydrating of thirst in the Sinai Desert in the twinkling of an eye. Any German with the slightest trace of grey matter kept well away from the Racial Purity Commission.

'Let us see some of your men at work,' says Porta

obligingly, and sets a course towards the butchering unit. 'I shall prove to you, Herr Stabsfeldwebel, that intelligence is required to lead such a unit. How many drivelling idiots do you find who decide to change their trade and buy a butcher's shop. Think, if a cobbler, who had never sold anything but leather boots, suddenly began to perform behind the counter of a butcher's shop! *Some* hams the fool would cut for us! He might even supply to your own favourite establishment where you and other *eisbein** enthusiasts meet every Thursday. You'd look funny when you found your *eisbein* to be the snout of a Polish wild pig, thanks to your cobbler/butcher. But you are perhaps a good-hearted person who prefers to think the best of his fellow-men, so you try just a little of this strange caricature of *eisbein* lying on your plate. If you are not a very well-disciplined Prussian gentlemen you will then throw the whole mess in the face of the waiter and empty the French mustard over the fat North German hausfrau sitting nearby who has been lucky enough to get *proper eisbein*. Imagine the trouble that can come of such a former cobbler's change of profession. If the restaurant is one where true German culture predominates then the menu will consist of nothing but *eisbein mit sauerkraut* every Thursday evening, and you will not be the only disappointed guest. One of the most dangerous things on this earth is a disappointed *eisbein-fan*.

'What *is* this?' roars Porta with simulated rage, bringing his fist down on a piece of meat with a bang which makes Brumme's butchers jump.

'A hindquarter,' answers Brumme dejectedly. It was a cut which had been set aside for the Oberstabsintendant who always shut his eyes during the army check.

'*Now!* I've heard everything!' screams Porta in outrage. 'I'm sickened! Any tradesman can see that this is a *ruined* hindquarter! Herr Stabsfeldwebel, I shall soon be forced to state my straightforward opinion of the unmilitary conditions obtaining here. If the Führer demands a juicy roast,

* *Eisbein*: Salted and boiled shank of pork. (Also pig's trotters.)

136

you'll be in trouble if you let one of your Moses Dragoons cut it for him. An insult to Germany's leader – who has no liking for Jews.'

'There are no Jews in my section,' Brumme defends himself sullenly, making a great attempt to hide his rage behind an impeccable military front.

'You cannot be certain of that,' answers Porta coldly. 'But now, say one of your pork satellites cuts a Führer roast and does not know that Adolf hates shreds and sinews.'

'I thought the Führer was a vegetarian,' protests Brumme wonderingly.

'Every streak pig has the right to believe whatever he wishes in our National Socialist society,' instructs Porta with a lifted finger. 'He must merely always believe in the Führer. But you would perhaps wish to forbid the Commander-in-Chief the right to a roast without sinews?'

'No, God forbid?' shouts Brumme frightenedly. 'If the Führer were to order a roast I would cut it myself,' he declares proudly and grips the cutting-knife resolutely. 'I would cut it like so!'

The knife flashes and gleams and amazingly quickly a roast of dreams lies on the table.

Porta smiles contemptuously, takes a small magnifying glass from his pocket, presses the bloody meat testingly, and turns to Tiny with raised brows.

'What do you think of this piece of rat-bait?'

'Unfit for 'uman consumption,' lies Tiny shamelessly, with his mouth running saliva at the corners. 'Nothin' but bloody sinews! If I didn't know better I'd think it was the arsehole of a dried-up Jew suicide.'

'You hear, Herr Stabsfeldwebel?' smiles Porta. 'Before the war Creutzfeldt was leader of a special unit on the Reeperbahn. His district stretched to the far side of Königstrasse in Altona.'

'IV 2a, Gestapo Special Section,' thinks Brumme who had once owned a cosy little restaurant in Heyn Höyer Strasse. Two visits from IV 2a had cost him seven months. Now he must be careful. 'Dear God, let Germany lose this war too,' he prays silently.

'I will not maintain that it is a bad roast you have cut,' continues Porta, 'but is not a roast for the connoisseur! You are not in possession of the necessary scientific knowledge of anatomy. The Inspector General of Army Schools of Catering should give tradesmen such as army butchers, cooks, and bakers a better training. Even in our National Socialistic welfare state, there are many who need a swift and powerful kick in the slats. Welfare creates laziness and indifference. Everyone is looking for a comfortable chair in which he can plant his well-upholstered arse and wait for pension time to arrive. Herr Stabsfeldwebel, all this welfare is quite unnatural. It is best for man to have to chase after his food in the sweat of his brow. Then he is good and obedient and says thank you nicely when something is given to him.

'But what happens now, when everybody has an abundance of everything? They all want more and even envy their wives the little something they sometimes get from a generous outsider. A society like that breeds informers, provocateurs, and is the sure way to ruin! Socialism they call it! A paradise for pampered pets, is what I call it! Pah!'

Brumme refuses to believe his own ears. This is the sharpest criticism of the National Socialist regime he has heard to date. He is completely in agreement with Porta but isn't going to admit it. Porta sharpens the long butcher's knife with practiced strokes and pulls a whole side of beef over to him.

'A roast *cannot* be cut as you and your slaves do it. Have you never heard of sinews and muscles or the treacherous small bones?'

Brumme shakes his head and gives up trying to follow him.

'Think of the underskin,' shouts Porta, pleasurably. 'It is Nature's own secret building system used for everything which lives, whether on two legs or four, from a Sankt Pauli

138

whore to a striped East Galician sow. You would be completely on your arse, kicking, my dear Herr Stabsfeldwebel, if you were not provided with an inner skin. This is something every butcher must know, since without this knowledge he cannot excise a roast. It is a special gimmick which holds the whole affair together. Here a fine incision is required. I imagine you can follow me, Herr Stabsfeldwebel,' shouts Porta superciliously. 'A long lovely incision to the vena peniscellum. That has nothing to do with the penis. Do you know what the penis is, Herr Stabsfeldwebel?' he asks with a wide smile. Brumme, who by now resembles an overheated boiler which needs a valve opened to release surplus steam, is unable to answer.

'The penis,' continues Porta, 'is that comically limp piece of gristle which depends, swinging, between the legs of men, and is called, by uncultured persons, the prick. See now, we continue the cutting so, and we have a roast which could be put on show at any art exhibition, and, slapped on to a piece of canvas, would pull in a safe first prize in the shape of a gold medal. It's exactly the same as when they twist a rusty cycle-frame out of shape and weld a kettle where the handlebars usually are and then a part from a WC in place of the saddle. It is quite simply, Great Art! The wild dream of a DT patient which nobody understands *shit* about. Nevertheless any provincial Civic Council will, with pleasure, use the tax-payers' hard-earned money to obtain the wonder for exhibition in their home town culture park. Do you remember, Herr Stabsfeldwebel, that beautiful play which was acted at the Bergtheater with Emil Jannings in the role of the Great Elector. I am thinking of the third act where this national scoundrel is sitting with half a deer between his teeth and the juices from it running down over his jabot. Now this is not merely a play, Herr Stabsfeldwebel, but something which really happened, when the Great Elector lay encamped near the wine slopes of the mountains north of Salzburg, looking hungrily towards the castle. The cook, who had prepared the venison, was a master of masters, originally a butcher from

Berlin-Moabitt. He was promoted to Oberst with the right to wear a sword of honour decorated in the national colours.'

'Heavens,' says Brumme in confusion, 'can that really happen to a cook?'

'Very seldom,' answers Porta. 'As far as I know it has happened only twice in the history of the world. But here we have a really excellent roast,' he cries enthusiastically, patting the large piece of meat affectionately.

'It's a *real* roast,' praises Brumme in surprise. 'It really belongs on the table of the Commanding General but, since he knows nothing of its existence, I feel we should eat it ourselves and make a night of it.'

'I am not such a villain as to protest,' smiles Porta. 'Hunger has always been my greatest problem. Even when I have eaten my way through the pleasures of a well-laid table and convinced myself that I am satisfied, suddenly my eye will fall on a greedy pig packing himself with stuffed pigeon. Immediately my insatiable stomach begins to grown and the saliva floods between my teeth. At such a moment I am capable of committing murder to get my teeth into my neighbour's pigeon. Usually I can get a couple of bones quickly enough for my stomach to be fooled for a few minutes! After a belch or two I start off all over again.

'Sometimes I've said to myself: "Now you really can't get another morsel down you, Herr Porta!" But the smell of a well-prepared hare from the other side of the street is enough to set me going as if I'd been seasick fourteen days in a row with the lining of my stomach turned inside out. If I can't get it any other way then I'll degrade myself, the Holy Virgin aid me, to stealing the odorous hare out of the hands of a hungry scoundrel of an officer. This unbearable hunger has been my lot since birth. At home we had a padlock on the larder door. My brothers and sisters and I were known as "the Locusts". We were known all over Berlin, Herr Stabsfeldwebel. You may not believe me, but I could eat cartridge cases and wash them down with warm Polish water. For *me* food does not need to be of the best quality, such as German Army waste. If nothing

140

better is available I can make do with the French or Russian Army's muck. Ordinary home-cooking such as: sauerkraut, rice balls, butter-fried leeks, pease pudding and curried chicken can turn me into a hungry tiger. I dare not tell you what happens inside me when my eyes fall on mashed potatoes with those small cubes of pork, or a mixed fish pudding with various sauces. Herr Stabsfeldwebel, I must ask you to provide me with a double helping, when we sit down to table to celebrate this unexpected meeting. I think we understand one another!'

Brumme laughs long and noisily, without really knowing why but feeling it to be best.

'I've also got some bottles of '36 wine,' he fawns when he feels he has laughed long enough.

'My recruit year!' shouts Porta in a barrack square voice. 'The wine *belongs* to us!'

Stabsfeldwebel Brumme snatches the gigantic roast, presses it to his bosom, and rushes to the kitchen to prepare a banquet for himself and the secret commission.

As the meal progresses, the atmosphere becomes more and more friendly. After two hours they have only got to the meat course. They eat like Vikings of old with both fists firmly gripping great chunks of meat. The gnawed bones fly in graceful curves over their shoulders.

Porta eats and drinks as if he aims to split his liver apart in record time. Four times Tiny has to lie across the table while the other two thump him on the back to loosen a couple of pounds of meat stuck in his throat. But when Brumme also begins to choke and only misses death from suffocation by a hairsbreadth, they send for the medical orderly, to stand by in case of a repetition. He is given a normal ration to amuse himself with.

'The coolies have to eat,' explains Brumme largely, 'but who the hell says they have to be satisfied? We NCOs must keep the slaves down or we're finished. This stuff about "workers of the world unite" isn't my kind of thing. The only place they ought to be united is in a mass grave!'

'Little Sir Echo!' cries Porta as a resounding fart escapes from him between two great gulps of tender meat.

'These 'ere cultivated types as spell cunt with four bleedin' dots ain't for me neither,' says Tiny with his mouth full of juicy roast.

'No, by Jesus, you're right!' shouts Brumme with a scowl. 'Just like my boss, Oberintendant Blankenschild, who thinks Stabsfeldwebels are for wiping his arse on. If you could peel his skin off over his ears upwards you'd earn a place of honour at the NCO's table in Valhalla with the right to fill your boots up with German beer!'

'Tearing the arse off a Mongolian ape like him would be an easy matter for us,' boasts Porta throwing a cleanly gnawed thigh-bone over into the corner where the medical orderly is sitting.

'We'll rip 'is bleedin' belly up an' tie 'is guts round 'is ears, so 'e can only shit backwards,' Tiny whoops with laughter, and takes a long swig at a bottle. Half of it runs down over his chest.

'My boss is a fucked-up whoreson bastard who lives on regulations and shits out orders and paperwork like a dysentry patient on his death-bed,' snuffles Brumme raging. 'A nigger must've pissed in his grandmother's porridge.'

'Skoal!' shouts Porta and swings the big quart-pot over his head, before emptying it in one long slobbering draught.

They drink their own health collectively three times. They drink one another's individually, and demonstrate a raw heartiness not by any means to be confused with what is called friendship.

'I'll explain the position to you, comrade,' says Brumme confidentially, and helps a great lump of meat on its way down with a bottle of wine. 'That pig of a suet soldier is a treacherous jackal, a stinking red-arsed baboon, a dirty, depraved south sea cannibal, who ought've been eaten by his tribal enemies long ago. Now he puffs himself up in an Oberintendant uniform, the dirty bastard.' He snatches up a

piece of meat and forces it into his mouth. 'Bring the *tatar*!'*
he shouts through the open door to his men, who are all on
the alert. Most of them have been waiters in civilian life. One
of them has, in fact, been headwaiter at 'Kaminski'.† He is
Brumme's personal cupbearer. An insurance against the front
line and a hero's death. 'That stinking Arab,' Brumme
continues his report on the Oberintendant, 'is so greasy and
insinuating that his black conscience oozes right through his
skin. There's no doubt whatsoever. That cunt-eater is ready-
made material for a court-martial.'

'We'll look after him,' promises Porta readily, laying a
piece of ham on top of the *tatar*. 'Where in the name of hell
will the Fatherland be if that kind of meat-basher is allowed
to sit there quietly sabotaging the war effort?' He puts a bottle
to his lips and empties the whole contents down his throat
without any visible appearance of swallowing. He swills his
mouth out thoroughly with the last drops, ready for the fifth
course.

'Don't you run into a lot of unpleasant things when
you're making these inspections?' asks Brumme, digging Tiny
with brutal friendliness between the ribs.

'No, we know what we're doin'. We flatten 'em before
they open their yaps, but we've got 'eavy weapons back of us,
and know all the dirty tricks that's ever existed,' says Tiny
gently. 'And nobody's stupider than 'e was born!' He gets on
his feet and sings in a piercing voice:

> *A false friend flattered and lied,*
> *And angry and bitter I cried.*
> *I lost my heart and my mind;*
> *A Stabsfeldwebel swung in the wind.*

'Are there often inspections, here?' asks Porta interestedly.
'I'd heard it has been a long time since the last one?'

'Oh, it's not so long ago,' answers Brumme, sourly. 'The

---

* *Tatar*: scraped beef.
† Kaminski: Berlin luxury restaurant.

blasted Nosey Parker's have got their snouts in all over the place. We need a revolution! Sorry . . .' he adds politely, as he realizes that his innermost thoughts have run away with him.

'Quite all right,' smiles Porta in friendly fashion. 'Tell me, have you never been *taken*? I mean have you never been visited by a couple of con-men playing at being Control Commission auditors?'

There is a moment of threatening silence in the room, and then Brumme emits a long and violent roar. His face goes an unnatural shade of blue and his eyes pop halfway out of his head. Ten or a dozen blood clots must be on the way to ending his military career. Ten minutes or more are needed for him to come back to normal.

'God's death! If anybody had the nerve to try *that* on Stabsfeldwebel Brumme!' he gasps. 'I'd send the bastards to feed the heroes in single rations of mince meat.' He hammers his knife into a piece of meat lying on the table and hacks away at it madly. 'I'd cut their God-damned arseholes out! Like this! And this!'

'I'd recommend you be on your toes, nevertheless,' says Porta in his friendly manner. 'You've no idea how many of these swindlers there are about trying to con Supplies NCOs and civil servants. We've run across quite a few of them!'

'It won't happen to *me*,' Brumme assures him. 'I can smell that kind of gaol-bait, before they even start their spiel. That kind of thing should carry the death penalty. Mother-fuckers they are! Dying's too good for 'em!'

'Dead men are always good men,' intones Tiny unctuously.

After four and a half hours of unbroken eating they arrive at the dessert. A freshly-made apple charlotte. Porta takes half of it immediately, pours in half a bottle of cognac and stirs it to a thick soup which he drinks noisily.

'Enjoy life while you've still got it,' he grins. 'Both the Nazis and the Communists are trying hard to take it away from you!'

'If I'd known it was that dangerous, I'd never 'ave let meself get bleedin' born,' sighs Tiny sadly, throwing half a black pudding into his apple charlotte. He says it tastes wonderful.

The former head waiter from 'Kaminski' serves champagne. A bottle apiece. Less than a bottle a man is unthinkable at a German stag-party. Brumme has put on a deferentially doltish expression and addresses his guests as 'Old Goat,' and 'Noble Cow.'

'We should be friends for the rest of our lives,' decides Tiny waving his arms wildly to emphasize his honest intentions, 'and we will never wear brown shoes, to avoid being suspected of certain sympathies.'

They embrace and kiss one another on the cheeks in the Russian manner. They are, after all, in Russia.

'When you get to Hamburg, I'll introduce you to "Gerda the Gun",' promises Tiny. 'The thing she's got tucked away in 'er pants 'd make a bleedin' gorilla shed 'is 'air an' 'ide 'is prick in a bleedin' cactus.'

'My coolies fear me more than they fear death,' Brumme's beery bass rings to the farthest ends of the great slaughterhouse and echoes back again. He throws a meat-bone at the Sanitätsgefreiter.

'Hop like a kangaroo! Hop till you shit yourself!' he orders. Proudly he points to the medical orderly who begins to carry out the command immediately. What won't a man do to avoid the front. 'That's what they call discipline!' He bends confidentially over Tiny. 'I know just exactly how to kill an enemy so that he'll stay alive a long time and die badly!'

'So do we!' admits Tiny with a satanic laugh.

'In my unit there is good German order and discipline,' roars Brumme harshly and shows his clumsy dentures. Beery breath streams out like a banner from his open mouth. The medical orderly and the former headwaiter look as if they are ready to faint.

'Order is a good and wise thing,' smiles Porta, beginning again on the first course. 'So that here it is not necessary to

145

fear auditors who arrive without warning and stick their old tomatoes into your accounts and stocks. But you look to be an honest man, comrade Brumme!'

An oppressive silence sinks over the room. They watch one another like old experienced tom-cats preparing to go into battle.

'No idiot, with even a minimum of cunning, blows the war horn straight away,' says Porta mysteriously. 'Intelligent people like us prefer to employ the tactics of diplomacy. Why in the world should we take the broad road of idiocy when we can use the narrow path reserved for people with grey matter under their wigs.'

Brumme whinnies delightedly and long, even though he has not understood a word.

'I'll give you a nice parcel to take with you when you leave,' he promises willingly. 'I knew right away you were real Ironheads,' he adds grinning noisily. 'I *did* wonder once if you were a pair of sly wolves, out on a little con,' he grins with false heartiness and stares cunningly into Porta's sly blue eyes.

'Dear friend,' smiles Porta resignedly. 'Who hasn't been doubted since January 1933? Either you're a dangerous PU* or an even more dangerous patriot. We live in dangerous times. Duplicity is king. Those you least expect it of are scoundrels. As I told you earlier, Brumme, don't invite just anybody to sit at your table!'

'Did you volunteer for the armed forces!' asks Brumme confidentially, taking a large bite of meat.

'Volunteer, that's putting it strongly,' considers Porta, 'but on the other hand I have nothing against membership of the weapons club until things get better in Civvy Street. The uniform is good protection at present.'

After coffee and cognac they go out to inspect a new sausage machine.

'What do you think?' shouts Brumme proudly, as the

---

* PU (Politisch unzurverlässig): Politically unreliable.

machine, working at full pressure, spews sausages out in long strings.

'It's like a cow shitting in a warm shed,' says Porta without attempting to conceal his astonishment.

'My Stabsintendant is a holy pig,' confides Brumme, when they are sitting at the table again, confronting fresh-made sausage swimming in red wine.

'It's dangerous! Dangerous as 'ell!' roars Tiny, trying to drown himself out. 'In my experience keep away from the 'oly religious leaders 'ere in the Army. Bastards as believe in the life after bleedin' death don't give a shit for the few lousy years we 'ave 'ere on earth, an' take all sorts of bleedin' risks. They're sniffin' at an 'ero's death an' a place up there with Abra'am. A bleedin' 'eathen as only thinks about number one is better. 'E looks after the one life 'e's got an' 'olds back when things get tough. 'E won't let 'is slaves dirty their weapons usin' 'em on the neighbours' bleedin' coolies. Then there ain't no talk of all this revenge shit. Units what've got that kind of godless leaders almost always get back intact, whatever they've been through. Look at all the fallen padres we 'ave. They mumble a prayer and wander straight into the enemy lead an' they're up there with Abra'am before they know where they are.'

The feast of the unholy trinity really steps up the decibels a little after midnight.

Wir halten fest und treu zusammen
Hipp-hipp-hurra! Hipp-hipp-hurra!
Wir halten fest und treu zusammen
Hipp-hipp-hurra! Hipp-hipp-hurra!*

they sing, so loudly that they can be heard in the most distant huts.

At two o'clock in the morning they start mixing vodka in their beer and the female personnel are invited to join the

* *Wir halten fest und*, etc.: German song approximating to 'The more we are together, etc.'

party. They start immediately with strip poker. They're in a hurry. In the early hours of the morning a highly treasonable speech is made, which would have turned a court-martial white as a sheet. The Führer and his personal guard are discussed intimately in the role of corpses.

Tiny suggests that they should start by throwing red-hot cartridge cases into the mouth of the largest of them and watching the interesting grimaces as the cases cooled on his tongue. Later they could try some of the refinements the Christians had used to convince the heathen during the religious wars.

'By hell!' enthuses Brumme. 'I can't wait for it! Did y'ever see how the cardinals tortured the holy Emmanuel? There's a picture of it in the cathedral at Leipzig. They're jabbing him both here and there with red-hot sabres. The Popes can teach us a lot.'

It is late the next day when life comes back to them. they are, all three, lying in Brumme's antique bed, an heirloom from Bulgaria.

'God's death, Jesus Christ!' moans Brumme, grabbing at his hammering head with both hands. He groans. A long trembling cry of anguish.

'Oh the Devil!' cries Porta with unconcealed nausea and snatches a bottle from the floor. He drinks long and noisily.

Tiny falls off the bed with a thud, creeps like a wounded boar to the water bucket and pushes his whole head under the water. He drinks like a camel which has been wandering a month in the desert without water. His belly swells visibly. He doesn't stop until the bucket is empty.

Porta sits up in bed with bloodshot eyes and wonders if he is dead.

'I am quite against the sky pilots who preach about the holy communion of friends,' he explains to Brumme, who is lying over the foot of the bed making weird sounds. 'People like that are trying something underhanded,' he concludes, and throws up under the pillow.

'They oughta be shot!' echoes Tiny from the empty water bucket.

'Fire!' moans Brumme, wrenching his revolver from its holster and sending three shots into the ceiling. The signal for the headwaiter from 'Kaminski' to serve coffee. In bed, of course.

A couple of hours later moving farewells are being made. They are friends for life. Porta and Tiny go back to the regiment with bulging sacks of supplies across their shoulders.

Brumme stands at the door and watches them disappear into the drifting snow. He is not quite certain whether or not he has been conned by a couple of swindlers or has been lucky to get out of the clutches of a couple of tough Ironheads.

'If they've swindled me, by God I'll *shoot* the bastards!' he shouts, raging to himself, and his face goes quite a pretty shade of blue at the thought. But he decides to reply in comradely manner as Porta turns at the gate for the last time and waves a salute.

> 'We demand the death penalty for those who oppose our fight for the fellowship of the people. We demand the death penalty, likewise, for criminal traitors, usurers, defrauders and national parasites, without regard to belief or to race.'
>
> Taken from the National Socialist Party Programme.

Major Mikhal Gosztonow, partisan leader of the district of Minsk was a heavy-set brute of a man, hated by his subordinates. A man who had in his time waded through seas of corpses. His small furtive eyes examined the men around him in the little *izba*,* which stank of damp clothing and unwashed bodies. 'Tomorrow night we attack the village,' he said in a voice which brooked no refusal. He pointed with his machine-gun at an old man in a worn ragged coat, his feet bound in old cloths like thousands of other Russian peasants. 'Rasin, you'll see to it that your village is set fire to just after midnight. When everything is ablaze, and the Nazis are running around like blinded rats, we attack and liquidate the green swine.'

The old man, marked by a life of poverty and toil, wrung his hands in despair.

'*Tovaritsch gospodin*, what about our children, the old people and the sick? It's cold, and the winter gets crueller every day, *gospodin*, I don't remember a harder winter than this year!'

'Stop crying, *moujik*,[†] this is war,' roared the partisan major. 'We must all make sacrifices. Your life means nothing when you're fighting for the Soviet Fatherland. The Devil help you, old man, if your damned village isn't in flames shortly after midnight!' He drew his Nagan and smashed it brutally across the old man's face. Two teeth snapped and blood poured from his

---

* *Izba* (Russian): Peasant hut.
† *Moujik* (Russian): Peasant.

nose. 'You are *Staross*,* so don't forget your first duty is to our father Josef Stalin, who gives you bread and work! The Fatherland requires your services. You don't seem to realize this. Burn your pigsty of a village as I have ordered. And now: Get out!'

'They need a taste of the whip now and then,' grinned the major to the partisan leaders when the *Staross* had left the little room.

'Those swine let the Fascists sleep in their beds, sit with them at table, fill themselves with enemy food instead of dying honourably of hunger!'

He pushed a large piece of ham into his mouth and swallowed it like a stork swallowing a frog.

A bottle of French cognac was passed round. Left over from a raid on a German supply column.

'The knout is what's needed to keep these peasants down,' he continued in a hoarse voice. 'They help us, but only because they are more afraid of us than they are of the invaders. For us there is only victory or death. Don't forget this, any of you partisans who might just be thinking of going over,' he added threateningly. 'Any partisan the Germans get hold of gets tortured before they hang him. We can expect no help from anyone. Our war never stops, day or night. Our lives are worth nothing. We have nothing but our duty to the Fatherland and to Comrade Stalin to live for.'

7 | Before Moscow

In the icy cold of a jet-black night we creep from our foxholes and march forward to new positions over against the forest. Half unconscious we weave in disorderly column. We are wadded out with newspaper, the QMG-Clothing's latest idea. According to orders paper is just as warm as fur. A lot of orders are read out to us every day. About victories and heroic deeds. Nobody listens to them any more. The brave men who

* *Staross* (Russian): Mayor.

had the courage to lie down in the snow are dead. The not-so-brave, like us, keep on marching and let ourselves be misused, as has been the custom in all ages with the young.

The man marching beside you drops suddenly into the snow and lies there, his hand gripping his rifle. If you've a little strength still left in you, you bend down and break off his dog-tags so that the folks at home will know he's dead and won't spend years searching for him. Many die like this.

Fog comes creeping up from the river, and in our half-awake condition we see dream-figures coiling in it. Porta sees a giant table covered with the most wonderful kinds of food. He tells us that he sees whole battalions of Supplies soldiers piling tons of mashed potatoes and mountains of tiny cubes of pork on it.

'Jesus 'n Mary!' groans Tiny, snatching at a great chunk of *eisbein* which seems to swim past him dripping with fat. All his hand touches is Heide's icy, frost-covered pack.

'Wizened-up Chinese cunt!' he curses in disappointment, but a little later he tries again. Now it's a huge lump of roast pork, covered with apple sauce, which is sailing by in the fog. He stands quite still for a moment staring in astonishment at his empty fist. He can't believe it wasn't real. The hallucination is so realistic the smell of roast pork still seems to hang in the air.

Heide has just pushed a piece of frozen bread into his mouth and is chewing energetically on it.

'You've stole my bleedin' pork!' rages Tiny in disappointment, and grabs him by the neck.

'Get the hell away from me,' snarls Heide savagely. 'Don't give me the chance to get you for insubordination! I'd get pleasure out of it! Understand, you Jew psycho bastard?'

'Get fucked, brown-nose!' says Tiny unimpressed, pushing in between Porta and me.

When Heide's trigger finger starts to itch it's wise to keep your distance. He suffers from the kind of madness which, sooner or later, attacks every political fanatic.

'Black as the inside of a nigger's arsehole,' confirms Tiny a little later. 'Man can't even scratch 'is piles. Bleedin' arse is that froze-up your finger'd break off!'

'*Caramba*, do you see those domes shaped like onions?' shouts Barcelona Blom in amazement.

'We're *there*! We'll be thawing out tonight by the Kremlin stoves,' says Stege relievedly.

'An' fillin' our guts with *Kaslak* an' vodka,' cheers Tiny, beaming all over his frost-seamed face.

'Damned if it *isn't* Moscow,' mumbles the Old Man fascinated. He puffs hard at his silver-lidded pipe. 'Can you hear the bells? But why the bonfires in the streets?'

It isn't the bells of the Kremlin the Old Man can hear, nor is it bonfires in Moscow's streets he can see. It's the fiery fountains of shell-bursts, which sweep the whole terrain in a violent barrage. The fog dances and is split into long waving veils by the violence of the explosions.

The company advances towards the edge of the forest, at the double in a confused hobbling mob, with shrapnel flying about their ears. These shrapnel splinters smash joints as if they were glass. Shrapnel is the Devil's work. The splinters leave terribly large wounds which in this weather bring almost certain death.

'Forward!' shouts Oberleutnant Moser hoarsely. He stops a moment and leans tiredly on his machine-gun.

'He's sick,' says the Old Man quietly. 'The medical orderly told me he's pissing blood. His kidneys are shot. But he's not sick enough for hospitalization. You have to get your head shot off now to get into a bed!'

'Forward!' repeats Moser, the sweat pouring down over his ghastly face. Tiredly he lifts his arm and points out the attack objective.

'No. 5 Company. Forward!'

Knots of men storm forward. Every step is agony. Our boots are frozen hard as iron. The German military boot was not designed for a Russian winter.

Porta, of course, has long since exchanged his German infantry-boots for a pair of butter-soft yellow Lapp boots. He has liberated almost everything the heart could desire in the way of Russian equipment. Nobody can understand just how, but one way or another he always gets hold of the things he needs. The other day we went past Djil – it was just after we'd taken the railway line and were advancing on down towards the *kolchos*,* Porta stops suddenly. 'Hang on!' he says. 'It's my guess there's something worth snitching over in that barn.' He disappears quickly between the low buildings and reappears soon after with a sheep over his shoulder and a jar of vodka in his hand.

And now we are sitting in our hole in the snow filling up in readiness for the seven lean years.

'When you can turn up something like this, and a little sup now and then,' explains Porta with his mouth full of mutton, 'you can always get by in a World War. *Al*though I wouldn't complain if the knocking-off whistle went in an hour's time! You'd see a cloud of snow moving westwards at a very rapid rate! And in the middle of it would be Obergefreiter, by the grace of God, Joseph Porta. I'd like to see the lousy NKVD gang that'd be able to catch *me* when the Berlin magnet'd begun to tug away at me little old cock!'

But now we're hungry again. For us, the Army, will always be the place where we were hungry and short of sleep.

They say we're to cross the river. Then we go into quarters.

That's what we want. Two nights more of this murderous cold and it'll be all over with us. Warmth, above all warmth. It's the most important thing in life.

Great numbers of dead horses lie alongside the road. Their legs stick straight up in the air in an unreal manner. A whole cavalry regiment has been killed with one shot. Surprised by the Stalin Organ. An Organ strike bursts your lungs. You die so fast you don't even have time to go blue in the face. Nevertheless we still prefer the Organ to the *rasboms*.† You can hear the Organ's rockets and have a chance to run, but

---

* *Kolchos*: Collective.
† *Rasbom*: Blast bomb (compressed air).

the *rasbom*'s there before you know it. You hear the detonation at the same time the sound of the discharge reaches you. Now they've starting fusing them for air burst. Heide affirms that this type of bomb or shell is forbidden by international agreement. But then so is the flamethrower, not to mention the explosive bullet that tears half your head off.

Heide has a little book bound in red in which the provisions of the Versailles Treaty with regard to forbidden weapons are printed, and every time we come across something forbidden he writes down the date, the time and the witnesses names in a black book.

He says that at the right time, he will place his book at the disposal of the international commission which will try war criminals.

'You were born to shit against the wind!' jeers Porta. 'Do you think anybody'll bother listening to a Nazi unteroffizier who's lived on an exclusive diet of swastikas all his life and painted his prick brown to make sure he'll only make Nazi kids when he fucks!'

The forest is ringing with frost. Ice crystals whirr through the air and the snow lies thickly everywhere.

'What a country to make war in,' says Barcelona, depressed. 'Even a skiing fantatic'd be cured of his liking for winter sports for the rest of his life.'

We keep falling into deep snowdrifts from which we need help to extricate ourselves. The Professor is nearly going crazy. Without his glasses he is almost blind and now the snow continually covers them. He blunders around until finally we tie him to Barcelona. We've got fond of this little idiot of a Norwegian student. At first we took the piss out of him. Not so much because he volunteered, we nearly all did that, but because he came to us from the SS. We never really discovered why. There are rumours that he's a quarter-Jew. That's one good reason, at any rate, for the SS throwing him out. We have three quarter-Jews with us. Porta says he's a half-Jew but that's only to annoy Heide. He says they always sat at table with their hats on in his family and held an economy council every Friday, before the Sabbath began.

We keep stopping all the time. The enemy barrage is terrible. It looks as if the Russians are throwing in everything but the lavatory seat to keep us from getting across the river.

Shells falling in snow sound funny. A queer sort of splashy thump sounds from far away. Then a column of snow shoots up into the air. They've executed three from our division. It was read out to us this morning. They always do that when somebody's due to be hanged. These execution notices made an impression on us at first, but now we're used to them.

'Executions are necessary in wartime,' explains Porta, as we stand in front of the gallows with its three swinging corpses. 'They are what educated people call pedagogic. They make carbine coolies like us lose interest in getting up to funny business. The track of a good army is marked by its gallows.'

'Speed, speed!' orders Oberleutnant Moser.

'Faster, faster,' scream the section leaders furiously, raising their clenched fists above their heads in the signal for: 'Forward! Quick march!' The artillery fire is to be 'ducked under' as the Army calls the manoeuvre. It *sounds* easy. Marshal your forces close to where the shells are dropping, and execute a quick forward movement *under* the barrage. There is a lot of stuff like this in military manuals. The fat HDV is the German Army's bible. There are even people who run their private lives according to HDV. Iron Gustav at Torgau, for example, has brought his wife almost to the verge of madness. Like a good housewife she prefers to change the bed-linen every fourteen days. Iron Gustav won't permit it. According to HDV, prison personnel change every six weeks, and prisoners every eight weeks. In Iron Gustav's home they take a bath every Saturday between 10 and 12 o'clock. The water is 18° C., neither more nor less, and bathing is carried out, of course, under the shower and lasts for exactly seven minutes. After twenty years of married life the good woman is *still* unable to understand why they mustn't use their bath-tub, and this despite the fact that her husband has explained to her countless times that bath-tubs are for officers only. Over Iron Gustav's front door, in beautiful gothic letters, is the inscription *ICH DIENE*.* And this is the motto the family has to follow. Soldiers spring up from the snow and start off on the race with death. We pant under the heavy weight of weapons. Suddenly the road grows steep.

We use bushes and saplings to pull ourselves up the slope. An infantry Gefreiter just in front of me gets his. He stops as if he has run into a wall. His carbine flies up into the air, he falls backwards and rolls down the hill, over and over and over in a cloud of snow. His body is stopped by a bush, his steel helmet rolls on by itself. His hair is yellow as corn, and shows up against the snow like a newly-opened sunflower.

I stop for a second to look back down at him before following the others.

The MG-fire grows still fiercer. They are firing from above us.

The MG salvoes tear long splinters from the trees. Great pieces of stone and ice come howling transversely in amongst us.

No. 5 Company seek cover in the scrub. With practiced speed machine-guns are mounted to cover No. 7 Company, the spearhead. Below the heights the heavy company places its mortars and soon after we hear the cosy: Plop! Plop! of our own mortar bombs. Enemy mortars sound terrible, but ours have a wonderfully comforting sound.

'Fix bayonets! Prepare to advance singly!' comes the order.

'Hold on to your guts, Ivan Stinkanovich, I'm comin' to carve 'em out of you!' shouts Tiny drawing his short bayonet from its sheath. He is off at an amazing speed under Heide's covering fire.

Muzzle-flashes from the Russian fortifications make a long necklace of light. Heide relieves me at No. 1. I'm a grenade specialist and must now go forward and attempt to blow up the machine-gun nest. It'll have to be fast. I throw five

* *ICH DIENE* (German): I serve.

157

grenades, one straight after the other. They fall where I want them to. One by the heavy MG, which is now on continuous fire. One a little to the right where the command group is lying, and the rest behind, where the ammunition is stacked.

Porta shoots from the hip as he runs. Tiny follows him with the light grey bowler jammed down on his head. He affects to believe that it makes enemy bullets veer away from him in sheer horror.

'Get your finger out!' screams the Old Man furiously. 'Use your grenades! Stop that Maxim!'

'Bugger off!' I answer, and stay down.

The heavy Maxim is firing so that even a fly would get itself killed if it were mad enough to run across the snow.

'Forward, or you're for court-martial!' shouts the Old Man, raging.

The Maxim gets a stoppage and, tight with nervousness, I spring up and run forward.

I throw my grenades on the run. The heavy machine-gun is blown high into the air together with the gunner.

Our legs move under us like racing pistons. The blood-stained bayonets gleam dully on the end of our guns.

We tumble into the enemy entrenchment. Now it's not half so dangerous, as long as you don't run blindly down the straights.

We know to perfection how to roll up a trench with hand grenades. The enemy mustn't be given time to think. The first three minutes in the trench are decisive. I throw a grenade into each dug-out as I pass. Explosions crash behind me. A group is about to leave the trench as I round a corner. My last grenade drops in amongst them and explodes with a vicious crack. There is blood everywhere on the snow. I tear the sub' from my shoulder and empty a magazine into those who are still moving. Then I drop down between a couple of torn-open bodies.

'You did very nicely!' says the Old Man, appreciatively.

' 'E'll 'ave 'is name mentioned on the bleedin' wireless as an 'ero some day,' jeers Tiny with a grin. 'Then they'll find out afterwards 'e's a bleedin' Yid an' 'ang 'im with the Star of David spinnin' merrily on the end of 'is prick!' He throws his MG quickly up over the lip of the trench and opens fire on the fleeing Russians who are rolling in panic down the slope.

'Cease firing!' orders Oberleutnant Moser. 'Five minutes rest!' We drop where we stand. Most of us fall asleep.

Half unconscious I hear Porta explaining something to Stege about a donkey which had to cross the Landwehr canal, an exercise in which the military observers had decided all bridges had been blown.

'Everything would have gone off all right,' I heard Porta say, 'if only the bloody donkey hadn't been *white*! It was immediately suspected of being a spy for international Jewry. . . .'

I fell asleep and unfortunately heard no more. When I asked Porta, later, for the end of the story, he had forgotten it and denied ever having known a Jewish spy in the shape of a white donkey.

'2 Section take the lead. Take up your arms! Get moving! Forward, you sad sacks!' orders Oberleutnant Moser.

Mortar grenades fall around us. We look back and are glad we are spearheading the advance. A wall of fire and steel rises where our trench has been. The heavy Russian artillery is spotted in on it.

'There's the river,' says the Old Man, with relief, pointing with his Mpi.

We can't realize that this dirty brown ditch is the Nara. Even the ice, which is screwed up into hillocks, is a filthy brown.

'So this is the trickle of piss we've been chasing after for the last few weeks,' mumbles Porta wonderingly. 'I can well understand never having heard of it.'

'Rinse, please!' grins Tiny, as he urinates in the river.

'Nara!' mumbles Oberleutnant Moser. 'So we've made it. We're *that* close to Moscow.'

'Can we take the tram in, please, Herr Oberleutnant?' asks Porta. 'I've got *such* pains in my knees.'

We have become noticeably more disillusioned recently. Even though we have gone from victory to victory, passed endless columns of prisoners and seen mountains of captured equipment, Heide is still the only one of us who believes in the ultimate victory.

'I don't give a sod who wins this war,' says Porta. 'When I get back to Berlin they can all fuck a pig far as I'm concerned!'

No. 3 Company begins the river crossing. We give them covering fire with automatic weapons. They are almost half-way over when suddenly it's as if the whole river explodes. Yellow, stinking watery mud flies hundreds of feet into the air. A seemingly endless sheet of flame spreads out to all sides, and great chunks of ice are thrown far into the forest. No. 3 Company is gone without a trace under the gurgling, bubbling water.

The Stalin Organ starts up. It sounds as if every planet in the Solar System is on its way towards earth, and it looks like it. The entire sky is covered with the long fiery tails of great rockets like shooting stars.

Where they strike every living thing is annihilated.

'The bloody swine,' curses Heide indignantly.

'Why?' asks Stege in surprise. 'They're only using what they've got. They won't stop till we're spitted and roasted!'

'These *untermensch* will never live to see that!' shouts Heide fanatically.

'Don't be too sure,' grins Porta. 'I do believe they've given your Führer an unpleasant surprise.'

'He's your Führer too, *isn't he*?' shouts Heide threateningly.

'So *he* says at any rate. These Austrians have always been good at persuading themselves. Their mountains give them a superiority complex.'

'Joseph Porta I intend to make a duty report to the NSFO. Take warning of that!' screams Heide, his eyes flaming.

'Be a good little boy now, and bend you 'ead down so's Daddy can put a bullet through it,' says Tiny pleasantly, pressing his gun against Heide's neck.

160

'You wouldn't dare,' howls Heide, dodging to cover behind the Old Man.

'Bet your sweet life I *would* dare,' answers Tiny, with a perfectly diabolical look on his face. 'You wouldn't believe what I'd dare do now that I've put on the Wehrmacht uniform! Prepare to be shot. I don't like these long drawn out executions.'

'Stop that *piss*!' orders the Old Man, knocking the muzzle of Tiny's Mpi down. 'That's no toy you've been issued with.'

'I *do* 'ave a lot of fun playin' with it though,' says Tiny pleasantly.

'I'll have you shaved with the big razor,' shouts Heide desperately. 'Threatening an Unteroffizier in the German Army is not a cheap amusement, Obergefreiter Creutzfeldt! It's bloody *dear*!'

'No. 2 Section follow me!' commands the Old Man curtly.

Porta stumbles over a body, a dead German major with the Knight's Cross round his neck.

'The heroes are all dying!' mumbles Tiny, seating himself comfortably on the body. He takes a long pull at his water bottle before handing it on to us.

'Where in the name of hell did you get this?' coughs Porta gripping his throat which burns as if he had swallowed acid.

'Can't you take it?' grins Tiny. 'It's a naphtha and reindeer piss cocktail.'

'Where'd you get it?' asks Porta doubtfully, sniffing at the bottle which gives off a dreadful aroma.

'A present from a departed comrade commissar who thought I might need somethin' with a kick in it before I knocked on the gates of the Kremlin,' grins Tiny, clicking his tongue.

'What the devil are you men doing sitting here staring?' shouts a strange Feldwebel briskly.

'Giving the dead major here, sir, extreme unction, sir, if you please, sir,' shouts Porta in military parade-ground manner.

Tiny sticks his water-bottle between the dead major's lips.

' 'E's gone,' he sobs aloud, and falls on his knees with folded hands.

The Feldwebel is visibly confused. He doesn't know what to think. On the other hand he doesn't feel he can start bawling them out with a major present – even a dead major!

'Get along with you, quick,' he orders tamely and disappears between the trees.

' 'Ero!' grunts Tiny, brushing the snow from his trousers.

'Have you looked?' asks Porta suddenly.

'Oly Mother o' Gawd from the slums o' Jerusalem. I bleedin' near forgot!' howls Tiny shocked, and with a sharp tug he opens the major's mouth.

Three gold teeth.

'What the devil have you three been farting about at?' grumbles the Old Man.

'Court-martial 'em,' suggests Heide in comradely fashion.

'We've been giving extreme unction to a hero with the Knight's Cross, a major of Jaegers,' intones Porta in his 'holy' voice.

'Amen!' echoes Tiny virtuously from the background.

'Liars!' snarls the Old Man. 'Breathe out! What the devil have you been drinking? What a hell of a stink!'

'We shared the oil with the dead hero,' answers Porta, with an insincere parson's smile, crossing himself.

Suddenly a machine-gun comes down on us and breaks up the interesting entertainment.

Shadowy shapes disappear hastily into the brush. A few indistinguishable words come from the darkness.

I throw a hand-grenade. Heartrending screams come from the thick underbrush.

'Come death, come . . .' hums the Legionnaire satanically, and empties a magazine at some flitting shapes.

'Light!' commands the Old Man brusquely.

Stege holds his signal pistol high above his head. With a crack the phosphorous flare explodes replacing the darkness with stark white light.

'Cease fire!' shouts the Old Man furiosly. 'Here Panzer Regiment 27 z.b.V!'

'Here Rifle Regiment 106. Password?' comes from the other side.

'Rotten apple!' answers the Old Man.

'Running rat!' comes immediately from the heavy brush.

'Runnin' prick! sounds closer,' considers Tiny insubordinately. We get up, go slowly over towards the brush, and suddenly find ourselves face to face with the Feldwebel from before.

'*You* again!' he roars in an enraged voice.

'Herr Feldwebel, sir, Obergefreiter Joseph Porta, always at your service with last rites, sir! According to Regulations the dying defender of the Fatherland has the right to prayer, oil and a final shot over the open grave, sir!'

'I think you are doing your best to get yourself on a court-martial,' raged the Feldwebel, reddening.

'Beg to report, Herr Feldwebel, sir, that I have seen service with the Army Courts Martial at Torgau, Glatz and Germersheim. At 6 Army HQ at Münster I was responsible for changing the water in the decanters. Beg to report, Herr Feldwebel, Herr Kriegsgerichtsrat Dornbusch drank like a hole in the sand.'

'You ought to be choked with your own shit,' states the Feldwebel, disappearing with his men into the darkness.

'Lot o' bleedin' idiots,' says Tiny, 'lettin' theirselves get shot at by their own mates!'

'That sort of thing happens quite often in war,' explains Porta waving his arms about. 'We live in surprising times. There was once a Herr Bauer who had a house in the hills outside Eger. In 1915 he became a one-man unit. They made him a Cornet and sent him off to the 2nd Imperial Jaeger Regiment. But when Cornet Bauer couldn't find the Imperial Jaegers in Galicia – they'd been sent in the meantime to Italy to defend the Fatherland there – this intrepid man decided to form himself into a separate individual unit and develop a new kind of strategy to be used against the Czar's Cossacks. . . .'

Just then we run into the arms of another company and we hear no more about the heroic Cornet Bauer from the Eger Mountains.

'Good thing you got here, Feldwebel,' thunders an Oberleutnant with a black patch over his eye. 'The Reds have mined the river and blown the bridge.'

'Very good, Herr Oberleutnant!' answers the Old Man tamely, thinking to himself, 'Wish you'd gone with it!'

'But they didn't manage to drop the bridge entirely,' continues the Oberleutnant. 'So now it's up to us to get across before the bastards realize they've left us some bridge. Move straight across with your section and establish a bridgehead. I'll follow with my company. On your way, Feldwebel!'

'Yes, sir!' replies the Old Man apathetically, and moves towards the bridge with the section behind him. What good explaining to the officer that we were not under his command. He regards us as sent from heaven to do his dirty work. He'll get the kudos for the bridgehead, we'll do the paying – in blood – *ours*!

'You first,' orders the Old Man, pointing at Porta with his gun.

'Go fuck a pig!' says Porta disrespectfully. 'If the Bohemian Boy, Adolf, came in person with all his Party Uncles and ordered me to step out onto that bridge I would still veto the idea. What about Julius? He's a born hero!'

'Do you think I'm mad?' protests Heide furiously.

'Well, now you ask. Your being a PG's* enough. Membership's the first step up the suicide ladder.'

'Stop *talking* about that blasted Party. Save it for after the war,' snarls the Old Man impatiently. 'Get *on*, Porta! It's bloody Moscow we're after now! Take position at the third pillar! Sven you'll help him. You can throw hand-grenades

---

* PG Parteigenosse (German): Party Member.

from there!' He throws a sack of grenades at me. A present from the Oberleutnant with the black patch.

We edge our way carefully along an iron girder. It's covered with ice and several times we almost fall off. Besides the grenades I have both ammunition bags to carry.

'Should've joined the bicycle dragoons,' grins Porta, 'we'd have pedalled over in no time on the Wehrmacht model 1903 with turned-up handlebars and valuable improvements such as the free wheel, pneumatic tyres and adjustable shithouse.'

A machine-gun spits tracer at us from the opposite bank.

'A nice welcome,' shouts Porta, raising his top-hat to them politely. At last we reach the pillar and take up position.

With unbelievable slowness Porta inserts the belt and pours half a bottle of Russian frost oil over the lock.

'The greasier, the easier,' he grins. 'I learnt that from a Chinese wholesaler dealing in cunt in the year 1937. He handed out two pounds of vaseline to his workers every Saturday morning so they didn't feel the pistons going in and out.'

There is a heavy bump above our heads. It's Tiny throwing himself down with the SMG.

' 'Ere we are then, my sons, 'ow d'you like the view? *Some* people'd pay money for it!'

'*Hombre*,' groans Barcelona. 'It's just like old times when we were pissing about on the Ebro trying to take the spaghettis in the black shirts.'

A mortar bomb explodes close in front of us and blows half the pillar away.

Two of the section get hit and disappear into the unbelievably filthy waters of the river. A 20 mm automatic cannon begins to jolt away from the far bank. It's a wicked weapon. The small shells tear great jagged shards from the concrete and send them flying like shrapnel around our ears. Two heavy Maxims sight in on us.

'Think I'll go home,' says Porta rolling his eyes skywards. 'There's too much going on here for a peace-loving Berliner.'

'Retire,' orders the Old Man with a taut expression on his face.

We begin to run back, but the patch-eyed Oberleutnant appears and fires on us with his submachine-gun. We decide to stay where we are.

'Hold on, boys!' shouts a voice from the bank. 'The flamethrowers are on the way.'

'I'll 'old on to 'is bollocks for 'im, if I ever get close enough,' promises Tiny, and sprays the far side where the 20 mm gunner seems to be going mad.

But the flamethrowers *do* come. Flamethrowers and explosive charges. They shoot across the river on strange machines which seem to be a cross between battle pontoons and self-propelled sleds.

We follow them and storm the forward pill-boxes, where the Russians fight back more fiercely than we've ever experienced before. They're komsomols from the industrial areas.

I've been given a sack of the new grenade type. The Pioneer-Leutnant warns me solemnly. 'A little of that liquid on your hands and the flesh is gone. We tried it on a dog once and couldn't believe our own eyes. Three somersaults and a long howl, and a skeleton was all that was left.'

I'm all alone with my sack. The others keep well away from me. Together with two pioneers I press forward towards the nearest pill-box. It's one of the big ones with a lift in it.

The weapons dome rises up like a mole-hill and a snug-nosed gun spews flame. The dome sinks back into the ground. When it appears again I throw two of the red cross grenades at it.

The heavy steel seems to melt away. We feel the fumes biting at our lungs and eyes, even though we are wearing the new Czech gasmasks. 'I'm off!' says one of the Pioneers laconically. 'This is sheer insanity!'

'Stay where you are,' wheezes the other holding the nozzle of the flamethrower against his chest. 'Don't forget you're a penal posting! They ought to have liquidated you in Germersheim, you lousy traitor! The Führer sent you here to tighten your ring. You'll never see Moscow!'

I keep out of it. It's none of my business if a busted Leutnant gets a punishment posting to Combat Pioneers. Far as I'm concerned they can liquidate him, or do what they like with him.

I run forward to the next shell hole, throw two red cross grenades and press myself down into the crater.

The pioneers catch up with me. One of them lifts his flamethrower and sends a long hissing burst of fire at the pill-box.

At the same time the former Leutnant vaults up out of the crater and runs towards the Russians with lifted arms.

'Give him a grenade!' howls the other.

'Get fucked!' I answer. 'If he's going to get killed it won't be by me!'

'*Tovaritsch, tovaritsch, nicht schiessen*,' shouts the Pioneer desperately, only a few yards from the Russian position.

I will him to get away with it. If he comes back it will be to a horrible death in solitary at Germersheim. Not many people know what happens in Germersheim, but No. 5 Company was guard company there just after the French campaign. The chief of the Special Section, Oberfeldwebel Schön, wasn't a good man to get across. He once came close to breaking Tiny's back for throwing an oak desk at him. Tiny's still a little crooked in the spine as a result of that comradely pat on the back. They called it that to avoid having to make a report to the Commandant of the prison. Oberstleutnant Ratcliffe. A more hated officer never lived. The permanent staff, the guard company *and* the prisoners were in complete agreement about that. In every other respect we weren't. Germersheim was the scene of a merciless three-sided war, and of the three sides the guard company was best-off. No company stayed on duty there for more than three months. The permanent staff had it worst. They were life prisoners – with keys. None of them dared to move outside the prison alone, for fear of running across a former prisoner back in rank and using his leave to revisit the military prison.

Porta and I met a Leutnant once who had so many medal-ribbons he looked like a walking advertisement for a paint and colour shop. One night, far behind the Russian lines, he told us that he intended to go back to Germersheim to square accounts with three Feldwebels on the permanent staff.

'I'll make him hit me first,' he grinned revengefully.

'Yes indeed,' says Porta, 'I can see very well without glasses. You intend to meet the Feldwebels in a private's rig. It's an expensive game striking an officer. Even when you don't know he *is* one.' But the Leutnant never made Germersheim. The very same night the ski-troops got him.

It's funny how torturers almost always get away with it. They commit one legal murder after another, and every day they make more and more enemies who want to kill them, but it happens very infrequently. In their seventies you can run across them as jolly old pensioners with grandchildren on their knees.

The Pioneer-Gefreiter lifts his flamethrower, sights care-fully in on the former Leutnant who is now very close to the Russian position.

'Ten times damned bloody traitor,' he snarls, his voice sounding hollow and far away inside the gasmask. His finger presses down on the trigger.

Like a blowlamp at full pressure the flame licks out over the uneven ground.

Small oily flames bob and flicker in front of the Russian position. They're all that's left of the Leutnant. Two seconds more and he would have made it.

I don't pity him. He's been a fool. Leaving the German Wehrmacht is an operation which needs careful planning. The Leutnant got no more than he deserved. He had been in Germersheim under the care of Oberfeldwebel Schön and should have known he was under observation. The attack rolls on. We fight our way through a whole world of nothing but pill-boxes. The outer defences of Moscow. Villages are blown up time and again. We have to fight for every yard of ground. New bridges are thrown over the river and tanks, field artillery, special units, heavy artillery go rolling over them in long columns towards the Moscow skyline clearly visible in the distance.

We fight through the night against broken armies which refuse to give up. We have to literally liquidate each unit. There is nothing left of the buildings. The Russians employ scorched earth tactics in retreat. They would rather destroy everything than leave it for us.

Every hour the cold becomes more terrible. 52 degrees below zero. We have no frost oil for our automatic weapons. We tie hot stones around the locks to prevent them freezing. Our lives depend on our light and heavy machine-guns.

Coffee-grinders, old biplanes with small bombs attached to the fuselage, come out as soon as darkness falls. We can hear them coming and as long as their motors bang and cough there is no danger. When they stop we take cover. A rushing in the air, a shadow flitting over the snow, and soon after an explosion followed by the cries of the wounded.

Porta shot one down the other night. The pilot killed three of ours before shooting himself, so now we are cured of approaching shot-down Russian pilots. We light a large fire. It's dangerous but the cold is insupportable and we must have hot stones for the machine-guns.

A few moments after our fire flames up the small, devilish 75 mms are on to us. The Russian forward artillery spotters can't help seeing the fire, and where there's fire there's us.

'My marrow's freezing to fucking ice!' moans Porta pushing a hot stone inside his greatcoat.

'Jesus, it's cold,' Stege cries despairingly, hopping from one foot to the other. 'Gimme a wound and let me get out of this. I'd give a leg for a warm hospital bed.'

Barcelona rubs his face carefully, thinking of his nose which is already going dangerously white.

'Not so rough, or you'll lose your strawberry!' Porta warns

him. 'Rub it with snow! It's the only way to thaw out a frozen horn!'

Barcelona wouldn't be the first to lose his nose. Suddenly it's in your hand and all you've got left is a hole.

'Bloody *lice*!' shouts Porta scratching madly away like a flea-ridden dog. 'They won't leave you alone until there's icicles hanging from your bollocks. Soon as you get warm again and roll up to get a bit of shuteye they're running and fucking about all over you again!'

'*C'est la guerre*,' answer the Legionnaire. 'Even the red lice are against us!'

I push a hot stone in under my uniform. As soon as it touches my skin I begin to itch. The lice go for the heat, too.

'These minipartisans have been told about Stalin's orders,' explains Barcelona. 'Don't give the Fascist invader a second's peace!'

'Then they shouldn't be bothering *me*,' comments Porta. 'I've never been a Fascist! Tell 'em to march on over to Julius! He's pissfull of rich brown Nazi blood!'

'It feels queer getting to Moscow,' says Stege. 'Six months ago none of us would've believed it. Now we've just got to get into the town,' he continues, 'and we'll have peace inside fourteen days. Stalin'll go soft when we march into the Red Square!'

'The Kremlin's farther off than you think,' says Porta, clapping his hands vigorously.

'We can *see* the bloody place,' protests Stege angrily.

'We could see England, too,' answers Porta drily, 'but did we ever get there? The Party and the Generals boasted a blue streak. The lords would be put to work as shepherds and whatnot. Buckingham Palace'd be turned into an officers' knocker. We Germans suffer from an incurable case of swollen head complex. "God punish England," said the Kaiser when he found he couldn't do it himself. Now Adolf's searching for Moses' rod to part the waters, but it's kept in a glass case in the British Museum in London! It's my modest belief that he's gonna get a shellacking like nobody's business here at Moscow. Haven't you ever noticed what a funny lot these house painters are? Quite a lot of them are ring-snatchers. Look at Luetnant Prick on the gun section. His firm in Berlin are house painters. We got at cross purposes with one another the other day.

'"We'll meet at Canossa," he shouts after me. "You'll get to know me better!"

'Not on your bloody life he won't! Everybody's knows "Canossa", that little homo' bar on Gendarmenmarkt. Nobody from over there dares to go into "the Crooked Dog" on the other side. If Leutnant Prick were to drop in to "the Dog" they'd have a whole whitewash brush up his arse crossways quicker'n shit. *And* it'd be one of the cheap ones that leave stripes on the ceiling.'

'Victory is just around the corner,' shouts Barcelona confidently. 'Tomorrow night we'll be stuffing the Moscow whores, and in a week's time we'll be off on leave!'

'You'll get wiser,' Porta grins a disillusioned grin. 'Adolf's Travel Bureau'll give us all enough sleepless nights yet to last us the rest of our lives.'

When we're relieved the Russians begin to cover the area with mortars and field artillery.

The concussions follow one another without pause and great craters open in the snow-covered terrain. Russian infantry swarm out of the forest.

'*Uhraeh, Stalino, uhraeh, Stalino!*' comes in an animal roar.

Worn-out German units emerge from the ruins. Flares whistle skywards and illuminate the attacking hordes streaming endlessly from amongst the trees.

With feverish haste we bring our machine-guns into position. Bayonets wink in the ghostly illumination from countless explosions. Grenades are armed and lie ready to hand on the breastwork with porcelain rings dangling. If they get through it's all up with us. There aren't enough of us left to win a hand-to-hand fight. There are only a few remaining of those who formed up for the attack on 22 June. The others make a pathway of bodies from Brest-Litovsk via

Minsk to Kiev and from Kiev to Moscow. Thousands of them are floating as corpses in the Volga and Dnieper. Greater Germany, and the Führer's, honoured dead!

Out of the red-black mist comes an infantryman laughing madly. With a scream he throws his carbine away and creeps along close to the ground like a wounded animal. A steel rain of shells whips up the earth around him. Nobody tries to stop him. It's no business of ours. Even the Watchdogs can see he's out of his mind. Those piercing screams are unmistakable. They can't be simulated. The Watchdogs might take him to a field hospital but they *might* also shoot him through the back of the neck with a P-38 just to get rid of him.

Hundreds of MGs spit tracer across the terrain. Rank by rank the Russians fall to the deadly fire and are replaced by others who pick up their weapons and continue the advance. Every armed rank is followed by two ranks without weapons. A swaying forest of men in khaki.

The commissars are easy to recognize. They're the ones who wear fur caps with a gilt hammer and sickle in the star and the green cross, symbol of ruthless power. God help the Soviet soldier who hesitates to go forward. The commissars look after him.

Hand grenades whirl through the air. Our rearward lines of communication have been destroyed by Russian commandos. We are cut off and have to use runners to maintain contact. To be sent out as a runner is almost certain death.

The Russians attack in close order with bayonets at the ready. Automatic weapons hammer tracer incessantly into their closed ranks.

'At this rate we're going to kill the entire Russian Army,' says Heide. 'Their leaders must be insane!'

'Are they hell!' answers Porta. 'They're cool as the Russian winter. To them men are cheaper than ammunition. Before we've killed the half of them we'll have nothing left to shoot *with*. We're not the first who've tried. Russia cannot be conquered.'

'That's Russian Communist shit,' shouts Heide indignantly. 'I ought to set the MPs on you!'

'And I ought to put my foot up your arse!' replies Porta sending a long burst away at a dangerous-looking Russian group.

Two Russians appear suddenly amongst us. Oberleutnant Moser and the Old Man are close to being bayoneted; then Tiny grabs the two militia-men by their throats and strangles them. One-handed!

We are about to leave our position when a section of combat artillery rolls up. They stop and fire and trundle on. The shells drop amongst the attacking mass of infantry. The artillery are using incendiaries and instantly the waving forest of soldiers is a roaring sea of flame.

The attackers sway back. Their commissars shoot into them but without effect. They begin to withdraw in panic flight.

A soldier here and there, then a whole column. Suddenly the battlefield is empty.

Stacks of corpses are left behind. Parts of bodies hang on the frozen bushes. Bloody entrails flap in the wind.

We clean our weapons and refill magazines. We are feverishly busy. Nobody knows how soon they'll be back.

Motor sleds from Supplies come buzzing out of the forest towards us. We help them off-load ammunition. They are older men who were with the infantry in the last war. To protect them they have been put into Supplies. There they only have mines and the partisans to worry about. To our eyes they seem like old, old men who have stopped talking about girls and sit writing letters to some worn-out wife at home who has the air-raids to worry about. Many of them have sons our age among the fighting troops.

Just after darkness falls the enemy attack again but the artillery unit is still with us and takes a heavy toll of their infantry as they march forward in close column, shoulder to shoulder. The butcher's work continues all night, the fighting swaying back and forth over the open ground. We crawl over ever-growing heaps of bodies; pull ourselves up by stiffened arms which point accusingly to the heavens.

Towards morning the Russians manage to force their way through our automatic fire and we prepare for the final battle. Unexpectedly the weather comes to our aid. A howling storm sweeps across the river and drowns everything in driving snow which makes it impossible to tell friend and enemy apart. We feel our way forward, shout for the password. If the answer doesn't come quickly enough a bayonet rips into the shadowy figure in front. The fastest talker lives longest.

Quite often you find your bayonet opening up a comrade's guts, but this doesn't worry you. The main object is to stay alive. They didn't teach this kind of war in training school.

We're not human anymore but a kind of arctic animal, killing to stay alive. Whenever we get a break we spend it sharpening our combat weapons. They are keen enough by now to shave with. We have cloths wound around our faces, so that only our eyes show, as protection against the cold. The oil in the locks of our weapons freezes in a few seconds, and all the MGs are out of commission. In the fearful battle which now ensues our best weapons are sharpened out spades. We use those taken from the bodies of the Russian infantry. They are stiffer, and considerably better for the job than the German collapsible spade. A German spade, in a hand like Tiny's, breaks at the first stroke whilst the stouter Russian job stands up well to this kind of work. Catch them right, just under the ear, and off goes a head with one stroke. Be careful, above all, not to aim at the collar, since the stroke will be partially stopped by thick uniform material.

We fight hand-to-hand, with spade in one hand and pistol in the other. Run quickly from shell-hole to shell-hole, crouch on one knee like beasts of prey, ready to spring again as soon as we've got our wind and our blood has stopped pounding in our veins. The heavy artillery lays down a close barrage. Even the Corps Commanders far in the rear have discovered that they are in serious danger. That's why we get artillery support.

Clouds of smoke and flame rise from the forest. Trees are cut down as if with a giant scythe. the Russians take cover behind their own dead. A body gives as good protection as a sand-bag. In war you learn to use whatever is ready to hand. At the front nobody has time for moral tenets. But the soldiers aren't to be blamed for that. Let the blame fall on the politicians who have led them down the road to ruin.

The firing and the pressure of the attack, dies away. The screams of the wounded can be heard now. One of them is lying right in front of us. He screams all through the morning and we get so desperate that we send rifle grenades out towards where we think he is, but every time the snow spurts up and we think we've finished him there he is again with his longdrawn, heartbreaking wail. The Old Man thinks he must have got an explosive bullet in the gut. That kind of wound takes a long time to kill a man. It can't be a lung wound. He'd have been suffocated long since. A lung wound hurts terribly but means a quick death. The best wound is a piece of shrapnel in the thigh. All he blood has run out of you before you even realize you're going to die. Stomach and head wounds are the worst. They take a long time to kill a man. Even if we risk a couple of lives and bring him in the hospital can't save him. We get nervous, scream, and shout curses at him. We begin to discuss him. What sort of a chap is he? He's a German we know. '*Mutti, Mutti, hilf mir!* he's shouting all the time. If it was one of *their* boys he'd have been shouting: '*Matj!*' He must be young or he wouldn't be calling for his mother. The older ones call for their wives.

Just before darkness falls the Old Man asks for volunteers to go out and pick him up.

Nobody steps forward.

'Bastards!' snarls the Old Man, swinging a stretcher up onto his shoulder.

Moser tries to stop him.

The Old Man hits out insubordinately at the Oberleutnant.

'Shit!' rasps Porta tearing the stretcher away from him. 'Come on Tiny, we'll bring that bloody opera singer in! And when we get him here we'll break his skull. He might be a volunteer who thinks war's just a nice rough game for men.'

Bent-backed they run forward through no-man's-land. Tiny is waving a white flag. The enemy have had enough of the screaming, just as we have.

The firing stops. They disappear into a shell-funnel. Suddenly a German howitzer opens up:

'R-u-u-u-u-um! Buuuuum!'

The wickedly sharp splinters fly through the air. It's not pleasant for a couple of infantrymen to find themselves on the receiving end of howitzer fire.

Oberleutnant Moser sends runners back to the artillery. The Russian commander on the other side waves a white flag. The enemy artillery is stilled. Only our own artillery is still firing.

Suddenly the howitzers are quiet.

Porta springs from a soot-blackened shell-hole only a few yards from the enemy trenches.

The badly wounded infantryman is only seventeen. The Old Man was right. He's got a banger in the gut.

The boy dies soon after Porta and Tiny get him in, even though he gets one of our precious blood transfusions and a big shot of morphine.

We scrape snow over his body. We haven't time to bury him properly.

We crawl over in turn to one of the many fires. Thaw out our weapons and warm our frozen joints a little.

The Russian troops have been supplied with face-masks against the cold. We have only our scarves, so we rob the Russian bodies of their face-masks and felt boots.

'It's the first of December, today,' announces Julius Heide solemnly. 'The war will soon be over!'

'How the hell do *you* know?' asks Porta. 'You got a direct line to Stalin?'

'The Führer has said that the *untermensch* will have been crushed and the war concluded by Christmas!' says Heide with conviction.

'Is there anything Adolf the Austrian *hasn't* said?' sighs Porta. Laughter ripples round the fires. It's easy to hear that the company present doesn't consist entirely of Party members.

'*Mon Dieu*, how cold it is!' mumbles the Legionnaire, and throws a piece of wood onto the fire so that the flames shoot up and send sparks flying into the darkness.

From the forest a machine-gun barks. It sounds comically harmless in comparison with the shell-fire.

More fires are kindled. A couple of mortars begin to spit bombs at us. They come in great arching curves, but they are too far away for us to bother with them as yet.

Stege looks nervously in the direction the explosions are coming from.

'Ivan's finger got the itch,' he mumbles. 'Must be about time we got our fingers out and found us a comfortable shell hole.'

'Breathe easy, *mon ami*,' says the Legionnaire, calmly. 'It takes a while for them to get the range. When they begin to drop by the fires closest to them it's time for us to make a move.'

'What the hell are we waiting here for anyway!' Barcelona curses viciously.

'Orders, *mon ami*,' answers the Legionnaire laconically. '*C'est la guerre!*'

'See! See!' shouts Barcelona furiously, 'Orders! Orders! That's the rotten Army for you. Soon as you're in the door it's orders, orders, orders! Shit by numbers, they say, and you *shit* by numbers! Stand up and get shot, they say, and up you get with your fingers down your seams and you *let* yourself get shot! And all because some bastard with silver braid has given an *order*!'

'Those aluminium stars seem to be weighing heavily on you, Feldwebel Blom,' grins Porta, 'but they're easy to get rid of! Just tell 'em you're not playing any more. At Germersheim they're specialists at snatching the stars off people's shoulders!'

A mortar bomb falls on a fire over by the forest.

We look nervously in that direction and listen to the screams of the wounded.

The sinister slobbering comes again from the trees. There are more on the way. We hear the long hissing whistle followed by a grating whine, that tells us a mortar bomb is on the way. Now it's: Move, brother! The bastard'll fall within a radius of fifty yards from us. Even before we've reached cover we hear the explosion, and shrapnel buzzes through the air like angry wasps. The shock has hardly passed before the next one's on its way.

I have only have risen to make for cover when it falls in front of me. Before I can get down I'm underneath an avalanche of snow. Like a mobile snowball I roll over to Porta and Stege who have dropped into the hole the bomb has left. It's warm. Melted snow trickles down the sides.

'Slop – plop!' sounds from within the forest. Then the longdrawn whistle, the terrible roar of the strike and a wave of hot air passes over us like a giant's breath.

Twirling like a dry leaf in a November storm I'm thrown through the air far out into no-man's-land where my flight is stopped brutally by a barbed wire fence-post. When I come to myself again, I can still hear the slobbering of the mortars firing from the blackness of the firs.

Desperately I try to dig myself in with my hands behind the slender post. The bombs seem to be coming directly at me. The explosion is so violent that it blasts all the breath from my lungs.

'Plop-Plop!' the mortar goes again.

I run madly back towards our position. I'm running a race with the grating whistle above me, roll head-over-heels down to the others just as the bomb explodes behind me and fills

178

our hole with snow. 'Come death, come now,' the Legionnaire hums his macabre battle hymn.

Suddenly the mortar fire ceases. We gather in the village. The section has shrunk to twelve. Sourly the Old Man requires a name-check of the twenty-three missing. He has to account for losses. It doesn't mean much that they've fallen, but the Section Commander has to prove it. If not the Military Police are advised of their names as possible deserters. Nobody is allowed to get away with deserting from the German Army. In the First World War 8,916 men deserted from the Army, but only 7 got away scot-free. The MPs are proud of this record, and make use of it as a deterrent in the Second World War, but some still make the attempt.

We covered the last one for seven days, before we sent the report through to the regiment. His wife had written that the sea was coming through the dykes. It had reached the hay and was rotting it from below. If only you were here, Herbert, she'd ended her letter. And that was her man's death warrant. Herbert Damkuhl, the farmer, started off home, but was picked up at Brest-Litovsk. He'd only been reported missing nineteen hours. He was sent to Paderborn for court-martial and sentenced to death. One rainy morning in Sennelager they shot him. The *peloton* consisted of twelve Landesschütze under the command of a sleepy Leutnant who'd learnt how to shoot deserters in the First World War. Behind the broken dykes in Friesland the hay continued to rot.

The Legionnaire is holding his long, French water-bottle made of leather, over the fire to thaw out the contents. You can hear the ice rattling inside when he shakes it. Silently we watch him at work. He places a delicate porcelain cup in front of him and pours warm coffee into it. He's lived a long time amongst Frenchmen and likes to point out the fact that he is not *quite* the same as we are.

'Almost like sitting in the Café de la Paix on a May evening,' he dreams, rolling a cigarette. He does it with the earnest attention of a Spaniard. The final operation is the adhesion of a Russian mouthpiece, which gives it a particular aroma.

'God be thanked! Tomorrow we'll be in Moscow,' says Julius Heide, rubbing his boots with a Kiwi cloth. They are already highly-polished. He parts his hair carefully before replacing his helmet. Then he cleans his pistol. Heide is always 'according to regulations', even when he's in bed.

'Well we can't stay here anyway,' says Barcelona, holding his hand out for his share of the little Legionnaire's coffee.

The Legionnaire regards the black grains with a longing expression in his eyes.

'Paris, Paris, Paris in May. The girls wearing dresses so thin that you can see right through them and which the tiniest zephyr can lift. The whole world visiting one another at the Café de la Pais. *C'est la vie!* If you have never known it you've still got something left to live for.'

'*I've* been there,' declares Tiny, unimpressed. 'They asked me to leave. I was that drunk it was comin' outa me ears. While we was talkin' it over with a lot of Frenchies the 'ead 'unters turned up an' closed the show. They accused me o' bringin' the German Wehrmacht into disrespect in the eyes o' the bleedin' Frenchies. As if they coulda 'eld us in more disrespect'n they did already! They 'it me a whack over the 'ead with a bleedin' great bunch o' keys, an' said I was a psycho, which is about right I reckon. I got a paper 'as says so at any rate. They went blue in the bleedin' face when I explained to 'em 'ow we're all more or less mouldly under the bleedin' lid but some can 'ide it better'n others. Them as is cleverest gets stars on their shoulders, I told 'em. You shoulda seen the bleedin' Watchdog major go straight up through 'is 'air without even takin' 'is tin 'at off. I got 8 days 'ard on the spot for insultin' a German officer when on duty.

'Then Staff bleedin' Gren, the bastard, give me the treatment, till I was willin' to testify to bein' the one an' only psycho in the *en*tire German bleedin' army. After that I 'ad no desire *at* all to sit in their stuck-up Café de la pissin' Paix watchin' all them bleedin' ring-snatchers an' cock-suckers sellin' their line o' goods! Gawd strike me down if I ever see so many tight arses in me life as I did the five minutes I 'ad to look around in!'

A series of mortar bombs cuts him short.

For the fourth time the Professor is thrown out into the wire.

This time a boot is literally blown off his foot. He's screaming like a madman when we get to him. He's lost his glasses. Being unable to see drives him wild.

'Get your pecker up, matey. Think if it'd been your old napper you'd lost,' shouts Tiny, cheeringly. 'You don't need to see in a war. Go for the sound! The action's where the bleedin' noise is!'

Our second-in-command, Leutnant Jansen, lies groaning at the bottom of the trench. We've covered him with a couple of greatcoats taken from the dead but he's shivering and has a high fever. He groans continually from excruciating pains in his kidneys. Even though he is 2 i/c he's still younger than most of us. He came to the unit straight from the officer factory. What he knows he's learnt from us.

The Leutnant watches us with childish fear. He's been at the front long enough to know what *he* is to us. Trouble! If we wish him dead it's not to be wondered at. Whilst we're stuck here it doesn't make much difference, but as soon as the battle starts rolling again, one way or the other, he's a burden on us. He knows that sooner or later we're going to have to roll him in a greatcoat, give him a packet of cigarettes and leave him to freeze to death quietly.

'Done!' cries Porta. 'He snuffs it within three days!'

We discover Jansen watching us and feel ashamed. Look away and busy ourselves with the automatic weapons.

The Old Man sits down by the Leutnant's side, rolls a plug of tobacco into place behind his teeth, and spits at a snow hare which is sitting on the edge of the trench wagging its ears at us.

'How's it going?' he asks, pushing a gasmask bag under the young officer's neck.

'Bad!' answers Jansen tiredly, wiping a hand over his wet brow. 'Have you written me off?'

'Balls, why'd we do that?'

'Porta took three days!'

'Some bet about a bottle of vodka,' laughs the Old Man, throwing a snowball at Porta.

'They were betting on how long I'll last. Porta gave me three days,' mumbles the Leutnant, stubbornly.

'Herr Leutnant, pull yourself together now. Don't forget you're 2 i/c. You're duty bound to show an example!'

'I'll finish myself,' says the Leutnant firmly. 'I'm sick! I'm *trouble*!'

'Come, come now,' the Old Man soothes him. 'It's not that bad. What was your job in civilian life?'

'I was something in a bank,' answers the Leutnant tiredly. 'I'm not suited to be an officer. You should've been an officer, Feldwebel.'

The Old Man laughs aloud. It's the last thing he could ever imagine happening. He's never understood how he came to be a Feldwebel, even though he is a born leader.

'What's Ivan up to?' asks Jansen.

'I was over at No. 3 last night and heard them examining prisoners,' answers the Old Man despondently. 'The other lot are marshalling everything they can get hold of. New troops with the best possible winter clothing and equipment. Countless battalions of Siberiaks. First class fighters who've been promised the earth if they crush the Fascists. Hundreds of T-34s ready to roll. If what the prisoners say is true, we ought to lose no time packing up and getting away from here.' The Old Man pushes a new plug behind his teeth, takes the magazine off his submachine-gun and examines it critically. 'Still no orders from regiment?' he asks.

'None yet,' answers Jansen, shaking with a new attack of fever. 'Something'll come through. They can't just take off and leave us here.'

'Yes, they *can*,' answers the Old Man, 'and I believe they will. What's a lousy company against the safety of a regiment! The good of the majority comes before the good of the individual, says the Party.'

'To hell with the Party, the Führer and this whole bloody war,' whispers Leutnant Jansen through chattering teeth.

Violent artillery fire cuts short the conversation. A seething cloud of smoke cloaks everything. Men are blown from their holes and strewn about the snow. A few get up and run until they are caught again and blown higher than the flaming tree tops. In the wink of an eye frozen snow and earth is turned into a boiling broth whipped up by glowing metal.

We retreat at speed, racing through thick, steamy mist. The Russians cannot follow us through the sea of flame. We throw hand grenades behind us, shoot into the flames.

An Oberst sits against a tree, his teeth showing in an obscene deathshead grin. Both his arms are gone. The Cossacks dash past, sabres gleaming, and disappear into the smoke.

A German artillery limber rushes past as fast as the horses can go. There is a long thunderous roar and it disappears. The horses fall screaming from the sky, their legs splaying outwards, to splash to a bloody gruel on the ground.

The earth opens up in front of us like the mouth of a roaring volcano. Stone, earth and snow fly far away through the riven air. A giant crater, large enough to hold a four storey building, is torn out of the ground. A lorry comes flying through the air. The driver is still at the wheel as if he is steering it. With a crunching sound, it lands at the bottom of the crater in a heap of tangled metal.

A soldier runs towards us. His insides trailing like ghastly snakes behind him. His mouth is one great gaping, screaming hole. He stumbles over his own entrails, falls, gets up, and runs on until he disappears in a flaming explosion.

A two-storey house hangs seemingly suspended in the air, above a company. It falls and house and soldiers mingle to an unrecognizable mash. Long tree trunks with parts of bodies hanging between their branches come flying through the air with inconceivable force and bore themselves into the ground like giant javelins. A salvo of shells turns them to firewood.

Porta and I are lugging the heavy machine-gun. Tiny has Leutnant Jansen over one shoulder like a sack.

We take up position behind the ruined village. A swarm of Jabos hoses the battleground clean of stragglers.

> 'It is no longer necessary for the Courts to give a decision. An order from the Führer is sufficient where the execution of criminals, for crimes against the state or for parasitism, is concerned.'
>
> Reichsführer Himmler to Police President
> SS-Gruppenführer Kurt Daluege, 3 January 1942.

At Headquarters Hitler raged for the third hour without pause. 'Cowards, traitors, bunglers,' he howled, at the officers sitting in silence along both sides of the heavy oak table.

Marschall Keitel fiddled with a pencil. General Olbricht watched a fly crawling around on the great war chart. It edged its way between the coloured pins and flags and stopped on a large red spot: Moscow. General-oberst Jodl leafed through documents concerning the disappointing tank production. Reichsmarschall Göring sketched ideas for new uniforms. SS-Reichsführer Himmler noted energetically the confusion of orders flowing from Hitler.

'Guderian is to be dismissed!' he roared. 'Hoepner, that criminal dilletante, must go too!'

'Very good!' mumbled the Chief of Personnel, General der Infanterie von Burgerdorf, making a note in a pocket diary.

'Have I not ordered the troops to hold on and to fight fanatically to the last bullet?' screamed Hitler. 'And what happens? No sooner do these *untermensch* begin to fire back at them my miserable soldiers flee like frightened hares! I blush for the German people. If I did not feel myself called to lead them I would resign immediately!' He kicked viciously at a chair sending it flying across the ankles of General Fellgiebel, who could not restrain a half-smothered exclamation of pain.

Hitler sent the Liaison Chief a deadly look.

'Fieldmarschall von Bock is to be removed from his command, and I forbid him ever again to show himself in uniform.

Halder has informed me that we have lost one million and one hundred thousand fallen and seriously wounded, but it is no more than they have deserved! Catastrophe I hear? No, a weeding-out! Only cowardly swine let themselves be annihilated by these *untermensch*. I forbid that any man from the middle echelon be decorated or promoted until such time as he has rehabilitated himself by service on other sections of the front!'

Hitler ordered thirty-eight more generals removed, twelve to be executed.

Ruthlessly he raged on, demanding the blood of others in payment for the failure of his own reckless plans.

Panzer General Model came close to losing his life when he explained that Napoleon's armies had also attacked Russia on 22 June and were in Moscow by 14 September, 86 days later. And this was done on foot whilst, by 14 September 1941, Hitler's Panzer Troops were still 220 miles from Moscow.

For fully five minutes Hitler stood like a stone statue staring at the little general. Then he exploded into a long wailing scream and threw a bundle of documents at his head.

'Do you dare to say that the Führer of Greater Germany is inferior to that comical little Corsican gangster? A person who only became an officer by reason of the times he lived in! Only the degenerate French could be proud of such an individual. Model, you are dismissed! Never show yourself before me again! You have insulted Germany!'

A week later Hitler was forced to order Model to take command of the retreat. Six other generals had refused it. Hitler had almost to go on his knees to his army leaders. Two of them were sent to concentration camps, but did not give in.

Hitler stuck at nothing to demonstrate his power and cruelty. Troops sent to the front were given orders to fire on the traitors who had opened the line of battle to the enemy. Countless soldiers who had fought desperately to break the Russian bear-hug were executed by their own side. Without trial they were lined up against a wall and butchered. Those without weapons were lost. If they protested a rifle-butt smashed their mouths shut before they fell to the whipping bullets of a firing-squad.

8 | The Mongol Captain

Chief Mechanic Wolf* has ventured out to the front line. Puffing badly, he seats himself on a gun carriage and thoughtfully ignites one of the special cigars which only he and the generals at HQ smoke. He has the largest private haulage company in the German Army. You can buy *anything* from him – especially if you can pay in hard currency.

Two fierce wolfhounds lie down watchfully in front of him. Their yellow eyes inspect us hungrily. A snap of their master's fingers and they'd tear us to pieces. An expensive officer's fur-coat gives him the look of an operetta general playing in a theatre in some Vienna side-street. His buttons and badges are pure silver. He is, of course, wearing a tall fur cap, and a sabre which couldn't cut a radish in two. Anybody else would be punished for being so irregularly dressed.

Nobody but Porta dares to cross swords with Chief Mechanic Wolf. For anyone else it would mean a painful death – by starvation!

'What the devil do *you* want, me old Sprocket Dragoon?' asks Porta suspiciously.

Wolf grins condescendingly, flashing all his gold teeth at once. It's not that his teeth are bad. Quite the opposite; but he thinks a mouthful of gold teeth a mark of position. When we captured a Russian Mobile Dentistry Unit complete with personnel Wolf had all his teeth covered with gold. Before then he'd been sparing with his smiles.

Now he's always grinning.

'I've come to say goodbye,' he smiles, falsely.

'You leaving?' enthuses Porta.

'*Njet*, not me. You!' he smiles cunningly.

'How'd you criminals get the word?' asks Porta suspiciously, gripped by a sinister foreboding.

If Wolf dares the perils of the front line to bring the message it can't be just to please Porta.

* Wolf: See *Comrades of War.*

'None of your business where it came from but, as you ought to know, a chief Mech. has his network,' answers Wolf, superciliously. 'What about those three Zim tractors you've stolen? You won't need 'em where you're going. So what about a quick little deal? I can offer you a first class battle pack for every man in No. 2 Section, plus a *kalashnikov* and double ammunition. A 150 kilo ration sack extra for yourself. You'll need it badly in the near future. But it's up to yourself if you'd rather move off with three days coolie rations and not a bacon rind more. You'll get that hungry they'll be able to hear your belly screaming back in Berlin.'

'Spit it out, you wicked, wicked man,' says Porta growing suspicious. 'Where am I going?'

Thoughtfully, Wolf cuts himself a slice of salami. He doesn't attempt to hide how much he is enjoying Porta's anxiety.

'A Zim 5-tonner for it!' he says, after having swallowed the sausage and picked his teeth clean with the point of his knife.

'Kiss my arse, chum!' replies Porta, in a careless tone, spinning his pistol dangerously. 'That Zim's my return ticket to Berlin.'

'Thanks for the information,' says Wolf, showing all his teeth in a triumphant grin. 'I wasn't sure. You got a 150 mm howitzer battery stowed away's the rumour!'

'There's plenty of shithouse rumours going the rounds,' answers Porta slowly. 'What the hell'd I want with howitzers? Am I a gunner?'

'You know what it's all about,' says Wolf in a rough but almost friendly tone. 'The German Wehrmacht's got its arse dangling gently but firmly in the snow. There's gonna be more'n a shortage of guns. You can get what you ask for an SP-battery soon as you feel like showing your hand, son.'

'They'd commandeer it soon as I made the offer,' declares Porta, trying, as hard as he can, to look naive.

Wolf screams with laughter and takes a swig from a silver hip-flask without offering it round.

'Balls, my good son! *You* know how to turn that one.'

'Mind you don't choke on it,' answers Porta sourly. 'The German skeet-club'll be moving smartly backwards p.d.q., and Ivan don't give a French fuck for your wagon park. The day they march you off to Kolyma I'll go with you as a volunteer just to enjoy watching you kick it slowly in the lead mines! They'll cut the tails off your bloody wolves and stick'em up your arse so far you'll never get 'em down again and can get a job as crossing-sweeper when the war's over!'

'Shit, son!' replies Wolf, easily. 'All my wagons are in a nice safe place already, you'll be glad to know! All I need your Zim for is to haul the last of them out. I've got a nice place fixed up at Libau, son. Good harbour. If it should happen our victorious army advances too far backwards I can always take a boat to Sweden. They've got a Socialist government there and feel it their duty to take in us boys from the cruel world outside and look after us.'

'How the hell did you manage it?' asks Porta with open admiration.

'Easy for a Chief Mechanic in Transport. Movement in Russia ain't difficult if you've been through the Army Hauptfeldwebel School, and know what it's all about,' explains Wolf looking down his nose slyly.

'Someday they'll hang you,' says Porta in friendly admiration, without attempting to conceal that it wouldn't worry *him* when it happened.

'Never,' says Wolf, grinning, 'but I'm convinced you'll end *your* dirty little life on the end of a rope. If I'm there I'll do you a service. I'll cut you down before the crows get at you, son!'

'Know what *you* are, you fucked-up son of a mangey wolf and a clapped-out dingo, you're due to die for Führer, family, if you could get one, and Fatherland,' comes from Porta with bitter emphasis. 'You're the wickedest bastard I've ever met in all my life.'

'*Basura*,'* shouts Barcelona, happily.

'Can it, bastard!' snarls Wolf, turning his snapping green

* *Basura* (Spanish): Dustbin (Porta is emptying it on Wolf.)

189

eyes on Barcelona. 'How'd you like a case of Spanish oranges jacked up your arse, son? How'd you like to shit orange-juice the next twelve months?'

'You're a sick cat, brother!' says Barcelona in a dry tone. 'Keep on shitting in your straw till it smells as bad as you do!'

'It's on the record, Feldwebel Blom,' Wolf smiles villainously. 'This war ain't nothing to what's coming when it's all over! Porta, we gonna do a deal or ain't we?' he continues, without changing his tone. 'The little Zim for what I can tell you!'

'I'll fuck your mother if you like, Wolf!' says Porta in a condescending voice.

'She wouldn't get anything out of it, son!' says Wolf proudly, patting himself with a heavily perfumed handkerchief. 'She's a lady.'

'You stink like a bucket of slops from a Chinese knocker,' says Porta, holding his nose and grimacing.

' 'E couldn't earn a sausage draggin' 'is brownie on the town even with tight-arsed pants an' a red ribbon round his charlie,' shouts Tiny, slapping his thighs and roaring with laughter.

'Last chance,' says Wolf, preferring to ignore the insult. 'I'm your *only* chance!'

Porta laughs loud and long.

'If a man only had one chance in this bloody campaign of love and liberation, I'd have died and risen again more than a few times.'

'You a cousin of Rothschild, or something?' smiles Wolf, with a superior air. 'You're itching to know what I've got.'

'Fuck off,' growls Porta, spitting carelessly into the wind.

'Let's stop playing games, Porta, and get to business. I'm willing to admit getting your Zims is my big problem.'

'Too right, son,' says Porta, slitting his eyes. '*You've* got a problem. *I* ain't. That makes a big difference. Why should I give you my Zims? We both know the big shots're getting homesick, and the price of tracks and half-tracks *with* petrol is rocketing. I've still got *my* Zims because I know prices ain't

190

topped yet. But since I'm a good-hearted sort of chap I'll let you have a five ton, three-axle job with*out* tracks, if you like?'

'What'd I like about that kind of shit?' asks Wolf, hurt. 'It wouldn't move an inch in all this bloody Commie snow. For the last time: One ready-to-move tracked Zim with forty-five gallons in the tank. I'm an honest man, Porta, I treat my friends the way they deserve.'

'You sound like somebody chatting-up a bint who's ready to believe any kind of shit long as you've got stars on your shoulders,' says Porta, with some dignity.

'Let's operate on 'im with a Bolshie bleedin' bayonet,' suggests Tiny, loudly and undiplomatically.

'That Hamburg boy of yours'll never grow up,' confides Wolf to Stege. 'The son of a proletarian thinks everything can be worked out with fists.'

'Don't insult *me*, Mr Chief bleedin' Mechanic, or I'll dig your bleedin' gut out,' warns Tiny, letting a finger run along the sharpened edge of his spade.

'Shut it, dryshitter!' is all Wolf condescends to remark. After a long and secretive palaver Porta and Wolf come to an agreement and Porta brings up the Zims. Wolf goes over them carefully. He's looking for time-bombs. Satisfied, he offers schnapps all round.

'You don't really deserve it,' he turns to Tiny, 'but since you'll soon be leaving this vale of tears, well here's one for the road, sonny! You'll be happy to know that you're going to the Brandenburg Regiment,' he adds, maliciously.

'Sounds like some SS mob,' considers Barcelona.

'Dope,' grins Wolf, tolerantly. 'The SS wouldn't touch you shower with a shithouse broom. If you went down on your bended knees to 'em they wouldn't have you lot. The Brandenburg Regiment, friends, is the arsehole of the main sewer. A regiment of suicide squads where only five percent speak German. The rest are deserters and enemy traitors. When I heard the good news I opened a bottle of champagne, I can tell you. I really intended to save it for Victory Day, but—'

'Oberst Inka won't stand for it,' shouts Porta indignantly. 'He'll go right to the bloody top!'

'He *has* done, and they spit in his eye,' laughs Wolf, noisily and long. 'The good God of Germany has destined you to turn up your toes on the banks of the Moscow River.'

'What the hell do they want *us* to do with the Brandenburgers?' asks Porta, doubtfully.

'They've suffered a hell of a lot of losses lately,' explains Wolf, with fitting sorrow in his voice. 'The holes are being filled up with the scum of the Army and Navy. That's why your little friendly society's going to 'em. You're going to Moscow to send up a couple of factories.'

'The Luftwaffe can do that easier,' says Porta. 'They can pulverize the whole bloody lot without losing a drop of valuable German blood.'

'They won't lose a drop of that anyway,' Wolf grins, satanically. 'You and the other white niggers don't count for as much as a cup of Jew piss. They'll give you plenty of plastic demolition charges and a yellow monkey to show you the way. A half-human shit-eater more treacherous than any of those bastards you read about in the Bible.'

The telephone rattles long and angrily. Wolf takes it and hands it gracefully to the Old Man.

'The shithouse is on fire, I reckon, boys!' he says, in a fatherly tone, patting Porta on the shoulder with false friendliness. 'Your section commander's being called in for his last communion! I'd be a lying son-of-a-bitch if I said I was sorry. I've been looking forward, ever since we first met, back in '36, to seeing you off on a real death or glory job, but I'm not really a wicked chap, just a cool calculating business man. You gotta be if you want to stay alive. Inside here,' he thumps his breast theatrically, 'there's a big heart beating, and in it there's a little membrane throbbing for you too, Porta. So I wish you a quick death without too much suffering, even though you deserve a slow and painful one, and a candle will burn for you in the cathedral of my heart when you have passed on. You should be proud, man! You are going to fall in defence of the Fatherland on ground soaked in historical traditions!'

'You're not a human being, Wolf. You're a non-com soaked in primitive bloody Army traditions, and a typical Wehrmacht product,' shouts Porta viciously, to hide his growing fear.

'I haven't got the time, Obergefreiter Porta,' states Wolf, coldly. 'What about the rest of your tractors, and your guns? I'll take them off your hands, if you like, for old times' sake!'

'I can use your services,' Porta smiles a superior smile, 'but they can't pay for my vehicles. Let's do it a different way. I'll buy your supplies – on bills of exchange!'

Wolf falls off the gun, laughing madly.

'You've missed your vocation. You should've been a clown in a Goddamn circus, you should. People'd die laughing. Bills of *exchange! Yours!* Five miles from the Kremlin! *And* when you're on your way up the steps of the scaffold for your last shave! Think I've got softening of the brain? Me, who's never had an iron pot on it in my whole career! I didn't go into the bloody Army to fight for Führer, Family and Fatherland. I came in to do *business*. Bills! Not this boy! A mortgage maybe, if I'm pushed, and then only for officers from Oberst upwards and against security in land or property.'

'Anybody ever tell you what a giant-sized shitbag you are?' asks Porta, sarcastically.

'Plenty,' grins Wolf self-satisfied. 'I've got it in writing too, but I'm like the Yids, I don't give a fuck long as the money drops on time. So, Porta, what about those tractors and guns?'

The field telephone breaks in. Porta lifts the receiver as nonchalantly as the president of a world-famous bank. He listens for a moment with closed face. Then replaces the receiver on the hook with an elegant turn of the wrist.

'The market's closed,' he grins with much satisfaction. 'No more deals, *tovaritsch* Wolf! Back to your hole in Libau, son! Your continued presence here is turning my stomach. You are a stinking skunk!'

'What'd they say on the blower?' asks Wolf, inquisitively, his face slowly reddening.

'GEKADOS,'* smiles Porta, slyly. 'You'd have a stroke if I told you!'

'If you believe everything you hear through that crazy bloody ear-trumpet, you're stupider than I'd thought,' shouts Wolf, angrily.

'Sail off to your Royal Swedish Democracy,' jeers Porta. 'Your presence bores me! Buy a mirror and take a good look at yourself, my son. You'll never go for a shit with the lights on anymore.' Wolf rises threateningly. He looks like a dangerous carnivore whose prey has slipped away right under its nose.

'If you're planning anything clever just let me put you straight! Wherever you go I'll have you by the balls, boy!'

'Careful, even if you do belong to the *Herronvolk* you can burst if you blow yourself up too big,' says Porta, chortling with merriment. He pulls out a pack of cards and begins to deal.

'Feed 'im a dose of rat poison,' suggests Tiny, confidentially.

'You may be big and strong as an ox, but you're dumber'n a stillborn calf,' roars Wolf, losing control of himself. 'I could crush you like a sick nit when and where I felt like it!'

'Wicked bastard, ain't 'e?' says Tiny casually, playing a king.

A squad of Brandenburgers wearing Russian ski-trooper uniforms reports to the Old Man. A little later a small slant-eyed Mongol arrives, his face split in a white-toothed grin. He is wearing an NKVD captain's uniform, short black leather caps, a leather belt with two cross-straps, and a large Nagan on his left hip. Under his arm he is hugging a *kalashnikov* like a happy mother holding her infant child.

'Vasilij,' he introduces himself, shaking hands all round. 'By *Kunfu*,† here stink good of schnapps,' he cries, sniffing loudly. 'Vasilij like schnapps too! Bad pinic no schnapps!' He

---

* GEKADOS (Geheime Kommandosachen) (German): Military Secrets.
† *Kunfu*: Confucius.

194

empties Porta's bottle rapidly, and rolls himself in a ground-sheet. 'We no go through Communist position until all dark. Best at Starodanil where weak-minds from Karabats lying. They shit pants when dark comes. We come say: "Dam big NKVD check!" They frightened. People from Karabats always on wrong side. Deal with traitors and sell grifas.'

'Sounds interesting,' says Porta, expectantly.

'Now I sleep!' decides Vasilij, pulling his camouflage jacket up over his head. 'Two o'clock you wake up. I lead you dangerous action. Big boom Moscow. Then you fuck me all ways, on foot, on 'orseback!'

Thirty seconds later he is snoring loudly.

'Where the hell did that odd-ball come from?' asks Barcelona wonderingly.

'He ought to be liquidated,' considers Heide, not troubling to conceal his disgust.

The Old Man unfolds a town plan of Moscow and begins to discuss our task with a Brandenburger Feldwebel.

'*Hals und Beinbruch!*'* says Oberst Hinka. He has come out to see us off.

'Get back in one piece. *Don't* let yourselves get captured in those Russian uniforms. You all know what they do to agents and raiders.'

'When I was with 35 Panzer Regiment at Bamberg I had the job of carrying water to the married officers' quarters,' Porta is telling a story as we lie in the pre-action area. 'We had a strict CO insisted that all officers parade with their companies for inspection, at 7 o'clock every morning. At 7:30 I started to deliver water to the first of the quarters, Leutnant Pütz, 3 Company. I'd usually finished shagging his wife by 8 o'clock, and moved on, with my water to Feldwebel Ernst's quarters. *His* wife'd had as much as she could take by a little after 8.30. By 10.30 I'd had so much high-grade officer cunt I was near turning homo at the thought of more. But at 2 o'clock me and my little friend had to start our rounds again.

* *Hals und Beinbruch* (German): 'Break your neck and leg.' An expression equivalent to 'Good luck,' by opposites.

195

That was when I had to beat the sofa for Major Linkowsky's wife, who was a very religious woman. She and her husband were a temporary posting to us from 1 Cavalry at Königsberg. She told me every day that she never got anything at Königsberg but she was making up for it at Bamberg. It was in Bamberg I started to collect panties and this caused trouble when the Secret Police turned up looking for some larcenist or other. The snap-brim and leather coat boys ordered a general search, and turned up my collection, all with names on. The wives, of course, didn't recognize any of them as theirs. But one of the snap-brims was an Obergefreiter who hated officers. They sent the whole collection to the Police Central Laboratories in Berlin and after the Alex-boys had had a long strong sniff at them the good ladies had had it. When our CO, Oberst Hackmeister, had spelled his way through the Reischkriminalpolizei report they say he shot straight up out of his boots and swallowed his monocle on the way. It ended up as a window-pane in his arse, and it required the attention of an Army glazier to get it out. All the officers who'd been cuck'd were given punishment postings to distant border regiments. Some wanted a divorce but Army Personnel forbade it. Officers should be able to maintain discipline in their own homes. If necessary, chastity belts could be supplied from QM stores.'

'What about you?' asks Barcelona inquisitively. 'You couldn't stay at Bamberg after all that!'

'No, they sent me to Westphalia to 11 Panzer at Paderborn but I was never a water carrier again. I was turned into a machine-gunner in an experimental battalion. That wasn't so bad, either, I oiled locks. We had a Hauptfeldwebel in 9 Company who collected pubic hair. He used to keep it in small boxes, with a photo of the scalped lady inside the lid.'

'Shut it,' orders the Old Man crossly. 'We want to sleep. To hell with you and your Bamberg bitches!'

Three hours later an infantryman wakes us.

'Whassa time?' ask the Old Man sleepily.

'Two-thirty, Herr Feldwebel,' stammers the unhappy man.

'You were supposed to call us at 2 o'clock,' shouts the Old Man sharply, pulling on his boots.

'You've been asleep on guard, soldier,' states Heide, with the look of an avenging angel. 'I'm booking you for neglect of duty. It can cost you your head!' Heide loves executions.

Barcelona gets up slowly and stretches himself, so that his bones crack. The Brandenburger Feldwebel's submachine-gun falls to the ground. Immediately a row starts.

We slip through the lines and march straight down into a Russian trench.

'Captain Vasilij raves at the Russian lieutenant in real NKVD style, and threatens him with Kolyma.

It begins to blow. Snow drives into our faces in great clouds. I have a pebble in my boot. At first I try to forget it but this only makes me think about it all the time. It feels like a boulder. I sit down by a milestone and feel hard done by.

'*Qu'as tu*?' asks the Legionnaire irritably, bending over me.

'Got a stone in my boot.'

'*Mille diables*, is that all!' he curses. 'You ought to try Germersheim where you do morning drill with your boots filled with gravel.'

He helps me off with the boot. The stone is so tiny you wouldn't believe it. Such a little thing to be so painful.

'*Tu es con*,' he jeers. 'To cry over so little!'

At the Danilovskoye cemetery we take a rest after an exhausting march into the teeth of the storm.

Porta suggests shooting dice but nobody feels like it so he plays against himself and wins every time.

'Soon make big bang,' explains Vasilij, in high good humour, 'but watch out for real NKVD devils. They catch, German turnip roll. War over!'

As we double over the broad Varshavskoe Street a long column of T-34s rolls past us, so closely that we can feel the warmth of the exhausts like a hot wind on our faces.

'Why can't we move along the river bank?' asks the Old Man, crossly. 'It'd be a lot quicker and we could move under cover of the warehouses.'

'*Nix karosch*,'* shouts Vasilij, grinning his big, shiny-toothed grin. 'Dam dangerous part! Dumb German go there, big knife shave turnip in Ljubjanka. NKVD devils watch good. Big German General say Vasilij: "you show dam commando soldiers factory. They make boom!" Vasilij always do what general say. You no do what Vasilij say, Feldwebel, Vasilij trot off to big general, say you traitor! Hitler please with Vasilij, give big Order. People make big eyes when Vasilij home in Chita.'

'I'm beginning to love that yellow monkey,' grins Porta appreciatively.

'Nip 'is ol' nut off an' you've got yourself a free pass into Paradise,' considers Tiny. 'I don't reckon friend Abraham loves '*im* much.'

'I do *not* like him,' says Heide, sulkily. 'He's not sincere.'

'Do you really like anyone, apart from your Führer?' asks Porta frigidly.

'What do you mean by that?' comes threateningly from Heide.

'I mean you'd kiss old laced-up boots on the arse if you got the chance!'

'Laced-up boots is insulting to the Führer,' states Heide. 'It is a disparaging reference to the Austrian people.'

'Austrian people?' asks Stege. 'What's that? It's called *Ostmark* now!'

'His Führer had to call it that to make himself a German citizen!' grins Porta noisily.

'That's the worst I've heard yet,' gasps Heide excitedly. 'It'll cost you your nut, boy, when my Duty Report gets to the NSFO!'

'Let's get on, Vasilij,' the Old Man hurries him impatiently. 'Let's get that factory blown up and get back. I don't like wandering about here like this!'

'You reach dam shitty Zim factory soon enough,' Vasilij assures him. '*Kunfu* say: "Better go quickly, come safe to

* *Nix karosch* (Russian): No good.

goal." We no *Tekaui*,* reach *Beijing*† next Sunday. We go big circle. Go straight way like you want and bom! bom! bom! dumb German turnip get hole in!'

'All right then let's go in a big circle,' says the Old Man wearily, 'as long as we reach the factory today and can be back early tomorrow morning. I don't fancy this caper!'

'You got shit in turnip? We no see factory before three days. We wait, all dark, send shitty factory up in sky. Today dam big guard wait us. NKVD know crazy German about. When we not come today, tomorrow, they think we no come at all! They think we go home.'

'How the devil do *you* know what they'll think?' asks the Branderburger Feldwebel wonderingly.

'Mongol man know many things. He know what crazy Commie pig think. I see spy bitch in German lines. When me back, dam *prasstitutka*‡ get funny long rope round neck.'

'Why in the world didn't you report it immediately?' asks the Legionnaire, not understanding.

'Only idiot kill spy on spot,' explains Vasilij, with a cunning expression in his shoe-button eyes. 'Wise Mongol man from Harbin keep watch Commie bitch. She show us other spies, we blow hole in all one time. Very simple!'

'Do you mean we're going to be here in Moscow for several days?' asks the Old Man, in a voice which clearly shows his misgivings.

'Moscow nice city. People come dam long way see dam nice city!'

'What a nice feller, he is to be sure,' Porta laughs heartily. 'If his countrymen are all like him, I'll never go to China!'

'Listen, Vasilij,' says the Old Man, bending over the map of Moscow. 'Why not go down Starodanil Boulevard and cross over towards the docks along the Moscow river?'

'You crazy,' grins Vasilij friendlily. '*Mulkt sakt manna hail*§

---

* *Tekuai* (Chinese): Express train.
† *Beijing* (Chinese): Peking.
‡ *Prasstitutka* (Russian): Whore.
§ *Mulkt sakt* etc. (Tibetan): Zone strictly out of bounds.

You get Commie bullet in Nazi gut and factory no go boom up to sky. Great Kunfu tell Vasilij: "Go NKVD, say Vasilij catch bad German Vasilij hero with big Soviet Order!" You go Starodanil Boulevard me no know you. Mongol man never so dumb as dumb white man think.'

'Don't hide his opinion of us very well, does he?' grins Porta.

We hide in a little park which runs alongside the Boulevard whilst a large section of troops marches by.

'What do you suggest then, Vasilij?' asks the Old Man. 'You're in command.'

'*Njet, njet, tovaritsch* Feldwebel, I no like have command. Him general say: "Vasilij you take commando soldier to power station. You bring survivors back to Hitler Army after make big boom." Me shitty easy what you do. You say: "Vasilij go home." We go back, no carry out orders. Vasilij tell NKVD devils all he know about action. Get Red Star on chest. Maybe too pardon from *tjurjma*.'*

'What do you say, you yellow devil?' shouts Porta, flying up. 'Have you broken gaol?'

'*Da, da,*' Vasilij admits pleasantly as if it were the best joke in the world that an escaped convict was our guide in Moscow.

'All clever *plljudji*† put in cage. Big honour in Soviet paradise.'

'*Merde alors!*' cries the Legionnaire, visibly shaken. 'Do you mean to say you've broken gaol and there's a posse on your track?'

'*Da, da,*' grins Vasilij, quite unruffled. 'That make me dam faithful guide for Nazis. Him general never ask: "You be in *tjurjma*?" My father, big wise Mongol, live in Chita. He say to eighteen sons: You never admit you *strafnik* if crazy pig no ask." Him general ask: "Can you show way, Vasilij?" and I say: "*Da, da!*" Me say: "*Njet,*" me tell big lie.'

---

* *Tjurjma* (Russian): Prison.
† *Plljudji* (Russian): People.

'*Bande des cons*,' groans the Legionnaire. 'A wanted criminal leading the way. Allah have mercy on us!'

'Be easy, soldier,' consoles Vasilij. 'Crazy cop no time look for *strafnik* leave gaol no say goodbye. *Politsyja** out get shot Hitler soldier. This good thing!'

'What were you in for?' asks Barcelona interestedly. 'Nothing serious, I hope.'

'Vasilij good man. No do wicked thing. Only little thing. Cut throat dumb, shitty woman sleep with Mayor and sell Vasilij horse to Jew in Chita.'

'Wife-murder!' gasps Porta, 'and that he calls a little thing! God knows what he'd call a big thing!'

'Can we trust the little yellow ape at all?' growls Heide suspiciously. 'He doesn't even attempt to hide that it'd be to his advantage to turn us in to the NKVD.'

'Don't be nervous, *mon ami*,' the Legionnaire quiets him. 'I know these little devils from Indochina. They came to us through the Gobi Desert. Some stayed a long while.

'If they didn't like it with us they just quietly went over to the enemy and changed uniforms. They are mad about their God. Most of them carry a small image of Buddha on their person. It's forbidden in the Soviet. That's why they hate the Reds and everything to do with them. If *we* don't do what he wants he'll turn us over to the NKVD or the Gestapo without a qualm. He'll choose sides according to his own best advantage.

'Chopping the head off an unfaithful wife is nothing to him.' He turns to Vasilij and fires off a mouthful of Chinese.

Vasilij doubles up with laughter, pulls a *kukhri*! from his waistband and swings it proudly round his head.

'I thought so,' laughs the Legionnaire, convinced. 'He's been three years with the Ghurkas.'

'And five years in the nick,' notes Porta sarcastically. 'How old *is* that little yellow orang-utan, anyway?'

'*Je ne sais pas*,' answers the Legionnaire with a shrug. 'He

---

* *Politsyja* (Russian): Police.

probably doesn't know himself. Most of them hardly seem to age at all after they reach twenty-five. Even when they've got to be a hundred they still look twenty-five. They use vegetable lotions on their skin, live almost exclusively on raw meat, and are eternally happy. They'll still grin while you're hanging them. As long as they have a Buddha image about them nothing else matters. Being punished for cutting the throat of an unfaithful wife is something he understands as little as if it had been a goat he'd slaughtered. The woman is a possession. Something he owns, like a piece of furniture or livestock.'

'And this is the man we've got to entrust our lives to?' moans Stege despairingly. 'He'll sell us out as soon as he gets the chance!'

'His hatred of the Soviets will cause him to be faithful to us,' continues the little Legionnaire confidently. 'That hatred could send him a hundred times round the world on foot if need be.'

'We've no choice at all,' says the Old Man, shortly, and turns to Vasilij who is rolling a cigarette from a leaf of a German Bible.

'What do you suggest?' he asks. 'We have agreed that you make the decisions.'

'You clever man. Not so squarehead like other German,' says Vasilij happily. 'We make big swing, come nice old bridge, big tourist attraction. On other side river Tanganskaye Prison. There we find shitty old NKVD. They know all people afraid big political cage. Only crazy idiot willing go near.'

' 'E's right enough about idiots an' prisons, anyway,' cries Tiny pleased.

'NKVD man think same way,' says Vasilij enthusiastically, throwing his arms out wide. 'When funny Russians march by they think we guard on torpedo factory in Kozhukhovo so they no put out dirty big policeman hand and ask for *propusk*.* I walk like big boss, salute like fine Soviet officer salute who want lick arse NKVD.'

* *Propusk* (Russian): Pass.

202

'What happens when we've got past the prison?' asks the Old Man, worriedly, pulling his fur hood up over his head so that the large Red Star is hidden.

'Then we march towards power station,' explains Vasilij, as if he were sketching out a tour of the sights of Moscow. 'We go down Dubrovsky Passage. Go past NKVD guard and take short-cut, over old train track and all that shit, to Ugrezhskaya Station. NKVD guard no see us. They sleep always. Me and good friend steal lorry with lot nice things there one time. NKVD find out what happen three days later. They sleep. Very dangerous street. They think nothing happen and most time they right. Only not when NKVD come bring friends.' He bends forward, laughing loudly.

'Why can't we take the straight road down Simonovoslo-bodsk Street?' asks the Old Man, irritated by Vasilij's pidgin. 'Ugrezhskaya Station is well out of our way.'

'Vasilij think you clever man, *tovaritsch* Feldwebel! NKVD shitty big factory down by Moscow river where make secret things. Straight way forbidden way, *Nejmtsamat!** Also forbidden see secret shit they make.'

'What the devil *do* they make?' asks the Brandenburger Feldwebel, interestedly.

'Good friend of Vasilij from Chita, NKVD lieutenant, he tell Vasilij what Soviet make in secret factory.'

'What the hell *is* it, then?' asks Stege, impatiently.

'Not good German turnips know too much,' Vasilij brushes the question aside. 'Only tell Nazi scientist. Him pay good. When war over, me share all with shitty NKVD lieutenant from Chita.'

'I never could take to chaps who grin all the time,' says Barcelona. 'They're false as Majorca pearls!'

'We *not* go along Moscow river,' continues Vasilij, untroubledly. 'Many wicked NKVD. We come they shoot like hell. German soldier get filled Soviet lead. NKVD catch and torture so bad you glad when shaved with big knife in

---

* *Nejmtsamat* (Mongolian): Strictly forbidden.

Ljubjanka. Better take long way round with Vasilij than lose hair and German turnip both.'

We aren't far past the churchyard when we run straight into the arms of a three-man NKVD patrol. Their leader, a very young and very energetic corporal, with a battle-stripe, puts forward his hand in the international gesture of police all over the world – Let me see your papers!

The corporal addresses himself officiously to the Brandenburger Feldwebel who doesn't understand a word.

Vasilij pushes him to one side, gives the corporal a friendly pat on the arm and hands him a Russian soldier's identity book. A tank section rattles down the street, almost hidden in the driving snow.

The corporal rants at Vasilij, banging the book in his hand angrily. Something seems to be missing. Despite German thoroughness they have probably forgotten a rubber stamp somewhere. Two things the Russians and the Germans have in common; a superfluity of paper, and rubber stamps.

'*Job Tvojemadj!*' curses Vasilij, tapping his Captain Commissar's red star.

'*Propusk comandatura,*' howls the corporal, beside himself.

'Be a good boy, now, *brat*,* or I'll have to ask my Commandant to send you to Kolyma with ten kicks up the backside first for delaying an important mission!' Vasilij commands.

'*Propusk!*' screams the corporal stubbornly, putting out his big policeman's hand, with the thick, black leather glove, again. Vasilij throws up his hands hopelessly and unbuttons his fur jacket as if he were finding some papers.

'You brought it on yourself, *brat*,' he says sorrowfully. 'Your mother will cry for you!'

A blade flashes and the corporal's head is rolling along the pavement, the cigarette still between his lips. The headless body sways a moment, and a jet of blood spouts from the neck.

* *Brat* (Russian): Brother.

The Legionnaire and Tiny are on the two paralysed NKVD men like lightning. Combat knives glint. *Kalashnikovs* rattle to the pavement. A column of T-34s roars past. Leatherclad heads can vaguely be seen poking up from the turrets.

We push the bodies into a cellarway where they are quickly covered by snow.

Vasilij kicks the corporal's head through the window of a ground-floor flat, where it frightens the life out of two sleeping cats. He slaps his thighs and roars with laughter at the sight of the cats going spitting and squalling through the snow.

'Let's get out of here,' gasps the Old Man, shocked.

We rush down narrow side-streets, crawl over fences and find ourselves suddenly in the middle of a mob of people, being held in check by an NKVD section with submachine-guns at the ready. The end of the street is blocked by two T-34s.

'Shit!' whispers Vasilij. 'Crazy arseholes been looting. NKVD catch, now make example. Shoot one in three so Moscow people understand looting risky work.'

An NKVD man calls to us authoritatively.

Vasilij reports himself smartly as being a guard officer on duty.

'*Propusk,*' snarls the NKVD officer, coldly unimpressed, and looks casually at our papers. 'Get your people together and get the hell out of here!' he orders.

'We're on our way, *tovaritsch,*' grins Vasilij, and begins to curse and swear at us in true Russian Army style.

The first civilians are already being liquidated as we turn the corner. Looters get short shrift. In Berlin as well as Moscow. Tomorrow their names will be posted on red handbills on the street corners as a warning to others.

'See the way 'e lopped the 'ead off the NKVD corporal,' says Tiny respectfully. 'Alois the Axe from Bernhard-Noecht Strasse couldn't 'ave done it better, an' 'e was good, when in practice. Nine 'eads 'e took off before the bleedin' Kripos diddled 'im. Nass an' 'is blood'ounds was really after grifas smugglers and 'ad just drove into the elevator at Gate 3 on Landungsbrücke when out of a dark corner comes a 'ore's 'ead 'oppin' an' dancin' right up to the feet of Inspector Nass. I see it myself. I was just on the way with a basketful of fish.'

'What the devil? Have you dealt in fish as well?' asks Porta, wonderingly.

'I was in Green Gunther's 'aulage set-up. All the 'erring was filled with grifas. I 'ad to keep kickin' all the time at one of Nass's bleedin' police dogs as kept sniffin' away like a mad thing at me an' my delivery bike. Nass an' the Kripo bulls thought it was the fish 'e was after. Schaefer's with a bit of Dobermann in 'em are mad on *Gefüllte Fische*,* the Yid scoff. They won't 'ave Dobermann's as police dogs no more 'cause they reckon they're imitation Schaefer's bred special by international Jewry. I was sittin' one evenin' mindin' my own business, in "Wind Force II", when in comes four bleedin' great Yid Dobermanns drippin' at the jaws. They'd been after a coupla German crooks all the way over from Gänsemarkt, but crossin' the 'Ansa Platz they'd suddenly got wind of the *Brust Flanken*† our 'alf-Jew cook was puttin' together, an' off they went, an' to 'ell with the villains. They shot into that kitchen so fast there was no doubt left they 'ad Jew blood in 'em. This cook'd just got 'is discharge from the army.

'The Wehrmacht slung 'im outa the skeet-club soon as they found 'im to 'ave false blood in 'is veins. An' was 'e sorry? Not on our life 'e wasn't! The *Brust Flanken* was on for that very reason. Any'ow the Kripo bulls went barmy when they found their four-legged mates sittin' round this Yid cook an' 'is oven. The immitation Schaefers were discharged without pension. They shoulda been glad they didn't get the bleedin' gas-chamber.

'"In the name of the Führer, I arrest you all!" screamed Nass, wakin' up the echoes in the elevator.

'But they soon let us loose again, when they found Alois

---

* *Gefüllte Fische* (German): Stuffed fish.

† *Brust Flanken* (Yiddish): Corned beef – Beef a la mode or Allemand.

the Axe rolled up under a lorry. Nass just got 'is napper out the way of the axe in time. If 'e 'adn't it'd've been the first time for years anybody's seen Otto Nas without 'is snap-brim on. They got at least twenty pairs of cuffs, chains and Gawd knows what else on Alois before you could say Jack Robinson. When we got to the bottom they threw us all out of the elevator. Nass an' 'is posse couldn't get back to the station fast enough, to get the news out to the reporters. They'd been after the Sankt Pauli axe murderer for four years an' 'ere 'e was served up on a plate with all the evidence needed, ready for Marabu's* executioner. Nass got 'imself a big swelled-up napper all right that day. They called 'im sharpwitted in all the papers. 'E never told 'em just 'ow it 'appened, you see. They even give 'im a decoration for it. 'E was on special duty at 'eadquarters as a luxury inspector on permanent day duty, but they threw 'im out before long. 'Is worn-out old leather coat didn't fit in at the mornin' conferences.'

A long column of strangely uniformed soldiers went past us, moving towards the bridges over the Moscow.

'Suicide companies,' Vasilij explains with a casual gesture. 'Hole-in-head from Tanganskaya.† Them pardoned. No go Kolyma. Shoot crazy Germans instead. Stalin clever man. Him not shoot shitty politicals stick neck out ask better deal. Stalin say: Them want die hero. Let crazy Germans knock off. Soviet no problem, no charge.'

At Pavlet Station there is a road block swarming with NKVD. Even large military units moving in order of march are checked. A bulldog of a colonel with straps crossed over his chest steps towards us with a *kalashnikov* under his arm.

'Holy Virgin, be merciful to us,' groans the Old Man, resignedly.

At the corner of Marko Street four officers are neck-shot. The bodies are thrown into an open lorry waiting on the pavement. Bloody icicles hang from its sideboards.

We disappear up Tatarsk Street with Vasilij, grinning

* Marabu: See *'Assignment Gestapo.'*
† Tanganskaya: Notorious Russian political prison.

happily, in the lead. Completely unworried he leads us to the middle of the bridge where they are sluicing people through the barriers.

'It won't go,' groans Julius Heide, fearfully. 'They only need to ask one of us something, anything at all, and we're lost. The Red Army don't enlist deaf mutes!'

'I'm playin' barmy,' declared Tiny, rolling his eyes.

'Not necessary,' says Julius. 'You're born to the part. Can't understand why they haven't gassed you long ago with the rest of the mental defectives.'

The Old Man and the Legionnaire ready their Mpis. They obviously expect to have to fight.

'If they uncover us, use your peacemakers for all you're worth!' whispers the Old Man. 'It's our only chance! If they catch us in Russian uniforms they'll cut us to pieces slowly before they let us die!'

'Amen,' says Porta, crossing himself. 'Light a candle for poor old Porta.'

Even Vasilij seems to grow thoughtful after having talked to an NKVD sergeant, sitting half-asleep on a vehicle.

'Shitty NKVD catch other German Brandenburger commando,' he whispers. 'You ready fix with chopper, make many bodies! Now come big row! NKVD know crazy Nazis on tourist trip Moscow! Hell, shitty much danger for us. Come here phony paper, stolen uniform!'

'What a bloody prospect,' whispers Porta, nervously. 'I'd rather be at home. Let's fall out smartly and let Ivan keep this bloody rotten power station!'

The Old Man considers it and looks enquiringly at Vasilij.

Vasilij replies with a wide, white smile which can mean anything or nothing.

'No-o-o,' says the Old Man, thoughtfully. 'That yellow chimpanzee isn't just a guide, he's also our jailer. He'll let us be liquidated if we give way now.'

Vasilij grins and slaps the Old Man on the shoulder.

'You very clever, Feldwebel. Wise man go with Vasilij so German turnip stay on shoulders!'

'Long as you don't lose yours,' mumbles the Old Man ominously.

'Me no care about own turnip,' grins Vasilij, happily. 'Me no have face longer great Kunfu want. When Kunfu make choice you go.' He pulls Tiny by the arm. 'You strong Russian bear, smash Red skull one blow. You stay with Vasilij, come back to village with turnip on, play games with *djaevusch-ka*.* You no do what I say, you choke on old whore *rjaegully*!'†

Tiny, who doesn't understand half of it, nods violently and swears a solemn oath of allegiance with three fingers raised.

How we got through I can't remember. A sergeant wipes me across the face, which all the green crosses seem to find amusing.

When we finally reach the Kozhukhovo quarter a swarm of our own Stukas come howling out of low cloud cover.

Heavy bombs explode all around us, pulverizing buildings and the railway area. Finally they saturate the district with incendiaries and sweep it with their machine-guns.

'Stukas do work for us,' whoops Vasilij, enthusiastically. 'All NKVD in cellar, protect Commie lives. Now we fix plastic bomb, blow Stalin factory up under NKVD arse. Walk back Hitler army, have good sleep ready next trip.'

A Brandenburger Gefreiter falls between two concrete blocks and when we try to pull him free one of the blocks slips and catches him. His screams go echoing through the night.

The Brandenburger Feldwebel puts his pistol to his neck. It's a silenced Beretta specially made for the job. Commando soldiers are finished if they can't keep up. Nobody must be allowed to fall into enemy hands alive.

We roll more concrete over the spot where the Gefreiter's body lies jammed. Perhaps their patrols won't find him right away. The bombs have broken down the wall round the Zim

* *Djaevuschka* (Russian): Girls.
† *Rjaegully* (Russian): menstruation.

factory at several points. We go in from Lizina Street. We should have gone through Tyufalev Street but Vasilij, who has reconnoitred it, says we can't go that way. There's a whole column of light armour halted there. Whether they're really an NKVD guard company watching for saboteurs he can't say. But the vehicles have no corps designation and are manned. Even with our two Degtyarev anti-tank rifles we can't take on these armoured vehicles in a fight. We decide to go the other way.

Vasilij agrees with the Old Man and the Brandenburger Feldwebel that we march in in column of threes like a unit. He thinks his NKVD captain's uniform will get us in, and we have, in any case, a *propusk* giving us priority permission to enter the Zim works. There's a risk they may have instituted a password, and we can't guess what *that* is. It can be the most logical, or the craziest, combination. They might, for example, shout 'Ivan the Terrible' and the right answer be 'Dead rat'.

Vasilij takes a look at the entrance point. We're lying between some goods wagons in the Kozhukhovo Station, from where we can see them moving the wounded from Kashirskaya Hospital which has been set on fire by the incendiaries.

'Gawd, take a look at the cunt in there,' mumbles Tiny, who is lying there watching the nurses through artillery glasses. 'Jesus Christ almighty what a fuckin' arse *she's* got on 'er. It's screamin' for it. Gawd, 'ow I could rip it up 'er right now.'

A short silent struggle for the glasses ensues.

'Jesus me old rollockers are playing up!' giggles Porta. 'It's been a long time since me old pal's had a new fur-coat on!'

'You shoulda banged it up that sow at Klimskaja the way I done before we slaughtered it,' says Tiny, 'Just shut your eyes an' imagine it's a lovely bit of 'Amburg cunt as's gone to a ball without 'er drawers on.'

'Shitty NKVD go up through hair,' Vasilij comes up panting. He's just been on an investigatory tour. 'Many dumb Commies lose life in air raid, but we no make big boom now. Them take wounded away. NKVD come with armoured cars. Me think good wait one hour. Kunfu say: "Never move too fast." Take easy, keep turnip on shoulders. Me learn codeword. We march in to attention. Move in one hour, maybe keep head while yet. Them shout "war". We shout "green apple" and march on. Then not look close. Shitty pig colonel say password while me listen under car. Them know crazy Brandenburger in Moscow. Him cut prick off and eat without salt, say shitty colonel. So not good pet prisoner. Better more legs fast when bomb go up. Them be crazy in head, chase shitty dumb German all over Moscow.'

'Shouldn't wonder when we've just blown a factory out from under 'em,' remarks Stege drily.

'What you see?' asks Vasilij pushing his machine-gun into Tiny's shoulder. All this time the big man has been lying with the field glasses glued to his eyes.

'Soviet cunt,' breathes Tiny, with a lustful grin. 'When they go up the stairs, I can see up their skirts. Should've joined the fuckin' medicine-men. Be more fun stickin' glass cigars up dirty great soldiers brownies than racin' round blowin' up bleedin' factories.'

'Vasilij have little look at nanny! Long time since little boy have good time in nice warm house.'

Before Tiny realizes properly what is happening Vasilij has taken the glasses. But he soon has them back.

'Me make suggestion,' says Vasilij, 'make clever plan. Take Commie nurse back home Hitler Army. Say them know secret medicine things. We have good fun before we give to General. They shout rape, we shout Dirty Commie propaganda. What you say?'

'He ought to be in the Ministry of Propaganda,' grins Porta. 'I could find it in my heart to promote him brother to me.'

'When shitty war over, peace break out, we throw chopper down, you go with Vasilij on big trip my cousin Hong Kong. Him have eating-house "Little Hen." Many China man come selling forbidden thing. Cousin make big eating. First serve *Tang-ts'u-yu*. That be sweet pickled fish. Then we eat beautiful *Fuh-rung-chi-p-ien*. That be velvet hen with shrimp. Now finish first course, give good appetite *Pao-yang-reo*, back of sheep with vegetable. We take little rest now, go then to *Cheng-chiao-tze*, steamed spring roll. Now many pretty nanny come from joy-house and play game with us, we wash throat with *sake*.'

'Can you learn to eat with chopsticks?' asks Tiny doubtfully. He tries to pick up a piece of ice with two bayonets, but keeps dropping it. 'Can't even pick up a bleedin' piece of ice,' he breaks out irritably. ' 'Ow the 'ell'd you ever get a mouthful of rice 'tween your choppers?'

'Let's move,' says the Old Man, tightening his shoulder straps.

Detonators and P-2 sticks are shared out. As soon as the oiled paper covering is torn from a couple of sticks of explosive a heavy odour of marzipan spreads around us.

'Queer how a little roll of dough like this can blow up a whole factory,' says Barcelona, pushing pencil detonators into sawdust bags.

'No fumbling now!' says the Old Man, sternly. 'If you get wounded and can't keep up, then finish yourselves. The straight trip to Heaven's better than the detour through the NKVD interrogation cells!'

'You sound like a bloody parson,' jeers Heide. 'You forgot the Amen!'

'I wouldn't in the least mind leaving *you* behind with a wound,' snarls the Old Man. 'It'd be interesting to see whether you'd have the nerve to finish yourself! Wouldn't you think the Führer'd expect it of you?'

'They'll mash our bollocks for us,' says Porta, laconically.

'They'll have a job with Tiny. His are as tough as the balls on a granite boar. They'll have to machine 'em down with special tools!'

'Shitty NKVD got such tool,' Vasilij informs them, happily. 'NKVD got *all* tool for them job in Ljubjanka. Very

212

clever people. Got all thing make hole-in-head German sing pretty song for NKVD.'

The back of the factory is on fire. Three large fire-engines stand just inside the gates, and brass-helmeted firemen are rolling our hoses.

'The things you do see in wartime!' whispers Tiny, thrilled. 'I love fire-engines. I'd really rather've been a fireman 'n join the Army. But they wouldn't 'ave me 'cause I'd 'ad a trip inside for a bit of arson as didn't even catch light properly an' was only attempted really.'

'What were *you* trying to burn?' asks Porta, with interest.

'Davidswacht Police Station! Them wicked bastards caught me red'anded when I was stackin' it. A trick cyclist save me from the nick. Said I 'ad a complex about coppers in uniforms. If 'e'd said I 'ad a complex about Inspector Otto bleedin' Mass 'e'd 'ave been a lot closer. I ain't really got anythin' against Schupos.* There's many a little warnin' note I've 'ah stuck in me 'and when I been called in to 'ave a coffee with Otto. I 'eard, not so long since from a chum from 'Amburg, as Nass was due for a trip. 'E'd 'eard 'e was posted to Copen'agen. If 'e does I 'ope the bleedin' Danish underground turns 'is toes up for 'im. If they don't, then they ain't the Vikings there's such a lot o' talk about.'

'Shut your face, Tiny,' whispers the Old Man. 'You're making enough row to be heard in the Kremlin. If those chaps on the gate as much as hear us draw breath in German they'll open up with their choppers straight off.'

'It's bloody dangerous with all these different languages,' mumbles Tiny. 'If everybody talked German there'd be no trouble. The Russians've got you straight away. All they need to do is ask you to say the "Our Father" in Russki and where are you? Out on your arse!'

'Do the Commies all know the "Our Father",' wonders Stege. 'It's supposed to be forbidden.'

'If it's forbidden then everybody in Russian *does* know it,'

---

* Schupo (Schutzpolizei) (German): Uniformed police.

says Porta. 'They learn it from their grandmothers before they can walk even. Old whores always go holy when they're getting towards the end.'

We tramp in step through the gates. No trouble. The Germans and the Russians both goose-step.

An NKVD sergeant stands to attention and salutes Vasilij, who is marching on the flank with his *kalashnikov* regimentally slanted across his chest.

A white finger of light from one of the watch towers falls across us for a moment.

'Arseholes tight, boys,' whispers Porta. 'I can't stand the smell of shit!'

A column passes us. The lieutenant in charge gives Vasilij a comradely slap on the back. They both laugh loudly.

Vasilij rejoins us a little later.

'Him lieutenant much glad. Catch big group Brandenburg commando today. Now they fetch tools grind bollocks off so they tell secret Hitler things! Him lieutenant say me come with. See prisoners make funny faces! No time, say Vasilij, big important job on. That no lie!'

On a large open square at least 500 brand-new T-34's stand ready for the front.

'What about organizing a couple of chariots, so we can roll home first-class?' suggests Porta.

'Not a bad idea,' answers the Old Man in a low voice. 'See if they're armed and munitioned?'

Porta is up in the nearest tank quick as a weasel, whips the hatch off, lays his Mpi aside on the shielding, and is down the hatch in a flash.

Tiny lets his hand run gently over the broad tracks.

'Jesus, boys, what a vehicle! If we'd only 'ad a coupla thousand of *them*! What a battlewaggon! See 'er slippers! An' 'er lovely round arsepart. Just like an expensive French 'ore!'

'With these T-34's Ivan's going to win his war,' says Stege decidedly.

'Victory doubter,' fizzes Heide appalled. 'I intend to make a Duty Report to the NSFO. Comparing German weapons unfavourably to those of the enemy is high treason. It'll cost you your head.'

'Cut it out, Julius,' whispers Tiny, 'or maybe I'll just 'and you over to the NKVD for special treatment!'

'They'll experiment on him and mash him together with an incorrigible Commie. They'll get a whole new Party out of it,' grins Barcelona, pleased at the fantastic thought.

'Him Julius crazy in turnip,' states Vasilij. 'Him no understand *shit*! This way all political idiot. Them think them only one think right think!'

'Not enough in there to fill the hole in a frog's arse,' reports Porta, twisting up out the hatch. 'Not even gas. Julius'll have to *push* us home!'

The whole section grins at the thought.

'Your lot seems nervous,' the Brandenburger Feldwebel turns viciously on the Old Man. 'Reckon I'd as soon do this job alone.'

'Hear, hear!' comes from Porta. 'Let's go!'

'Shut it! Let's get on with it,' snarls the Old Man. 'Twenty minutes from now you're all outside the gates! You know the fuse length of these pencils. The first'll go off in half an hour. Get your fingers out, and *move*! If we're lucky there'll be a bang they can hear in Berlin!'

'What about layin' a chunk o' marzipan under this lot?' asks Tiny. 'Then we won't meet them at the front, anyrate!'

'No,' answers the Old Man. 'Can't afford it. We'd have to fix marzipan on the tracks. Blowing the coffins themselves is no good.'

We move about amongst busy NKVD men and workers. The factory seems to be in wild confusion.

A worker says something to us.

'*Job tvojemadj!*' answers Porta rebuffingly, and the worker hurries on.

I am sweating so much with fear that my clothes stick to my body.

Porta walks quietly into a large power station. An NKVD corporal looks after him curiously. I ready my Mpi and keep an eye on the guard. Even if I have to shoot it won't be heard in the thunder of the machinery. The noise is so violent it makes your head throb with pain. It is unbelievable people can work here day and night without going mad.

Porta comes out of the power station wiping his hands professionally on a piece of waste. He wads it and throws it at the NKVD corporal, with a big grin. The corporal catches it and throws it back. They play at this for a few minutes. I almost scream with nervousness. Porta must be crazy.

I don't know whether I ought to salute the corporal or not. They should have given us a better briefing on Red Army service regulations. I decide to salute in a semi-friendly way. I can't believe he'll bother to book me if I'm wrong so better a casually cheeky salute than none at all. Corporals, no matter the uniform, are always touchy about salutes.

He stares at me for a moment and makes a step forward, stops, nods condescendingly and waves me away. I smile a friendly smile to him but his face remains frozen. An NKVD corporal doesn't smile to a private soldier.

We walk on through the factory as if we owned it. Porta stops and points upwards.

I look up and move quickly to one side. A giant crane is dropping a complete T-34 down on to my head.

A long row of railway wagons is shunted out of the factory. Each wagon carries a T-34. Wet paint gleams in the arcs.

Headquarters should see this, I think to myself. Then maybe they'd realize the Red Army wasn't beaten yet by a long way. In the Zim factory alone there are enough tanks to equip five divisions. When *they* begin to roll then God help the Wehrmacht.

Quickly we jump onto a wagon going to Shop 9. One of my sacks of marzipan begins to slip. A passing worker pushes it back under my arm with a friendly smile. I get a firmer grip on it.

We drop off just before we get to Shop 9. The stillness outside the shops feels like a punch in the solar plexus.

In the Gun Shop, where tank turrets lie in stacks, the noise is deafening. Even a gun-shot would be drowned in it.

Porta is well in front of me, talking and gesticulating with two workpeople. It's impossible to hear what he's saying. Every word is drowned in the noise of the machines. We understand quite a lot of Russian but not enough to manage a conversation.

An electric locomotive shunts railway wagons into the workshop. Firemen with brass helmets run past pulling hand-drawn fire pumps after them.

A railwayman shoves me irritably and shouts something or other. '*Job tvojemadj!*' I scream in his ear.

He shakes his fist at me. I point my *kalashnikov* at him. He immediately becomes friendly and apologetic. An NKVD man with a *kalashnikov* is always in the right.

The flats slacken speed and I duck under them. Porta is pushing a stick of marzipan under a steel-converter from which there comes a thunderous bubbling of molten metal.

A red warning lamp winks, up under the ceiling. What does it mean? Do they know we're here?

A squad of NKVD soldiers hastens across the shop floor and out through a small door.

Porta leads a couple of wires into a fuse-box. My job is to cover him. I've removed the blue caps from the grenades, ready for use. Cheekily he cadges a cigarette from a worker who has just finished rolling it in a little machine.

The man grins and gives him a light. Porta offers him a cheroot.

'*Germanskij ssigara!* he roars.

'*Spasibo*,'* the worker howls back, lighting up and drawing the smoke deeply into his lungs.

In Russia a steelworker like him doesn't get many luxuries. I feel almost like warning him to get out before the explosion. Why couldn't they have sent us to the Kremlin instead. There'd have been some sense in *that* !

* *Spasibo* (Russian): Thanks.

217

A new NKVD squad goes by at the double going in the opposite direction to the previous one. They look excited. Have they caught any of us?

A sergeant stops and waves at us.

Porta makes a Russian gesture which is the equivalent of '*Job tvojemadj!*'

The sergeant hurries on. When a Russian doesn't obey an order he must be covered by another order. Every Russian in uniform knows that.

A line of T-34s move out of the shop on their own tracks. We catch the tow hooks and pull ourselves up by the infantry grip. At the doors NKVD men shout at us and threaten us with their machine-guns. We wave them off with the casual Russian gesture you use when you've got authority behind you.

Two NKVD people try to mount the tank we are on, but the T-34 increases speed and doesn't stop until we reach a side road. A colonel goes down the column counting the tanks. We disappear quickly down a narrow passage which leads us to a large open square.

Porta sits down on a gun carriage and lights a cigarette.

'I think things are getting dangerous,' he says, with a forced smile.

'In three minutes time the first caps'll blow and the whole bloody knocker'll crack open.'

'Got *your* shit in place?' asks the Old Man, coming over to us from the armaments shop.

'You'll find out soon enough,' grins Porta. 'Hold onto your pants, Dad, or you'll get blown clean out of 'em.'

'Let's get out of here,' snarls the Old Man. 'It's getting too warm.'

We jump a passing wagon train and roll out of the great factory. By the ruined flak-tower we drop off. Some of the others are already there.

Tiny shows us a cap with the green NKVD star and a colonel's gold braid on it.

'This'll fetch a packet on the Reeperbahn,' he says happily.

'Eighteen gold teeth, too. The last six I 'ad to smash 'is face in to get!'

'You push deep in snow hole,' says Vasilij, with an Asiatic grin. 'Vasilij set bomb. Chemical grenade. Hold tight to snow. You no want fly Hong Kong, get eat for German puppy-dog in "Little Hen".' A siren sounds alarmingly and NKVD troops swarm suddenly onto the thick walls above our heads.

'*Stoi koi*,'* comes confusedly from the factory streets.

'What the devil are they up to, now?' enquires Porta fearfully, looking up at the high wall.

'Got all yours?' the Old Man asks the Brandenburger Feldwebel.

'Any of you shit missing?' snarls the Feldwebel to his men.

'All here,' comes the reply after a quick count.

'*Mon Dieu*, something must have happened to make them sound the alarm,' says the Legionnaire, nervously.

Shots crash suddenly from the walls. Violent explosions can be heard from the town.

The firing increases. The night is ripped open by an intense, crackling sheet of fire.

'To the river!' screams Barcelona, excitedly.

'*Njet, njet!*' shouts Vasilij, warningly. 'Back railway. Shitty NKVD all run river! Hell much danger meet there! NKVD much annoyed now!'

A flare bursts over our heads and illuminates the scene with a ghastly blue-white light.

Porta drops into a deep bomb crater.

'Lie still!' he whispers warningly to me. 'Don't move!' The flare seems to last for ever. I get cramp in one leg, but daren't move. Finally it dies. I dig myself down into the snow with both hands and feet. A Brandenburg Obergefreiter rolls panting down to us. His face has been slashed open showing his teeth in an unnatural grin.

'Why did *you* volunteer for the Crazy Club?' asks Porta, giving him a suck at a grifa.

* *Stoi koi* (Russian): Stop immediately.

'We were told to,' answers the Obergefreiter. 'It was in Poland. We were only a battalion then.'

'We're always "*told*" to do everything,' sighs Porta tiredly. The whole of the western sky flames a blinding yellow-red. A long thunderous roar, followed by a colossal blast of air, rolls over us, blankets us! Three more explosions follow in quick succession. Then comes a wave of heat like a breath from hell's ovens. Then all is quiet. A whole row of searchlights go up on the walls.

Countless beams wander nervously over the terrain. An LMG hammers long bursts towards the big sewer where the Old Man wouldn't let us take cover.

An automatic cannon starts up, spitting tracer shells over towards the hospital. They have obviously no idea of where we are.

'Two minutes!' whispers the Old Man. 'Get your hands down! It'll be like a volcano erupting!'

The Brandenburger Feldwebel scratches himself nervously under the arm.

A long string of orders can be heard through the firing. Vasilij listens in a half-crouching position.

'NKVD no shoot more! Saboteur pigs caught! Better we go dam quick! NKVD much annoyed now! More annoyed when we blow factory!'

'Stay down!' snarls the Old Man furiously. 'Don't move!'

A new order comes from the tower.

'Him commander say, they no shoot more, go get crazy dam Nazis, shave balls off slow,' translates Vasilij, casually.

A squad of NKVD soldiers doubles out of the gates. Only a few of the guard have emerged when the blow comes. A hollow long drawn-out explosion sounds inside the factory and suddenly the night is light as day. A blinding fountain of flames flashes up towards the sky. For a fraction of a second we see the NKVD soldiers silhouetted against a fantastic blue backdrop. Then they're gone but only to appear again against the background of an even greater white glare. All other sounds are drowned in a long series of thundering explosions. A giant hand seems to lift the ground and a rose-red mushroom cloud roils up and spreads out above the factory. In only seconds everything is changed. We are thrown through the air like leaves and whirled down the slopes leading to the Moscow river. None of us can grasp what is happening. Sobbing, deafened, blinded and with blood streaming down our faces we slowly find one another again.

The first I see is Tiny. He is digging the Old Man out of a giant snowdrift. At first we think the Old Man is dead, but, thank God, he is only knocked-out.

'Some bang!' gasps Porta, crawling out of a deep hole. A shell splinter has cut a permanent parting straight across his thick red hair.

Tiny nearly goes mad when he finds a hole in his water bottle. All the vodka has run out.

Down by the river, and over by the hospital, we find most of ours, but eight Brandenburgers are missing. We find one of them smashed to pieces under an ice-floe. Gerhard, one of ours, a farmer from Friesland, who'd been promised leave when we got back, has disappeared completely. Caught in the final blast wave, probably. All that's left of the Zim factory is a black smoke-cloud rising, thick and choking, from a jumble of concrete blocks and twisted girders. The torpedo factory across the street is a volcano of flame. The snow around us begins to melt, and water floods down from the heights. The heat is almost insupportable. The whole top floor of the hospital has been shorn away as if by a giant knife. The railway station is gone and a telegraph pole has driven through the roof of the ferry-house and down into the ground like a giant spear. We can see no people. They must have been pulverized. Our marzipan has started a terrible chain of explosions. The action has been more effective than could ever have been imagined.

'What in the world happened?' asks the Old Man quietly.

'*Merde alors!* We must have set off some ammunition stores,' guesses the Legionnaire. 'But there must have been highly inflammable material there as well. That chalky-white fire on the other side of the river looks like phosphorous.'

'Poor bastards,' says Barcelona. 'I'm sorry for them. They never wanted this lousy war any more than we did.'

'We bang factory good!' says Vasilij, with a soft chuckling laugh. 'Me see inside. All kaput! Shitty T-34 gone. Railway gone. Biggest boom Vasilij ever hear in life! Get maybe big Order for big boom!'

'Order, *mon camarade!*' snarls the Legionnaire. 'I'll be more than happy to get back alive! Let's get moving! They know we can't be far away.'

'Bye-bye, chums!' shouts Porta. 'Must rush!' He's already on his way in a cloud of snow.

As we cut across the Danilovskaya Quay, air raid sirens begin to howl. Hundreds of searchlights rake the sky, and anti-aircraft guns begin to bark viciously.

'Crazy Commie think we air-raid,' grins Vasilij unworried. 'Best for shitty NKVD it not Brandenburger make big boom! *Natschaljniks** in Kremlin annoyed with crazy NKVD, they let factory go boom under nose! Hard find good excuse save turnip!'

'Listen!' says Porta, stopping abruptly.

'JU 87s, Stukas,' says Tiny.

'No, Heinkels,' contradicts Stege. 'They don't knock like JU 87s.'

'Jesus'n Mary!' says Barcelona. 'There's a hell of a lot of 'em. It won't be pleasant being where they drop their load!'

A fiery umbrella of explosions raises itself above the Kremlin. Most of the AA seems to be placed there.

A nerve-tearing howl splits the night.

'Stukas, all right!' says Porta.

Bomb explosions sound from the northeast.

'Move!' the Old Man hurries us.

'Past Danilov churchyard best,' suggests Vasilij, 'so we come Serpukhovsky Boulevard. Go down to Krovjanka river,

---

* *Natschaljniks* (Russian): Bosses.

so straight home! Gorky Park much shitty Commie soldier! Best not see us. Vasilij think we home morning night. If not, we dead with NKVD! Great *Kunfu* know! Him say, maybe: Shitty Nazi soldier go home, not leave pretty head Ljubjan-ka.'

'All very simple,' sighs the Old Man tiredly. 'With God's help and a little sweat you can manage most things.'

We lose our way and suddenly find ourselves in the middle of Smolenskaya Place and can see right down to the Kremlin.

For a moment we stand in amazement and look at the bulbous towers, shining like diamonds in the winter morning sun.

'Looking at that could make a man almost want to be a Russian,' says Porta, enchanted.

Vasilij is suddenly nervous. He has the Mongol's sure instinct for danger.

'Not look shitty Kremlin too much! Dam dangerous! There all half-Commie chop to dog meat! Big tricky Commie NKVD sit there, warm arsehole! We get shitty quick out here! Chita man say: See Kremlin no see much more in life!'

We cut down to the Moscow at the Borodinsky Bridge. A whole line of lorries filled with prisoners is standing there. They're obviously emptying their nets here. There are quite a lot of uniforms among the prisoners on the vehicles.

'Shitty dam NKVD HQ,' says Vasilij, 'not good go there! Them arrest general if no like face! Vasilij lousy captain! Kick arse captain like butcher kick stray dog! Vasilij shout, wave them! You run dam fast Smolensky Street! Them think we chase bad men! No lose turnip, maybe!'

We run as fast as our legs can carry us down the narrow street. Vasilij is just behind us, running as if his feet had wings.

'Quick into yard,' he shouts. 'Shitty NKVD come with machine-gun. Not think we chase bad men!'

We rush madly through a yard and swing over a series of fences. A policeman shouts at us and draws his pistol, but before he can pull the trigger the Legionnaire's steel wire is round his neck and the life is choked out of him.

We push the body into a dustbin out of sight of passers-by. Tiny wants to try on the uniform.

'I've always wanted to be a pavement admiral. Now I got the chance over 'ere with Ivan and you won't let me! Call yourselves mates! I could spit in your bleedin' eye, every one of you!'

'You crazy take shitty policeman coat,' says Vasilij. 'Policemen pigeon-shit on Red Square, say NKVD man. You be glad you green on uniform. In Soviet paradise, green only colour. No green on shoulder soon no turnip!'

One of the Brandenburgers goes mad suddenly. He runs in circles screaming in German.

One of his own party is on him like lightning and slashes his throat open. Screams die away in a hideous rattle.

On Suvorovsky Boulevard we go into an Intourist office, the door of which is standing invitingly open.

'We're closed,' says a tight-lipped elderly woman with hair tied in a bun at the back.

'*Je te pisse au cul!*'* snarls the Legionnaire wickedly, bringing the back of his hand across her face.

'*Germanskij!*' she whispers hoarsely in terror, falling back into her chair so hard that it cracks warningly. 'Germanskij,' she repeats, staring at us with bugging eyes.

'No, love, we're the last of the Mohicans,' grins Porta, 'Come to take your scalp!' He chucks her under the double chin. 'A well-upholstered overweight sow like you is just what I need. It'll feel like a great gate pressing down over you, and I can assure you, my dear, that the key'll find its way into the keyhole every time!'

A BT-5 tank with the characteristically high turret stops outside. The Commandant tries to see through the almost frozen windows.

'Watch it!' warns Barcelona. 'If he gets suspicious he'll put a banger into us!'

* *Je te pisse* etc: (French): I'll piss up your arse!

The tank backs onto the pavement with a scrabbling of tracks. The wind pleads at the frozen windows, powdering them with snow. The tank's engine roars and it scrapes noisily along the wall.

A piercing scream from the fat woman makes us jump with shock. She vaults amazingly over the counter, slides across the floor and bangs into a cabinet, which falls, spreading papers all over the floor. She screams, terrifyingly, again.

With a long leap the Legionnaire is on top of her. She rolls away under a desk, where she gets hold of a metal lamp and throws it at the window. Vasilij intercepts it.

'Let air out of shitty dam bitch quick! She dam shitty dangerous!' The woman springs straight over the Legionnaire and hits the Old Man like a battering-ram. He goes one way, his Mpi clatters the other.

I try to catch her feet, but get a kick in the face so that I see stars. Porta grabs her by the jacket but she slips out of it and screams for the third time.

If the tank's motor hadn't been speeded up to a roar they couldn't have helped hearing her.

She's nearly at the door when Tiny gets an arm round her and shoves his combat knife into her between the neck and shoulder. The broad blade sinks slowly into her body. It catches! Irritably he wobbles it loose! Blood pumps up over his hand in short spurts!

The woman struggles like a wild animal in his iron grip. Carefully he withdraws the knife and drives it with all his force between her breasts.

'What the 'ell's wrong with you, sister?' he growls with a kind of brutal friendliness. 'It's too late now. You've signed your own pass!'

He presses his knee into her back and with a quick practiced movement slits her throat.

A half-smothered guttural noise bubbles from the gaping slash in her throat, then she goes limp in his arms.

A great pool of blood spreads across the floor and sinks into the carpet.

Tiny looks at the body for a moment; wipes the knife and his hands on her dress.

'Holy Mother of Kazan!' he mumbles. 'It's a thing I'll never get bleedin' used to! No wonder they give you the last shave for it in peace-time!' He throws up into a bucket standing by the wall.

'*C'est la guerre, mon ami,*' says the Legionnaire, indifferently.

'Get her out of sight,' orders the Old Man, his face like stone. Porta and I push her into a cupboard. A green coat with worn fur trimmings is hanging there. On a shelf above, an old-fashioned brown hat with a feather.

'Crazy woman no scream, no die,' says Vasilij laconically, opening a packet of sandwiches he has found in a drawer. He offers them round. There's enough for one apiece.

'Pity she die! Make good food!' says Vasilij, with his mouth full. 'Goat milk cheese and red salad, good!'

When we leave the travel bureau we hang the 'Closed' sign inside the door.

At Smolenskaya we take cover from a big parade of troops taking the oath with their commanding general. Here we split up from the Brandenburgers and arrange a rendezvous a little way behind the Russian front line.

We go on down Lenskaya Quay and hide in the Zoological Gardens for the night. Porta, Tiny and Vasilij go in advance through the Krasnopresnensky park. They are to wait for us at the first lake. There we cross the river. Crossing the railway on this side is impossible. We have to go south of Kutuzovo Station, up over the Pakionnaye heights and from there to the Mozhaishkoe road. Several hours go by and we've heard nothing from them. The Old Man decides to move the entire section down towards the park in as spread order as possible. Their silence can mean that they are either taken prisoner or dead.

'Nobody fires without my express orders,' he snarls. 'If it

226

comes to a fight use close combat weapons only! The sound of a shot carries a hell of a distance in this frost!'

After a lengthy search we find them by the long lake. They are hiding behind a huge statue, set up on the top of a hill, from where they have an excellent view.

'What the devil are you doing farting about here?' scolds the Old Man. 'Why haven't I had a report?'

'Take a pew and let peace sink over you,' grins Porta easily, putting the glasses to his eyes. 'The bridge is still occupied. A German louse couldn't get across. But we're all right here!' he adds, with a lascivious chuckle.

Tiny is panting and scratching feverishly at his crutch. He too has his eyes pressed to the glasses.

'Gawd's truth,' he whispers. 'This is better'n a bleedin' cunt exhibition!'

'Dam shitty nice nanny! Vasilij think we go meet!' says Vasilij, and whinnies lecherously.

'What the devil *are* you looking at?' asks the Old Man irritably, tearing the glasses from Tiny. 'Now I've seen *everything*,' he mumbles, a flush of rage mounting from his neck up into his face. 'Have you three crazy bastards been lying here watching bloody girls all day long?'

'Know of any better occupation?' asks Porta. '*I'm* satisfied with the entertainment!'

'Feldwebel, Vasilij think good plan we go down catch soldier women. Then we take shitty long rest on soft groundsheet before trot back by dam HKL!'

'God damn you sons of pigs,' curses the Old Man viciously. 'You're that bloody randy you'll be fuckin' the statue next.'

'They're taking showers over in that house,' grins Porta and points to a long red house with lighted windows, even now in daytime.

'We can see the 'ole of their bleedin' bodies,' giggles Tiny without removing his eye from the glasses he is sharing with Vasilij.

'Shitty good nanny,' says Vasilij. 'Them shave off hairs!

227

No give crab! Chita girl all shave! China man no like weed round garage! Come take little look, Feldwebel! Wife Berlin no give shit! No get baby, make lovely music, with only look!'

'By God,' the Old Man swears, viciously. 'We'll soon have to be asking the enemy to order his women soldiers to draw the blinds when they strip off.'

'Let's have a look,' says Barcelona, taking the glasses from Porta.

Soon the whole section is enjoying the sight in rotation. The girls are singing and chattering away.

'What are they saying?' asks Porta, throwing his Mpi behind him. It is getting in his way!

'Not understand all,' answers Vasilij. 'Talk dialect! Grenadier women from Caucasus! Not talk proper language!'

'Why are they bathing all the time?' asks Stege in wonder. 'They practically live in that shower-room.'

'Them shitty shitty from Caucasus! Stink like goat! Vasilij thinks. Wash much now! Moscowman not like stinky woman!'

'Do you mean to say they give it to the bleedin' goats in the Caucasus?' asks Tiny. 'What a bleedin' waste!'

'Do *now* with goat! All men gone war!' answers Vasilij.

'There'll be hell to pay if they catch us peeping,' says the Old Man doubtfully. 'Women have a sense for that kind of thing.'

'We use sleepy-gun them keep mouth shut tight,' considers Vasilij, optimistically. 'You no be sour, Feldwebel! Take look! Not every day see so good thing in time war!'

'What about makin' a little check-up,' suggests Tiny. 'They ain't gonna say no to green braid!'

'Vasilij think plan good,' says Vasilij, beginning to climb to his feet.

'Holy Mother of Kazan,' moans Barcelona. 'Have you seen what's coming our way? I'm near fainting when I think what she's hiding under that uniform.'

'Jesus, Son of God Almighty!' cries Porta, his jaw falling. 'She's bloody well coming over here! Open your flies, boys, and get ready for shopping at the fur counter. It's not every day it comes calling in wartime!'

'We've got to get away,' half-shouts the Old Man. 'If she sees us she'll give the alarm!'

'You forget, we belong to that tough NKVD lot,' says Porta, calmingly. 'We're like snakes and other forms of political reptile. People are hypnotized at a glance.'

'Oh Hell! I'm scared,' pipes the Professor. He is down at the bottom of a deep hole with his fur cap pulled over his ears. He must think like an ostrich. When he can't see them, then they can't see him either!

'It's all right,' says Tiny, licking his lips expectantly. 'Just sit still, like an old tomcat sittin' 'avin' a shit on a 'ot tin roof.'

'If one of those girls comes by here,' says Barcelona, 'then you must forgive me, because I will not be able to help myself!'

'She'll get herself a gang-bang that quick you'd think it was a flock of sparrows!' grins Porta.

'Moscow ain't so bad when you get used to it,' says Tiny. 'I'm sorry, really, we're leavin'. It's like bein' in a 'ospital in a way. When you been there a bit you don't even want to go outside! 'Ow'd you lot feel about changin' FPO numbers?'

'You must have your balls where your brains ought to be,' says Barcelona. 'They'd knock us off in a minute or I'll eat my helmet!'

'Up on your feet!' orders the Old Man, sharply. 'We're moving to the top end of the lake. They can't see us there.'

Slowly and unwillingly we follow the Old Man. We were doing all right.

From our new hiding place we can see a lot further into the park, right over to the railway station, but we can't see the bathroom anymore. We can see a woman officer changing her uniform but only half of us get a look before she's finished. We've only three pairs of glasses to go the rounds between twenty men. We quarrel continually about who's next.

We make ourselves comfortable, loosen our equipment,

wrap ourselves in our long Russian greatcoats, pull the fur collars up round our ears and build up a little wall of snow around us to keep off the keen wind.

'Just like Christmas!' says Porta. 'What about it. Let's hang a few cartridge belts on this fir tree here, and play Christmas Eve. Then we could go over and get some of those grenade tossers and dance round the tree with 'em.'

Four girl soldiers come along arm in arm, singing. They wobble out on a narrow jetty with girlish squeals, knock a hole in the ice and pull up a long line. There are half a dozen perch wriggling on it.

'I thought fish slept in the bleedin' winter!' cries Tiny in amazement.

'Why should they?' asks Heide. '*You* don't go to sleep just because it's cold.'

'You're bleedin' *stupid*!' shouts Tiny, contemptuously. 'Bears bleedin' well sleep in the winter, don't they? They fill their bleedin' gut all summer, then they roll up in a ball soon as the snow comes, and snore til the sun an' warm comes back again. There's plenty more animals as do that too, ain't there? Then why's it so bleedin' funny, you brown-nosed bastard, if I think bleedin' fish do, eh?'

The girls pull in another line, but with only a roach on it, and that such a small one they leave it on the hook for bait. They bait the other line again and let it down through the hole. Then they cover it with grass mats to make it easier to find again.

They sit down for a moment on a stone stub close to the bank. After a while they get up and walk straight over towards our hiding place.

We lie quiet as mice, hardly daring to breathe we're so excited.

A few yards away from us they stop and haul some boxes from under a low shelter. They are slim, clean-looking girls. One of them is really beautiful with masses of golden hair which makes her side-cap look too small.

Tiny drops the glasses! They roll noisily down the slope.

The sound makes them look over towards us. They don't know it, but their lives are hanging by a thread. Two steps more towards us and we'll take them and then rape them before we kill them! That's war! Even with a gun pointed at us the Old Man couldn't prevent it.

A group of girls under command of a fat woman sergeant march past us and disappear behind the trees over towards Selsoyu Street.

'Let's capture them!' suggests Porta, lecherously. 'It'll only be two of us to each one of them. It ain't bad stuff. I'll take the fat 'un with the tapes. Jesus, I've never shagged a sergeant before, and now I can do it without getting me rod brown!' He laughs, so loudly that the four girls over by the shelter get up and look questioningly towards us.

'You mad bastard!' scolds the Old Man, raging. 'Now you've done it! Get 'em if they start to make a run for the barracks. They mustn't be allowed to give the alarm.'

The girls settle down again.

Suddenly Tiny throws a snowball and hits one of them on the back of the neck.

'Jesus, no!' groans the Old Man, and throws his gun down on the snow in despair.

'Hoo-oo-oo-hoo!' howls Tiny, throwing another snowball.

'Vasilij stand up. Girls see NKVD uniform. Pissy much danger now!' says Vasilij nervously. 'You ready with strangle-wire nanny try run!' He gets to his feet, and waves his fur cap above his head.

The girls cry out with pleasure and four snowballs are on their way towards Vasilij.

Soon after we are all throwing snowballs.

The Old Man leans against a tree with a sour look on his face. 'The maddest bloody lot on the whole of the Eastern Front! Playing with snowballs while they're on a desperate commando raid behind the enemy lines! I can't even report it! Nobody'd believe it!'

A hard snowball hits him slap in the face. He hesitates,

231

and is about to shout but checks himself. Instead he throws a snowball back at them.

The girls scream with laughter every time they score a hit and we hit them almost every time.

The party from before comes back and joins in the battle.

Girlish screams and shouts of laughter can be heard a long way off. The snowfight doesn't stop until darkness falls. They wave goodbye to us. A last snowball flies through the air and catches the fat sergeant squarely on the nape of the neck. She turns round and shakes her fist at us.

Porta jumps up and down like a giant frog shouting like a happy boy. He is quite smitten with the fat girl.

'This is the best long distance warm-up I've ever struck!' he shouts excitedly.

An hour later we're on our way. We cross the ice by the Dorogomilovsky churchyard, and pass a great pile of bodies awaiting burial. Casualties from the air-raid and the artillery attacks. We move round a small house and are challenged by a guard.

'Better me speak,' whispers Vasilij. 'He no get dead scare, shout out!'

In the wink of an eye the Legionnaire has strangled the officious guard. We throw his body, still warm, up to the others.

Tiny turns over one of the bodies.

'What about a little gold minin', eh?' he asks, nudging Porta.

'Just try it!' snarls the Old Man pointing his gun at him. 'Try it! That's if you want to join the great majority of the Goddam pile here!'

'Fuck *me*, but you're difficult!' shouts Tiny, irritated. 'The face you been goin' round with just lately ain't good for our nerves, you know. It's psychological cruelty, that's what it is. You can get *divorced* for that!'

By the film studios we run into a large column of militia. An old major blows himself up to the size of a general and demands *propusk*.

He can't see our badges in the dark and Vasilij has to make it clear to him that he is talking to the NKVD and risking a long holiday in Ljubjanka and Kolyma. Without more discussion we march off. Vasilij on the flank of the column.

The major remains, standing stiff as a poker at the salute, for as long as we are in sight.

As soon as we're across the railway line we run as fast as our legs can carry us. You never know what an old officer like that can hit on when he's had time to do a bit of thinking.

On the Mozhaishkoe road we hitch on to a large troop unit, so that it looks as if we belong to them, and are soon in open country.

A storm blows up that makes every step a battle. Mountains of snow drive across the road. We hold on to one another's belts to avoid getting lost in the white hell of the blizzard. We take a couple of hours rest in a deserted sheepfold and reach the front area the following day. There we meet the Brandenburgers who are nervous, and vocally irritable, at having been kept waiting.

The rest of our trip up to the front line goes off without any brushes with the Russians. They have their hands full preparing an important offensive. All sorts of units are on the move. The whole area behind the front line is fluid.

'Damn good us, they busy make shitty big attack,' says a satisfied Vasilij. 'Them no time squash crazy German louse.'

We creep out through the Russian lines when night falls and reach our own forward positions shortly after dawn.

The Brandenburg Feldwebel is the first into the trench, but there isn't a sign of our people.

Porta runs to the command dug-out. Empty. No SMGs in the nests. A ruined baseplate is all that is left of the mortar group alongside it.

'*Fritz, Fritz, idisodar,*' sounds behind me and an MG hammers tracer the length of the trench. In a second we are down and shooting down the straight with everything we've got.

A party of Russians fall back as if struck by a battering-ram.

Grenades fly through the air and explode hollowly. Torn-off human limbs are blasted along the lip of the trench and sink soggily into the breast-work.

'Get moving!' cries the Old Man. 'I'll cover you. Run for your lives!' Quickly we are up and over the lip of the trench and storm southwards. Behind us machne-guns crackle.

I fall over a body, a fallen Brandenburger, and slide into a shell-hole filled with dead. Frozen arms and legs point accusingly at the sky. Crooked fingers seem to catch at me. It's as if they are saying 'How dare *you* remain alive when *we* are dead?'

Porta jumps across the hole. I try to go after him but slide back twice down the icy sides. The ice is red. Frozen blood. A beautiful sight, really, only to be seen in war. The Old Man is right when he says: 'Even in war there are moments of beauty.' The Russians are right on our heels with their inviting call: '*Fritz, Fritz, idisodar!*'

We keep on at top speed over a wasteland carpeted with the dead. We almost jump down into a Russian position but they fire too soon, and we manage to turn off.

Tiny leaps down into a shell hole and turning like a top in midleap has his LMG in position as he lands.

The leading Russians fall only a few yards from him.

I stop for a moment to throw a few grenades. It's like rolling up a trench. As if in slow motion I see Russians blown to pieces. A torn-off hand flies past my head. Then we're off towards the west again. Our people must be *some*where. They've probably only straightened the front.

A few yards in front of me is the Brandenburger Feldwebel running with long athletic strides. I stop suddenly as if I had run into a giant fist. The earth gapes in front of me. A column of flame shoots up into the air and the Feldwebel goes up with it. He seems to spin like a ball juggled on the tip of the flame. His body lands at my feet with the sound of a wet cloth. The mine he has sprung has blown off both his feet. Nothing can be done for him. Blood pulses in thick jets from veins and arteries. I hasten past without looking at him. His screams follow me. It is best for the badly wounded to die quickly! Often, though, it takes them a wickedly long time.

Finally we reach our own trenches. Firing commences from both ends.

'Cease fire! Cease fire!' screams the Old Man, desperately. 'We are Brandenburgers!'

A boyish Leutnant, with *Hitler Jugend* eyes, sticks his head cautiously from a corner of the trench and demands the password.

'Get fucked!' shouts Porta insubordinately and takes cover immediately. They might be just frightened enough to shoot. Nothing is so dangerous and unpredictable as terrified soldiers led by an inexperienced officer.

'Are you German?' comes a shout from the corner where the Leutnant seems to be.

'Come out 'ere, you wicked bastard!' shouts Tiny, 'an' I'll prove it to you before I strangle you!'

A potato-masher whirls through the air and explodes in front of Vasilij throwing him several yards into the air. He falls with a heavy thud and a streaming pool of blood grows under him.

'Them crazy shitty German we run to,' he groans. 'You kill for me! Vasilij go Great *Kunfu*. Great pity no know how war end and we no eat velvet hen with cousin in Hong Kong.' His body arches like a stretched bow. He struggles to get to his feet. Gets halfway, presses the Old Man by the hand. '*Dasvidanja*, Feldwebel!' He is dead!

An uncontrollable rage grips us. With submachine-guns chattering we rush the trench containing the Leutnant and his men. In seconds we have disarmed them. The young Leutnant presses himself against the trench wall, white in the face.

The little Legionnaire literally cuts his uniform off him with his Moorish knife.

'Don't kill him!' shouts the Old Man, warningly. 'He's only a boy!'

'That little shit murdered Vasilij,' screams Porta furiously.

235

Before the Old Man can hinder it the Leutnant is thrown to the other end of the trench.

A Feldwebel springs at Porta and gets his throat cut in a flash.

We stand on the edge of the trench with armed grenades and guns at the ready.

'Down on your faces! Hands behind your neck!' shouts the Old Man. 'Or you're dead men!' The whole trench complement goes down.

'And we're supposed to win a war with this kind of material,' says the Old Man, shaking his head, despairingly. 'Who was it said our German soldiers were marvellous? God preserve us!'

Oberst Hinka arrives shortly after with a group of officers. He welcomes us back, almost embracing Porta, and hears our report in silence.

Cigarettes and schnapps are passed round.

'You've given this trench complement a terrible shock,' laughs Hinka. 'Why did you not follow my orders?' he turns severely to the Leutnant, who is keeping his distance. 'You knew we were expecting a commando group back!'

'They were in Russian uniforms and could not give the password,' the Leutnant defends himself, redfaced.

'Did you expect them to arrive in dress uniform with a pass in a cleft stick?' shouts Hinka.

'I thought . . .'

'You'll come to explain what you thought,' answers Hinka, turning on his heel.

'Bastard!' hisses Porta, spitting at the Leutnant's feet. The young officer tries to say something.

'Just one word,' snarls Porta, lifting the butt of his weapon. 'One word that's all! And I'll smash your silly HJ face in!'

We bury Vasilij on a height from which the towers of Moscow can be seen in silhouette. A Brandenburger plays the Dead March. His submachine-gun and his kukhri go with him to the grave. Only women go unarmed to Great *Kunfu*.

In the evening we march back to 27 Panzer Regiment. Chief Mechanic Wolf can't believe his own eyes when he sees Porta alive.

'God strike me dead!' he shouts. 'And I've paid for three candles for you on the field altar!'

He is so shocked that he invites us to dine on roast wild-pig that evening. We eat till we nearly burst. All next day we spend sitting in the latrines playing dice. They even have to bring us our meals there. It's not worth getting up. Everything runs straight through us. That wild-pig must have been sick. Maybe that was why Wolf invited *us* to dinner.

> 'Traitors must be rooted out, and the children of
> traitors; nothing of them, nothing at all, must be
> allowed to remain.'
>
> Adolf Hitler to SS-Obergruppenführer Heydrich
> 7 February 1942.

A little past 3 o'clock on the morning of 11 January 1942, two men, in long leather coats and wearing black steel helmets, rang long and impatiently on the door of a flat on Admiral-von-Tirpitz-Ufer, across from the Potzdamer Brücke. When no reply came they began to bang with their fists on the tall oak panels of the door.

'What do you people want? The Herr General went to bed long ago. What is this hooligan behaviour? I am Regierungsrat Dr Esmer. I can assure you a complaint will be made tomorrow!'

'Get out!' snarled one of the black-helmeted men, 'if you don't want to jump through the hoop yourself!'

The Regierungsrat noticed, for the first time, the silver collar dogs with the SS emblem. He seemed to shrink into himself and retired quickly into his flat. In the dubious safety of their marriage bed his wife berated him violently.

The following day the Regierungsrat reported sick and left on a recreational visit to Bad Gastein.

A servant opened the door of the General's flat.

'We wish to speak to General Ställ,' barked one of the SS officers, pushing the servant roughly aside.

'Gentlemen!' mumbled the servant plaintively.

'Shut your mouth!' answered Hauptsturmführer Ernst.

The servant fell into a chair and stared open-mouthed after the two tall, lean officers who walked straight into the general's study without knocking. In the twenty years he had been in service here no one had ever dared to do that. The General was an aristocrat who kept strictly to the forms of etiquette.

'Are you General-Leutnant Ställ?' asked SS-Sturmbahnführer Lechner, stony-faced.

'I am,' replied the astonished General, getting up slowly from his desk chair.

'The Führer has sentenced you to death for dereliction of duty and sabotage of orders! You have, without permission, given your division orders to retreat.'

'Are you mad, man?' was all the General managed to get out before four pistol shots followed one another in quick succession.

A piercing scream rang through the house. Frau Ställ came rushing in and threw herself desperately across her husband's body.

'The swine is still alive,' said the Hauptsturmführer, and tore the woman away from the dying General.

Lifting the head by the hair he pressed his pistol muzzle against the neck. Two shots cracked hollowly from the heavy service revolver.

The General's face splintered like glass. Brains and blood spattered across a painting of his children. His body writhed briefly.

'Dead!' confirmed the Hauptsturmführer brusquely, holstering his Walther.

'Heil Hitler!' They saluted with raised arms and left the flat without hurrying.

A black Mercedes with an SS-Unterscharführer at the wheel waited in the street.

'And now?' asked the Sturmbahnführer, leaning back into the soft cushioning.

'To Dahlem,' growled the Hauptsturmführer.

The black car disappeared swiftly across the Landwehrkanal.

9 | The Generals Depart

A long threatening rumble from the Russian side of the front wakes us from an uneasy sleep.

'*Mille diables*,' shouts the Legionnaire, shocked into

wakefulness. 'What in the world is that?'

'Hundreds of batteries firing!' answers the Old Man and listens nervously.

'Who said Ivan was finished?' mumbles Porta.

'What a lot o' gunpowder Ivan must 'ave,' says Tiny. ' 'Ope the bastards ain't goin' to start a big 'un. Sounds bleedin' like it!'

'That shower's coming right at our heads,' says Barcelona with foreboding.

The far away metallic ringing increases to a roar. Thousands of shells are coming closer in a mounting crescendo of sound. We're out of our bunks and down on the floor in a second. We envy the lice at times like this. Shells don't bother *them*. The shells fall with a murderous noise, tearing at the earth. In an inferno of flame, earth, ice and razor-sharp splinters of steel fly hundreds of yards from the striking point. When a shell falls on to a position it simply disappears.

The mounting thunder of exploding shells beats at us from all sides. The earth, air, river, snow, forest; the town of Lenino; everything about us, seems to be changed in a moment into a giant anvil ringing incessantly under the strokes of gigantic triphammers.

Explosions of unbelievable power claw and rip at the frozen ground. Dirt, snow, whole trees are thrown up into the air, balancing on volcanoes of flame which seem to originate in the very bowels of the earth. Poisonous smoke rolls backwards and forwards across the wounded soil. Wherever we look there is a greenish broth of melted snow, blood and shredded human flesh. We are in the midst of a deadly cauldron.

The dug-out bobs and dances like a cork in a high sea. Men go mad. We knock them about, our own recipe for the treatment of shock. The forest burns. The ice on the river is splintered and black waters fountain upwards. This river is to be the graveyard of many Russian and German soldiers. I press myself hard into the floor of the dug-out, flat as a dry leaf. Shell splinters whine through the narrow windows. The sandbags we blocked them with have been blown away long ago. The dug-out cracks and groans. Can its heavy timbers stand up to this?

A new shell, one of the big coal-scuttles, literally throws the dug-out into the air. I can feel a scream welling up from the pit of my belly. It won't be long before my nerves go.

'Jesus!' shouts Porta. 'He's showing us all his samples today!'

'I don't like it,' says Tiny. 'If one o' them pointed boxes 'its us on the 'ead, you can all throw your bleedin' toothbrushes away. 'Cause you're all gonna need new teeth.'

The Old Man turns the handle of the telephone, and whistles into the mouthpiece.

'What're you ringing for?' asks Porta. 'If it's a taxi you want then I'm willing to go halves. Probably be a long wait though on a rough night like this!'

'I've got to get hold of the company commander,' snarls the Old Man. 'I want orders! This is a big attack.'

It seems as if the noise of the shells moves back a little.

'Curtain,' we shout all together, grabbing at our equipment.

'Attack,' confirms the Old Man confidently, puffing at his silver-lidded pipe.

'Where would these Soviet *untermensch* get the men and material to mount an attack?' jeers Heide. 'The Führer has said they are crushed. The rest of the war will be a parade-ground exercise.'

'There's the door,' grins Porta. 'Quick march, Julius! I'd like to see the boys from here who'll go on parade with you!'

Magazines are prepared. Pockets filled with ammunition. Potato-mashers down our jackboots. Magnetic bombs ready.

We live from second to second, minute to minute, readying ourselves for death in that bellowing inferno.

The company is on the march. A shell howls down from the sky and the road in front of us is gone. Comrades are blown into the fields. Most of them are dead. Soon after, the survivors are on the march again, looking for faces known to them, finding few or none. They form new acquaintances. Until a new shower of shells come from the clouds. Now they become 'difficult', dare not form the slightest of ties with anyone.

We take cover in shell-holes, dodge the swarming thousands of devilish things which infest the air, storm on with flashing bayonets, split faces with our sharpened spades, queue at the cook wagon for a bowl of nettle soup, go to the medics to have a wound dressed. Everybody dreams of a white bed in a hospital at home. The Medical Sergeant grins jeeringly and sends us back into hell!

With three aspirins and a light dressing on his flesh-wound the wounded man marches on, is picked up by a strange unit and made company runner, dashes with messages from shell-hole to shell-hole through the barrage and over mine-strewn terrain until he is again wounded or perhaps killed. He moves from unit to unit. Seldom sees a letter. When one does arrive his longing and his homesickness rip his nerves to shreds. His entire twenty-year life collapses around him. Get out of it, he tells himself. The Fatherland, what's that? I don't owe it anything. And now it wants my life! He swings his belongings on to his back and walks off. The Watchdogs liquidate a number of deserters. Penal troops from OT* fill up the graves. Deserting the colours goes out of fashion for him. Mass execution as a deterrent has worked, and brought his reason back.

'Were you leaving us?' they ask him confidentially at the company, as he throws his equipment roughly into a corner.

'What do you take me for?' he lies, with a laugh.

'Are we really goin' to give up this lovely place?' asks Tiny. 'Bleedin' 'ell, we could've seen the winter through real nice in 'ere!' He looks around him sadly.

'Stay on, if you fancy it,' grins Stege. '*I'm* off, anyway!'

A terribly close strike makes the dug-out bounce like a

* O.T. (Organization Todt): Work battalions.

rubber ball. The roof falls in on one side. The stove-pipe breaks off in sections, and the room fills with a choking smoke which puts out the Hindenburg candles.

'I must get through to the commander,' says the Old Man, snatching up his gun. 'There's a mass attack on the way!'

'*Hamdoulla*,'* shouts the Legionnaire. 'There won't be as much as a button left of you, if you go out there!'

'It's a big 'un' mumbles the Old Man, taking an extra big bite of his plug, before sitting down again. 'He's presenting his bill. It won't be pleasant!'

'It's the Jews fault!' shouts Heide, fanatically. 'They started it all by crucifying Jesus!' Nobody bothers to answer him. He is only barking senselessly like any other dog.

'Last time I was on leave I picked up a dose,' says Feldwebel Jacobo, gratuitously. 'It all started very promisingly in the "Zigeunerkeller". That's where I ran into Sylvia. Her husband, a ground-staff pilot in the Luftwaffe had been posted missing, but *we* didn't miss him. Sylvia took my load out in the toilets. It was a solemn occasion, I can tell you. The orchestra was playing *Düstere Sonntag* † all the time we were on the job. Later on that evening I gave it to Lisa while the ladies' orchestra was playing *Mädchen wie schön*.‡ They certainly get you in the mood at the "Zigeunerkeller", and I took one for the road with the girl driver of the cycle-taxi that took me home. My wife was out when I crawled into bed. She's very pretty with everything in just the right places. She's the kind a man can only have shares in. Real good stuff, like her, you can never keep all to yourself. When she got home, she got the whole gun, even though she *was* dog-tired. She'd been with an Oberst from the night-fighters. They say they get really lecherous up there fighting above the clouds. My wife had got a bit more than she fancied, anyway, but after a bit she warmed up and began to tell me that a Feldwebel was a lot better than an officer.'

* *Hamdoulla* (Arabic): Slowly.
† *Düstere Sonntag* (German): Blue Sunday.
‡ *Mädchen wie schön* (German): Girl, how lovely.

'Is your wife a racehorse, or something?' asks Porta with interest.

'Not really,' smiles the Feldwebel, 'though she *is* very good on the run-in. We must live, and preferably live well, so when you've got a good product why not sell it?' He pulls a photograph from his pay-book. 'See here. My wife's a frigate; she sails straight for any gold-plated bollard she sees on the horizon. You can bet your sweet life Grethe's got a paying guest in our marriage bed right this minute.'

'And you stand for it?' cries Heide disgustedly. 'I'd have her picked up by the MPs. The Führer says unfaithful wives should be sent to the brothels. They are unworthy of being allowed to live in our National Socialist society. Germany must be cleansed of whoredom!'

'They'll be some dreadful types, them that are left!' grins Porta.

The Old Man turns the handle of the telephone desperately and whistles into the receiver.

'Who the hell are you so anxious to get hold of?' asks Porta. 'Nice piece of crumpet?'

'The OC damn your eyes,' curses the Old Man, taking a new bite at his plug. 'We've got to have orders,' he growls.

'Make up your own,' says Porta. 'It'll all be the same in the end. We're going backwards! The trip home has begun, and I'd be a lying bastard if I said I was sorry!'

'Crazy bastard!' the Old Man swings the handle again. 'The line's gone,' he growls. '2 Section, two men! Get it fixed. I've got to speak to the OC.'

'*Merde* not now?' protests the Legionnaire. 'It's madness. Fix it one place and it'll go in another and we'll go with it.'

'Let's get out,' suggests Porta, draping another belt of cartridges round his chest.

'Two men,' orders the Old Man, roughly. 'I want the OC!' Two signallers are detailed from 2 Section. An Unteroffizier and a Gefreiter. Carelessly they put on their helmets and adjust their gasmasks. There are as many poisonous vapours out there as if we were under a gas attack.

244

Bending low they work their way through the hell of exploding shells. The Unteroffizier in front with the cable running through his fingers. They find the first break, repair it, test with their own apparatus. Still dead! They move on, dodging shells all the time. Find the next break.

'Stop,' snarls the Unteroffizier. He scrapes the wire clean with his combat knife and twists the ends together. Insulating tape binds them. Seven times they have to repeat this job before the Old Man gets his connection.

'Very good, sir,' he shouts into the telephone. 'Yes! Hold the line at all costs! A mass attack, Herr Oberleutnant, sorry, Herr Major! I thought I was speaking to Company, sir! 2 Platoon, 5 Company, Feldwebel Beier, here, sir! Platoon torn to pieces. Fifteen men. Very good, Herr Major, understood! My neck? What I've got in front, Herr Major? Don't know, sir! Army Corps I should think. No, sir! Not being insolent sir! This connection's cost me five men, you puffed-up bastard!' he concludes, but not until after he has broken the connection.

We stare at him expectantly. Now it's up to him. Will he follow the battalion commander's orders, or do the only sensible thing and get out in a hurry.

He takes a new chew of tobacco and begins to study the chart, pushing the plug around between his teeth and pulling thoughtfully at his beetroot of a nose.

'Take up your positions,' he snarls, 'and take all your equipment with you.'

'Oh, no!' groans Porta. 'We're going to be heroes.'

'You heard the orders! Hold on at all costs!' the Old Man says, defensively. 'We're the last crap Greater Germany's got left! The commander gives the orders, but it's Ivan who makes the decisions!'

'This lovely dug-out,' moans Tiny. 'We'll never 'ave another like it! Oh, fuck it all!'

'Stop it cry-baby,' scolds Porta. 'You can build a new one when we get a break. With a verandah, and a swimming pool too, if you like!'

From the east, across the Lenino road, the thunder of mortars and the scream of tank tracks can be heard. Quickly we ready our equipment: hand-grenades, signal pistols, mines, bandoliers, sharpened spades, combat knives, magnetic bombs.

We wait patiently, our nerves tight, and listen to the scream of tracks from the far side of the road.

A flare explodes throwing its white dead light over the torn earth. The countless dead seem to begin to move and get up. Slowly the light dies, but immediately a new flare bursts. The front is nervous.

An artillery dump gets a direct hit and a rosy light spreads above the woodland area.

They come in packed masses. Infantry in white camouflage hoods. Legs, thousands of legs in jackboots, storm through the snow. Everywhere you look boots are tramping.

'Uhraeh Stalino! Uhraeh Stalino!' comes the hoarse battle-cry. As if at one word of command every automatic weapon commences firing into the human wall crossing no-man's-land.

They are mowed down like corn.

New infantry forces rise from the snow and storm forward with bayonets at the ready.

That night Marshal Tsjukon joined the troops at the front, and did not return to the Kremlin until the Germans were beaten!

The second wave of Russian attackers take up the bodies of the dead and use them as shields as they continue to advance towards the German positions.

The slaughterers burst like a hurricane from the clouds and drop their bombs. The attack breaks down. The snow is dyed red with blood. The survivors flee in groups, running for their lives.

Tracer hammers into bodies making them jump and jerk as if they were still alive.

The panic stricken Russians are stopped by the NKVD units. With gun butts and shots they send them back into the attack again. They run heavily through the snow with their long greatcoats flapping behind them.

'*Uhraeh Stalino! Uhraeh Stalino!* On to the victory for the Great Communist Fatherland! Long live Stalin!'

With our automatic weapons adjusted to waist-high fire we prepare to receive the new attack. The human wave is pushed back by the murderous fire. The Russian ranks break in confusion.

'Forward, you cowardly dogs!' roars a commissar, firing ruthlessly into his own men.'

Other commissars follow his example. The packed hordes panic. They fly, trampling the commissars underfoot. They are no longer soldiers. They are terrified animals with the fear of death in them. Run, run from the slaughter yard. But both the butchers in front and the butchers behind them are without mercy. Shell-bursts smash showers of snow and earth across our faces. A shell blows up half a trench. With a nerve-shattering howling the shells rain down blanketing our positions.

A boy stands next to me, the last man of a whole company. He looks at me with frightened eyes, smiling with the pale lips of a corpse. Even though he hasn't been out here very long he has already experienced a whole world of horror.

The curtain of fire moves slowly forward. We rip our machine-guns free of their mountings and crawl down into the tiny dug-outs.

Now they're right over us, whining, howling, roaring, thundering. Earth shoots up in cascades like water.

'Holy Mother,' prays the boy, kneeling with hands pressed together in front of him. I keep an eye on him. His nerves will break soon. He'll run straight out into the rain of shells. I grip the barrel of my submachine-gun, ready to knock him out. If I hit too hard I'll crack his skull. But then, won't it be all the same if *I* kill him or if the Russians do the job? According to Regulations I'm supposed to try to stop him.

A shrill scream, and a huge column of fire lifts itself immediately behind us.

My machine-gun has disappeared without trace. I feel as if every bone in my body is broken. The boy is lying half across me. They're firing air bursts and heavy calibre HE.

A terrible sight meets my eyes. The sea of bodies is turned to a trembling, sucking morass of flesh and blood. Shells are exploding wherever I look. I am still frightened but my fear is under control. I have been turned into a deadly killing machine. I hold the LMG, with its long triangular bayonet, at the ready.

'Jesus Christ!' screams the young infantryman. 'I'm hurt! I'm hit!' He humps his body along the floor of the trench like a wounded reptile. I try to get a grip on him, but he slips away from me and runs out into no-man's-land.

'Oh God! I'm blind!' he falls on his knees, his hands clasped to the place where his eyes had been.

A long whine cuts into my ear drums. I flop down quickly. It is one of the smaller calibre high explosive shells which cause frightful personnel damage. All kinds of debris rain down onto my back and my hunched shoulders. I feel down my body. All there? You don't feel the loss of a member straight away. I lift my head cautiously. Where the young infantryman had knelt there is now a great soot-blackened hole.

I'm pretty safe if I don't get a direct hit. Dead and dying lie all around me. I listen intently. Artillery fire is more than an indescribable noise. It's a book the old hand at the front can read in. This artillery fire tells me that a new attack is being mounted and that the enemy infantry are already on the way. I peer cautiously over the lip of the trench.

Something's moving. An enemy patrol? No it's a fir tree, flattened to the ground by the pressure of heated air. The little fir is almost the only surviving tree. All the forest giants have gone long ago. A foolish thought flashes through my brain. If that stubborn little fir can live through this then I can too!

'Down,' I scream at the tree. A big HE is on the way. Snow and clods of earth rain down on me. Carefully I look up again. The tree is still there. Stubbornly it sways back to the vertical. It shows up startlingly green against all that white.

Crouching over, with his old artillery helmet on his head, the silver-lidded pipe clenched between his teeth, the Old Man runs from man to man. He has a piece of sausage for me.

'How's it going?' he asks.

'Scared to death!' I smile wretchedly.

He takes the pipe from his mouth and looks out at the deep crater where the infantry boy disappeared.

'They've had a go at you all right! And nothing's happened?'

'Nothing much. An infantryman they'd blinded got blown to bits.'

'Anybody we knew?'

'No, not really.'

'Oh well, never mind. It happens all the time. *Hals-und-Bein-bruch*, son!' And the Old Man disappears round the corner of the trench.

The Old Man's alive still! Nothing much can happen to us then.

'All the luck there is in the world, and the Old Man's section's got the lot!' Porta always says.

When it gets a bit quieter I'll try to find the dead infantryman's dog-tags. His people ought to know he's gone.

Now they're using light field guns and mortars. They're deadly dangerous but not so unforseeable. If you take a little thought you can move about between the falls. Porta can tell exactly where the shells are going to hit as soon as he's heard the muzzle report. Inexperienced people often mistake the actual discharge for the muzzle report.

'Rumm! Rumm!' It sounds crazy but the *first* sound you hear is the muzzle report. I've got 22 seconds, but that's more than enough to get to the comparative safety of a shell-hole. It's not often a shell drops in the same hole. It can hit the edge and slide down the side but I've never heard of one

249

hitting dead on in the bottom, and I'm right in the bottom of an HE manufactured hole.

The mortar bombs explode above my head with an infernal din. These 80 mm mortars are wicked things. They blow all sorts of rubbish in all directions and you can never feel completely safe from them. Right in front of me lie the infantryman's dog-tags. There's a little piece of greasy string still hanging from them. I pick them up.

Infanterie Ersatzbattalion 89,

Fenner, Eswald,

geb. 9.8.24.

Now his family will at least get to know that he has died for Führer and Fatherland. If they are patriotic they will also believe the euphemism 'fighting bravely'! They'll never hear the truth from me. Their son died a hero. Sooner or later this will be some solace to them. It is for all Germans. Every German family should have its hero.

I crawl back to my MG emplacement. The artillery fire is now dropping in front of the trench again. Shell splinters whistle above me. My little tree is still standing.

Suddenly the shell-fire stops. The silence is frightening. Small fires here and there flicker out. A scream comes. Long, complaining, wild.

'E-e-e-e-ya! E-e-e-e-ya! *Germanskij sabaka!* * *Russkij* come get you!'

A machine-gun chatters viciously. A couple more start talking. Tracer tracks whistle across no-man's-land. The scream comes again. Long, horrible, wailing. Impossible to believe such a devilish sound can come from human throats.

'*Germanskij*, we come get you. Make dog meat you! You never leave Russia! Fritze, throw down your gun! We catch with gun we cut prick and ears off!'

The machine-guns bark in protest, blowing long lines of tracer into the Russian positions.

'Come and get pissed on, brother Ivan!' screams Porta,

* *Sabaka* (Russian): Dog.

making a megaphone of his hands. 'Come on you Mongol shits! You'll go back without your balls!'

'You scare, Fritze, tonight I come get you!'

'Big-head!' Porta howls back. 'Be a man and come on *now*! You can keep your prick and take it back home on a lead!'

A blinding burst of flame and I'm thrown high into the air. I smash down into a pool of blood, bones and snow. Slowly I come to myself and realize I am lying in front of the Russian positions. I can hear them talking quite clearly. Some grenade-throwers light up the scene now and then. Not far from where I'm lying there must be a field battery. I hear the bangs repeatedly. They are nearly shaking my eyes out, my head and my ears are deafened. In the muzzle-flash I can see the wire in front of the Russian lines.

As the short grey winter day passes, the bodies in front of me seem to grow smaller. The Russian cold eats everything up. Night comes and drips frost. The killing frost of death.

Cautiously I begin to crawl. Fear bores like a knife at my brain. Am I crawling in the right direction? There are Siberiaks in front of us. They wouldn't make pleasant hosts to drop in on.

Tensely I crawl on, flattening when a glare goes off above my head, and taking cover in shell-holes when the firing gets heavier.

By the light of the tracers I search for my next cover. Wherever I look there's wire, devilish damned barbed-wire. Often a half destroyed body hangs on it, flapping bloody arms and legs at me.

I hear German voices, but by then I've been crawling round for hours in this mad lunar landscape. I drop my head down on to the butt of my weapon and cry. The field guns and mortars are still firing. The Germans are shelling our backward area heavily. German batteries reply to the Russians, but more often than not they drop short.

Porta and the Legionnaire slide down into my hole. They are out looking for me.

'Are you wounded, *mon ami*? How we have searched for you!' says the Legionnaire breathlessly.

Porta hands me his filled water-bottle.

'Where the hell have you been farting about? The Old Man's already reported you missing. They promised us a bang at the Old Man of the Steppe's daughter if we found you.'

By the light of the rockets we see something moving over by the wire. We are about to raise our weapons when Tiny comes rolling over the lip of the shell-hole with a stretcher under his arm.

'You shockin' shower o' bastards!' he bellows angrily. 'I crawl around riskin' me one an' only bleedin' life to find you lot an' 'ere you sit 'ittin' the bottle an' scratchin' your bleedin' arses!'

A couple of hours later we're sitting by the cook-wagon on margarine boxes, with our belts round our necks and our trousers down round our ankles, shooting dice. Every so often we look at one another with happy, satisfied eyes. What more can one ask for: a set of dice, a dixie of beans, a good latrine, a stove to warm your naked backside, and the shelling a good long way off.

Tiny hands me a fat cigar. He's got two of them on the go at the same time. He stole a whole box not so long ago when he was temporary driver for the general commanding the division.

I've still got the dead seventeen year old infantryman on my mind. I feel guilty for letting him get away from me. The next day I speak to the Old Man about it. He listens to me silently, puffing away at his old silver-lidded pipe and spitting tobacco-juice regularly. He's the only man I've ever met who smokes a pipe and chews tobacco at the same time. He takes me over to watch the snipers, murderers with Feldwebel stars. For several minutes we watch their results through glasses. Ruthless murder. We go over to the cook-wagon. There are mountains of sauerkraut. We sit down with the cook. Unteroffizier Kleinhammer, and fill ourselves with sauerkraut and mashed potatoes.

'This business of killing is quite an ordinary thing,' explains the Old Man slowly. 'Every time one of the enemy gets killed there's one less to knock *us* on the head. Some even say war's needed, to maintain the balance between birth and death rates.'

All through the night the air shakes with the noise of engines from the other side.

'Ivan's warming up his T-34s,' says Porta, laconically.

'They'll be coming in a couple of hours time,' says the Old Man pulling thoughtfully at his spud-nose. He recommends us to get hold of all the mines and magnetic bombs we can scrape together.

A short violent bout of Russian artillery fire drops behind our lines and silences our guns.

They come up over the rise at full speed, their broad tracks throwing up the snow behind them in great clouds. The gun-muzzles flash incessantly and high explosive shells crash into the thinly-manned German line.

'Steady!' the Old Man warns us. 'Stay down and let 'em roll over you! then go at 'em with mines and magnetic bombs!' The German positions are quickly flattened and the tanks penetrate far behind the lines. An 88 mm flak battery wheezes, on the other side of the river, as it sinks into position for anti-tank fire.

Eighteen T-34s go up in flames. The charred bodies of their crews lie around them. Their supporting infantry is cut down by the concentrated defensive fire of our automatics. The remaining tanks retire, breaking through where our line is weakest.

Russian troops have got through at countless points and are behind the front. T-34s supported by camouflaged ski-troops roll furiously towards the west, flattening the German reserve positions. The ski-troops mop up after the tanks.

In Schalamowo a Divisional HQ is packing up. Long columns of vehicles are ready to move off. The Divisional Commander, in his long fur coat, gives his Chief-of-Staff the order to take over.

'The position is to be held to the last man and the last bullet. This attack is the enemy writhing in his death throes,' the Commander explains to his Chief-of-Staff, a young major straight from the War Academy.

'Very good, Herr General, I understand. An elastic withdrawal to tempt the enemy into a trap where we will divide him into small pockets and destroy him! A genial move,' adds the young General Staff officer with enthusiasm.

'Exactly,' answers the general, buttoning his fur coat. 'I trust you to look after things in my absence. You must be hard with the men, or discipline will break down. They've sent us a lot of bad material lately. Do the job well and you'll soon make Oberst-Leutnant!'

'Thank you very much, Herr General!'

They shake hands solemnly. The young major feels in fine fettle, and decides to make a visit to the front line when the general has left. It will make a good impression on the fighting forces.

The general drives away bravely in his fur coat and his three-axled Mercedes.

'*Auf Wiedersehen, Herr General!*' shouts the major, saluting stiffly.

'I certainly hope *not*,' mumbles the general to himself. The major would be an unpleasant witness to have around should his sudden departure ever be investigated.

A couple of miles further on, in a thickly-wooded area, the general makes a halt. Through his artillery glasses he examines, with professional interest, a group of T-34s attacking the chateau, which the major is obviously defending. With a crooked smile he makes the sign to resume the march. He takes a pick-me-up from his built-in bar and smiles to himself. This is the third division he has lost, fighting bravely, of course. They'll *have* to give him the Knight's Cross now. It will look nice alongside 'Blaue Max',* which he

---

* '*Blaue Max*' (German): Pet name for the Kaiser's most valued order, *Pour le merité.*

picked up as Chief-of-Staff of an infantry division in Flanders in 1917.

The Divisional Field Police have gone in advance. They are commanded by the toughest Watchdog major in the whole of the German Army. If he cannot clear the road for the Divisional Commander's Mercedes then nobody can.

The Adjutant, a womanish Rittmeister with a voice as soft as boiled asparagus, turns with a servile air from his seat by the driver:

'Herr General, we left perhaps too early? If you will excuse me saying so we could have used our divisional reserves to make some excellent antitank blocks at the crossroads.'

The general does not reply, but notes somewhere in the recesses of his mind a resolve to kick this young homosexual puppy up into an antitank command as soon as the opportunity arises. Adjutants who are capable of thinking are dangerous to have around. They should obey orders and otherwise keep their mouths shut. He lights a cigar, but stiffens at the first pull. The village they are approaching is on fire.

'Stop!' he orders, sharply, and gets out and goes a little way up the road. The adjutant hands him the glasses. In cold silence he observes the T-34s down by the village, and reads, with a jeering smile on his lips, the inscription chalked on the turrets: 'Kill the invaders, the Fascist plague!' He lowers the glasses.

'Give me your submachine-gun, Rittmeister. Seems to be German tanks. Must belong to our neighbours, 2 PD. Take the car and go and see what's happening. Obergefreiter Stolz will stay with me! You drive. And hurry back!'

'Very good, Herr General,' replies the Adjutant, clicking his heels together.

The driver, an active old Obergefreiter, gets out of the Mercedes with a grin on his face. He knows the tanks are not German but says nothing. If the officers want to do away with one another it's not his business. Silently he picks up a bundle of hand-grenades.

'What do you want with those?' asks the Rittmeister in his high voice.

'Throw them at Ivan,' the Obergefreiter grins broadly.

'I'll remember you, Obergefreiter,' pipes the Rittmeister. 'You've been the longest time on HQ staff!'

'So have you, Miss Rittmeister,' thinks the Obergefreiter jumping spryly across the ditch with an LMG under his arm. Before he became the general's driver, he was a top-class machine-gunner. He won't move without an LMG. From the ditch he watches the general, standing thoughtfully up on the road.

'That fat, cowardly little bastard ought to be court-martialled if anybody ought. But they can't touch him or the whole lot'd collapse. He's a general. When he deserts it's called making a tactical withdrawal and he gets decorated for it,' he thinks, and spits, grinning, against the wind.

The Mercedes is flattened by a T-34 a mile up the road, but the adjutant dies happy. He thinks he is falling like a German hero.

The general is promoted to General-Leutnant, the Obergefreiter is left in the ditch, and watches the various units marching past.

He waits patiently until a wagon train from a Corps Supplies Depot passes. With a unit like that you can buy your way across Europe, if necessary.

He lies down to sleep on a butcher's wagon. The only thing that can wake him now is a stopped motor. During a retreat a vehicle which is not moving is a dangerous thing to be in.

Twenty-two days later he meets his general again. These two understand one another. The Obergefreiter makes a long well-considered report of fighting with enemy ski-troops. The general gets his longed-for Knight's Cross and the Obergefreiter, who according to his report has shown great bravery during the tactical withdrawal, gets an EK.I.* They get a new division, this time Panzer Grenadiers.

* EK. I. (Eiserne Kreuz erster Klasse) (German): Iron Cross First Class.

256

The general is promoted to General-leutenant, the Obergefreiter gets another stripe and they drive round in a new three-axled Mercedes planning new elastic withdrawals. They have got a new Chief-of-Staff and a new adjutant, and they enjoy their war in a new chateau where the noise of the guns is too far away to disturb their sleep.

'War's not so bad. You just have to know how to manage things,' the Obergefreiter explains to a friend. 'Only stupid people get in the way of bullets!'

At Lokotnja T-34s surprise the entire HQ staff of 78 ID packing up. Before the staff realize what is happening everything is turned to a heap of scrap-iron and corpses.

The T-34s roll on through the back areas killing everything in their path.

At L-of-C units far behind the lines you hear the cry: 'Ivan's broken through! The T-34s have reached the motorroads!' One battery commander from 252 ID stands his ground. He collects the scared stragglers and makes them dig in around his 105 mm gun battery. With dropped muzzles he fires high explosive shells into the advancing masses of infantry. He retreats, the soldiers pulling the guns themselves.

Muscles and sinews tear under the inhuman strain. At the edge of a forest the artillery Oberleutnant brings his guns into position for the last time.

'Load three,' he orders, 'Five in salvoes!'

Breeches close! The guns roar! Carriages hop and shudder! Shells ring into the breeches again. Again and again the muzzles spout flame.

The battery fires for over an hour. Then the ammunition runs out. The crews roll their guns over in front of the infantry positions but cannot stop the T-34s for more than a few minutes.

Blood and crushed bodies and equipment making a blot on the snow, mark the end of the Oberleutnant's battery. The Russian Panzer Infantry sit on the rear shielding of the T-34s.

The Otto engines roar at top speed, and the tracks whine a triumphant song of victory.

A horse depot is rolled over and wounded horses fly into the forest with entrails hanging from their bellies, until they go rolling head over heels. Ski-troops cut fresh collops of meat from the horses' bodies and swallow them raw in Eskimo fashion. They grin happily with bloody mouths. On a full belly you can fight on. Raw meat gives a man strength.

Over a hundred miles behind the German front the T-34s drive through the 243rd Reserve Field Hospital. Nurses go around here in crisp white uniforms. Everything is quiet here, the Reds will never come back. Without warning the T-34s arrive.

From the tank turrets leatherclad tank commanders watch the murderous attack.

A bloody nurse's cape flies from the wireless antenna of the command vehicle. The ski-troops, following up, kill everything the T-34s have missed. Enthusiastically they gulp down medical alcohol, eat as much as they can from the Supplies Depot and urinate on what they have to leave, before racing on.

On that terrible night of 5 December 1941, the German steel ring around Moscow is broken. In the streets of Moscow, Russian battle units lie in readiness. Endless rows of T-34s, the paint on them scarcely dry, wait with motors running. Behind thousands of guns, from the smallest to the largest calibre, mountains of shells lie stacked. The gunners stand ready, lanyard in hand, as the second-hands of watches tick rapidly round.

The gun commanders raise their arms, and as they fall hundreds of guns roar out simultaneously, with a crash the world has never heard the equal of.

More artillery has been brought together on this front than the armies of all the countries engaged in the whole of the First World War were in possession of. Chalk falls from the ceilings of every house in Moscow. The bulbed domes of the Kremlim shake. Even the Communist leaders shake with fear. This terrific noise would frighten the very Devil in hell himself. The night becomes as light as the clearest day. Flames flash from every gun-muzzle. At dawn the battle planes come. They come in swarms, flying so low they nearly take Moscow's chimney-pots with them. Nobody cheers. Nobody shouts hurrah. People turn to one another with a fearful question in their eyes.

'If we don't kill all the *Germanskijs* now, tonight, what will they do to us in reprisal?'

At 10.30, on the morning of 5 December, one and a half million Russian infantry men are ready for the attack. A sea of men. One and a half million against six hundred thousand German infantry.

Three hours later a quarter of them have fallen.

The windows of Moscow rattle to the roaring of tank motors. The heat from countless exhausts can be felt several miles away. With ruthless speed they move forward. The roads are slippery with mashed bodies. Bloody doll-rags of humanity hang from the sides of every vehicle.

On 2 Panzer Division's sector of the front, twenty-three T-34s are destroyed in twenty minutes. But the German Panzer Division pays for it with 90 percent casualties and every single one of its tanks.

On other sectors the T-34s break through the German lines almost without resistance, and drive into the L-of-C area. Divisional HQs are simply rolled over and flattened.

Everywhere is heard the frightened cry. 'Panzer, Panzer!'

Padres, cooks, quartermasters, medical officers, supplies troops, clerks, to whom until now the front line has only been a distant rumble of artillery in the east, mill about in a confusion bordering on madness.

Like lightning they pack up, fill their vehicles with petrol, and drive madly towards the west.

'Panzer!' The cry paralyses the rear echelon. Hardly one of them has ever seen a T-34 and never expected to do so, at least not manned with a Russian crew.

Even faster than the steel noses of the T-34s can poke

themselves into German affairs, runs rumour, spreading fear and terror.

Highly-placed officers go amok. They are the kind of people who have talked a lot about a war they had never really taken part in. Many break down and have to be carried to their cars by their faithful batmen. None of them has less than two.

They order their men to their posts, and make a moving speech to these brave soldiers before leaving, to get help, as they say. A high-ranking officer must go himself, for another high-ranking officer to be convinced that help is really needed. A Leutnant could never convince an Oberst. You must have an Oberst to do that.

Others put their Walthers theatrically into their mouths and pull the trigger. But not before the T-34's Ottos can be heard on the outskirts of the village and there is no chance of retreating.

On the desk the obligatory farewell letter. 'My Führer I have done my duty! Heil Hitler!'

The letter seldom reaches the Führer. Usually some Russian soldier uses it to wipe his backside on.

'All hell's broken loose. The front line is simply dissolving!' report others.

'50 Army Corps has been liquidated,' whispers an Oberst confidentially to a General-Major, who immediately begins to prepare for a rapid move westwards.

The survivors of an Artillery Regiment state confidently that there isn't a German soldier left between them and the Kremlin.

Panic spreads with the speed of fire on the steppe. Very soon there are no German troops anywhere within a hundred miles of the front.

Every man capable of moving at all is on his way towards the west. The wounded have to take care of themselves. Blind soldiers carry wounded comrades on their backs. The blind using the eyes of the legless. Madmen stand by the side of the road shouting 'Heil!' with raised arm every time the car of a red-tabbed General flashes past.

Nobody worries about the front-line troops standing far to the east at the gates of Moscow. All lines of communication are broken. The line-units re-equip themselves with Russian leavings. Very soon only Russian arms and ammunition are to be seen. Front-line units battle on in pockets surrounded by a sea of enemy.

'Can't raise a damned thing!' says Oberleutnant Moser furiously, banging the telephone down viciously.

'No, Herr Oberleutnant,' answers the Signals Feldwebel. 'The line is intact, but there is no one there to take the call.'

Porta throws six sixes.

Tiny cries out, shaken. He has lost fifty gold teeth and says he is cleaned out. Porta knows he has two more bags of them hidden away under his shirt. It's not long before Tiny 'accidentally' discovers a couple more teeth.

The Signals Feldwebel tries to get through to battalion again.

'They've made a run for it!' says Porta, without looking round. 'Goodnight Amalia. The money's on the window-sill and your maidenhead's hanging on a nail!'

'You're insulting the honour of the German officer class,' screams Heide furiously. 'A German battalion commander doesn't run from Soviet *untermensch*. He destroys them. Herr Oberleutnant, I wish to report Obergefreiter Porta!'

'Try to keep your mouth shut, just for a moment, Unteroffizier Heide. 'You make me more nervous than the Russian infantry. Go out and check the sentries!'

'Herr Oberleutnant! Order received and noted! Unteroffizier Heide to check sentries!'

'Would you mind putting your head in the way of a Russian lead pill, while you're up there?' grins Porta, pointedly.

'Do you want it to be understood that you would like to see a German unteroffizier murdered?' asks Heide from the doorway, as he adjusts his belt to the regimentally correct tautness.

'No!' grins Porta. 'I'm protecting us against the plague!'

'Not understood,' mumbles Heide, blankly, and disappears.

'What *did* you mean by that?' asks Tiny scratching his broad rump. 'Julius got somethin' catchin'?'

'Yes, brown plague!' answers Porta, with a broad grin.

'Oh, that!' says Tiny, looking wise, but still not understanding a word. 'Is it dangerous?' he asks after a lengthy silence.

'Quiet down there!' comes sharply from Oberleutnant Moser. 'I won't have you always on the back of Unteroffizier Heide. He can't help being one of the faithful.'

'Gawd! Is 'e a bleedin' missionary?' shouts Tiny incredulously. 'I never knew that. I thought 'e was only Nazi bleedin' barmy.'

'That's right,' smiles Porta condescendingly. 'Don't try to think. You'll get a headache at both ends!'

'But it must be awful for Julius with two kinds o' barminess. One lot for Adolf an' the other lot for Jesus,' considers Tiny sympathetically. 'I'd go to a bleedin' trick cyclist an' get 'im to give me some pills against it if I was 'im.'

Between two violent bursts of shelling a breathless runner tumbles in on us. 'Report, Herr Oberleutnant, Battalion Commander fallen with entire staff. Battalion consists of only 160 men! Orders from Regiment: Company to retreat to new front line. New orders on arrival at Nifgorod!' with a click of his heels the runner concludes his report and continues on to No. 3 Battalion. He runs from shell-hole to shell-hole, literally dodging between the shells.

We never see him again. A runner's life is a short one at the front.

'Move!' orders Oberleutnant Moser. 'All equipment. Beier place the explosive charges! We don't want to make Ivan a present of anything!'

262

Porta hangs a giant charge up in the doorway. God help the man who opens it!

Tiny pushes a stick of dynamite into a hollow log and puts it on top of the log-pile temptingly ready to hand.

'Pity if Ivan was to get chilly!' he says, and bends over grinning with laughter.

A piece of half-rotten meat is laid in the middle of the table with a short fuse. If it's touched the whole dug-out will go up.

'They'll be sorry they couldn't stand the stink when they throw that out,' laughs Porta in happy anticipation.

We position a bundle of grenades underneath a body. If they move it the grenades will go off.

On a tree we've hung a large picture of Hitler. No Soviet soldier could resist tearing it down. When he does he'll have set off a stack of 6 inch shells two hundred yards further along the trench. Barcelona nails a crucifix to a door and connects it to fifty small charges.

'Anybody can see you don't like commissars,' grins Porta. 'Very clever indeed. No Russian foot slogger'll touch that crucifix. He'll bow his head and cross himself, but the dear heathen of an NKVD commissar'll go straight for it. Remove that shit – boom! – no more commissar! Far away in the Siberian villages it'll be rumoured how Christ looks after the godless! I do believe Saint Peter'll give you a medal for this when you get to Heaven.'

'It's really a pity we can't sit up in a tree and watch what happens when they move in,' says Stege.

'Come and see what *I've* done,' says Porta pulling him over to the latrine. 'Take a seat on one of these planks for a comfortable shit and I promise you you'll get your arse polished like never before. Before you've even slacked off your ring, twenty-five 105 mms'll ensure you'll never be troubled with piles again. I've attached the plank to a Bowden cable. And there's another little finesse here that'll make you split your sides. The boys who're waiting for a shit jump straight down into the split trench when the bang

263

comes, and *then* there'll be a *new* bang, because I've put the rest of our shells under the planks down there. They won't forget *that* trip to the shithouse in a hurry.'

'I think we'd better not fall into the hands of the people you're doing this to!' says Barcelona drily.

'We're not going to,' grins Porta, unworried. 'Ivan just can't run that fast!'

'Fingers out!' shouts the Old Man. 'Ivan's on his way! Porta, drop that supplies sack! Take grenades instead!'

'Can't eat grenades when I'm hungry,' answers Porta, 'and hungry's what I always am!'

'You can't defend yourself with 'em!' shouts the Old Man angrily.

'What the hell'd I want to defend myself for if I was dying of hunger?' shouts Porta, hanging on to his supplies sack.

The advance party is already over the river when we hear the firing of a Stalin Organ in the distance.

'Get on! Faster, faster!' shouts the Oberleutnant, impatiently chasing us. 'They'll be here in a minute!'

Most of us are across by the time they start to drop into the river. Black water is thrown high into the air, and yard-thick ice-floes fly into the forest.

Barcelona screams terribly from out on the ice. The blast has thrown him into a fissure. His screams turn to a gurgle as he disappears under the icy water.

In seconds we have tied our slings together. Porta snaps the hook on to his belt and crawls out over the ice to where Barcelona has disappeared.

Tiny and I are anchor-men. Others come running to our assistance.

Barcelona appears and disappears again under the ice.

Porta drops into the water and gives a shocked cry. The water is so cold it feels like red-hot pincers tearing great chunks of flesh from his body.

'Crybabies,' roars Tiny, enraged. 'Gimme the line!'

'Where the hell can I make it fast?' I ask, in confusion.

'Wrap it round your prick, if you can't find anything

264

better,' he yells, irritably. '*My* bleedin' iron could 'ave a T-34 parked on show on it!'

When I leap back again, two or three great ice-floes break away, but by some miracle I don't go into the water.

The Old Man pulls me to the bank and gives me a terrible scolding.

Tiny is lying on the floe and pulls Porta up to him. Together they get a grip on Barcelona and haul him out by the feet like a sack of potatoes.

'Some weather for a river picnic,' coughs Porta breathlessly. 'Jesus, but it's *cold*!'

We make a ring of fires and put Porta and Barcelona in the middle of them.

When Barcelona stands up water pours from his buttonholes.

'Jesus'n Mary,' cries Porta. 'You're like a leaky bucket! I wouldn't have believed you could've held so much!'

We force Barcelona to roll naked in the snow. We've got to get his blood circulating. He's alive but he's like ice inside. You don't take a bath in the Moscow at 52 below and live, without the roughest kind of first aid treatment. He cries, sobs, curses us, but we are merciless. We're going to take our Spanish orange farmer home with us. In a couple of hours we've saved him. Porta has looked after himself. He has put on a dead German major's uniform, and insists on Tiny saluting him every time he passes, which he does continually. At last this gets too much even for Tiny. He demands a posting to another division. There's too much saluting in 6 Panzer.

We reach a deep ravine and Moser orders us to swing ourselves over on the overhanging branches. The last man, Gefreiter Kono, disappears into the depths with a scream, as the branch breaks..

'They might have warned us,' grumbles Barcelona. 'Save their own bloody skins and *piss* on us!'

'We have never retreated before,' states Heide, proudly. 'The decadent German aristocracy is behind this. The Führer should have slaughtered every one of the noble swine long ago.'

'German soldiers only learn how to attack,' says Moser. 'The word retreat is unknown at the German officer factories.'

'Considered immoral, I suppose?' sighs the Old Man disillusionedly.

'Of course,' Porta laughs contemptuously. 'It's bad for fighting morale, but all the heroes are getting so tired they soon won't give a fuck which way they're going!'

'You talk like a lot of bleedin' books,' growls Tiny. 'Let's talk about bints instead.'

'How *was* that Russian nurse you raped the other day?' asks Porta, scratching himself under the arm, where his lice have their favourite place of rendezvous.

'Dry as a 'ambone that's been 'angin' 'undred years in the rotten pantry,' grumbles Tiny, disappointed. 'They don't understand 'ow to make the most of their big moments in this country. It's somethin' *I've* been experimentin' with for years.'

'*What* have you been experimenting with?' asks Porta, in astonishment.

' 'Ores an' orgies, of course,' answers Tiny, irritably. 'When you're goin' to arrange an orgie the first things to lay on are buckets o' wollop an' a bunch o' itchy-arsed bints. It's best if the bints roll up about an hour's time after the boys've filled their gut. Me an' a mate o' mine 'ad a quiet place at Hein Hoyer Strasse, 19. The shack belonged to the Yid fur bloke, Leo, properly, but 'e nipped off smart when Adolf started comin' round the bleedin' mountain. Even though 'e *was* always dressed in black, 'e wasn't a bit like Reichs-'Eini's black boys, an', of course, there ain't no really normal people as are!'

'You'll answer for those opinions, Obergefreiter Creutz-feldt! Your cup will soon be filled to overflowing!' shouts Heide solemnly.

'Must've run over long ago,' replies Tiny, consideringly.

'All them reports you're goin' to put in I reckon there'll be a big paper shortage when we get back. But just give your jaw a rest for a bit, Julius. Stick a couple o' bullets in your ear-'oles and think of somethin' else. Well, when we *started* 'avin orgies we didn't understand it much and just pulled in passin' crumpet off the street. This meant we only got casual customers,' continues Tiny. 'There was even some as asked for credit. A bleedin' nit from Bolivia wandered in one night straight from the bleedin' jungle. 'E thought it was all free an' we 'ad to throw 'im out.

'"*Cerdo, cerdo*," 'e 'owls from the other side o' the road, and we thought this was some kind o' political party cry at first. But soon as we found out that it meant "swine", we rung over to the boys at Davids Strasse. "There's a pointy-'eaded bastard from South America down on the street shoutin' 'Adolf, *cerdo*! Adolf, *cerdo*!'", we said.

'"That's nice," says the desk-man, with the sleep still in 'is eyes. "'Ope 'e keeps on with it!"

'"What's it mean then?" we ask 'im

'"Look it up in a Spanish dictionary," 'e suggests. "Probably the Spanish for 'Eil!'".

'But they must've looked it up for themselves,' continues Tiny, ''cause they was all there with blue lights, truncheons, the lot, in under seven bleedin' minutes. That "cerdo" bleedin' Indian got whipped off quicker'n the devil takin' a nun off on Easter mornin'!'

'Pick up your arms! Single file after me!' orders Oberleutnant Moser.

A couple of miles further on we are fired on from the darkness of the forest. A rain of bullets cuts the bark from the trees around us, ricochets plow channels in the frozen snow. The moon hides behind a cloud. The impenetrable darkness is split by flashes from hand-weapons.

Tiny has taken up position with the LMG behind a large fir. He is firing whenever he sees a muzzle-flash.

'Move, boy!' he snarls at the Professor. 'Don't you know

we're fightin' for Newropa an' *lebensraum*! *Untermensch* must be wiped out to make room for more Germans!'

The firing dies away slowly and the sound of running feet can be heard disappearing into the forest. Frozen twigs snap loudly.

'Sections space out!' orders the Oberleutnant. 'No. 2 Section take the lead. The enemy will try to split us at the break in the woods but we've got to get through. All wounded will be taken with us. If a single one is left behind I'll have every NCO court-martialled. I hope I have made myself perfectly clear?'

The company advances in open order. We are continually forced to take cover from furious bursts of MG fire. Why not surrender? On the Eastern Front nobody surrenders.

Three men from No. 4 are wounded. Unteroffizier Lehnart gets his knee plowed open by an explosive bullet. He cannot stand on the leg, but we make him a support out of a carbine tied tightly to it so that the butt serves him as a foot. He groans loudly at every step, but it's better than being left lying in the snow.

It's unbelievable what a human being can endure. We have often observed this with wounded men. Leutnant Gilbert walked several miles holding his entrails in place with his hands. Oberschütz Zöbel crawled across a ploughed field with a smashed hip. Pioneer Blaske hobbled to the main dressing station with his whole face shot away and one leg crushed. Not to speak of Hauptfeldwebel Bauer, who dragged himself to the doctors with both feet hanging around his neck on a string. He thought they could be sewn on again. Fahnenjunker West, his father was a general by the way, lay out in no-man's-land for three days, spitted on the posts of the barbed-wire with his lungs hanging out of his back expanding and contracting like great balloons. Porta and I brought him in. He lived four days at the dressing station. I could go on and on like this.

We have become experienced veterans, although most of us are no more than twenty-two. We know all about how to kill people. We know, too, whether or not a wounded man will make it. We have a name for every way in which a man can be wounded: Full lung perforation, lung penetration, flesh wound, belly perforation, explosive scrapes, infantry stab, grenade lesions, disjointing shot. We have sixty different names for the various kinds of head wound. Our anatomical knowledge is astounding. In a clearing in the forest a halt is called to get the company together. Signals Feldwebel Bloch has had his shoulder torn open by a ricochet. The bleeding is ugly. With the help of a sling Sanitäts-soldat Tafel manages to stop the bleeding. He works quickly and professionally. Tiny helps him, handing him the required instruments. He sews up the wound with skilled fingers.

'You'll be all right now, Herr Feldwebel,' he says moodily, as he finishes dressing the shoulder.

'You're quite a bleedin' bone carpenter,' exclaims Tiny, astonished.

'You might say that,' answers Tafel, looking away. Tafel came to the unit straight from Germersheim.

'I mean like a real doctor feller as can turn an honest copper fixin' up a singed prick that's been out ploughin' up the open market,' continues Tiny.

'All right then!' snaps Tafel, irritated.

'*Are* you a real doctor with diplomas an' university degrees an' all that?' shouts Tiny enthusiastically.

'Yes, I *am*! So what? Now I'm a Sanitätsgefreiter and that's enough of that.'

'Porta,' screams Tiny. 'Our bleedin' Sani's a real gut-scraper. Come an' take a look at 'im. Some unit we got!'

'If you're a real doctor, why the hell aren't you an officer?' asks Porta wonderingly. 'What did they send you to Germer-sheim for?'

'Oh, very well!' replies Tafel unwillingly. 'I knew you'd find out sooner or later. But I'm not going to make a public confession to you lot. You can ask me to go, and I'll go, because there's just one thing you can note down, and that's the simple fact that I look after you because it's my duty and

269

apart from that I just couldn't care less what happens to you!'

'Herr Oberleutnant,' shouts Tiny, in pretended horror. 'Our Sani's run his head into a newspaper. He don't care a fart if you're playin' the 'arp tomorrow or not!'

'I didn't say that,' says the Sani indignantly.

'You said you couldn't care less about us,' Porta breaks in.

'If it means so much to you,' replies the Sanitäts-Gefreiter, sullenly. 'All right; I was a doctor.'

'Then you're still a doctor,' states the Old Man, puffing hard on his silver-lidded pipe.

'I am not allowed to work as a doctor. It's surprising they let me work as a medical orderly.'

'Did somebody go an' drop dead while you was pressin' 'is bollocks?' asks Tiny interestedly.

'Shut up,' snarls the Old Man, 'You can't understand what it's all about anyway, that's certain.'

'No, thank Gawd,' sighs Tiny happily. 'The bleedin' upper classes make such a lot o' bleedin' piss over fuck-all. Things they fix with a couple o' loose teeth, on the Reeperbahn.'

'Are you quite finished?' asks Porta. 'How you do go on!'

'I had a great many wealthy patients, hypochondriacs every one of them,' continues Tafel, wearily. 'After a while they began to irritate me. An upper class lady had invented some of the most mysterious illnesses. I sent her to Bad Gastein to get rid of her and gave her a sealed letter to my colleague and friend, the doctor at the health resort. He is also a medical orderly now.'

'Did you give her the letter to take with her?' gasps Porta. 'You must've been out of your bloody mind!'

'Clear as mud,' chortles Tiny, pleased. 'This old mare's gone 'ome fast as 'er pumps could carry 'er 'an steamed the bleedin' letter open. Who wouldn't? Everybody wants to know what's wrong with 'em.'

'What the devil did you put in it?' asks Stege.

'It was foolish, but I was so annoyed with the bitch that I wrote to my friend: Herewith Europe's most hopeless case of malingering. There is nothing wrong with her but too much leisure and too much money. Dip her in your warm swindle bath with ten pounds of kitchen salt in it and then pack her down in the most stinking mud you've got. Both she and her husband are the parasites of the age. Write her a huge bill and she will think you are a genius.'

'Very well,' nods Porta. 'I don't even need to put on my glasses. One night there's a knock on your door, and with classic stupidity you open it instead of shinning out of the back window and over the balcony. Even a newborn babe from Weding would have known that a couple of snap-brims in leather coat were marking time outside your door.'

'Yes,' admits Tafel, tiredly.

'An' who *was* this psycho-dame's feller?' asks Tiny, with interest.

'SS-Brigadenführer,' answers Tafel. It sounds as if he is saying 'Death!'

'You're more'n bleedin' stupid,' says Tiny, contemptuously. 'They must've scraped you out with a bleedin' spoon at the maternity clinic.'

'Why didn't you give her a trip on the banana express?' asks Porta. 'What d'you think she was paying you for, anyway?'

'Leave him alone, now!' snarls Oberleutnant Moser. 'Let's get a move on. The new German positions can't be far off. There can't be more than a day's march to them.'

'The cowardly swine are already in Berlin,' says Stege, pessimistically.

'So would we be,' grins Porta, 'If we'd had the chance.' No. 3 Section is sent out on reconnaissance. They curse bitterly as they disappear across the creaking snow.

'Maybe they'll go in the wrong direction,' says Barcelona, listlessly, 'and walk deeper and deeper into the snow.'

'West is always right for us,' answers Porta, sawing a piece of a long Russian loaf which is frozen to the hardness of iron. He shares it out amongst those closest in the leading section.

A recruit stretches out his hand.

Porta raps him on the knuckles with his bayonet.

'There are ninety million people in Greater Germany, Adolf says, and this section can't feed them all! Ring to your Führer and tell him you're hungry!'

'West,' mumbles Stege, tiredly. 'You don't hear anything else these days. Before it was always East.'

'You'll get used to marching West,' says Tiny, letting go a gigantic fart. 'Maybe Adolf'll want us to liberate the Berliners and get the Party some *lebensraum* on the bleedin' Rhine!' He bends over whooping madly, one shout of laughter following the other, as if he'll never stop. The threat of defeat seems comical to him.

The company marches on, through frozen swamps, over heights and through thick forests. Sniper groups and partisan units are met and beaten off.

'We'll get through,' says the Old Man to Oberleutnant Moser, during a short break. 'Long as we've got ammunition, we'll use our guns for all they're worth!'

'An' when we've banged off all our powder then we'll tear Ivan's ring out an' pull it down over 'is bleedin' napper,' remarks Tiny from the darkness.

'What about surrendering?' asks Wachtmeister Bloch.

'I'd rather pull the devil by the tail!' says Porta.

'Gawd but was I lucky to get into this bleedin' Army,' grins Tiny. 'Even though I 'ave got to be Obergefreiter you mustn't think I've gone militarist!'

'We don't!' laughs Porta.

'Come on, move!' orders Moser, sharply. 'Close up! Keep touch with the man behind you! Keep alert up in front!'

'That man's a bloody sadist,' grumbles Stege. 'The war-mad bastard never gives us a second's peace.'

A patrol comes panting back. 'Three miles on there's a village where a tank regiment has gone into quarters,' reports Unteroffizier Basel.

'Hell and damnation!' curses Oberleutnant Moser. 'What's on the other side of the village?'

'We don't know,' answers Basel.

272

'What the hell do you think I sent you out on patrol for, man?' Moser flares up hysterically.

'Herr Oberleutnant, I believe the forest ends a mile further on. Two T-34s are guarding the village on this side.'

'Why, then, do you tell me you don't know where they are?' thunders Oberleutnant Moser, his face going a dark red.

'Goin' on for evenin' we come to this one-night-stand 'otel, where you can rent a bed for an hour at a time,' Tiny is explaining to a circle of listeners. 'Well, we'd organized a white Mercedes on the Reeperbahn, so we were travellin' in style. The first thing me bleedin' eye falls on when I wakes up in the mornin' is a bunch o' light-coloured parsley tucked away between a couple o' fat thighs. What the 'ell, I think, 'ave you gone to sleep in a knocker? So I feels about, cautious-like, to see if it really was a bit of crumpet I was parked alongside of, an' who should pop up out of the bedclothes but "Strauss Waltzes" from Kastanien Alleé. 'Er, you know, as bangs the old joanna to death in "Passaten".

'"Mornin', 'ubby," she says, fresh as you please.

'"Morning, pedal-pusher," says I, listenin' fascinated to the blackbirds singin' in the pear tree outside the window.

'"Bein' married is lovely," she says a bit later.

'"Don't know," I says, "Never tried it!"

'She starts off again, chewin' away at me old bonce, and we take another trip in the gondola while the kettle's boilin' for coffee.

'"What's all this talk about marriage? 'Ave you gone an' got yourself 'itched up some whacked-up womb-snatcher or other?"

'"You're *funny*," she says, clickin' 'er loose teeth at me. "Don't you tell me you've no memory of us two bein' chained together in 'oly matrimony yesterday night? Cause if you *'ave* then Mum 'ere's got a few nasty tricks to show you, as some Japanese wrestlers I once knew give me a rough ol' knowledge of."

'"Chained together?" I yell. "You got softenin' o' the

brain, or somethin' girl? I don't need no bleedin' contract to get 'old o' *my* ration o' crumpet. I'd never dream of it."

'A slave of the bleedin' silver salver in a white nanny jacket turns up then bearin' a couple o' jugs o' niggerpiss on a tray.

'"Congratulations, dear guests," the silly bitch whinnies at us. "This must be the most wonderful mass-wedding ever known to 'istory. The entire village got absolutely stinko, and they're all still stewed as newts. The landlord is in bed with Otto, our prize boar. 'E's just said goodbye to friends and family with a bottle of 'Dead Man's Chest', best Jamaica. Never even *felt* Otto eatin' the trousers off 'im!"

'Slow but sure the ol' memory starts to go retro. The mayor, a little ol' fat feller, kept on askin' us if we was really serious about goin' in for this one man one cunt business, an' in my condition at the time I wasn't to be talked out of it. Nobody as knows 'ow to think with 'is shoes off could ever even dream o' gettin' spliced to ol' "Strauss Waltzes".

'"Any more been slipped into booster gear?" I asks.

'"The lot!" she says an' laughs that much she drops 'er bottom set into one o' these jugs o' niggerpiss."

'"Emil the Pusher, too?" I asks, for that at least ought to be an impossibility. 'E was the eagerest 'emmorhoid-buster in the 'ole of 'Amburg and 'id 'imself every time 'e see a pair of womens drawers 'angin out to dry.'

'"Emil too," smiles Ruth an' pushes 'er bottoms into place with a sound like a 'ippopotamus shittin' in choppy water.

'Now the 'umour of it 'its me. All us bridegrooms get together down in the sawdust bar and discuss things, an' agree on 'ow we're goin' to get out of it. We give the key o' the Mercedes to "Ida the Rider" an' tell 'er to drive straight to the Commerzbank on Kaiser Platz in Darmstadt an' wait for us there.

'All the sheet-workers are in that car like lightnin' when they 'ear the name Commerzbank. They reckon we're goin' to pick up some change. They're off as if the Vice Squad's on their tails.

'Emil grins like a poof while 'e's ringin' up the Schupo's to tell 'em a bunch o' crook amazons is on the way in a white ol' Mercedes, to wring out the Commerzbank on Kaiser Platz. What a reception them brides got. It was worthy of Mexican bleedin' general.'

'Pick up your weapons! On your feet!' Moser chases us impatiently.

'If we have to bite out the throat of every single Soviet soldier we meet we've got to get through!'

'Good appetite,' grins Porta, 'I've had *my* dinner, thank-you very much!'

'In Bernhard Nocht Strasse there was a big bleeder as bit a pro's throat out,' says Tiny, excitedly. 'All the bleedin' pimps got together an' was goin' to lynch 'im.'

'Shut it!' shouts the Old Man irritably. 'Your blasted voice can be heard for miles! Try taking a deep breath!'

Soon after, the forest begins to thin out. The trees are small and bent. A forest fire must have raged here. An ominous silence is all around us. We feel as if every bush and tree has eyes. With nerves at full stretch we sneak forward with weapons at the ready.

'A village,' whispers Stege fearfully, throwing himself down behind a snow bank.

Everything seems deserted, but the wind carries the sound of diesels and the rattle of tank tracks to us.

The fog comes billowing in shroud-like waves. In places only the tops of the trees can be seen.

'No good,' whispers the Old Man, examining the village through the glasses. 'They'll mow us down if we go closer.'

'It's our only chance,' says the CO drily. 'We've got good cover from the fog.' He looks back at the company which is spread about in small groups in the snow. He raises a clenched fist, the sign for 'Forward march!'.

We get up slowly, creaking in every bone. Moser and the Old Man are already off. Their steps creak in the snow, and their weapons knock against their helmets. The small noises sound loud in the silence.

The fog closes in. The lead-men disappear now and then in the clammy veil.

'Getting into this man's shit army's like shootin' a double six,' whispers Porta, sourly. 'God if I'd only been born without a prick!'

The noise of the tanks increases. It sounds quite close now.

'Christ!' whispers Barcelona. 'Must be how it feels before the head cashier drops his bloody chopper for the last shave.' We move forward in single file in a long column, going as fast as we can in the deep powdery snow.

'Gawd!' growls Tiny, shocked. 'We're runnin' straight into the arms of the bleedin enemy!'

'Keep a little more to the right,' whispers the Old Man, hoarsely. Oberleutnant Moser is bent almost double. His breath whistles through his nostrils. It takes all your strength to march in deep, loose snow. Every time you lift your foot to take a fresh step you think it's your last. You weep, beg to be allowed to lie where you drop. The snow-drifts seem bottomless.

A row of ski-troops flashes past with capes flapping. They're so close to us that they shower us with loose snow. 'Sheeee! Sheeee!' whisper the skis and then they are gone, almost before we realize they were there at all.

Without a sound the company drops down in the snow, ready for battle.

'I don't think they saw us,' whispers the Legionnaire, trying to conceal his uneasiness.

'Can't be certain,' says the Old Man, pulling at his spud of a nose, and taking a new bite of his plug.

'Why the hell'd they pass so close?' asks Porta thoughtfully. 'They've got something cooking for us!'

'They know what they're up to,' answers the Old Man, wisely. 'Half the company nearly died of fright just at the sight of them!'

'Forward,' orders Moser, raising his fist above his head. 'As long as we aren't attacked, we keep going forward.'

276

The Command Group takes the lead. They have the SMG mounted on a small sled. It's easier that way.

'We *must* reach the new front line before long,' considers Oberleutnant Moser.

'You never know,' says Porta, sceptically. 'When an army, with generals and all, gets on the move, it's like a railway wagon, rolling down-hill by its own weight. It's not easy to stop. They may even take up the new front before Berlin. That'd be pleasant. We could take the train home to Bornholmer Strasse in the breaks. It's mad running a war miles from home when you could have it just as well on your own doorstep. You'd never think of going all the way to Hamburg just to give a bloke a black eye if you lived in Berlin.'

'I'm piss-scared,' whispers Barcelona.

'Those ski-bastards are waiting in ambush somewhere near here. They saw us all right! Hell, they weren't a yard away from us. Soldiers can be slow on the uptake, but nobody could be *that* slow!'

As we cross the top of a height, tracer spits at us from the hedge-rows where the ski troops have taken up position.

'I'll take the bastards on the flank!' shouts the Signals Feldwebel. '4 Section follow me! Move! Move!'

'Feldwebel Beier! Attack the middle with No. 2 Section,' orders Moser. 'I'll take the rest of the company over the hills! Fix bayonets! Forward march! March!'

Porta covers us with the LMG. His well-directed fire keeps the heads of the ski-troopers down.

We use grenades to force our way through the hedge. Half-a-score bodies are lying there in pools of blood. We tear the white camouflage hoods from the bodies. We need them badly.

'Quick, let's get on!' cries Oberleutnant Moser. 'We've got to be a long way from here by the time they get back!'

Our own dead lie in the snow, staring unseeingly up at the cold grey heavens.

With a muffled thud a shell explodes in front of us. We

dig ourselves feverishly into the snow. Loose snow is good cover against both infantry fire and shell splinters.

A T-34 waddles out of the fog, making straight for us. Even the snow cannot deaden the scream of its tracks. It stops with a jerk and fires. A lightning bolt of flame shoots from the muzzle opening. Even before we hear the report the shell explodes immediately behind us. Gefreiter Lolik screams horribly. The sound of the scream tells us that his lungs are hanging out of his body. His whole back must have been shot away.

'It's all over,' groans the Professor, resignedly, wiping the heavy glass of his spectacles. Tears freeze to ice as they run down his cheeks.

'You must 'ave got snow in your whistle,' says Tiny. 'It ain't over, until our bleedin' 'emorrhoids are 'angin' on a cloud. Go back an' fetch that magnetic mine, an' I'll show you 'ow the English knock the top off a egg.'

'You don't want me to go back now?' asks the Professor, terrified.

'Believe you me, I *do*!' grins Tiny, wickedly. 'Get goin', you Norwegian sild, you, or I'll drop one o' your own bleedin' mountains on the back o' your neck, so you'll shit gravel. Get movin'. Want your prick to get frozen over with Ivan? Never 'eard of Kolyma, son?'

'Good God, I could get killed!' protests the Professor, with horrified eyes.

'Of course, what d'you think you're 'ere for? If there ain't a lot o' bleedin' casualties in a war then it ain't been a good war!'

The Professor crawls back, his teeth chattering, to fetch the mine. Looking more than ever like some terrible prehistoric monster, the tank fires again. The shell bursts violently in front of us.

Slowly the steel monster crawls nearer. Its forward machine-guns send their tracer into the snow in front of us.

The professor comes panting back with two mines. He wouldn't want to make that trip again.

'We-e-e-ll!' rumbles Tiny satisfied. 'One mine's enough for me, but maybe you'd like to take a T-34 yourself, so you can go back to your bleedin' mountains with cunt magnets on your chest?'

'No never!' moans the Professor. 'I was the biggest idiot the world's ever seen ever to get myself into your shit army.'

'Now you mention it,' smiles Tiny, 'I can't understand what you wanted to get in with the Prussians for. They don't give a fuck for people like you! To a Prussian anythin' as ain't Prussian's just shit!'

'They can all fuck me,' says the Professor, coarsely.

'Tain't likely!' says Tiny.

The T-34 closes in and sends a stream of explosive shells into the hills.

'Make yourself as little as a fly in a cow's arse,' advises Tiny.

'Don't run. That's all them Soviet boys in that tin-can are waitin' for. Then they've got you.'

The gun roars again and a deep blackened hole opens in the hill. Tiny pulls his feet up under him, and presses the T-mine to his body. Tight as a steel spring he waits patiently until he is within the tank's blind area. With the mine under his arm he springs forward through the deep snow.

The T-34 throws large chunks of ice up into the air. The frozen earth shakes. Machine-gun bullets buzz over the spot where Tiny lies ready for the next spring.

'Cover him,' I shout desperately.

'Got a PAK-gun in your back pocket?' asks Porta drily. 'Think a T-34'll notice this poxed-up peashooter?' he kicks the LMG viciously. 'A tank like that works on Tiny like a bowl of fresh cream does on a hungry tom-cat.'

'God, turn me to a mouse,' prays the Professor. His teeth chatter like castanets in his mouth.

'An ant'd be better,' I reply, pressing myself deeper into the snow.

'What about a lump of shit?' asks Porta. 'Fit us to a T.'

'Humans are too big to have a chance,' says the Professor.

'We've only got to move our eyes and those fellows in the tank can see it.'

Bullets buzz around us and hop over the snow. I press my hands to my ears. The scream of the tracks is driving me crazy. Inexorably the tank comes closer. Its infernal thunder is like a song of death. I want to dig down into the ground with teeth and hands like a mole, but dare not. The slightest movement and ice-cold eyes behind the T-34's viewing-slots will discover us.

Porta pulls a magnetic charge over to him and makes it ready.

'Where the devil's Tiny?' asks Stege, worried.

'Taking a bloody nap,' grins Porta. 'He's the kind that would, too!'

But Tiny isn't asleep. He is lying in wait for the steel colossus waddling towards him. Calmly he looks at the huge turret and the grey cement-covered steel sides. From the viewing slits MG-fire blazes. Broad and low-slung the tank rolls up over the last hill.

I can feel the broad tracks catching and crushing me into the snow. I have to take a firm hold on myself to fight the urge to get up and run.

Tiny pulls his legs up under him ready to spring up on to the grey monster. Who would think it was a bum from the Reeperbahn, one of those they call a social loser, lying there about to perform a deed of heroism which generals would recoil from in fear. Poor boys make the best soldiers.

Now the tank is only eight yards away.

Tiny crawls towards it. The heavy T-mine leaves a broad track in the snow behind him.

Every man in the company is following him tensely. He is pulling the mine after him on a rope. With a long cat-like spring he is up and moving fast towards the roaring tank. Now he is inside the six yard zone within which the T-34 is blind. He swings the mine above his head like a discus thrower. No other man in the company has his strength. The mine flies through the air, with the rope trailing after it, and hits the tank directly below the turret. Tiny lifts his bowler and disappears into a hole in the snow.

The tank stops with a jerk, as if it had run into an invisible wall. A hurricane of fire lifts towards the sky and a terrific explosion throws twisted fragments of metal far out into the forest. A black mushroom of smoke blooms above the flaming column. Russian tank infantry run heavily forward through the snow in an attempt to get up to us.

Tiny's SMG chatters. He knocks his bowler further down over his eyes.

The Russians go down like nine-pins. The wounded try to crawl away, but are killed by our concentrated fire.

The SMG wheezes and smokes. Its barrel is red-hot. Tiny kicks it viciously when it has a stoppage.

'German propaganda shit,' he curses, raging. 'Gimme a Russian Maxim! *It'll* fire as long as you can keep the cooler filled with piss!'

Oberleutnant Moser gets up and swings his arms over his head in the signal to move on him.

'Let's get out of here before they send a squadron after us!' We circle the village to the north cutting the throats of the advanced sentries before they can give the alarm. Desperately we hasten on through underbrush and thorns. Fear lends us wings.

We have five more wounded to look after. One of them soon dies. His insides literally fall out. We leave him sitting up against a tree, his glazed eyes looking towards the west.

'Adolf ought to see him!' says Porta.

With bursting lungs we push on into the forest. It's safer than the open fields. The cold fog closes behind us like a wet shroud. Russian orders sound and we hear the heavy Otto's speeded violently up.

Terror drives us on. Every muscle in our bodies burns as if it were on fire.

A couple of hours later Oberleutnant Moser gives the order for fifteen minutes rest.

Panting and worn-out we drop where we stand. Despite

281

the inhuman cold our tired faces drip with sweat and our clothes stick to our bodies.

'Bloody *lice*,' curses Porta, wriggling his body despairingly inside his clothes. 'Soon as there's the least bit of warmth those prickless partisans chase around like mad things. It's as if you were in the middle of a mini-size world war.'

'Maybe you are,' says Tiny, holding up two overweight specimens for examination. 'This feller 'ere with the red cross on 'is back is a bleedin' Commie louse. This grey bastard's a Nazi. They ain't so crazy. If they get 'ungry they stop an' 'ave a go at the bleedin' battlefield till they're full up. What do we do. We can't eat earth an' bleedin' trees. Lice are cleverer'n we are!'

'*Mille diables*, you can't fight a war in a cabbage-patch,' protests the Legionnaire.

'Could if the bleedin' generals'd take the trouble to think about it,' considers Tiny, 'but the big-'eaded bastards can't be bothered.'

There isn't a sound to be heard. Only the wind moans complainingly in the tops of the fir trees.

Moser spreads out a dirty chart and calls the Old Man over to him. 'See here, Beier! The village we've just passed is Nievskojo.' he points it out on the chart with his pencil, 'and here's the village Divisional HQ was quartered in. I don't expect they're still there though.'

'No, I dare say not,' smiles the Old Man. 'Staff officers don't like to hear shells howling around them!'

'If only we knew where the German front-line is now!' continues the Oberleutnant.

'German front?' says Porta. 'Who says there *is* a German front?'

'You can't believe the whole lot's gone bust?' asks Barcelona nervously.

'Not unbelievable,' answers Porta. 'Germany always breaks down at some time or other. It's in the tradition. So we could just as well break down when we've reached Moscow as later. Then comes the time when a lot of people'll give everything they've got just to disappear quietly, and generals'll swap their stars with pleasure for a Gefreiter's woollen stripes.'

'Why we got GOTT MIT UNS on our belt-buckles?' asks Tiny, naively.

'Cos He's the only one who *is* with us,' explains Porta. 'He sees to it we don't win. To stop us getting too big for our breeches. Soon as we've had a good bang on the nut, we're nice, pleasant people again. For the next twenty-five years or so.'

'Is that a bleedin' fact?' mumbles Tiny. 'Are we really such a lot o' shits in Germany?' He runs a big dirty hand over his face.

'You know, when I come to think of it, all the Germans *I* know *are* rotten bastards!'

'Thanks for the recommendation,' says Porta.

'I don't mean you an' bleedin' me an' most of us lot 'ere, but the bleedin' *German* for Christ's sake! You *know* what I mean. It's piss difficult when you begin to think about it, ain't it?' he adds, a little later.

'As I've told you before, son, the best thing you can do with *your* brain is to pack it up nicely and post it off home. Then let others do the thinking for you,' advises Porta.

'Be easiest,' Tiny admits.

'Take up arms! Single file after me!' orders Moser, pushing the chart into his report-case. 'We'll be through before dawn,' he promises, optimistically.

The wind pipes through the forest carrying great blankets of snow with it. Trees creak with cold and burst with sharp reports.

We march all through the night and most of the following day. It's getting dark, the creeping Russian twilight which seems to fall silently from the grey clouds above us.

The wind whips ice crystals at us and the merciless frost lays a mask of rime over our faces. We look like monsters from some fantasy world.

Two steps more, you say to yourself, and I'll let myself drop. But still you go on. Fear of Russian revenge drives you

283

on. We lie rolled together in the snow, trying to find warmth from one another, while we listen to the sounds that come from the darkness. Giant firs and pines rise around us like jeering giants.

'What time is it?' asks the Legionnaire, who is completely covered with driven snow.

'Two and one to carry,' snarls Porta, boring himself still closer in between the Old Man and Tiny. He's so thin the frost goes straight to his bones.

'*Naldinah Zubanamouck*,'* snarls the Legionnaire.

An artillery Gefreiter is calling for his mother. Both his feet are frozen. We take turns to carry him hanging between two men. Many of us have frost sores, and hop along with the help of a stick. Porta considers we have died a couple of days ago and are just zombies moving on automatically. Like headless hens. We've marched so much in our lives that we keep on moving our feet a couple of days after we're actually dead!

'Think we'll march straight into 'eaven?' asks Tiny, rubbing his hands cautiously over the wet, open frost sores on his face.

'*Non, mon ami!*' says the Legionnaire quietly. 'There we shall have peace! *Vive la mort!*'

'Gawd love us!' says Tiny, feebly. 'Do you mean we'll get a permanent pass for ever? An' can go for a shit when we want to, without 'avin' to ask nobody?'

'*Bien sûr,*' answers the Legionnaire, in a convinced tone.

'I'm on my way,' Tiny breaks out. 'Jesus Christ, 'ow I'm gonna *enjoy* bein' dead!'

* *Naldinah* etc. (Arabic): Insulting expression.

> '**The dead are daubed with slime, and the murder-
> ers have an alibi. The executioner not only kills,
> but also preaches over the dead. Old Germany,
> you have not deserved this!**'
>
> Le Temps, 3 July 1934 (After the massacre of 30 June)

Broad, patrician Bellevue Allée is empty of people one Sunday
morning in May 1942. The trees have begun to bud a few days
earlier. Everything is dressed in translucent green. It is as if the
city begins to breathe again after the hard winter.

A grey Horch swings into the allée followed by three black
Mercedes. They stop in the middle of the road outside an old,
aristocratic residence. Men in long coats and grey SS caps
spring smartly out and run up the steps, with a little man in a
blue-grey uniform in the lead, Adolf Hitler.

On the third floor they knock hard on a door. 'Berger' is the
name on the small brass plate. The door does not open
immediately and one of the officers kicks it in.

Hitler rushes in with a pistol in his hand.

A tall powerfully-built man in a silk dressing-gown comes
from another room.

'Mein Führer!' he cries in astonishment.

'Traitor!' screams Hitler springing forward and catching
General Berger by the throat. 'Traitor! Cowardly swine! I arrest
you!' He strikes the general twice across the face and spits a
mouthful of vulgarisms at him. Then he lifts his Walther,
empties the magazine rapidly, turns on his heel and almost flies
from the apartment with coat-tails flapping behind him.

SS-Hauptsturmführer Rochner confides later to a friend that
the Führer reminded him of a bat. The confidence costs him his
life. He is shot by his own comrades in Dachau.

Neighbours who have heard the sound of shots stand

fearfully at their half-open doors. They are brutally pushed back by the SS officers of Hitler's guard.

Studienrat Walter Blume, who reproaches them, is ruthlessly shot down before the eyes of his wife and three grandchildren. When his wife resists, her face is smashed by a blow from a pistol.

10 | The Partisan Girl

'It's the fifteenth day,' says the Old Man to Oberleutnant Moser. 'If we don't catch up with our boys soon we've had it. Over half the company's suffering from frost bite. Most of them with gangrene. Twenty-three men are wounded. Four won't live through the night.'

'I know,' Moser nods darkly. 'I won't last much longer myself. But if they catch us here behind their lines they'll execute us on the spot. We've *got* to catch up!'

'If we can,' replies the Old Man. 'It won't be long before even rifle-butts won't keep the men moving.'

'It's just hell,' mumbles the Oberleutnant, and rolls himself in his greatcoat.

Porta nudges me.

Tired and frozen stiff with cold I get up on my elbow to see what he wants. I was just getting comfortable in a snow-drift alongside Barcelona.

He hands me a black, frozen potato and a sardine as hard as a rock.

I try to smile in acknowledgement but the smile turns to a cry of pain. You can't smile when your mouth is frozen to ice.

Carefully I push the sardine in onto my tongue, where it slowly thaws out. It tastes wonderful. A little meal like this can be made to last a long while if you know how, and you soon learn the trick of it in Russia. I put the potato in my pocket. I'm keeping it for later.

'Where the devil *is* that front-line?' asks the Legionnaire. 'It can't be much farther now.'

'That record'll soon be worn out,' rumbles Tiny, breaking great lumps of ice away from his beard. His feet are frost-bitten too. For the last three days he hasn't been able to feel his toes when he moves them. Gangrene, which eats you up horribly from the inside, begins like that.

Nobody dares to take off his boots and treat the ruined feet. The flesh can come off together with the boot. Many of us can already say goodbye to both feet if we don't get treatment soon.

'Butcher,' shouts Tiny to Tafel. 'Can you chop off a 'ind paw without killin' a man?'

'Of course,' replies the Sani, carelessly. 'But how would you get along without feet?'

'I suppose you're right,' says Tiny resignedly. 'It's this bleedin' stink though. Makes me sick as a bleedin' owl.'

'I'm staying here,' says the Signals Feldwebel suddenly.

'Are you crazy?' cries the Old Man.

'*As-tu perdu les pedales?*'* says the Legionnaire. 'It's madness to give up now!'

'Keep your pecker up,' shouts Stege from his hole in the snow. 'Tomorrow evening we'll be home. You'll be in the hospital. Clean white sheets, regular meals and *warmth*, son!'

'No,' growls the Feldwebel, angrily. 'I've had enough. I'm sick of all the lies they've filled us up with. I'm staying here. You'll go faster without me, too. If I live it'll be as a cripple and that's no life for me.'

'Only the dead will be left behind,' says Oberleutnant Moser firmly.

'As long as you're breathing you're going with us.'

'Then what?' asks the Signals Feldwebel with a sneer.

'That's up to the doctors,' answers the OC, shortly.

During the next twenty-four hours we are only able to

---

* *As-tu* etc. (French): Have you slipped off the pedals?

move in short marches. Continually we are forced to rest. Eight bodies lie behind us in the snow. During a rest Feldwebel Loew pushes his bayonet quietly into his stomach. A short gurgling scream and he is dead.

Stege has fever and screams in delirium. The bandage around his head is a bloody sheet of ice. We roll him in two Russian greatcoats but he still shakes with cold.

'Water,' he begs in a weak voice.

The Old Man pushes a little snow between his ruined lips. He swallows it thirstily.

'Think we'll get him through?' asks Barcelona, worriedly, putting a piece of frozen bread into his mouth.

'*Naturellement*,' snaps the Legionnaire.

'Hear me now,' shouts Moser standing up. 'You *must* pull yourselves together! If we stay here much longer we'll freeze to death. Come along now, up on your feet! Pick up your weapons and follow me! March! Left, right, left, right!'

With the utmost difficulty we get to our feet. Some fall again immediately. The forest seems to spin around us like a merry-go-round. Tiny grins foolishly:

'*Auf der Reeperbahn nachts um halb eins . . .*' he starts to sing meaninglessly.

'Just let me get back,' he whispers viciously, 'so I can give Otto the bleedin' bull somethin' to remember Tiny by.'

'I don't think you and Inspector Nass can really do without one another,' considers the Legionnaire.

'It *would* be a bit borin' on the Reeperbahn without Otto roarin' out o' the Davids Wacht every so often and livenin' things up,' says Tiny. 'You ought to see the fun when there's been a real good Sankt Pauli murder. The Davids Wacht Station lights up like a Christmas tree. The 'ole crew's on deck an' Otto flyin' around like a fart in a colindar. 'E almost always 'as to give up an' to go on 'is knees to the big boys at Stadthausbrücke fur 'elp, an' when *that* happens all us wide boys make straight for the wide open spaces until the case is closed one way or the other. Otto always starts off with a parade of the known villains from the Reeperbahn.'

288

'"Now you're for it," he roars out in welcome, spittin' out the window. "This time you'll be leavin' your 'ead in Fuhlsbüttel!"

'When 'e 'as to let us go again, 'e always gets into the throes of a deep depression an' threatens to retire. That's just 'is gas, though. Otto'd kick the bucket right off if 'e 'adn't got Davids Wacht to play with.'

The Old Man and Moser help the Signals Feldwebel to his feet and hand him the heavy poles he uses as crutches.

'Come on, mate,' says the Old Man, sending a long brown stream of spittle out into the snow.

The Signals Feldwebel nods and hobbles forward, half supporting himself on the Old Man's shoulder.

Slowly the company gets moving. The OC is in the lead with his Mpi at the ready.

Almost every minute one of us falls forward like a log, face down in the snow. We get him to his feet, shout at him, hit him until he livens up enough to stagger on. Some are dead though even before they reach the ground.

Towards evening a fat little infantry Obergefreiter runs amok. He is the only man left of a party that joined us a few days ago. He's kept us all awake with his jokes and funny stories. Suddenly he's out in the brush like lightning and opening up on us with his Mpi. The company scatters to cover.

'Come out you spawn of hell,' screams the fat little soldier, shooting away for all he's worth.

Two Engineers get behind him and snatch his weapon away from him, but he grabs up a Russian *kalashnikov* and runs off at full speed into the forest. His voice can be heard more and more faintly in the distance until the forest swallows it up altogether.

It's no use going after him. It would be a useless waste of invaluable energy.

'Company, follow me! March!' commands Oberleutnant Moser harhsly. We go on for two hours more. Then we can go no further.

'A short rest,' orders Moser, unwillingly. 'Nobody to lie down! Lean against a tree! Support one another! You can rest standing. Horses can do it, so can you!'

'They've got four legs,' protests Porta, leaning tiredly against a large fir.

'If you lie down you'll be dead within minutes,' continues Moser, unperturbedly.

With hanging arms we lean against trees, press up close to one another for support. Slowly the deathly weariness eases, and we fall into an unquiet sleep standing up. Fatigue and cold stiffen our limbs.

I take out a piece of frozen bread I've found on a corpse. I'm about to put it into my mouth but decide to save it and take a mouthful of snow instead. It may be a long time before I find anything eatable again. Just knowing I have a piece of bread in my pocket stiffens my spine and deadens the pangs of hunger. In the course of the night two of us freeze to death standing. We leave them propped against the tree just as they died. A pair of frozen caricatures of humanity. The Old Man breaks off their identity discs and puts them away in his pocket along with all the others.

Not one of us but doesn't have the thought that it would be easier to drop into the snow and finish it once and for all. No more of this hell we've been thrown into in the name of the Fatherland.

'Come on in the name of Satan!' screams Moser furiously. 'Get your fingers out you lazy dogs!' He lifts the stubby-nosed *kalashnikov*.

'March or I'll shoot you down where you stand!' he threatens. 'I'll *gut*-shoot you,' he adds when we stay down and ignore him. He pushes his gun into Barcelona, whom he considers the weakest link in the Old Man's section. 'Get going,' he says quietly but coldly.

'Get fucked!' says Barcelona. 'Win your own war! Count me out!'

'I'll give you a count of three,' snarls Moser, icily, 'and then I'll give it to you!'

Barcelona leans apathetically against a tree and begins to clean his nails with a bayonet.

'I'll shoot!' repeats Moser threateningly. His whole body is trembling with rage.

'You don't dare,' grins Barcelona. 'I'm going to wait here for Ivan. I'm tired of Adolf's marathon race. If you're clever, Herr Oberleutnant, you'll keep me company!'

'Take him!' recommends Heide excitedly. 'Liquidate that traitor to the Fatherland.'

'Shut it, you brown-arsed bastard!' shouts Porta, knocking him flat on his back in the snow.

A threatening mumble comes from the company. Most of them are on Barcelona's side.

'I shall forget all this nonsense if you take up your arms immediately and follow my orders,' promises Moser in a comradely tone.

'You can piddle up and down your back,' says Barcelona, jeeringly. 'And when you get tired of doing that you can take a trip to the Führer's HQ and piss all over Adolf with very best regards from me.'

'One,' Moser begins to count.

'You bloody great German hero, you,' cries Barcelona, uncertainly. 'You can't do it to an unarmed man.'

'Two,' hisses Moser desperately, his finger whitening on the trigger.

Porta swings his Mpi into position. The muzzle is pointed straight at Oberleutnant Moser.

If Barcelona doesn't give way a massacre will take place here in a few seconds. There is no doubt at all that the Oberleutnant will shoot, but it's just as certain that he himself will be dead before his magazine is empty.

'Made up your mind, Feldwebel?'

'If it amuses you then turn on your Goddam lullaby-maker,' says Barcelona, apparently indifferent.

'You asked for it,' hisses Moser and crooks his finger on the trigger.

There is the sound of a shot and a bullet chops a neat furrow in Oberleutnant Moser's fur cap.

'Come death, come . . .' hums the Legionnaire, playing smilingly with the sling of his Mpi. '*Vive la mort!*'

Without another word Barcelona swings his equipment up onto his shoulder and grins sheepishly.

Moser breathes in deeply in relief. He clicks the safety catch on his weapon to 'safe'.

'Come along! Let's improve the pace,' he shouts with an effort, avoiding Barcelona's eyes.

Slowly and creakingly the company gets on the move.

Tiny staggers forward on his rotting feet. 'Gawd! Oh Gawd! That bleedin' 'urts! I'll be glad when they chop the bleedin' things off!'

'Then you won't be able to run any more,' states Porta cheerily.

'To 'ell with that! I never did like runnin' anyway!'

'But you won't be able to go dancing when you get back to the Reeperbahn!'

'Never learned 'ow!' answers Tiny complacently. 'Only thing I ever used 'em for seriously was to march on, and that I can do without any time. So you see I really 'ave no use for 'em at all. Don't like runnin', can't dance, an' simply 'ate marchin'. It'd be the best thing ever 'appened to me if I was to get rid o' them bleeders.'

'Think the birds'll still crawl into bed with you when you're short of a pair of trotters?' asks Porta, doubtfully.

'I'll give 'em such a yarn about the 'eroic deed I lost 'em doin' as their mouths'll water that much with admiration they won't 'ave bleedin' time to notice what I'm up to with 'em. It ain't the feet as counts when you're rowin' along in the old sleepin' canoe, y'know.'

'You're not so crazy, maybe!' says Porta, thinking aloud.

It takes us almost two hours to cover a miserable two miles. Even Moser seems to be getting to the end of his resources. He drops to the ground like an empty sack just like the rest of us.

I take out my little frozen piece of bread. Everybody is watching me closely. I look at it, take a bite, and pass it on to Porta. It goes all round the group. A bite for each of us. Should I have eaten it when no one was looking? On the march, perhaps? I couldn't have done it. Not and stay with the company when we got back. To eat when they have nothing would have meant I could never have looked them in the face again. This comradeship is all we have left. It can make the difference between dying and getting through alive.

'What would you do, Porta, if the war were to end right this minute?' asks the Professor.

'It won't,' states Porta categorically. 'It'll last a thousand years and a summer.'

'Not on your life,' protests the Professor. 'The end of this war'll come suddenly. Just like a railway accident. What *would* you do now, Porta, if they came up to you and said the war was over?'

'Son, I'd find myself a demobilized Russian lady of like mind, and I'd do my level best to make her think that hostilities had broken out all over again.'

'Is that really all you'd do?' asks the Professor, wonderingly.

'Don't you think it'd be nice?' grins Porta. 'It's more than enough for most of us. Even the biggest buck nigger in existence!'

'And you?' the Professor turns to Tiny.

'Same as Porta,' replies Tiny, sucking on a lump of ice. 'Crumpet's the most important thing in this world. If they supplied us with it when we was out in the field I just wouldn't care if the war was to last a 'undred years. Comin' back to your question there's just a possibility I might take time out before I got on the job to bash a bleedin' general!'

'They send you to jail for that,' says Barcelona.

'Thirty days for disturbin' of the peace,' answers Tiny, optimistically. 'That I'd do with pleasure just to 'ave the fun of kickin' one o' them red-tabbed bastards in the crutch.'

'I'd take the Royal Suite at the "Vier Jahreszeiten" and then I'd die laughing at the sight of their faces when I couldn't pay the bill,' announces Barcelona, his face lightning up at the thought.

'I would enroll immediately as a student at the War Academy,' says Heide, with decision.

'You must have a University Entrance Examination before you can get those red stripes up, *mon ami*,' says the Legionnaire.

'I want those red stripes and I mean to have them!' shouts Heide, bitterly. 'My father was a drunkard who spent most of his life in one or the other Prussian jail. My mother was forced to wash other people's dirty clothes, and scrub floors for the fine folk. I have sworn to reach the very highest rank and then I will revenge myself on those swine!'

'Where are you going to get the money you'll need to live on while you're getting your exam?' asks the practical Porta.

'They hold back seventy-five percent of my pay. That's in War Bonds at twenty percent. I've been doing it ever since 1937.'

'There weren't any War Bonds in 1937,' says Porta, protestingly.

'No, there weren't,' says Heide, 'but we had the five year plan. When they're paid out I'll have a nice little nest-egg.' He pulls his blue State Bankbook proudly from his pocket and lets it go round. It contains nothing but entries in black ink.

'By Heaven!' shouts Porta in amazement. 'No red figures. When you open mine you have to put on your sunglasses to protect your eyes from the glare!'

' 'Ow d'you know you're suited for it?' asks Tiny naively.

'I'm suited,' states Julius, categorically. 'I'll be Chief-of-Staff of a division when you're called up again in ten years time.'

'We won't bleedin' well salute *you*,' says Tiny coldly.

'I wouldn't want you to,' says Heide, superciliously.

'You mean you wouldn't even recognize us when you've made Chief-of-Staff?' gapes Tiny, thickly.

'I won't be able to,' answers Heide proudly. 'I shall belong to a different class to you. A man has to burn his boats behind him eventually!'

'Will you tighten your mouth like Iron Gustav?' asks Tiny, looking at Heide as admiringly as if Julius were already on the General Staff.

'Tightening your mouth has nothing to do with it,' answers Heide with a self-satisfied mien. 'It's a question of personal pride.'

'Will you go round with a monocle screwed into your eye like old "Arse an' Boots"* used to?' asks Porta.

'If my sight should weaken, which I doubt, I would use a monocle as is the Prussian habit. I am absolutely against officers wearing spectacles. Spectacles are only for the coolies who work in offices.'

Passing through a frozen swamp we fall in with an infantry platoon led by a brutal-looking Feldwebel.

'Where are you men from?' shouts Moser, in surprise.

'We're what's left of 37 Infantry Regiment, 1st Battalion,' replies the Oberfeldwebel brusquely, spitting into the snow.

'Who do you think you are, Feldwebel?' says Moser, sharply. 'Have you forgotten how to report to an officer in a proper manner? Pull yourself together, man! You're speaking to an officer now!'

The Oberfeldwebel stares at the officer for a moment. His brutal face works with rage. Then he brings his heels together with a smart click, his left hand goes to the sling of his weapon and the right presses tightly down along the seam of his trousers in properly regimental manner.

'Herr Oberleutnant,' he roars in a parade-ground voice. 'Oberfeldwebel Klockdorf and nineteen other ranks, the remainder of 37 Infantry Regiment, 1st Battalion, reporting for duty, sir!'

* 'Arse and Boots': see *Wheels of Terror*.

'That's better,' smiles the Oberleutnant. 'We are also a remainder. The German Wehrmacht seem to be holding a remainders sale at the moment!'

'Did you really expect anything else?' asks Porta half-audibly. 'Any fool could've guessed how it was all going to end.'

Moser hears Porta's remark and steps closer to the Oberfeldwebel. 'Have you any idea at all of what is happening in this area?'

'No, Herr Oberleutnant. The only thing I know with certainty is that the German Army is getting the shit knocked out of it, sir!'

'You know nothing, then?' shouts Moser. 'Don't you read Wehrmacht reports? It's your duty to do so! Orders from above! Well above!'

A tired laugh goes round the ranks of the company.

The Oberfeldwebel looks at Moser in astonishment. Is he dealing with a madman? How's this going to end? But German soldiers are used to dealing with madmen. He takes a deep breath and clicks his heels an extra time. Mad Prussians like that sort of thing.

'Herr Oberleutnant I have a man in the platoon who was an Unteroffizier on the Staff of the Division. He tells me we are preparing a new front further to the west.'

'What a mine of news you are, man!' Moser grins broadly. 'So we're preparing a new front further to the west, are we? In front of Berlin, perhaps?'

'Very possible, Herr Oberleutnant. Unless they've decided Paris would be better, sir?'

Late at night we march into what appears to be a ghost village without a sign of life. Small huts peep out fearfully from between mountains of snow.

Porta is the first to discover smoke coming from the chimneys.

Signs of life!

'There's somebody talkin,' says Tiny, listening intently.

'Are you sure?' asks Moser, sceptically.

'When Tiny says he can hear something then there's something to hear!' states Porta emphatically. 'That boy can hear a hummingbird farting on its nest. *And* hear it twenty miles against the wind.'

'Russian or German?' asks the Legionnaire.

'Russian. It's women natterin'.'

'What are they saying?' asks the Legionnaire.

'I don't understand their foreign piss,' answers Tiny. 'Can't understand why these bastards can't speak proper German. Talkin' foreign's sneaky.'

'Very good!' decides the Oberleutnant. 'We'll spend the night here after we've cleaned it out.'

At the thought of warmth and something to eat the company livens up amazingly. There must be something eatable in a whole village.

Porta picks up a bread-bag and runs through it with practiced fingers. It's empty. He throws it down in disgust. With weapons at the ready we search the huts. We take no chances. Fire at the slightest sound. Even children would be shot down if we felt they were dangerous, and children *can* be dangerous here in Russia. Before now a five-year old child has bombed an entire company to death. In that respect there is little difference between Russia and Germany.

'Take care!' shouts Moser warningly, as we enter a tileworks with the Old Man in the lead.

'Hell!' says Porta. 'It's as dark in here as the inside of a nigger-woman's cunt!'

'Shut it!' whispers Tiny, stopping as if he had run into a brick wall. 'There's somethin' wrong in 'ere!'

'*Tu me fais chier,*'* whispers the Legionnaire, going down on one knee behind a stack of tiles.

'Some murderin' bastard cocked a gun!' answers Tiny, staring intently into the darkness.

'Are you sure?' asks Heide anxiously. He has a grenade ready to throw in his hand.

* *Tu me fais chier* (French): You make me shit (French Army slang for: You make me tired).

'Go an' 'ave a look,' whispers Tiny almost inaudibly.

We drop to the ground with every nerve taut.

'Close your eyes,' whispers the Old Man. 'I'm gonna let off a flare.'

There is a hollow report as the flare goes up into the ceiling.

Cautiously we open our eyes. The blue-white light burns them like fire.

Porta comes halfway to his feet and with the LMG pressed tightly into his hip lets off a burst. The belt flaps like a wounded snake. Tracer lines out and up into a distant corner of the tileworks.

Piercing female shrieks drown out the chatter of the machine-gun. An Mpi stutters viciously from a beam. A hand-grenade rolls to Tiny's feet. Quickly he picks it up and throws it back. With a roar it explodes in the air.

I throw a potato-masher. Everything goes quiet.

Over in the corner we find six women in Red Army officer uniform. The head of one of them is shorn off cleanly as if by a giant knife. It lies quite naturally in a pool of dark blood. The eyes almost seem to be looking at us, examining us.

'Nice-lookin' bint,' says Tiny, picking up the head. He sniffs at the hair. 'What a lovely smell o' woman. Pity the Fatherland requires a bloke to kill pretty little things like 'er.' He spins the head and examines the profile with connoisseurmien. Blood runs from the shorn-off neck down onto his wrist.

'Rough, tearin' the 'eads off pretty women!' He lays the head carefully under the girl's arm.

'When people were beheaded in the old days, they used to bury them with their heads between their legs,' explains Heide.

'Pretty girls, too?' asks Tiny.

'Everybody,' states Heide firmly.

'You'd think it was a bleedin' cock-sucker on the job!' Tiny grins long and loud.

'On Devil's Island the executioner holds up the head by the ears and says: Justice has been done in the name of the people of France!' explains the Legionnaire.

'Lord love us!' cries Porta, 'and I thought the Frenchies were a cultured lot!'

'But it is only criminals who are treated in this way, *mon ami*,' the Legionnaire goes to the defence of French culture.

'Only criminals,' mumbles the Old Man. 'You can't tell these days whether you're a criminal or a hero. They change the bloody rules every day.'

'Yes they do 'urry things, nowadays,' says Tiny, looking over at Heide accusingly. 'Glad *I* ain't a member of the bleedin' Party.'

'What do you mean by that?' comes threateningly from Heide.

'What I say,' grins Tiny, pleased.

'Come along,' shouts Oberleutnant Moser. 'Feldwebel Beier! Put some gunpowder under that gang of yours!'

'Remove fingers! Get your arses in gear!' shouts the Old Man. 'Peace hasn't broken out yet, you know!'

In short order the village is ransacked. Civilians come out of hiding. Everybody protests hatred of the Communists, and their great pleasure at seeing Germans.

'These people must've been Nazis before Adolf even heard of it,' Porta considers. He catches hold of an old woman, who isn't as old as she looks. '*Matj*,* you no like Commie partisan. You love Nazi!'

'Up with your right arm, old thing, and shout after me: "*Heil Hitler, grosses Arschloch!*"'†

They shout it gladly without having the least idea of what it means.

'I've never heard anything like it!' Heide explodes. 'If the Führer only knew what was going on!'

'Stop that nonsense,' orders Moser, irritably. 'Tell them to boil potatoes, and get some big fires going.'

* *Matj* (Russian): Mother.
† *Grosses Arschloch* (German): Big arsehole.

Porta explains to the Russian women that they are to boil potatoes and not spare the firewood.

The Old Man is bellowing at an artillery Obergefreiter who has been so foolish as to remove his boots. With a lost look the artilleryman stares at the fleshless white bones of his feet. Sanitäter Tafel throws up his hands in despair.

'I'll have to amputate! Boiling water!'

'Can you do it?' asks Moser sceptically.

'I can't *not* do it,' replies the Sani. 'He can't be left here and we can't shoot him either!'

'Nobody is to take off his boots,' shouts the company commander. 'That's an order!'

'Gawd, if 'e was to start marchin' off on them 'e'd scare the life out o' bleedin' Ivan!' cries Tiny. 'They think 'e was the old man with the scythe comin' after 'em!'

The artillery Obergefreiter is strapped to a table with rifle slings. A woman brings boiling water. She helps the Sani as well as she can. Her husband and two sons are with the Red Army, she tells us.

The operation takes an hour. Before evening the Obergefreiter dies without regaining consciousness.

We lower him into an antitank trench and shovel snow over him. We hang his helmet on a stick and the Old Man adds his identity discs to the growing collection in his pocket.

We stuff ourselves with hot potatoes. They taste wonderful. After a while we feel as if we were born anew, and don't even grumble when we have to go out on guard. The posts are double-manned. Thirty minutes on. Nobody can stand the cold for a longer period.

Moser decides to march at 7 o'clock. This will give us three hours before light, and we should be able to get a good distance from the village in case the villagers alarm the local partisans. They'll have to do this, in all probability, to avoid being liquidated for aiding the enemy.

Oberfeldwebel Klockdorf suggests, cynically, that it

300

would be wisest to shoot all the civilians before we march off. 'Dead men tell no tales,' he says with a grin.

'You weird bastard!' Porta stares at him. 'We can't knock off all these old *matjeri*!'*

'Why not?' asks Klockdorf. 'It's them or us. What're they worth? People over fifty ought to be put away, anyhow! Heydrich made the suggestion once!'

'I'll make a point of calling on your fiftieth birthday, chum,' Porta promises him, indignantly, 'just to see if you mightn't have changed your opinion.'

'Puncture that bastard!' growls Tiny.

A little past midnight it's our turn on guard. It's bitingly cold, and has just begun to snow. Visibility is no more than a couple of yards.

Porta and I have the post on the north side of the village. The Sani has excused Tiny guard duty, because of his feet. Half the period is over when Oberfeldwebel Klockdorf comes out of the darkness with two men behind him dragging a young woman between them.

'Found a knocker?' asks Porta, examining the girl with interest.

'*Ein Flintenweib*,'† grins the Oberfeldwebel sadistically, pushing his Mpi into the young woman's stomach.

'And you're taking her to the OC, of course?' asks Porta with a sly look.

'Like fuck we are!' answers Klockdorf, coarsely. 'What's it to do with him? We'll put this hellcat away right here on the spot.'

'She's too good to waste on the worms,' says Porta. 'Let me have her, instead.'

'Don't try anything with her!' Klockdorf warns him. 'She's poisonous as a snake!' He bends down over the girl, who cannot be more than twenty years of age. 'Now then, you dirty little whore. This is where you get your brains blown out!'

* *Matjeri* (Russian): Mothers.
† *Ein Flintenweib* (German): Army slang for a partisan woman.

'But you're going to die slowly, girl! We're going to gut-shoot you first!'

'Nazi,' she hisses, spitting at his face. 'You never leave Russia alive!'

Klockdorf drives his fist into her groin and she doubles up with a moaning scream.

'You wicked bitch! You'll regret that! I'll break every bone in your Commie body before I kill you!' he rages, white in the face.

'Kick her cunt up into her throat,' suggests a Gefreiter of Pioneers, cheerfully. 'I know her kind. In Minsk we used to drag 'em after the vehicles on a tow-rope.'

His friend, an Oberschütze from the cavalry, lets out a high-pitched laugh.

'In Riga we used to hang 'em up by the feet, and when their screams got to annoying us we'd send the executioner to rip out their tongues with his pincers.'

'Any of you got a thin rope?' asks Klockdorf, with a wicked glint in his eyes. 'I'll show you how far the neck of a bitch like this can be stretched by somebody who knows how!'

'I've got some,' says the cavalryman eagerly, pulling a length of telephone wire from his pocket.

'Just the job!' grins Klockdorf, looping it with almost tender care around the young girl's neck.

'There's a beam over there,' says the cavalryman, pointing to a hut. 'She'll just be able to touch the ground with her toes. Jesus this is going to be good! She'll struggle. Christ but it's something to see when they spin 'em off and the rope begins to strangle 'em!'

'Come on girl!' says Klockdorf, pleasantly, pushing the prisoner along with the butt of his gun.

The telephone wire is over the beam when Oberleutnant Moser and the Old Man come out of the darkness.

'Hold on Oberfeld! What's going on here?' asks Moser, threateningly. 'What in Heaven's name are you up to?'

'We've snaffled a *Flintenweib*,' says Klockdorf, with a

forced smile. He doesn't quite know how to take Moser. He is a type of officer Klockdorf's never run into before.

'I see,' nods Moser, a growing coldness in his eyes, 'and what is a *Flintenweib*? I don't recall seeing the term in any Army Regulation. What about making a properly-worded report to your commander, Oberfeldwebel?'

Hate literally drips from every pore in Klockdorf's body as he brings his heels together unwillingly and spits out his words: 'Herr Oberleutnant, Oberfeldwebel Klockdorf begs to report his arrival with a captured partisan woman!'

'Better,' replies Moser, with a sneering smile. 'And you have appointed yourself judge and executioner and established a field court, all out of your own little head. Get the hell out of here you filthy insubordinate swine before I forget myself, and keep well out of my way, by God, or I'll have a court on *you*, with Oberfeldwebel Beier as my assisting judge!'

'Want me to neck 'im?' asks Porta, eagerly, cocking his gun. 'Be the best job of work I've done in the whole of this bloody war!'

'Get out of my sight, man!' shouts the Oberleutnant, savagely, 'or I'll give Porta the order he's asking for, and have him shoot you down like the vicious rat you are!'

Klockdorf disappears quickly, with his two henchmen at his heels.

The Old Man lets down the girl. She gapes at the Oberleutnant, and cannot understand what is happening. If their positions had been reversed she would have done the same as Klockdorf.

'Beier,' continues Moser. 'Keep an eye on those pigs of men. The slightest infringement of discipline on the part of Klockdorf you're to liquidate him!'

'Be a pleasure!' growls the Old Man. 'Hear that Porta? You and Tiny are to see to that!'

'Inside twenty-four hours we'll have his prick for you on a velvet cushion!' grins Porta. 'Tiny'll be on his track within ten minutes, and you know what that means!'

'I have not given you an order to commit murder!' says the Oberleutnant, sharply.

'Killing a thing like that's not murder,' says Porta, cheerfully. 'It's the duty of every citizen to exterminate rats! You can be fined, in fact, for *not* doing it!'

'What's to be done with *her*?' asks the Old Man, pointing to the girl who is still wearing the telephone wire round her neck.

'Shoot her?' cries Heide brutally. 'According to international agreement and the rules of war it is legal to shoot any civilian who takes up arms. The Führer has also said that Bolsheviks are to be destroyed by every possible means.'

'Kick that man's arse!' suggests Porta, without trying to make it clear whether it's Heide or the Führer he means.

'I regret what has happened to you,' says Moser politely to the girl when she has been brought into the hut. 'You will, of course, be brought before a properly appointed court-martial. Nothing will happen to you as long as you are with my company.' Porta translates into his broken Russian, but it is obvious that the girl understands German.

'Beg to report, Herr Oberleutnant,' says Porta, grinning, 'this soldier lady requests you go and get fucked, sir, and I am also to tell you, with the usual compliments, that you will not leave Russia alive!'

Moser shrugs his shoulders and goes to the other end of the room together with the Old Man. He cannot understand these political fanatics, and still thinks you can conduct a war like gentlemen.

Big logs crackle in the stove, sending waves of warmth out into the low-ceilinged room. Porta, of course, has got the place behind the stove. The partisan girl is in the corner behind him, so that, to escape, she'll have to crawl over him first.

The Legionnaire comes back from his spell of guard duty. He seems excited.

'Porta!' he calls softly.

'Here I am, in the maid's room,' grins Porta from behind the stove.

'*Saperlotte*,* hurry up and come,' whispers the Legionnaire. 'I've found a Supplies Depot!'

'*Kraft durch Freude! Die Strasse frei!*' gasps Porta. 'Get your balls swinging, son!'

'I'm with you,' says Tiny, wide awake in an instant, and rolling out of his blankets without waiting for an invitation.

Silently we leave the hut.

'What d'you think of *that*?' asks the Legionnaire, removing some planks.

With our mouths hanging open, we stare at case upon case, piled on top of one another. They have American inscriptions on them: 'America salutes the Russian People!'

Tentatively we lift the boxes.

'Tinned stuff,' says Porta, with his eyes glowing. 'Corned beef, pineapples, *pears by God my favourite food!*'

Suddenly Tiny tenses. He drops the case he is holding and is over behind a snowdrift in one long spring.

'Run like 'ell!' he howls. 'Tickin'!'

'Tickin – what's he mean by tickin?' asks Porta from down amongst the boxes. 'You'd think it was that boy's mind there was gangrene in and not his feet!'

'There's a bleedin' time bomb tickin' away right under your bleedin' feet!' wails Tiny, from the snowdrift.

Like lightning Porta is up and out of the hole. His legs drive like piston-rods. He literally bores his way into the snowdrift.

'Is it still ticking?' he asks Tiny. 'Couldn't it just have been a woodpecker trying to get at my pears?'

'I dunno,' replies Tiny, 'but it's tickin' all right. It'll blow any minute now, I reckon!'

'Time bombs ain't dangerous till they've *stopped* bloody ticking!' shouts Porta frantically, and is back down the hole like a ferret.

* *Saperlotte* (French Army jargon): denotes pleased surprise.

'They ain't gonna blow *all* my preserved pears to pieces!' he shouts, swinging a box up onto his shoulder. He has hardly reached the protection of the drift when it seems as if the whole inside of the world has exploded. A fiery column, of incredible force, shoots up towards the sky throwing boxes and tin cans in all directions. A rain of preserved fruit and shreds of meat falls on us. Tin cans, with edges like knives, fly like shrapnel between the huts.

'That was a dirty, bloody trick,' sighs Porta, disappointedly, as we stand looking down into the sooty crater. 'I won't forget Ivan for this for a long, long time!'

Tiny takes a taste of some of the meat, but it tastes of saltpetre. With a grimace he spits it out.

We open Porta's case of preserved pears, and our faces light up when we find it contains thirty tins. We've hardly got through one of them when Tiny gives a warning shout.

'It's tickin' again! Let's get out of this! The whole shithouse's goin' up!'

Like chaff blown before the wind we are over behind the big snowdrift.

The second explosion is bigger than the first.

A hut over on the far side of the Supplies Depot is blown into the air and disappears high above the trees. Molotov cocktails fly through the air. Phosphorous fires blaze up.

We are on our feet as soon as the sound of the explosion has died away, running back towards quarters, where the company is paralysed with shock.

Before we can even begin to tell them what has happened the sentries shout:

'Alarm! Partisans!'

Machine-guns and Mpis bark from the darkness and the screams of wounded ring through the night. Dark forms run from hut to hut. Glass tinkles and explosive bursts light up the darkness. Huts catch fire and burn fiercely.

'Come death, come now . . .' hums the Legionnaire, opening out the tripod of his LMG.

Black shadows flit across the large square by the statue of

Lenin. As they reach grenade distance Tiny's heavy machine-gun thunders, mowing them down in rows like corn. But there are a lot of them. They swarm in the narrow, crooked streets. Muzzles flame everywhere. The explosive bullets make terrible wounds.

By the statue of Lenin a commissar is shouting and waving his Mpi above his head.

I put all my weight behind the throw. The grenade explodes right over the commissar's head and slings him straight across the wide square. His weapon flies in the opposite direction.

'Masterly,' Porta smiles, and nods his appreciation.

I run forward, together with the Professor, who is carrying the grenade sacks for me. He feeds me with ready-armed grenades. I put so much into my first throw that now I can't do much over seventy yards. Still a good average distance for a grenade-thrower, though!

The partisans withdraw in a disorganized rout now that the loud-voiced commissar is dead.

The Legionnaire throws a T-mine into a hut. The house bursts open like a bag of flour dropped from a skyscraper. Suddenly everything goes quiet. The footsteps of men running can be heard receding into the forest.

Klockdorf liquidates two prisoners with shots through the back of the neck, and then smashes in their skulls with the butt of his weapon.

'What the hell are you doing?' screams Oberleutnant Moser at him furiously.

'Beg to report, Herr Oberleutnant, carrying out execution according to regulations. I caught these two men cutting the throat of the *Staross*.* He was protesting against them burning the village over the people's heads.'

'I intend to report you for sabotaging orders!' Moser flares up at him.

'Be a pleasure, sir!' grins the Oberfeldwebel, jeeringly. We have lost twelve men. Two sentries are found with their

* *Staross* (Russian): Mayor.

heads smashed in. Five men are wounded, one of them with a whole burst of machine-gun bullets in the stomach.

'Ready to move!' commands Moser. 'They'll be back as soon as they pull themselves together again and get over their first fright. We want to be on our way by then.'

We've been marching for about an hour when Moser suddenly remembers the partisan girl.

'Where is the girl?' he asks.

'Beg to report, sir, she's left for home, but asked me to give everybody her kindest, sir!' shouts Porta, happily.

'Do you mean to tell me you let her get away?' asks the OC, amazed at Porta's frankness.

'Not on your life, sir! I fancied her and offered her the chance as first lady at my little knocker in Friedrichsstrasse, but she got tough and tried to get hold of my iron. Then, when I was trying to find some rope to tie her up with she nipped smartly out the back door, and when I went after her pushed a pot down over my head and started banging away at me with a shovel. While this was going on she took her opportunity and moved off to the left into the forest. I shouted after her to tell her that you'd be very angry with her indeed, sir, when you found she'd gone AWOL. But the lady paid no attention to my despairing cries, whatsoever, sir, and is now probably at home in her house on the Street of a Thousand Arseholes, sir!'

'You're a problem to me, Porta,' sighs Moser. 'I really hope our ways soon part!'

'Probably they will before all that long, Herr Oberleutnant, sir!' says Porta. 'Officers don't usually last very long with our company, sir. Seems almost to have become a kind of tradition, sir!' he adds, smiling widely.

'I'll speak to you later, Porta,' Moser promises him. 'My God, how I'll speak to you!'

Three days later we reached a ruined village where only naked chimneys point like stone fingers to the sky.

'They're firing off red flares over there,' says the Old Man, pointing out the direction.

'C'est un bordel!'* says the Legionnaire, thinking with sad longing of red light districts.

'That sounds like a bit of all right,' yawns Porta, 'think of getting your old tip covered again. Mine could certainly do with a good thawing out!'

It's a grey, starless night, with a fast-driving cover of cloud. Showers of snow fall every so often. We lie for a while watching the lights away in the distance. They look very beautiful from here. The flares draw long coloured tails after them and explode in a star-burst of colour nuances.

'Ours!' states Moser, with assurance. 'Let's get on! It looks as if the Russians are pressing heavily. By tomorrow it may be too late!'

Suddenly the whole sky lights up. Shortly afterwards a rolling boom of many explosions running into one another reaches us. A fair-sized artillery duel must be in progress.

'What in God's name is going on along the front?' mumbles Moser, thoughtfully, after having observed the great flashes of light for a while.

'Maybe they're using up the last of the powder!' says Porta, trying to twist his mouth into a smile but achieving no more than a grimace.

'Section leaders to me!' orders Moser. 'I want you ready to move off in ten minutes time! In full battle order, please!' He adjusts the chin-strap of his helmet.

'What, in the middle of the night?' asks Feldwebel Kramm, unbelievingly. He joined us with eleven men only a few days ago.

'The Russians are swarming everywhere!'

'Show me somewhere they aren't, Feldwebel, and we'll go there!' says Moser, sarcastically.

'We march in ten minutes time! And we are going to get through even if we have to do it with only spades and bayonets!'

We have used our short rest to fill magazines and

* C'est un bordel (French): It's a brothel.

309

cartridge belts. Everybody is grumbling. It's as if we've lost our drive now that we're so close to reaching our goal.

'Hear me!' shouts the Oberleutnant, softly, when the company is paraded ready to move off. 'We are a fair-sized company, now. A good many units have joined us of all sorts, from clerks and caterers to rocket artillery and demolition experts. Now hear me, all of you! The German positions are no more than four or five miles from here. One last effort and we're home! We must leave now. Tomorrow morning might be too late. By then the enemy may have broken through the new lines. We must expect to have to fight hard, but there is no other way. Wounded will be taken with us, if there is the least possibility of doing it, but they must not be allowed to hold us back! Above all things. Maintain contact! We shall go forward in a walking hedgehog formation. 2 Section will take the lead. I trust you, Feldwebel Beier! Any questions?'

'What if the breakthrough fails, Herr Oberleutnant?' asks Oberfeldwebel Klockdorf.

'You'll soon find out, Klockdorf,' smiles the company commander, sarcastically. 'We'll be dead, Klockdorf!'

Tiny has got hold of a brand-new Russian machine-gun in beautiful condition. He hugs it, tenderly as a mother nursing her newly born infant.

Porta throws a tin of pears over to me. I swallow the contents and feel new strength flow into me.

We advance in a wedge across a stretch of open ground. Halfway over a raging machine-gun fire opens up on us from a group of trees and is supplemented by rifle fire from the flank.

Porta sweeps the foreground with machine-gun bursts, and covers us while we work our way forward towards the trees.

Moser dashes forward, closely followed by the command group. He stops a moment to throw a hand grenade.

Tiny jumps and passes the company going like a tank.

The machine gun hammers, grenades explode in the forest, screams and curses arise:

'*Job tvojemadj, germanskij, germanskij!*'

Branches and twigs crackle and snap under fast-moving feet. A burst from an MG knocks over two Pioneers. Sani bends to help them.

'Get on!' shouts Moser, pushing Tafel on in front of him.

No. 2 Section rolls over the Russian group, and finishes them off with spades and bayonets.

Tiny breaks the neck of a woman captain, with a chop from the edge of his hand, just as she lifts her gun to shoot him. Her head hangs crazily down her back as if she were trying to see herself from behind.

Panting, we rush forward through the loose snow. Often we go in up to the shoulders and have to be pulled out. The snow is like a bottomless swamp sucking you down into its depths. Three Russian infantrymen are stuck in the snow. Only their heads are showing above it. Klockdorf liquidates them with shots through the back of the neck. Blood-red rings colour the whiteness around them.

When we stop we find we have lost twenty-three men. A machine-gun section has disappeared without trace.

'Damnation!' curses Moser, bitterly. 'That wouldn't have happened if they'd kept in touch as ordered. Their names?'

Nobody knows them. They have only joined us quite lately.

'Nothing we can do about it,' decides Moser. 'We can't go looking for them. Once again, then! *Keep contact!* It's your one and only chance of getting through. Death is running with us!' Four times in succession Tiny falls into giant snowdrifts. He is as hard to get out of them as a horse would be. When it happens for the fourth time running he goes quite mad and fires a burst down into the snow in hysterical rage. He sends two bodies sailing into the forest.

'Out o' the way, you dead bastards! Out o' the way o' men an' the war! You've 'ad it, you 'ave, see!'

The Professor falls behind. His strength is quite gone. He falls sobbing into the snow.

The Legionnaire takes him by the arm and drags him along with him.

A little later he finds he has lost the ammunition bags, and wants to go back after them.

'Tiny'll kill me for losing the bags,' he moans, weeping.

'*Pas d'objections!*'* snarls the Legionnaire, dragging him on.

'You can pick up a couple of full ones when we hit Ivan again, which won't be long now.'

Shortly afterwards Tiny catches up with them. His rage at the snowdrifts has cooled somewhat, but breaks out again when he discovers the Professor has lost the ammunition.

'D'you mean to say you've thrown the ammo away?' he roars, pointing a big, dirty accusing finger at the Professor.

'I've lost the bags,' admits the Professor, feebly.

'Lost the bags!' howls Tiny, his great beery, bass voice echoing through the forest. ' 'E's lost the bags, 'e says. You 'aven't got the brains of a frozen bleedin' Bolshie monkey! You don't lose your bleedin' *ammo* in the middle of a bleedin' war! Where'd we be if everybody was to do that? There soon wouldn't be no war, *would* there? No ammo no bleedin' war! Where'd we be *then*? Go back an' find it! 'Ow'd you expect me to make coffins for Ivan without any nails to put in me bleedin' 'ammer? Want me to go rushin' at 'im without no ammo in me gun an' *frighten* 'im to bleedin' death? I've never 'eard nothin' like it! A loader what throws away all 'is bleedin' load! That's what you get for lettin' these barmy bleedin' arf-arsed alien bastards into your bleedin' army!'

'He stays here!' says the Legionnaire, decisively.

'Say that again!' says Tiny, unbelievingly. 'You must've swallowed a bleedin' date-stone when you was wanderin' round in Africa an' got a bleedin' mouldy date palm

---

* *Pas d'objections* (French): No nonsense.

growing up through your brain, mate! You're sabotagin' the Second World War. Thought o' that? You ain't still fartin' around with that gang of flat-footed Legionnaires you 'ad in the 'ot Sahara sun 'avin a 'igh ol' time watchin' them mirages of Arab cunt winkin' at you from the bleedin' clouds'

'Don't forget I am an Unteroffizier, Obergefreiter Creutz-feldt. I order your loader to stay here! *Compris?*'

'Oh you *do*, do you?' snarls Tiny, raging. 'All right then! I ain't got no alien loader any more, see? You can stick 'im straight up your rotten sand-filled arsehole if you should feel like it, and all 'is snow-capped, icy, bleedin' mountains after 'im, an' then you can get yourself transferred to the Engineers an' make a livin' shittin' gravel onto the roads for the rest o' the bleedin' war. That's what you can do, mate!'

He disappears into the forest with the Russian machine-gun under his arm like a walking stick. We can hear him for a long time, cursing Norway and Morocco as if those two countries were to blame entirely for the loss of his ammunition bags.

'Who the devil is that shouting?' asks Moser, who is bringing the company together again.

'It's Tiny,' grins Porta. 'He bit off a commissar's prick in the fighting in front of Moscow, and now he's just discovered he hasn't had his monthlies. He's cursing the Maternity Corps because they won't give him a free abortion.'

'Your section again, Beier!' snarls the Oberleutnant, viciously. 'It'll drive me out of my mind! Either you get out of 5 Company when we get back, and take that crazy crew of yours with you, or I ask for a posting away from the company altogether! I can't stand it any more!'

'There's a shower o' yellow Commie monkeys a mile the other side o' the coal-mine,' comes Tiny's deep voice, as he steps from the thick forest. 'They near shit themselves when I turned up an' took a couple o' bags of ammo away from 'em.' He swings the filled ammunition bags above his head.

' 'Ow about nippin' over an' fixin' 'em proper? They're only bleedin' militia, an' it'd be easy as stampin' on a frog.'

'God damn your eyes, man!' screams Moser. 'My cup of patience is running over!'

'Cup?' asks Tiny, looking round him. 'If they're dishin' out tots I'm due for a double ration. I was 'avin' me prick looked at last time we 'ad a ration issue.'

'Shut up, shut up, shut *up*!' rages Moser, taking a step towards Tiny and clicking over his safety-catch. 'Open your mouth just once more, Creutzfeldt, and it'll be the last thing you'll ever do in this world!'

Tiny goes over and stands by Porta.

'This bleedin' war's gettin' worse an' worse,' he says, injuredly. 'Ain't even allowed to open your mouth, now. 'Fore you know where you are it'll be forbidden to go for a shit!'

The company commander sends him a killing look. 'Let's get on,' he turns, resolutely, to the Old Man.

Now the artillery fire is thunderous. The Russian artillery positions can't be far away. Flashes show continuously above the trees.

Silently Porta holds up his hand in the signal for Halt! Without a sound the company sinks down in the snow.

A thunderous roar and a muzzle flash which makes everything light as day splits the darkness. A Russian heavy-calibre gun is firing only a few yards away from us. By the light of the flash we see the artillerymen rushing around preparing the gun for the next shot.

'*Mille diables*, a 380 mm!' whispers the Legionnaire. 'It will take them at least fifteen minutes to ready her again. Let's take them just before they're ready. Then they'll all be looking at the gun. They won't even feel themselves dying! *Vive la mort!*'

There is a jingle and rattle of steel on steel from over by the gun. Short, sharp commands are given, the loading crane groans under the weight of the heavy shell being hoisted up to the breech.

'Ready?' whispers the Old Man, drawing his combat knife from his boot.

'Like a hungry stork about to nip up a big fat frog,' answers Porta, splaying out the legs of his LMG.

Moser brings back his arm and throws a grenade into the middle of the gun crew. As the gunner falls he fires the gun. The chatter of our weapons is drowned in the muzzle report, and we dart forward.

I stumble across a body, come quickly to my feet, and roll down a steep incline. Thorns tear the skin of my hands and face to ribbons.

Porta is right on my heels. He twists like an eel as he falls, and fires a burst at some figures which come running along the top of the ridge. The tracer tracks seem to sweep them over backwards.

Tiny comes down with a rush like an avalanche, a Russian clutched tightly in his arms. They are thrown apart and come to their feet together with a roar. The Russian has a bayonet, but Tiny kicks him in the crutch and smashes his head open against a stone.

We rush on. A machine-gun hammers at us from a split-trench. Grenades explode snappingly, flares pop. In the twinkling of an eye we have taken the machine-gun nest. We are desperate men. They were blocking our way to safety.

The Signals Feldwebel is hit in the throat, and his blood spurts over me. He cries out hoarsely and tries to staunch the wound with snow. Too late! A main artery has been cut. Two SS-men fall into a Stalin trap, and are spitted on the rusty bayonets in the bottom of it. Their screaming can be heard a long way off. There's no time to take them with us. Breathlessly we arrive at a little cluster of sheds used by shepherds as shelter for them and their flocks.

Tiny is in the lead. He throws a grenade through the open doorway and drops into cover. The grenade explodes with a heavy thud.

'Hear anything?' asks Porta.

'Not as much as a fly scratchin' 'imself!' answers Tiny.

'Something smells,' says Porta, suspiciously.

'It ain't our friends the enemy,' mumbles Tiny, staring anxiously at the sheds. 'I'd be able to 'ear 'em breathin'!'

I raise the signal pistol and send up a flare. Slowly the umbrella of light sinks down, illuminating the huts. Still nothing to be seen.

The Old Man and the company commander come crawling over to us. 'What the devil are you waiting for?' asks Moser. 'Get on, you lazy sacks! There's not a minute to waste.' He is about to get up when Tiny restrains him.

' 'Arf-a-mo, sir, or I'm afraid we'll be parted from another before even *you'd* like! A black cat's walked through them sheds.'

'What do you mean, a black cat?' asks the Oberleutnant uncertainly, crawling further under cover.

'I don't know,' answers Tiny, thoughtfully, 'but there's been one in there.'

Some rear echelon soldiers come racing up from the hedgerows. We don't even know their names. We found them, almost dead from terror, in a pill-box three days ago.

'Get *down*!' shouts the Old Man, warningly. Ignoring the shout they rush madly on seemingly crazed with fear, shouting:

'*Tovaritsch, tovaritsch, nicht schiessen!*'*

They seem to think we are Russians. With hands held high above their heads they run straight for the huts.

'Holy Mother of Kazan,' mutters Porta. 'You think a Siberian commissar was gnawing at their arses the way they run!'

'Get down! Halt! shouts Moser, signalling to them with both arms.

'*Nicht schiessen, nicht schiessen, tovaritsch!*' is the only answer he gets.

The first of them has reached the huts and is about to kick open the door.

* *Tovaritsch* etc. (Russian...German): Comrade, comrade, don't shoot.

316

'Heads down!' cries Porta, terrified.

A volcano breaks loose. The huts disappear and a series of explosions follow on the first.

There is nothing left at all of the frightened soldiers.

'God save us,' cries Moser in amazement. 'What in the world was that?'

'A present from Stalin,' grins Porta, happily. 'When those Supplies heroes opened the door they set off the lot!'

'Jesus, what a bleedin' bang,' says Tiny, happily. 'I was right, about that cat. Ivan ain't bad at 'andin' out them Stalin Prizes! The echelon boys drop in every time. I can't for the life o' me understand 'ow anybody in 'is right mind'd dare go into a place like that. It's just made for Ivan to 'ave 'is little bit o' fun in.'

'Well, let's get on,' says Moser, shortly, pushing his Mpi under his arm.

'Let's just take another little breather for a minute, Herr Oberleutnant,' says Porta. 'Ivan's coming to see who it was took the Stalin Prize this time.'

'And 'ere's the winner, boys!' grits Tiny, opening up with his machine-gun.

A party of Russians fall screaming under the hail of bullets.

'Move!' shouts Porta, and off we go as fast as we can through the deep, powdery snow.

The Russian soldiers lie bleeding amongst the trees. One of them looks down in astonishment at his ripped body and moans softly to himself.

The company closes up. Moser orders a count of heads. Fourteen men missing. Only seventy-three of us left. Over three hundred lie dead behind us.

The company commander seems almost to be losing heart. His hand plays, thoughtfully, over his Mauser.

Tiny tries to roll a cigarette out of the fluff in his pocket, and manages to get a cigarette out of it. He takes a deep drag, holding the smoke in his mouth for a long time. Then he hands it on to Porta. There's a draw for all of us in

No. 2. Artillery thunders and shells whistle through the air towards the German positions. The whole of the western sky is a dancing sea of flames. At the horizon everything seems to be on fire.

'Who said the Red Army was beaten?' asks Porta, sarcastically.

'Oh cut it out,' growls the Old Man, irritably. 'It makes me sick to think of it.'

'If it's going to take much longer to get through,' continues Porta, 'you can scratch Joseph Porta, by the Grace of God, Obergefreiter, off the Greater German Army List.'

The Professor is completely beaten, and lies weeping in a snowhole. Tiny bends over him.

'It was bad shit for you gettin' into this lousy, bleedin' war, my son! But now you *are* in it I'd advise you to cork your life away, see? Keep close to me. I'll see you get back to your bleedin' mountains again.' He pushes half a pear into the Professor's mouth.

'Chew that slow, an' swallow the juice. It's as good as puttin' pepper up the backside of a lazy 'orse. Makes it want to run away from its own arsehole!'

Several times I get stuck in deep snowdrifts, and the others have to come back to pull me out. The soft, powdery snow is hellish stuff. At last I'm so worn out that I beg them to leave me where I lie. I cry, as the Professor cried before. For most of us, our supply of nervous energy is stretched to the breaking-point.

We go straight through a wide patch of thorny brush, which tears our skin and uniforms to ribbons. Blood streams down our faces, mingling with the sweat.

Slowly it stops snowing. A full moon shines through the clouds. The sky becomes almost clear. We can see a long way in front, and won't run into the enemy by accident, but it's easier for the Russians to see us, too. Our footsteps become strangely hollow. We stop fearfully and listen. It sounds as if we were walking on hollow tree-trunks.

'Bong! Bong!' it sounds at every step.

318

'Faster!' the Old Man is chasing us. 'Don't piss yourselves, my sons. We're only walking over a swamp. Lucky it's frozen.' Man-high reeds and swamp rushes hide us. This thick forest of swamp plants makes us feel safe. Suddenly we are in the middle of a village.

We go down by the nearest huts like lightning.

'*Stoi kto!*'* comes from the darkness. A submachine-gun spits tongues of flame. The burst smashes the face of Befreiter Böhle.

'Forward!' roars Moser. 'Fire at will!'

The sentries are swept away as every weapon speaks. We storm forward, throwing grenades through windows, kicking open doors, emptying magazines into sleeping soldiers. We go to cover behind great stacks of ammunition.

Thoughtlessly Porta slings a mine in amongst the boxes. The resulting explosion literally blasts us out of the village. In a second the whole place becomes a thunderous hell of flames, with explosion following on explosion.

'You are the biggest, stupidest idiot I have ever met in the whole of my life,' shouts Moser as he gets up cautiously, with blood streaming down his face.

'Nice little bang,' grins Porta, unworriedly. 'Ivan must've shit a new commissar when that went up.'

We have been marching some time down a narrow road churned up by tank tracks, when Tiny suddenly sinks to the ground.

'Panzers!' he whispers, pointing to a long row of T-34s waiting in readiness in between the trees.

'Got anything we can use for the Last Supper?' whispers Porta. 'Wish I'd been a better imitation of the Virgin Mary's Son!'

' 'E wasn't unlucky enough to get mixed up in a World War,' sighs Tiny, tiredly.

We make a wide detour round the T-34s, work our way through a wood consisting solely of saplings, and come out

---

* *Stoi kto!* (Russian): Halt!

again on a wide, open plain. In front of us are some hills which we will have to cross.

A long column of Russian lorries with blue black-out lights is moving slowly towards the west. Flares are going up everywhere. Klockdorf and the Old Man climb up to the top of the heights, while the remainder of the company stays under cover.

'We'll have to pass through a Russian position at the foot of those hills,' explains the Old Man, when they return.

'Move!' orders Moser sharply, changing the magazine on his Mpi. The company spreads out and moves crouching-over towards the heights. A phosphorus flare hangs, like a lamp without a wire, over the terrain, lighting it up with its ghostly illumination. We can see the lines of trenches and pill-boxes clearly.

Tracer bullets draw dotted lines across the uneven ground. We lie still in the snow for a moment to pull ourselves together. The Oberleutnant nudges the Old Man in the side. 'The last fence, Beier! Let's see that finishing post! Keep contact, for Heaven's sake!'

'The wounded?' asks the Old Man, carefully.

'Each man must make his own decision,' answers Moser, looking away.

We work our way in towards the positions. If they notice us, our chance of getting through will be zero.

'Where the devil *is* Ivan?' whispers Porta, amazed, when we reach the Russian positions and can see down the whole length of the trenches. There is no sign of a living creature anywhere.

'The position *must* be manned,' whispers Klockdorf nervously, clutching a potato-masher in his hand.

'The German lines are over there at the edge of the forest,' explains Moser quietly.

'Then Ivan can't be far away,' whispers Tiny. ' 'E's onto the arse of everythin' German!'

'Everybody here?' whispers Moser over his shoulder.

'All got your tickets ready to be handed over at the

entrance?' grins Porta, in a whisper, 'any of you try to sneak in you'll get fined heavily.'

Silently we crawl closer to the trench. Porta points with his Mpi.

'There's our old pal, Ivan. I was afraid for a minute there that he'd got tired of fighting us and gone off home by train.'

'Wouldn't seem like the same war,' whispers Tiny. 'Ivan wouldn't never do that to us.'

A group of Soviet troops is sitting right up against the edge of the trench, half covered with white camouflage tarpaulins. There are hundreds of them. It's incredible that they haven't seen us.

'Hand grenades,' whispers the Oberleutnant. 'All together?' Working quickly we screw the caps off the grenades.

'Throw!' orders Moser, softly.

Grenades whirl through the air and land with the effectiveness of artillery in the narrow trench.

The surprise is complete. Panic breaks out in the position. Expertly we roll up the trench and break through into no-man's-land.

A couple of mines explode. Human bodies are flung into the air on the tip of the explosion flame. Fire eating into their eyes. Skulls crushed like seashells under the wheels of a tractor. Porta and Barcelona cut the wire. We run straight into the arms of a Rusian spotter who immediately opens fire on us. In a giant spring Tiny is on him and garrottes him. He took five of us with him, though.

Porta and I are pulling Stege after us on a tarpaulin. He screams dreadfully as we pull him through and over the wire. He is one of the few wounded we still have with us. All the rest have been abandoned.

The Russians have got over the first shock of our attack. Shouts of command can be heard. Grenades whirl towards us and machine-guns sing their chattering song. Hundreds of flares hang in the sky above us.

With hands and feet we dig our way down into the snow.

It would be certain death to keep moving in this sea of light. How long do we lie there? Years? Months? Days? Hours? We'd be amazed if anybody were to tell us it was only minutes. Bullets whistle and snarl over our heads. Explosive shells bore into the snow and rip great holes in the frozen fields. We hug the ground desperately. I turn to the man beside me to find that all that is left of him is a great lump of quivering flesh. He made a joke just now when he saved me from a shell. I can hear they're using 80 mm mortars. Firing *katuschkas* which throw up earth like a breastwork in front of and behind us.

Moser makes a rush forward. The Legionnaire goes after him, but is thrown back by a burst of flame. He screams, pressing both hands to his face. Blood is pouring from between his fingers. I grasp his feet and pull him back under cover. One side of his face is gone completely. I bandage him as well as I can.

'I can't see!' he mumbles. 'I'm blinded! Give me my gun!'

'Balls, there's nothing wrong with your eyes. It's the bandage covering them, that's all,' I reply. 'Your left cheek's gone, nothing more. It'll give you at least three months at the rear. What the devil, Desert-rat, you're lucky!'

He doesn't believe me.

I have to lift the bandage carefully away from his eyes. He screams with joy when he finds he can see but I take his pistol from him anyway, for safety's sake. People with head wounds can get the craziest ideas. I take him by the hand when we continue our flight.

The Professor runs alongside me. He has lost his Mpi and is scared stiff of getting a court-martial.

I hear it coming. A deadly, whining whistle. I just manage to push the Legionnaire into a shell-hole and follow him myself. The Professor is worrying so much about his lost Mpi that he doesn't hear the shell until it strikes in front of him. His arm flies high into the air and falls beside him. Astonishedly he picks it up, and can't understand how it can be his. Blood streams from his shoulder. I try to staunch it. Make a tourniquet from the strap of his gasmask. He can't feel anything, he says. I powder the wound with sulfanilimide and try to call the others. Nobody hears me. Now I've two to look after. Let's hope I don't run into a Russian patrol. I have to carry my Mpi slung around my neck. Before I could ever get it into firing position I'd have been dead ten times over.

Suddenly the Professor begins to scream. The impact anaesthesia effect has worked off. He will soon be moving in a hell of pain. It hurts hellishly to have your arm torn off, but now, at least, his war worries are over. If they ask where his Mpi is he can say it went with his arm. Even the toughest of courts martial couldn't turn that one down, though I've no doubt some of them would like to be able to require both the limb and the weapon to be handed in to QM stores. Porta thinks it won't be long before loss of an arm will be regarded in the same way as equipment shortage, a form of sabotage. A soldier who has lost his arm cannot be used over again. Loss of a leg isn't so serious for the Army. After training in the use of an artificial leg the soldier can be utilized again in the Quartermaster branch. A man can be taught to march with a false leg. The Prussians have drill instructors – Feldwebels – who can turn almost complete invalids into acrobats.

105 mm shells roar over our heads. They sound like hundreds and hundreds of empty oil drums rolling down and down and down through a series of long, sloping tunnels.

A whole section, running a little in advance of me, goes up in flames. Fountains of snow and earth spout up with great, roiling clouds of smoke over towards the field path.

Porta works his way through the barbed wire. He is still dragging Stege after him on the tarpaulin. Suddenly he screams, and drops his Mpi as if it were red-hot. He goes down with both hands clutching at his stomach.

I throw myself across him, sobbing hysterically. For a moment I think he's dead, he's lying in such a strangely twisted position. One of his legs is turned the wrong way and lies along his back like a reversed rifle.

The Old Man rolls down to us together with Tiny.

Porta opens his eyes.

'I seem to have hit the jackpot! That was some bang! Where'd it get me?'

'In the leg,' says the Old Man quietly.

'In the leg?' cries Porta in astonishment. 'I've got pains in the chest and in the guts. I must have at least a hundred shell splinters in me!'

The Old Man slits his uniform up. There is no sign of a wound in his chest or stomach.

'Stop your tickling,' says Porta, beginning to laugh. 'I never could stand being tickled.'

The Old Man runs practiced fingers over his body. He looks at me and then at Porta's hip. It looks terrible. We have to use nearly all our first-aid packs.

Moser jumps down to us.

'What the devil are you up to?' He sees Porta and is silent. His mouth quivers. He is close to breaking-point. He lays aside his Mpi and passes a hand over Porta's wild red hair. 'It's not so bad, comrade. Now you'll go back to a hospital at home, and maybe you'll be able to stay on garrison duty for the rest of the war. As soon as we get in I'll put you in for an EK.I. If you want to be an Unteroffizier then you'll be one.'

'No thank you, sir,' grins Porta, modestly. 'An EK.I's all right, but garrison's not for yours truly. What'd happen to 2 Section without me? Starve to death, probably!'

I fetch the Legionnaire and the Professor from the shell-hole. 'Those boys too,' groans Moser. 'Are any of us going to get through this alive?'

When we move on, Tiny has Porta over his shoulder. The Old Man has Stege. Moser looks after the Professor and I have the Legionnaire.

We have got a good way on when I discover I have left my Mpi in the shell-hole. I have to go back for it. It's too

324

risky coming in without your weapon. Loss of limbs can be overlooked, but if you lose your weapon you pay for it with your head. I hand the Legionnaire over to Barcelona and wriggle back through the holes we have made in the wire. Suddenly I'm lost. Hysteria grips me. My nerves go. As if I were a raw recruit. I find myself in the middle of a minefield. Two connected mines are right in front of me. Touch one of them and hundreds of others with which they are connected will blow too. I go icy-cold. Lie still as a mouse for a moment. If I touch one of them there won't be as much as a button left of me. I pray to God in my terror.

I wriggle cautiously backwards. I leave half my greatcoat behind me on a wire-post. I roll towards a shell-hole to find at the last moment that it's been made into a Stalin trap. By the light of a flare I see the bayonets down there winking at me. If I'd rolled down into it I'd have had fifty of them through my body.

A little later I get caught in a barbed wire trap. You crawl into it and can't crawl out again. Thank God I am equipped with wire-cutters. I can thank Porta for that. I set them to the wire. If it's electrified I go up in a shower of blue sparks. I close my eyes and apply pressure to the cutters. The wire springs back, slashing across my face. The barbs cut deeply into the flesh. I hardly feel it. I only want to get out of the trap. I'm a sitting duck out here. If Ivan spots me he'll riddle me.

I'm out. I crawl through the hole but still don't know where I am. The frequency of the flares keeps me under cover. I crawl in circles. Lie still and try to steady my nerves. Try to get my bearings from the artillery fire, but can't hear the difference between strike and muzzle report.

A Maxim bursts out suddenly quite close to me. I'm nearly into a Russian position. It happens often enough out here. A man crawls down expectantly into a trench only to find he's dropped straight into the arms of the enemy.

I am close to giving up altogether when I find an Mpi. It's not mine, but now I've got a weapon equivalent to the one I drew from the QM. I feel quickly to make sure my 08 is still in its holster.

Oberleutnant Moser gives me a dressing-down when I make contact with the section again after almost an hour's absence. 'Where the devil have you been? A minute later and I'd have written you off!'

I let him rave. We'll be in in a few minutes. We can see our trenches clearly. Just back of the edge of the forest. Not far now!

Porta is unconscious. His leg joint is torn out at the hip, and they've tied a carbine to his leg to give it some kind of support. Tiny thinks they'll give him a silver hip, and then he'll always have something he can pawn if he gets desperate.

The Legionnaire asks for something to drink. We press snow between his lips.

'Come on,' mutters Moser. 'The last hurdle!'

Klockdorf is first man up. He runs forward, together with the cavalry Oberschütze who is so fond of watching hangings. Their feet seem hardly to touch the hard-packed snow and, obviously, they intend to cover the last few yards in one long jump. They never make it! Klockdorf runs straight into a minefield. The explosion throws his body high into the air, it falls and explodes more mines, is tossed repeatedly. The Oberschütze gets both legs blown away. By the time we reach him every drop of blood has drained from his body.

Now our own people open up. Machine-guns rattle and 40 mm light mortars spit bombs at us. We lose ten more men. I'm about to jump a shell-hole when a blow like a mighty fist catches me in the stomach. I spin round like a top, teeter on the edge of the shell-hole, and go down. At first I don't realize what has happened and am furiously angry. I think one of the others has knocked me down. Then a pain like a red-hot knife shoots up through my chest.

'What's up?' asks the Old Man, bending over me. 'What'd you want to get in the way of that for, now?'

'Am I hit?' I ask, wonderingly.

'You have had the honour of being on the receiving end of a German infantry bullet,' answers the Old Man. 'Stay here quietly. We'll come and pick you up as soon as we're in touch with our chaps.'

Half a ton of earth and snow showers down on us as a series of shells burst close by.

'Where did the bastard get me?' I ask. 'Oh hell, I'm *tired*!'

'You be glad it was a German bullet and not one of those Russian explosive jobs,' answers the Old Man. 'It's just an ordinary rifle bullet wound, son. Nothing to speak of!'

'All right for *you*,' I say. 'It hurts *me* like the very devil! Are you sure I've not been hit anywhere else? I'm boiling hot all up my back.'

'Maybe you've still got the bullet in you, and it's touching a bone. Don't eat snow. People with stomach wounds mustn't have liquids in any form,' warns the Old Man. He takes my pistol from me.

'No, let me keep it,' I plead. 'I won't do anything silly. I need it if Ivan turns up! I won't be taken prisoner!'

The Old Man thinks a moment, looking at me consideringly, and then returns the pistol to me. He pulls me up so that I'm sitting with my back propped against the wall of the shell-hole. It's a good position to meet anybody jumping down to me. Tracer lies across the terrain like a fiery shield. The whole front is active. Both sides think there is a big attack coming. I am alone. All by myself out in no-man's-land. Midway between the German and the Russian lines.

Where is Porta? Stege? The Legionnaire? And all the other wounded? The Old Man said they would leave us out here and come back for us later. That's sensible. Then the German machine-guns can give us covering fire, and above all, we won't have the risk of being massacred by our own people.

A long, burning pain shoots through my body. Fear gives me nightmares. I clutch the pistol tightly in my hand.

'*Job tvojemadj!*' That wasn't far from my shell-hole.

Somebody laughs. I try to dig myself down into the snow. Too difficult. My body hurts all over. I run a hand over my stomach and look at it. It's covered with blood. I lie still and play dead.

A fur cap comes into sight over the edge of the shell-hole. Black Mongol eyes examine me intently. He throws a piece of ice at me. Then he disappears. If the hole hadn't been so deep he'd have pushed his bayonet through me. Just to make sure.

I can still hear them. They're crawling around close to my hole.

'*Njet germanskijs!*'

'*Job Tovjemadj!*'

'*Piestre, piestre!*'* A harsh, commanding voice that one. A little later a scream comes. A long, wailing sound. It sounds like a belly-wound. A German MG-38 roars madly, than barks in short, brutal bursts.

The Old Man comes sliding down the side of my hole, catches me by the neck and throws me forward like a sack of flour. Brown boots and gaiters flash past. Russian feet! Black jackboots follow them. German feet!

A barrage of shells curtains off the whole front. A shell-burst batters me with snow and ice. A ricochet tears open my helmet.

Suddenly I'm in the German trenches. I look with glazed eyes at the infantryman who is holding a bottle to my lips and am about to drink when the Old Man knocks the bottle to one side.

'Belly wound,' he says in explanation to the Stabsfeldwe-bel.

'I see,' nods the old soldier, who has already been through one World War and knows the taste of defeat, and what comes after defeat.

* *Piestre* (Russian): Faster.

The wounded are carried down into a deep dug-out. The infantry commander presses the hands of every one of us, and hands out cigarettes. Junos.

'We really thought you were Ivan,' an old infantry Leutnant apologizes to Moser.

'That's all right,' replies Moser, tiredly, sucking cigarette smoke deeply into his lungs. 'I can't believe we've really made it,' he says, a little later. 'We've been through hell!'

We're transferred to lorries. At the Field Dressing Station the Old Man and Barcelona take leave of us.

Oberleutnant Moser stares out over the lip of a trench and follows a flare with his eyes. The sun is just coming up behind the Russian positions. It is a lovely morning. The frost tinkles. He lights a cigarette, concentrating on the job, and never feels the pain of the shell splinter which tears away his face. His hand loosens its grip on the Mpi which has become almost a part of him. His body bends slowly forward. Another shell burst buries him in earth and snow.

'I saw the boss go, just before I left,' says Tiny. We are lying in the hospital train. ' 'E got 'is wish, anyway. 'E's got away from us now!'

'C'est la guerre, mon ami!' says the Legionnaire, quietly.

'He promised me *Schwarzer Heinrich** but if he forgot it what's it matter,' says Porta slowly. He is being stretched, and rocks with every movement of the train.

'The doctor wouldn't cut off my trotters,' says Tiny, disappointedly, indicating a gigantic pair of feet swathed in bandages.

' 'Ave to march on 'em all me bleedin' life, I suppose. People who're born with a club-foot don't know 'ow lucky they are!'

'They've stuck a long tube right down into my stomach,' I tell them, pointing at the drain tube which sticks out of my throat.

The Professor is crying again. He doesn't want to go back

* *Schwarzer Heinrich* (German): Slang for EK.I.

to Norway with only one arm. The Oberartz has promised to send him to the recruit depot, but he doesn't believe it.

They take us off the hospital train at Lemberg goods station. We're going to be patched up in Poland before they'll allow us to be seen in Germany.

'Where are you from?' asks a tight-lipped hospital matron.

'From Moscow,' grins Porta, cheerfully. 'We've been sent here as a reward for good service to see the world's ugliest iodine and aspirin juggler!'

'I shall report you for this!' whines the dragon, insulted.

'You can borrow me old John Thomas to write the report with, if you like, love,' Porta laughs noisily, letting go a terrific fart, and with that pointing the final full-stop to our part in Hitler's Moscow campaign.

by Sven Hassel

Legion of the Damned
Wheels of Terror
Comrades of War
Marchbattalion
Assignment Gestapo
Monte Cassino
Liquidate Paris
SS General
Reign of Hell
Blitzfreeze
The Bloody Road to Death
Court Martial
OGPU Prison
The Commissar

Out of the red-black mist came an infantryman. He was laughing – madly – and then with a scream he threw away his carbine and crept close to the ground like a wounded animal. A steel rain of shells whipped up the earth around and he went on screaming. He was mad. No one could scream like that unless they were mad.

Then the MGs began to spit tracer fire and, rank by rank, the Russians fell to the ground. They fell in thousands, but there were more, always more behind them. They picked up the weapons of the dead and continued to advance, a hideous wave of death that rose from the corpse-strewn battlefield and surged towards the German lines . . .

This was Hitler's glorious conquest of Russia . . .